DYING
TO
TELL

thank you!

DYING
TO
TELL

THE DEAD DETECTIVE CASEFILES

Tj O'CONNOR

LEVEL
BEST BOOKS

Author Photo Credit: Tj O'Connor

Second edition

ISBN: 978-1-68512-761-9

Cover art by Level Best Designs

This book was professionally typeset on Reedsy.
Find out more at reedsy.com

For Sean, Ryan, and Shane
Chasing dreams is a long road.
It takes courage, stamina, and patience.
Don't give up—ever.

Praise for The Dead Detective Casefiles

"O'Connor's *The Dead Detective Casefiles* series is a *must read* for those who like mysteries with a dash of history, a hard-boiled twist, and a pinch of paranormal."—Heather Weidner, author of the Jules Keene Glamping Mysteries

"Tj O'Connor is a master storyteller who can have you gasping in suspense one moment and snorting coffee through your nose the next. In the Dead Detective Casefiles, he seamlessly merges mystery, humor, and paranormal so authentically that the reader never gives a second thought to the concept of the main character, Detective Oliver Tucker, actually being dead.

"I cannot put these books down. I love the characters, I love O'Connor's writing style, and while I can't wait to see what happens, I also don't want to reach the end and have to say goodbye to this engaging cast of characters."—Annette Dashofy, *USA Today* bestselling author of the Zoe Chambers Mystery Series.

Chapter One

Dying is as perilous as secrets and lies. Depending, of course, on who is keeping the secrets and who is telling the lies. Trust me, I'm in the secrets and lies business. I'm a homicide cop. Well, I was. Secrets and lies can lead to big problems—like murder—although it's not in the secrets or the lies themselves. It's that someone always wants to tell. The urge is like an addict needing a fix. You need to tell—you cannot help it—you have to tell. Sometimes it's out of guilt. Sometimes it's for revenge. Sometimes it's just spite. No matter, in the end, someone is always *dying to tell*.

And then bad things happen.

An auburn-haired beauty with green eyes—eyes that could hypnotize vampires—walked down the outdoor Old Town Winchester mall through a dusting of blowing December snow. She stopped momentarily to adjust her long wool overcoat over her athletic legs and curvaceous, bumpy body—a good bumpy. She looked around the mall, twice back from where she'd come, and turned down the sidewalk to the annex behind the First Bank and Trust of Frederick County. When she caught sight of me, her smile—one that normally could charm snakes—looked more like that of a cobra ready to strike.

I ran to catch up.

No, not because I'm obsessed with vampires or snake charmers. And no, I wasn't stalking this classy university professor on her way to some mysterious early morning appointment. She was my wife, and she *was* on her way to a mysterious appointment. I didn't know where or why. So,

1

being the former detective I was, I followed her.

"Angel, where you going?"

"To the bank." She reached the employee entrance door and stopped. "Why are you following me?"

Silly question. "Because you're going to the bank at seven in the morning. It's closed."

She checked her watch. "It's almost seven thirty."

"Haven't you ever heard of banker's hours? Who do you think is here this early?"

"Really, Tuck?" She rolled her eyes—a signal that my wit or charm had disarmed her. "I'll explain later at home."

"I'll wait. We can get pancakes."

"You hate pancakes. What's wrong with you lately? Are you spying on me?"

I did hate pancakes, but watching her eat steak and eggs—my favorite breakfast—was much more painful. "Spying, no. Me?"

"I didn't think the dead could be so frustrating."

Oh, did I mention I'm dead? No? I'm Tuck, formerly Detective Oliver Tucker of the Frederick County Sheriff's office. Now I'm just Tuck to my friends—those living and dead. I was a hotshot detective before I went to investigate noises in my house late one night. Those noises put a bullet in my heart. That was over a year ago. And it's taken me that long to come to terms with it. Sort of. It helped to catch the bastard who shot me and put an end to his killing spree. And it helps to have my wife, Angel, and Hercule, my black Lab, around, too. *Dead* and *gone* are two totally different things. I'm dead, but as Angel and Hercule will tell you—well, maybe not Hercule, he's a dog—I'm just not gone.

"Angel, listen, I..."

The steel security door at the employee entrance door burst open and banged against the brick annex wall. A masked gunman—a tall, strong-looking figure dressed in dark clothes and the traditional bank robber's balaclava—ran from the annex, turned, and fired a shot from a small revolver. He slipped on the sidewalk, freshly adorned with an inch of snow, and crashed to the ground. He cursed, jumped to his feet, and locked eyes on Angel.

"Run, Angel. Run!" I yelled.

Too late.

The gunman scrambled the three yards to us and grabbed Angel by the arm. "Come here!" He spun her around, pulled her to him like a shield, and faced the annex doorway.

A bank security guard emerged through the door, gun first. "Freeze! Let her go!"

The gunman fired two shots in rapid succession. One hit the security guard and the other slammed safely into the wall two feet beside him. The guard grunted, staggered back, and went down, striking his head on a stone flower planter beside the entrance.

"Angel, stay calm," I said. "I'll get you out of this."

"Tuck, help me!"

I dove for the gunman and took two vicious swings trying to free her. Both blows struck him in the face and neither caused him to flinch. I struck again—lashed a kick to his knee, a jab to the rib cage.

Two more body blows.

Nothing.

"Angel, fight. You have to fight. I can't help."

Angel was not a timid or slight woman and she erupted like a wildcat, taking the gunman by surprise. She twisted and fought against his grip and nearly broke free.

"Dammit, lady, stop!" He jammed the revolver to her cheek. "Or else."

"Tuck," she cried out, "help me! Tuck..."

Rage boiled over and the explosions started inside me everywhere. A second later, my fingers tingled and my body burned from the inside. Seconds were all I had. I lunged forward and struck the gunman in the throat with the heel of my hand. He staggered back, relaxing his grip around Angel. I struck two more vicious punches to his face and followed with a kick to his midsection.

"What the f—" He released her and turned in a circle, his eyes darting

3

around.

I struck two kidney punches and a sharp kick to the inside of one leg. He *umphed* and crumpled sideways down onto one knee. I crushed him with a two-fisted hammer punch to the back of his neck.

"Run, Angel—go!"

She was only four or five strides from the gunman when he lifted his revolver and took aim.

A gunshot split the air from behind us, searing a lightning bolt through me on its way to the bank robber. It struck him in the upper arm and spun him sideways. A second shot followed but missed him by mere inches. The gunman was stunned but regained his footing—his injury wasn't stopping him. He staggered back, lifted his revolver, and pulled off a shot before he ran around the rear of the bank annex and disappeared.

"Angel?" I spun around. "Are you all right?"

Apparently, she was fine.

A tall, square-jawed, distinguished man in a heavy wool overcoat stood beside her now. He had one arm around her, speaking slowly to her—consoling her—and his other arm hung to his side, a black, compart .45 semi-automatic handgun in his grasp. He looked like a younger Clooney, but perhaps better looking. I instantly distrusted him.

"I'm fine, Mr. Thorne, really." Angel slipped from his arm and went to the security guard lying on the snowy ground beside the annex door. She moved over him, checked his wounds, and tried to wake him. "Call an ambulance. He's been shot and is unconscious."

Thorne—a man I'd never seen before—pulled a cell phone from his overcoat pocket. "Right, and the police. Is Conti all right?"

"I'm not sure." She investigated a small, thin hole over the guard's left breast through his blue suit coat. From inside the coat, she pulled out a paperback book and held it up. "Agatha Christie saved his life—*Murder on the Orient Express.* The bullet hit this and didn't go through."

I put a hand on her shoulder to comfort her—or perhaps, to comfort he—or perhaps, to comfort me. The rage had passed, and with it, the last of my connection to the physical world. "Are you okay, babe? I..."

"I'm fine. Go see if anyone else is hurt inside." She caught Thorne eyeing her. "There may be more employees inside, right?"

"Not at this hour, no. Let's wait on the police."

No, I wasn't waiting.

A voice beckoned me into the bank and I followed. It wasn't a voice—not really—it was more like someone telegraphing words into my head: "It isn't over, kid, follow me."

The bank annex was dark. The faint morning light was barely enough to cast more than a dull haze through the lobby windows. I went through the grand lobby, down a long, dark corridor into the executive wing. At the end of the corridor were three offices. I stopped at the suite of William H. Mendelson, Chairman of the Board, First Bank and Trust of Frederick County—or so said the brass plaque below the oversized portrait of a silver-haired titan.

The voice from nowhere whispered, "Hurry up, kid. Inside."

I followed the voice into the pitch-black office and through a second doorway in the corner of the room—a closet, I thought—but it was the entrance to a stairwell leading down into more darkness. Two floors below, in a sub-basement, the stairwell opened to a wide landing at a heavy steel security gate that looked like a prison cell door. Beyond the gate was a small anteroom lit by a dim fluorescent light overhead. The gate was unlocked and open and the anteroom beyond was empty except for a small metal worktable and two battleship-gray chairs. In the rear of the room was a monstrous, turn-of-the-century steel vault door—the *nineteenth* century. To my surprise, the door was cracked open, and a sliver of eerie light from inside the vault etched the anteroom wall.

"Inside, Oliver." The voice was all around me now. "Go inside."

Oliver? "Who the hell are you?"

"Just go. Quit stalling."

I turned and found a strange man—a fellow wraith—leaning against the anteroom wall watching me—not in a casual way but trying to *appear* casual. He had one hand in a pocket of his leather bomber jacket, and he tipped a baseball cap that had a big "W" on it off his brow with the other.

"Trust me, kid. This isn't the way it looks." He threw a chin toward the vault. "Go on in. I've done my part. Now it's your turn."

Inside I found the Chairman of the First Bank and Trust of Frederick County.

William H. Mendelson always reminded me of Lionel Barrymore's Mr. Potter from *It's a Wonderful Life.* He was a starchy, arrogant old banker who made rare appearances around town. When he did, he never spoke, didn't wave, and never, ever smiled. And to those who knew him, he was never William or Bill—God, never Billy, either. He was Mr. Mendelson—or more often, the Chairman.

Like he was Frank Sinatra or something, right?

William sat behind a square steel counting table in the middle of the vault, facing the door. He was dressed in the same blue double-breasted suit he must have worn yesterday—from the smell, he'd been here a while. A dark blood stain ruined his starched white shirt and expensive silk tie—the result of a small-caliber bullet hole in his heart. Both hands rested on the tabletop like he was waiting for a sandwich—or pancakes—and they were stuck to the blackish gooey remains of his life.

And hanging in the vault air was the heavy, pungent odor of smoke.

The bomber-jacketed man—strangely familiar—said, "Remember, kid, it's not what you think."

"Hello, William," I said, looking at the murdered chairman. "I'm Tuck and I'll be investigating your murder. Perhaps you can tell me—what *should* I think?"

Chapter Two

The First Bank and Trust of Frederick County occupied one of the oldest buildings in Old Town Winchester—a historic town in northwestern Virginia whose roots were established before the American Revolution. The bank sat just off the town square in a brick and stone building guarded by marble columns at the entrance.

The bank annex—even older than the bank itself—sat behind the main bank and was connected by a covered brick courtyard. Both were now swarmed by sheriff's deputies and Winchester policemen processing the scene and searching for evidence.

I emerged from the strange subterranean vault and went looking for Angel. I found her inside an ambulance with a paramedic checking her over. The security guard, whose nametag read Larry Conti, sat beside her with an ice pack pressed against his temple. His face was a messy blue-black collage of bruises and his mouth sported two split lips that looked like a collagen treatment gone Frankenstein.

He'd gotten lucky with a bullet and taken a beating, but otherwise appeared fine.

Despite her harrowing morning, Angel looked like a winter-wonderland lingerie model. Minus the lingerie, of course—who would wear lingerie to a bank at seven in the morning? Beneath the long overcoat that lay beside her, she'd worn a well-fitted skirt and cotton top—fitted as in it swooned over her curves and hills and accentuated her sexy, womanly charms. Thankfully, no bullet holes or broken bones marred her centerfoldness—no, that's not a real word.

She smiled as she thanked the paramedic when he cleared her to go.

"Angel, are you all right?" I asked, stepping into the open ambulance door. "Back there, for a moment, I thought…"

"You should be so lucky. You'd love it if we were both dead. Then I could never escape you."

Ouch.

She glanced across the parking lot at an oversized detective stuffed into a dark brown barn coat interviewing the man who saved her life—Captain Oh-My-Hero—Mr. Thorne. She smiled at him and walked over to the security guard sitting on the gate of another ambulance beside hers.

"Are you all right, Larry?" she said. "You saved me, you know—you and Mr. Thorne. Thank you."

"It's my job, Professor." His words were slurred—the product of swollen lips and pain medication. "I'm glad you're okay. I'm sure lucky I brought that book to read at lunch."

Lucky was right. Dame Agatha took a bullet for him.

The paramedic pulled the blood pressure cuff off Conti's arm. "You're okay. You should come into the hospital to check for a concussion. You hit your head pretty hard and have a good gash there."

"Later, after I finish with the cops," he said. "Maybe."

Angel asked, "What happened in there, Larry?"

He shrugged and winced at the same time. "Got to work about six thirty and found the employee door unlocked. I went in to check it out. That guy jumped me just inside the door and took my gun. He beat the shi…"

"It's all right, Larry, my husband's a cop—was, I mean."

"Yeah, okay." He tried to smile but winced again. "He beat me up pretty good and kept yelling for me to show him the vault with the gold and stones. He was nuts—this is the bank annex. I told him the bank was next door."

"What else did he say?"

"Nothing." Larry slid off the gate onto the ground outside the ambulance. "He kept hitting me and yelling about the vault. He clipped me one last time and ran out. I got my backup gun and went after him. That's when we ran into you, I guess."

She climbed down from the ambulance. "You're a hero, Larry. Thank you again. Get better."

I said, "Angel, about William Mendelson. We gotta talk."

Neither she, Larry Conti, nor the paramedic paid me any attention.

Rude? No. And it wasn't because on this frigid, snowy December day I stood outside in the same clothes I've worn for nearly two years—jeans, an old black tee shirt, running shoes, and blue blazer. And it wasn't because I looked like a homeless guy begging for change or asking to move into your basement for the winter, either. It's because they don't see me—they don't know I'm here. You know, it's that whole "I'm dead" thing—dust, gone—well, *not* gone, not really. But dead all the same.

And I'm not hanging around haunting my beautiful wife just for spite, either. These days, I'm a dead detective. Or in some cases, a detective for the dead. When I was alive, I was a hotshot homicide cop. Now, dead, I'm still a hotshot homicide cop—it's just that my clients are nearly always dead or at least connected to someone who is dead. And sometimes, being on this side of life and death makes all the difference in the world for catching the bad guys. It doesn't pay much, but the satisfaction of nabbing a killer after he or she thinks they're in the clear is enough for me.

"Did you hear me? I found William Mendelson…"

Angel held up a hand. With the other, she lifted her cell phone to her ear—a ruse to speak with me in public—and walked away from the ambulance. Appearing to talk to herself in public makes her seem nuts, and that's not good for a well-known professor of American History.

"You've been following me a lot lately."

"What? No. Listen, Angel, I found William and he's—"

"Yes you were." Her eyes darkened the way they used to when I got caught sneaking in at oh-dark-thirty after a night howling at the moon with my cop pals. "Why? Can't I go to a meeting without you following me just once?"

"But, Angel, William—"

"I need my privacy, Tuck. I need space…me time. Normal-people time." She started to turn but looked back at me. "Unless you can do that spirit

9

thing—possession or reincarnation or whatever—into the body of a dashing French movie star. Then, I might overlook your irritating stunts."

"*Irritating?* Wait, *me time?* Without me?" Lately, Angel had the notion I followed her everywhere and listened in on her calls and hung around with her and her friends. Mostly, of course, because I did. Being a dead husband is tough. And after two years being none of the man I used to be, it was getting to me. "I heard you leave at six thirty and followed you—only for your protection. What are you doing down here at this hour?"

She rolled her eyes—we covered that, right? "William emailed me last night and wanted me here at seven thirty. So…"

"Angela," a husky, deep voice called—it was Bear. "If you checked out okay, we need to talk."

Most people's first impressions of Detective Theodore Braddock are that he's a big, bulky, gruff, grumbly kinda guy. It's amazing how perceptive people are. But Bear has redeeming qualities, too. He's fun, protective of Angel, and loyal. Okay, maybe I'm describing Hercule, but they're sort of the same. Hercule just listens better.

Bear was six-four and made the scale groan at two-fifty-plus. His hair was short and unstyled. He was powerfully built without any extra fries or cheeseburger flab, either. As he lumbered toward us, he looked tired and aggravated—perhaps because his face showed two days' growth of stubble on one side and clean-shaven razor burn on the other.

I always laugh at those movies where cops run from their homes after a "no one can save us but you" telephone call. The call always came while shaving and they never bothered to spend the extra sixty seconds to finish. Like a minute would end the world.

In Bear's case, I understood. His call was about Angel—bank robbery in progress, shots fired, Professor Angela Tucker at the scene. He'd probably left his house without closing his front door—probably left the sink water running, and probably ran over a dozen pedestrians to get here. He'd been my partner since the police academy and family since Angel and I married. And after my death, he'd been her rock and protector, too.

We were lucky he hadn't shown up in just his underwear and Glock.

"Angela," he said, "tell me again what you're doing down here this early."

He asked good questions, too.

She told him about her email from William Mendelson, then gave a detailed account of the greeting she got when she arrived. "And no, before you ask, I don't know what William wanted to see me about. I have no idea. Has anyone seen him yet?"

"I've got men searching the bank," Bear said, scribbling some notes in a small pocket notebook. "So far, we haven't found—"

I couldn't stand it. "He's dead."

Bear jumped and almost dropped his pen. He turned and locked eyes on me standing beside Angel. "For God's sake, will you wear a bell or something?"

"A bell?" Bear knows I'm around, but sometimes I have to speak to him to make the connection. Weird, right? "What for?"

"I hate it when you sneak up on me."

"I didn't sneak up on you. I've been here the whole time. You just didn't see me."

Now *he* rolled his eyes. "I'm still getting used to you."

"Why? We've been partners for almost twenty years."

"You're dead now."

"And you're not. Do you hear me complaining?"

He cursed. "What about Mendelson?"

"I've been trying to tell Angel, but she was too busy scolding me about—"

"Jesus, Tuck—what about Mendelson?"

"He's dead." I hooked a thumb toward the annex. "Somebody shot him in the bank, er, through the heart, really, but he's down in an old vault in the annex's sub-basement—sort of a secret sub-basement, too. You go through this closet in Mendelson's office and—"

"Murdered?" Bear's radio suddenly came alive as he said to Angel and me, "The bank robber killed old man Mendelson?"

"Detective Braddock," a voice called over the radio. "We…"

"You found Mendelson dead in a vault in some damned sub-basement," Bear snapped. "Secure the scene. I'm coming down."

"How the hell did you know that? I just found him."

Chapter Three

"What do you know about this place, Angela?" Bear said, leading the way into the annex. "What do you know about Thorne and the Mendelsons?"

"I just met Mr. Thorne. He seems like a wonderful man…"

"Wonderful?" Holy Captain Fantastic—she never called *me* wonderful. "You have two seconds of conversation and he's wonderful? During a shoot-out, no less?"

She held up her hand. "He just saved my life."

"That makes him lucky, not wonderful."

Angel ignored me and followed Bear across the lobby toward the dark corridor I'd gone down earlier.

I'd never been in the bank annex before this morning. In fact, I'd rarely—if ever—ventured into the First Bank and Trust of Frederick County at all. I'd known about it during my breathing days. Truth be told, I wasn't much of a bank person, or a checking account person, or a bill-paying person, either. And since Angel made more than three times what I had made as a cop, she handled all the finances. I did the other important stuff—like going to the gun range and barbecuing and guarding the plumber while he fixed what I broke. Manly stuff. I was more of a cash-in-hand guy.

The lobby was cavernous with marble floors and two-story-high mahogany walls adorned with paintings of local Winchester sights and renditions of famous local Civil War campaigns. I expected a fat-bellied, cigar-smoking rich guy in an expensive suit to wander out any moment with a bag of money to count. You know, the usual bank stuff.

13

Bear and Angel disappeared down the corridor and I followed it to the far end. With the lights on this time, I noticed a richly furnished waiting area and three oak office doors. On the far wall, adjacent to a mahogany receptionist desk, was an ornately framed door with a placard beside it that read "Chairman of the Board" under William Mendelson's portrait. The painting was of a stout bull of a man with slicked-back gray hair and dark eyes. He had a dull drone smile—the artist's attempt to breathe friendliness into an otherwise stark expression. The artist fooled no one.

Mendelson's office was still dark except for a single wall lamp at the back of the room that one of the policemen must have flipped on during their search. It had been pitch black when I'd passed through earlier. When I went inside, an ominous phantom lunged at me from behind the door.

"Holy shit!"

I backpedaled and would have slammed into a bookcase, but dead guys don't slam into anything. We just sort of, well, keep backpedaling.

Guarding the right of the office door was a ten-foot-high horrific monster—luckily not a vampire—that glared death and savagery as he lunged at me. Lucky for him he was just a statue. So I steadied myself and looked closer. The statue was neither monster nor beast, nor had it lunged at me—but it was thinking of it. It was a stone carving of some ancient Egyptian king or deity—I wouldn't recognize either one since the only things I knew about ancient Egypt I learned from Charlton Heston. The statue held a tall spear-like thing, and he was part-man, part-animal, with a curved face, long rectangular ears, and the body of a man. It wasn't Charlton Heston nor the death merchant I feared. But I was glad he was made of stone and on my side. He'd be a great ally in the pending vampire apocalypse.

Okay, yeah, I watch too much late-night television—the dead don't sleep, we just go to this dark, lonely "time-out" place. I hate it there, so I enrich myself with cable TV.

"No wonder no one likes Mendelson. Who has monsters around their office, Vincent Price?"

The stairwell door to the sub-basement waited in the corner of the room behind Mendelson's large antique cherry desk. Earlier I thought it was a closet. I followed voices down toward the vault chamber—again, the smoky air reached me but grew more pungent and dense as I neared the vault. A few more stairs and black smoke swirled around me and the heat was unbearable...

"Bear! Angel! Get out..." My warning was unnecessary, of course, because neither were anywhere in the basement. Well, not the basement I'd followed them to anyway.

Stepping off the stairs, the vault anteroom floor was nowhere beneath my feet—not because of the veil of smoke, but because I was not in the here and now. At the anteroom gate, I'd stepped into some other time—some other day—when William Mendelson's vault was the center of a storm.

This storm was a raging sea of flame and smoke churning around me like hell's front porch. The anteroom was engulfed in fire. Wooden shelves that lined the walls were awash in angry, growling flames. An old desk or table—I couldn't discern which—was consumed, too, and a nearby chair was toppled backward and almost ashes.

Muffled shouts descended the stairs as two bulky, masked figures emerged into the anteroom. Their masks were not any robber's disguise but respirators for firemen cloaked in heavy fire-protective ensembles.

"Is anyone down here?" One of the firemen called in muffled, hollow sounds through his mask. He stepped into the anteroom and glanced up. Flames chattered overhead across ancient wood joists as gnarled fire-fingers stabbed out at him. "Jesus, Tommy, we gotta get him fast." Another step forward. "Call out! Where are you?"

I could do no more than watch the two firemen inch into the furnace. My feet were immobile and my legs would not obey. Yet, movement was unnecessary, as neither fireman would be aware of my presence—they hadn't come to save me and were oblivious that I was mere feet from them watching their every move. I had a front-row seat for whatever I was to see and they had no clue I was in the audience. After all, I was not there. Not really.

A voice called from inside the open vault in choked, terrified spasms.

"Here...I'm...in here."

"We're coming. Get on the floor!"

Tommy lurched forward and used a long bar with a forked tongue on the end to push away a blazing fallen shelf blocking his path. The second fireman used his bar to lever the debris toward the wall, clearing an escape.

Violent swirls of smoke choked the room. The fire chattered and taunted the men as the surrendering joists crackled overhead.

"Gruber—I've got him."

Tommy emerged from the vault with a sooty, coughing body over his shoulder in the classic fireman's carry. He stumbled, twice fell to one knee, but regained his strength and tried to continue on.

"Wait!" Gruber—the other fireman—jumped back as a flaming ceiling-high shelf collapsed atop Tommy and his ward. "Tommy!"

I had to turn my head—not from the inferno's intensity, but from my certainty that at any moment the ceiling would follow the shelf down and finish the three men.

But there was a reprieve.

Gruber leapt into action and levered the engulfed shelf up and away. He grunted, reached into the smoke, and pulled Tommy and his charge free.

Tommy got to his knees and rolled the man off his shoulder to the floor. "Take him, Gruber, I gotta get my breath."

Gruber hefted the man over his shoulders with one powerful movement. "Come on, Tommy, follow me. We gotta get out of here. This place might be gone any second."

"Go, go," Tommy gasped and waved toward the security gate. "I'm right behind you."

Gruber hesitated, nodded, and disappeared into a wall of smoke.

Faltering wood groaned above and fire rained a gale down on Tommy's back.

"Get up, Tommy. The ceiling's coming down," I yelled, but the fireman couldn't hear me. I was losing touch with this place—this time. The room now turned around me like a carousel. The flames fluttered still and the smoke dissipated. I tried once more. "Go, Tommy. Get out before—"

Two heavy ceiling timbers crashed down. One struck the steel security gate and slammed it shut. The second fell against the gate, jamming between it and the wall.

Tommy was trapped.

"Gruber!" Tommy tried to lever the timber free. "Gruber!"

The room swirled into a blur before me. Lingering fingers of smoke faded and the room disappeared into nothing. An eye blink later, the overhead light shined ahead of me on the other side of the steel security gate that was now open and unbarred. I jumped toward Tommy—or toward where he'd been.

I never reached him...

My first step touched the anteroom floor and I faced the open steel security gate. The dim overhead lights were on and no shelves or flames surrounded me. The smoke was gone. The heat had cooled. Tommy and the burning timbers were no more—sent back to some point in time that was not my own.

"Damn." I shook off the vision that had tried to send a message. What that message meant was as mysterious and veiled to me as the events I'd just encountered.

These side trips from the here and now were not unfamiliar to me. Since returning from, well, from wherever it was really-dead people stay, I often was pulled elsewhere to watch vignettes of the past. I'm not talking about old reruns of westerns or *I Love Lucy*, mind you. The visions were hints and clues from the past—someone else's past—but they were never clear. It was just as it was moments ago: A flash of events. A secret needing to be told, sneaking out from somewhere to taunt me. And it was always up to me to figure out whether it meant anything or not.

Lucky me.

"Hey, Angel, am I glad to see you. I was just in a fire. Right here, too. Man, was it scary..."

Angel threw me a glance and shook her head—that meant *Be quiet and listen*. Of course, the two things I was not good at. "Gotcha."

Bear glanced over at me but said nothing. He stood in the open vault doorway beside Angel and a tall, almost too-thin African-American detective—Calvin Clemens. Behind Cal was Mr. Wonderful—Thorne—who stood watching.

Cal had been on Bear's team for years and was a solid cop. He was in his early thirties with close-cut hair, high cheekbones, and big round eyes. He wore a goatee and was dressed in jeans and an untucked black dress shirt beneath a dark sport coat. Unlike many of the cops on the team, he stayed to himself and did his job. He wasn't much for fanfare or bluster. My kind of cop.

"Cal," Bear said, flashing a penlight around the dimly lit vault, "get crime scene down here right away. And call the ME."

"Right. That robber cleaned this place out. Except for this safe, I guess." He gestured to an old railroad safe that looked like it was last used to keep money from Billy the Kid. It stood beside the counting table in the back corner of the vault. "Wonder what he got?"

"Poor William," Thorne said in a dry, steady voice. He didn't appear squeamish looking over the body. In fact, he seemed rather...*comfortable.* "After all he's been through—to be killed by a robber. I should find Marshal."

Bear noticed Thorne's calm, too. "You don't seem too upset, Thorne."

"Of course I'm upset, Detective." Thorne folded his arms. "But I am the Vice President and Chief Security Officer..."

"Yeah, yeah," Bear groaned. "I got that—twice already."

Thorne nodded. "Yes, of course. I should find Marshal—he's the bank president and William's son. He should have been here by now."

"Mr. Thorne," Angel said, "I'll help you find Marshal."

"It's Franklin, Professor." He smiled and I wanted to puke. "Or, may I call you Angela?"

"Of course."

Now I rolled my eyes. "Oh, come on. There's a dead guy in the vault and Captain Wonderful is making goo-goo eyes at you, Angel."

She took a deep breath. "We should let the *detectives* work." She led Thorne back through the anteroom gate and up the stairs.

When they were gone, Cal went to the rear of the anteroom and pulled out his cell phone. When he was out of earshot, I turned to Bear. "Hey, partner, do you smell the smoke?"

He looked around and took a deep snort of air. "No, should I?"

I gave him a quick summary of my vision of the fiery basement. "What do you think?"

"I think you watch too much TV."

"Yeah, I do, but that's not it." I went inside the vault door—Bear wouldn't venture in again until the crime scene team processed at least some of the scene. "This wasn't just a heist, you know that, right? I mean, fire or not."

"You sure?" Bear looked around. "What are you thinking?"

"William Mendelson knew his killer."

Chapter Four

"Are you sure?" Bear said. "You think he knew his killer by just peeking into this vault? Or did you do that hocus pocus crap again?"

I don't do hocus pocus—crap or not. "The killer stood behind him and shot him close up." I went into the vault and stood beside William's body and pointed to a spot on his back that Bear couldn't see. "The shot enters here—just to the right of the heart—and exits through the front. It probably clipped his heart and he bled out pretty fast."

"Right, the perp had to be standing behind him."

I nodded. "This vault isn't that big. William knew his killer, or he never would have let him get behind him—maybe if he were forced, but I don't think so. And there's no sign of a struggle. It's like he and the killer were looking at something on the desk." I pointed to the large, dark blood stain in the middle of the counting table in front of Mendelson. "And look at the blood stain. Something's been removed from that spot. Whatever they were looking at is gone. It was taken after the shooting."

"I saw that," Bear peered in at the table. "A file, I think—or a big book or something."

Blood covered a large portion of the counting table, along with William's hands, arms, and most of his shirt. Just beneath his fingers, however, was a rectangular bare spot that was virtually clean and blood free. When William Mendelson was killed, he bled out over himself and the table and everything on it. Whatever he and his killer had been looking at was taken afterward, leaving the void behind.

"Maybe a bank employee?" Bear said. "A big-shot customer or close friend?"

"Yeah, someone close to him." I threw a thumb toward the open vault door. "And I don't see that bank robber killing him and emptying the vault alone, do you? He ran out a half hour ago—empty-handed. Mendelson's body is cold and looks like he's been dead for hours. The timeline doesn't make sense."

Bear's mouth tightened as it did when he didn't like the news. "Not unless the robber was here for a while. Maybe he loaded up the stuff—whatever it was—and was making a dash for it when the guard arrived."

No, that didn't work either. "So, this robber—someone Mendelson knows—shows up to rob the bank annex in a ski mask and gun? Mendelson shows him something just before he gets killed? Then he runs off and collides with Conti? I don't think so."

Bear thought about that. "Conti arrived for work and found the employee door unlocked. When he came in to check, the robber jumped him, beat him up, and demanded to know where the vault was with the gold and stones. But yet, this vault is as empty as my refrigerator." He threw a chin at the tall, wide railroad safe in the corner. "Unless everything's still in there."

"Could be. But I don't think that guy robbed this place. Why beat up Conti asking where the vault was if he'd already emptied it?"

"Right. Doesn't fit." Bear looked around for the hundredth time as his face soured more and his jaw muscles twitched. "Another thing—what the hell was William doing in the bank at this hour? He's in his nineties and probably just a figurehead chairman, right?"

"Bankers don't work these kinds of hours, figureheads or not."

Bear knelt down and shined his penlight at an angle across the floor, scanning in all directions for any telltale sign of evidence. "You getting anything yet?" he asked.

Getting anything? "No, I'm not 'getting anything.' I'm a cop, not a gypsy fortune teller."

"You know what I mean."

Yeah, unfortunately, I did. Sometimes, the strangest things draw me in at a crime scene. It could be a piece of jewelry, a photograph, something personal to connect the dots in a crime and show me their secrets. Often those secrets are a piece of history behind the crime—or a piece of history from the object's owner. The secrets tell themselves to me, but they're not always clear. It's like watching a movie from the cheap seats. I can see but I can't participate, and too often, I don't get the whole show—just a small episode here or there. Once, when I was investigating my own murder, some stolen gold coins gave me a vision of the murderer at his first kill. I didn't know who it was and wouldn't for days—and only after more killing. It was confusing and without meaning till another clue put it all together.

Sometimes the little episode I watched was a big piece of the case.

And sometimes it was nothing at all.

I spent a few minutes poking and probing William's body—something Bear couldn't do without violating the crime scene. He couldn't touch anything; the crime team needed to photograph and process the scene before any detailed examination of the body or vault could be done. For now, a simple examination of the wound, a peek in a pocket here and there, and a check of the vault for any obvious evidence was the limit of his effort.

"Sorry, Bear. I got nothing. Unless you count the guy in the bomber jacket and Washington Senators ball cap."

"The what?"

I told Bear how I'd found William—after I reassured him I wasn't crazy. After all, telling him about a baseball cap–wearing ghost who led me to William's body would have sounded crazy...except that a dead guy was the one telling the story.

"Here we go again with your dead pals," Bear said, and when someone coughed just outside the vault door, he whirled around and found Cal Clemens watching him. "What, Cal?"

"Crime boys will be down in a flash." Cal grinned. "You guys okay in there?"

"We're fine—I'm fine." Bear cursed. "*I'm* fine."

Cal hid a smile and did a bad job of it. "Willy Mendelson was an okay guy. It broke my heart when I saw it was him."

CHAPTER FOUR

"Willy?" I said.

"You knew Mendelson, Cal?" Bear's eyebrows raised. "I didn't know you ran with the banking crowd."

"Hah, no, I don't, man." Cal flashed a smile made crooked by an arrested suspect a month ago. "One of my crew goes way back with Willy, though. And I see him around the club."

"Your crew? The club?" I gave Bear a *Where's the real Cal Clemens?* look. "Spence is out of town a few days and suddenly Cal has a crew and hangs with rich bankers at a club. And you think me hanging around is weird?"

Bear ignored me. "Make believe you lost me when you called him Willy, Cal."

Cal made the sign of the cross between his forehead, chest, and shoulders. "Yeah, sorry. I got this pal—Keys Hawkins—who owns a night club outside town. Keys and Willy go way back—all the way to the war."

"World War II," I said.

Bear nodded. "No shit."

Cal went on. "Willy and Keys are tight—real tight. Willy fought in Northern Africa and Europe. He met Keys in Egypt. Willy lied about his age to get into the Army, and Key's was just a kid himself playing in the Cairo nightclubs. They been pals since the forties. Keys is the only blues man; Willy can't play the spoons, but he's got a table there every weekend."

Bear's gears were grinding. "Mendelson hung out in some club with you guys?"

"Yeah, you should try it, too, Bear. It might loosen you up a little."

"Sure. Soon. Tell me about Mendelson."

Cal thought a moment. "I don't know him well. He comes in and chats us up sometimes. But mostly he and Keys go off and talk alone—you know, old-guy stuff. But Willy's cool. Him and Keys both. Keys is gonna take this hard. I'll tell him."

"Okay, and interview him, too." Bear eyed him. "Got it?"

"Yeah, no problem. Good thing Mikey is out for this one. Keys doesn't like Mikey."

I laughed. "No? I'm shocked."

23

Mike Spence was Cal's partner. Spence had a reputation as a, well, an irritant—like a piece of gravel up your ass. He didn't intend to be a jerk. Well, that's not true, he often did—but most of the time it just came naturally. Cal was the quiet, kind-hearted, easy-to-get-along-with partner. Mike was the other one.

"Okay, Cal, but when we're through here today, get with your pal Keys. Let's grab some coffee and we can talk through it. This one's a little weird."

Cal looked at William's body. "Weird like you talking to Tuck all the time? Or weird like we don't have any evidence?"

Bear eyed him. "I don't talk to Tuck."

"You were a bit ago, man." Cal smiled, patted Bear on the shoulder, and added, "But that's cool, man, that's cool. I get it. When I got shot last year, I was prayin' Tuck was still around. 'Cause, you know, if I had died, I'd come back and work with you, too."

Bear rolled his eyes. "Great. Just what I need—two of you."

Chapter Five

Karen Simms burst into the annex break room and went straight to Larry Conti and threw her arms around his shoulders. "Thank God you're all right. I just got here. I heard you got shot—almost killed. Someone robbed us? You stopped—"

"The Chairman's dead."

She leaned back from him as her face froze. "What?"

"He's dead." Larry sat at a small round dinette table sipping a cup of coffee and adjusting a bandage on his head. "Someone murdered him." Larry was perhaps thirty, with dark eyes that gave away his Mediterranean heritage. He stood and slipped his dark blue blazer off—pushing his finger through the bullet hole with a smile—and hung it on the back of his chair. "The robber jumped me and got my gun, but the Chairman was already dead."

"Are you sure?" Karen's lips didn't seem to move. "It wasn't..."

"No. It was him. They found him this morning."

She took a couple slow, shaky steps back and leaned against the kitchen counter. "The robber killed William? Oh my God."

"I guess so. Maybe. I don't know." Larry rubbed his jaw and rolled his head trying to loosen tense muscles. "That's the weird thing. When I got here this morning, I found the side door open. I went in and he jumped me. He kept asking where the vault and gold and stones were."

Karen slipped down into a chair across the table from him. "Gold and stones? And you didn't tell him where it was?"

"Nope. But he sure knew about the Chairman, right?" He sipped his coffee. "Anyway, the cops found him dead down in his vault. They don't

25

think the robber did it, though. And some lady was almost kidnapped, but Mr. Thorne stopped it all."

"The robber didn't kill William?"

"No."

"Who did?"

"Somebody here, maybe. Who else?"

Karen stood, went to the counter. She took her time and poured a cup of coffee, spooned in some sugar and a drop or two of cream. She stood facing the cabinet for a long time. She was tall, with a curvaceous, busty frame, and toned, tight muscles from hours each night at the gym. Right then she wished she could retreat to the gym for a run and workout. William murdered but not by the robber? Larry beaten—shot—but he kept the vault a secret? And Franklin Thorne was involved, too. He was supposed to be out of town. What was happening?

When she turned around, it struck her that Larry seemed calm and unfazed by the robbery. Was he that steely? Had she misjudged him all this time? Or was there another reason?

"Poor William." She tried to stay calm, but she could hear the fear in her voice cracking her words. "Larry, are you sure you're okay?

I'm worried about you." She brushed back her long blond hair and slipped her ski jacket off. When she gave Larry another warm embrace, she lingered a bit longer than she needed. She was thirty-one, just a year older than Larry. He had a soft spot for her. All the men at the bank did—well, almost all. But with Larry, it was different.

And it was important now.

"What happened, Larry? Did the robber get anything? The cops wouldn't tell me anything and told me to come in here and wait. I'm frightened."

"It'll be okay." He reached out and touched her arm, guiding her back into a chair beside him. "I'm not supposed to talk about it, Karen. You understand? But don't be afraid. It'll be all right—I'll make sure."

"I'm not a cop or someone like you, so I don't understand. It's just us, Larry, come on." She gripped his hand. "I'm afraid. You know William liked us—both of us. Not Marshal—he hates me. He'll fire me first chance he gets. And what if someone here killed William? What if..."

"It'll be all right, Karen. I promise. No one will hurt you. You're not going to get fired. And that guy won't be back, either. After he beat me up, he ran out and tried to take Professor Tucker hostage. Mr. Thorne shot the guy..."

"Who?"

"Tucker—she's from the university."

"Oh, yes, I took a class of hers last year." Karen's mouth went dry and she sipped her coffee. "Her husband was a cop—he was killed a couple years ago, right? What was she doing here before opening?"

He shrugged. "Beats me. When the robber ran outside, he grabbed her and tried to run. I tried to stop him, but he shot me." He stuck his finger through the hole in his uniform blazer again. "Thorne came out of nowhere and shot the guy. He just wounded him, though, and he got away."

"My God, Larry. Why didn't you tell him about the vault?"

He shook his head. "I tried to tell him the vault was at the bank—to get him out of the annex—but he knew all about William's secret vault. And he kept asking about gold and stones."

"Does William have those down there?"

"I don't know." He shrugged again. "The Chairman had a lot of stuff down there. Everyone knows—even though Thorne and Marshal think it's a big secret."

Karen leaned back and contemplated her coffee cup. In all the years she'd worked at the bank, no one ever spoke of William's secret vault, but everyone seemed to know—a whisper here, a sly comment there. No one had ever seen it, let alone been inside. Then, several months ago, William took her into his confidence. Since then, he'd relied on her for so many things—uncertain things. In time, his reliance on her grew until last week, when his last, biggest secret passed his lips. After hearing his story and seeing the proof of his past, William didn't seem so odd anymore—just scared. And that secret was to be feared.

And Larry knew as much as she did. Maybe *more*.

"Larry, has William shown you inside the vault?"

"Has he shown you?"

"He told me about it in case there was an emergency. But I've never seen inside."

"Me neither." Larry stood and refilled his coffee cup. "They asked about it, you know—the cops. They want to talk to me again later."

Franklin Thorne walked in, halting the conversation. "Karen, I need to speak with you."

"What's wrong, Mr. Thorne?"

"I can't say. Would you meet me in the main office in ten minutes, please? I need to access the safety deposit vault and I need your key."

"Yes, sir." When Thorne left, she looked at Larry. "This scares me to death. It could ruin everything."

"Why do you say that?"

"Because with the robbery and William's murder, they'll be poking and probing around at everything, right?"

"So? Karen, you're okay. You haven't done anything wrong."

She stood and went to the sink and put her coffee cup down. "Maybe we should tell the cops everything. You know, what we've seen."

"I don't know what we saw, Karen." Larry shook his head. "And neither do you. So, no. Don't do anything until we talk again. We should meet later, after you get away from Thorne and after I speak with the police again, okay?"

"Okay, meet me in the basement file room. Say an hour? And we don't say anything until then—to anyone—right?"

Larry nodded.

"I'm trusting you."

Larry tried to smile. "With your pal Thorne involved, I'm worried, too."

"There is no 'my pal.' It's you and me, Larry—you and me." She kissed his cheek and left the break room.

Thorne wanted to see her in six or seven minutes. She quickened her step and before she reached the lobby, she dug into her purse, found a key secreted in her makeup case, and turned right at a narrow corridor. As she did, someone ahead of her unlocked the steel door at the end of the corridor, marked "Security Room—Authorized Personnel Only." The person slipped inside and closed the door.

Franklin Thorne.

Chapter Six

"Okay, Thorne, you're the big-shot security guy around here: what do you think happened?" Bear dropped down at the conference room table across from Angel with a fresh cup of coffee. "Anything odd or out of the ordinary happen lately?"

Saying *odd* and *out of the ordinary* around me was like saying the Titanic was a boating accident. I said as much and made Bear smile for the first time all morning.

Angel, of course, rolled her eyes.

Bear asked, "Anything?"

Thorne—oblivious to my witty commentary—pursed his lips to think. He was in his mid-thirties or early forties. He had average weight on his six-one frame, and he wore a short-trimmed, stylish beard, and had large, piercing dark eyes. He was dressed in an immaculate dark suit and starched white shirt—both expensive and well fitted. He belonged in a men's fashion magazine, not this crime scene.

"No, Detective. I'm a little puzzled by it all."

"Murder always puzzles me." Bear sipped his coffee. "What part in particular?"

"Everything," Thorne said. "First, it would appear someone tried to rob the bank and came to the wrong building—they came to the annex. Why would anyone come here to rob us? They missed the bank by a hundred feet or more."

"The secret vault is why."

Thorne raised a finger. "My point, Detective. No one knew about the

30

Chairman's private vault—only Marshal and me. Obviously, they did as well. That surprises me."

"Marshal Mendelson—he's the bank president, right?"

"Yes, and now he's the bank's sole owner."

Interesting. I said, "Now, there's a motive, Bear."

"No shit," he cringed a little when he answered me aloud, but once again covered it well. "I guess he would be. What else?"

Angel sat sipping coffee and threw me the *Shut up and stop causing trouble* glance. If you're a guy, you know that look. If you're a woman, the look is part of your DNA.

"I don't know what William kept in there," Thorne said. "Some of his more valuable antique Egyptian collection, I imagine. But I didn't think anyone knew about it. Yet someone killed him there and robbed him."

"Egyptian?" I said. "Like the big monster beside his door?"

Bear repeated me.

Thorne laughed. "I nearly shot that statue when I went into his office the first time. But, actually, it's a replica—at least that's what he told me." Thorne glanced at Angel. "He fell in love with Egyptian history when he was over there. Seth is his favorite toy."

"Seth is the Egyptian God of chaos and destruction—other things, too." Angel gave Thorne a friendly smile. "I think Seth was related to my dear departed husband."

Thorne laughed again.

Not me. "Funny—until he eats someone. No one believed in ghosts around here until I got killed. Now who's laughing?" I turned to Bear. "We need to get in the safe, partner. Enough of this chitchat with Mr. Amazing."

"We need to open Mendelson's safe." Bear threw a thumb toward the conference room door. "After my crime techs finish with the vault, that is."

"Can't help you, Detective," Thorne said and shrugged. "I don't have the combination, and I doubt Marshal does either."

Bear cocked his head. "Doesn't anyone have it?"

"No. The Chairman was a strange, secretive old guy, Detective. As far as I know, he was the only one with the combination. And this morning was the first time I've even seen the inside of his vault."

Bear pulled out a pen and notepad from his pocket and made some notes. Strange, since I rarely see Bear take notes. He likes to delegate that to someone. It used to be me. "Okay, we'll get back to that. Anything else seem odd to you, Thorne?"

"Well, her." Thorne threw a chin toward Angel. "Angela's meeting is out of the ordinary. The Chairman worked all hours—sometimes all night. On what, I haven't a clue. But I've never known him to have meetings so early in the morning. And he always let security know if he did."

"And as I said, Bear," Angel said, "I don't know what the meeting was about. All he said was it was urgent, and I should be here at seven thirty—before the bank opened."

"See what I mean?" Thorne smiled at Angel again, as though they now had a secret no one could share. "Perhaps his death and Angela's meeting are connected."

"You think? Gee, Bear, no wonder Captain Wonderful is a vice president. A hush-hush meeting before the bank opens, a robbery of a secret vault no one knows about, and the boss is murdered in that secret vault. Gosh, I wonder if they're connected…"

Bear spit coffee onto the table and almost choked. "Sorry."

"That's all I'll say for now, Detective." Thorne shook his head. "I'd feel better if I waited until Marshal arrives. After all, he will feel this is a family matter."

"Yeah, about Marshal." Bear's eyes narrowed. "Where is he? It's going on eight thirty and he isn't here yet? You got here early."

Thorne frowned. "That's just accidental. Marshal and I were in Harrisonburg yesterday on business. I returned earlier this morning and came straight here. I wasn't supposed to be here until late this afternoon."

Bear's pen hovered over his notes.

Thorne got the hint. "I don't know about Marshal. He was with me last night and we were supposed to meet a client for breakfast. The client canceled late last night so we stayed over. I drove back this morning."

"With him?" I asked.

Bear repeated the question.

"No. He was there for two days and I joined him yesterday. I don't know what time he left today—he may have had more business in Harrisonburg. I left before six a.m. and drove straight here. Perhaps Marshal is still out of town. I simply don't know."

"Find out, will you?" Bear aimed his pen at the conference room door. "I need to speak with him soon."

"Of course." Thorne stood and picked up a thick manila shipping envelope from the chair beside him. I hadn't noticed it before. He slid it across the table to Bear. "There is one more thing. Something odd."

Bear picked up the envelope and read the hand-printed writing on the front. *"Emergency Instructions—Chairman William Mendelson's Eyes Only."*

"I have not opened it, of course," Thorne said. "I retrieved this from the bank's executive safety deposit box earlier with Miss Simms—she's our head teller. I went looking for the safe combination in case the Chairman placed it inside. Instead, I found this in the Chairman's personal folder."

Bear's eyes narrowed and his voice got curt. "You went into the safety deposit box and his personal folder? Don't you think you should have told me about it first, Thorne?"

"I'm telling you now. Miss Simms can vouch for my actions."

Bear tore open the envelope and dumped the contents out. Inside was a thick file labeled "Professor Angela Tucker, University of the Shenandoah Valley."

Angel's eyes went big. "Me? What on earth would William leave for me?"

"Let's find out." Bear opened the file.

There were several printouts of Internet stories surrounding World War II, and in particular, Allied operations in Northern Africa and the Middle East. Someone, presumably William Mendelson, had highlighted bits and pieces of text about German activities in and around Egypt. The phrase "Operation Salaam" was hand-scribed across a map of Cairo.

Thorne said, "It looks like William was doing research into the war. Mean anything to you, Angela?"

She shrugged. "I'm not familiar with any of it."

I said, "Maybe that's what your meeting was about—helping him with research. It must be pretty important to hide in a safety deposit box, though."

Bear repeated me, adding, "Sort of like he knew something was coming, huh?"

Thorne folded his arms. "Perhaps, but this is certainly not evidence. I'm sure Marshal will want the Chairman's papers returned—"

"It's evidence, Thorne." Bear gathered the papers and replaced them into the file. "He'll get it all back after the investigation."

"Yes, yes, of course," Thorne said with a forced smile. "But you have to understand. Suddenly, I find myself working for Marshal, not the Chairman. I must consider his expectations of me going forward."

"Sure. But he's not here and you don't know where he is, right?" Bear said.

Thorne shook his head.

"Then until he shows, I'll mind his interests." Bear noticed Thorne's empty leather holster peeking out from beneath his suit coat. "I find it odd you carry a weapon at work."

He nodded. "Really? Why, I'm the—"

"Vice president and ya-de-ya. I know."

Thorne's face tightened. "When may I expect my weapon back, Detective?"

"When ballistics is done and I clear the case—it's procedure." Bear eyed him. "Why, you plan on using it soon?"

"You can't be too prepared for a bank robbery." Thorne looked at Angel. "And you never know when you might have to save a brilliant, beautiful woman in distress."

Chapter Seven

A sandy-haired woman in an expensive Moncler coat stepped out of her Mercedes and looked across the parking lot at the glut of police cars behind the bank. She surveyed the area until she saw a familiar face—one of the bank tellers—sitting in an old Toyota across the street. The woman brushed her feathered hair from her face and walked over to the teller's car.

At the Toyota, she bent and knocked on the driver's side window, startling the young girl inside. The window rolled down and the smells of fresh coffee and cheap perfume drifted out.

"What's going on?"

"Oh, good morning, Ms.—"

"Call me Lee—everyone does. What's going on at the bank?"

"Someone tried to rob us." The teller gestured toward the bank and her voice got low and uneasy. "I shouldn't say—but I know you are a close friend of Mr. Mendelson—well, Mr. Mendelson was murdered."

"Murdered?" Lee leaned down to look into the teller's car window better. "Which Mendelson did the robbers kill—Marshal?"

"No, the police found the Chairman dead. But it wasn't the robber who killed him. At least, that's what I heard."

"*Wasn't the robber?*" Lee glanced toward two policemen watching her from the bank parking lot. "Did they catch him?"

"No, but almost. Larry got shot and Mr. Thorne shot the guy, but he got away."

"Who's Larry? A cop?"

"Nope. He's our security guard. Mr. Thorne shot the robber when he tried taking a hostage."

"Dear God." Lee checked her watch. She had to be back by ten, and this might change everything—especially if her *transactions* were involved. "Did the robber get much? Or did the security guard stop the robbery?"

"That's the funny thing, you know?" The teller leaned out the window. "That guy tried to rob the administration annex. You believe it? He wasn't even at the bank. I guess he knew."

"Knew what?"

"About the Mendelson's big secret." The teller took a long sip of coffee from her First Bank and Trust of Frederick County travel mug. "Which ain't secret."

"Big secret?" Lee tried to sound surprised. "What secret do the Mendelsons have?"

The teller's face lit up. "He has a private stash in the annex! Everyone talks about it, but it's supposed to be a big family secret. Some kind of safe or vault or something. Stuffed with cash and some kind of treasure."

Lee blinked several times. "Treasure? Really?"

"But I don't know—maybe it's just gossip. Anyway, bank's closed. Check back this afternoon."

Lee thanked her and returned to her Mercedes. She started the engine, turned down the Andrews Sisters CD, and activated her Blue-tooth. A moment later, an aged, tired voice answered.

"Good morning, my dear. Your lunch date hasn't changed plans, I hope?"

Lee watched a police cruiser pull out of the rear bank parking lot and drive slowly past. The policeman driving glanced over and made eye contact with her. She feigned a smile and focused on her call.

"No, Nicholas—at least, not yet. I'm at the bank and there's something you need to know."

Chapter Eight

Bear went to question everyone at the bank annex except the water cooler, and I didn't want to tag along. Neither did I want to sit around and watch Thorne ogle Angel, so I went snooping—er, investigating—on my own.

I had just stepped into the marble-tiled lobby when someone called me from across the lobby. "Don't you have some investigating to do, kid?"

The man in the bomber jacket was back. He stood at the entrance to the executive suite corridor where William's office was. Like before, he leaned against the wall with his ball cap perched on the back of his head. He wore an easy, friendly smile. He gestured for me to follow him and disappeared down the corridor.

I followed—carefully, as this was the kind of trap vampires and renegade Indians were known for. I found him in the middle of William Mendelson's office, looking at some old photographs hanging on the wall.

"Look around, kid," he said. "Following that big cop around ain't gonna solve this case. I remember following my boss out of a plane too soon and we got our chute lines all tangled and..."

"Who the hell are you, anyway?"

He winked. "My point is that some things are better done solo, you know what I mean? We'll talk later." And with that, he was gone.

I stopped inside the door and addressed Seth. "Watch yourself, pal. You're fake—I'm real. So back off."

William's office was like a museum. It was laden with historic trappings, most from Egypt and Greece, and memorabilia from William's WWII days.

There were wall hangings resembling ancient Egyptian scrolls and paintings, Egyptian figurines, and two tall statues in the rear of the room—one a birdlike man and the other a tall, chiseled pillar. There were smaller statues and artifacts lining bookshelves and display stands around the room, each overflowing with books, relics, and years of memories. I noted a shelf where a set of leather history books were lying on their face—imprints in the dust showed that two odd-shaped bookends had been removed. Strange.

I looked around for more anomalies but found only dozens of framed photographs hanging on the walls and propped up on shelves, replica model war planes, military medals, and patches. And of course, there was my new pal, Seth.

The office reminded me of a Smithsonian exhibit instead of a stuffy old banker's office.

And then, there it was—waiting for me on one of the bookshelves.

A photograph of a young William Mendelson sitting with three pals at a dusty, crowded streetside café during the war. He was much more than just young. He looked like a child in a military uniform. The photograph grew warm to my touch and pulled at me. When I looked back toward William's desk, there was a small figurine, perhaps a paperweight, lying on the expensive Persian carpet under the corner of his desk. I hadn't noticed it earlier, so I went for a closer look and found a stone carving of a bug.

"Hello there, why are you sitting on the floor?" Yes, I often talk to myself. It's a new habit—something of a twitch. It comes from having only two living people to talk to. And they tend to "shush" me a lot.

The figurine was not some cheap drugstore doodad. It was a heavy, expertly sculpted, ornate bug trimmed in gold inlay with tiny gemstones set into its body. Okay, not a bug like a slug or a cockroach. It was a scarab, an ancient Egyptian beetle. I know about scarabs not from my vast knowledge of Egypt, stonework, or history—I saw some scarabs eat a guy in a mummy movie a few years ago and it scared the crap out of me.

This scarab didn't appear dangerous or hungry, thank God. It lay on its back against the leg of the desk. It looked like it had fallen from the desktop and stayed where it landed. When I reached down and touched it, the room snapped to black...

The heat enveloped me like an oven. It wasn't just hot, it was oppressive, and I faltered a little and reached for the desk to support me. That was difficult because the desk was gone. Instead, there was a small square table surrounded by three tall-backed wicker fan chairs. The light ebbed around me and by the time I steadied my legs, William's office had transformed into a streetside café overlooking a dust-blown street where noise and commotion were everywhere. I was on the ground-floor terrace of a tall, four-story stone hotel. Men sat at tables similar to mine sipping small cups of some brew and tall glasses of water. Many were dressed in khaki military uniforms similar to the photographs in William's display case. A tall, dark-skinned waiter passed me, dressed in a long white Egyptian shirt—a thobe, I think it's called—that hung to his feet with a tasseled fez on his head. He carried a tray of chai glasses and pitchers of water.

Somewhere behind me, a piano played but no one listened.

The dust blew in from the street where an occasional old car drove by— and by *old* I mean 1930s old, with wide, round fenders and bulky, oversized bodies. Parked right outside the café entrance was a horse-drawn carriage with a bearded man, wearing a similar thobe and a turban, waiting for fares.

Where was I? And why?

I turned in a slow circle and tried to get my bearings. Around me were a couple dozen tables where men chatted and others sat alone reading newspapers or sipping drinks. I peeked at one of the newspapers and the date surprised me—1942. The chatter around me was English; the Queen's English, too, with a lot of *right-oh, jolly good,* and *cheers.* Passing waiters took orders from the Brits, nodded with a tip of the head, and walked away calling out the orders in loud Arabic.

A tall, thin, balding man dressed in a light linen suit that looked very Charlie Chan climbed the steps from the street and walked onto the terrace. He had weathered, dark skin and looked Egyptian. He carried a newspaper under his arm and stopped at the terrace entrance to look around.

A waiter greeted him in slow but well-mannered English. *"Salaam,* sir, good evening. Welcome to the Shepheard Hotel. How may I be of service?"

"*Salaam, salaam,*" the thin man responded. Then he sighted someone across the terrace and walked away. He negotiated the tables and met a heavier-set, shorter man at a rear table.

Why, I don't know, but I followed.

"Peter, thank you for seeing me," the thin man said, now in thick-accented English. "I trust you have not waited long."

"No, no." Peter gestured to a chair. "Not at all, Hussein. But, please, could this not wait until later at the houseboat?"

"No, I'm afraid not." Hussein ordered chai from a passing waiter and placed his newspaper on the table, took out a pack of cigarettes, lit one, and offered the pack to Peter. "Please, for you."

Peter took a cigarette and placed the pack in his shirt pocket. "Have you been to the cabaret? How is Hekmet? She is treating you like royalty, I hope?"

"I could not find her. She is too busy with our British friends."

Peter laughed and sipped at a tall glass of dark tea.

Hussein crossed his legs and looked around the terrace, studying a couple tables of uniformed military customers. "Very busy today. Are we still meeting our new young friend at the Kit Kat this evening?"

"Yes, of course." Peter picked up the newspaper and unfurled it in front of him. "He's bringing someone new tonight—Youssif is very well known at the Ministry of Antiquities. I believe he will fascinate you."

"Ah, very good. Then our young friend has been well received by our Western hosts?"

Peter nodded. "Very."

"That is good."

Peter removed something from his jacket pocket and placed it inside the newspaper, refolded the paper, and laid it back on the table. Hussein didn't wait for his chai but stood, tipped his head to Peter, picked up the newspaper, and wound his way back through the maze of café tables and back into the street.

Interesting. The old newspaper/cigarette pack switcheroo.

I followed Hussein as far as the terrace entrance. He kept going to the end of the block but twice stopped on the way and turned back toward me. But each time, he stopped again, turned, and continued on his way. Half a block down the street he climbed into a horse-drawn cart and waved at the driver to whisk him away. By the time I returned to look for Peter, his table was empty except for his tall glass of chai and a few coins on the tabletop.

I started toward the street to look for him, but with each step the light faded. Before I reached the end of the terrace, I succumbed to the darkness where no spoons rattled chai glasses and none of the Queen's English reached me.

Another step and the lightning flashed around me...

The sudden wash of cool air chilled me. When I opened my eyes, I was beside William's desk staring at the stone-carved scarab at my fingertips. Seth watched me from the doorway, and I'd swear he had a smirk on his wood snout.

"Okay, Seth, what was that all about?"

He didn't explain, of course, because unlike dead detectives and other spirits, carved Egyptian gods are not real.

Chapter Nine

Shaking off my trip down someone else's memory lane, I went looking for Angel and found her sitting in the annex's conference room alone. She sipped a cup of coffee and stared away at nothing—her deep-thinking pose. In her hand was the thick manila folder from William Mendelson's safety deposit box and several pages were spread out in front of her.

I slipped into a chair across from her. "Wait until I tell you about Cairo. It was great. I was at—"

"Shush. I'm going through the evidence Bear gave me."

Shush? Wait, did she say evidence? "So now you're his evidence consultant? I thought you were a university professor."

My wife ignored me and opened the file. In it were several pages of handwritten notes and some computer printouts similar to those spread across the table. "That's why Bear wants me to go through all these notes. Now quiet, I have a lot on my mind."

"Like Captain Charming? Major Majestic? General—"

"No, like the evidence and William's murder."

Oh, right. Well, I still had a secret. "Okay, I won't tell you about the Shepheard Hotel or the weird guys drinking tea. Well, they didn't actually drink tea, they passed secret—"

"Professor Tucker?" A woman poked her head into the conference room behind us. "May I speak with you?"

Angel looked relieved. "Certainly, come in."

I said, "I guess when you're a police evidence consultant, everyone wants to consult with you."

"Please, sit down," Angel said and gestured to a chair. "What can I do for you?"

The woman took a chair across the conference room table from Angel. "I'm Karen Simms, the head teller. I heard you were a friend of William's. I thought I might be able to speak to you—you know, woman to woman?"

"Of course, Karen. How can I help?"

Karen stared at the documents spread across the table. "Is this what was in that file I gave Mr. Thorne earlier? It looks like the same one I helped get from the safety deposit vault."

"It's evidence, Angel," I said. "Don't tell her too much."

"Yes." Angel scooped up the pages from the table and replaced them in the file. "But I cannot talk about it. What is it I can help you with, Karen?"

"Well, I'm not really sure how to handle all this." Karen folded her hands on the table and tried to find something between them to focus on. It ended up being the manila file. "But William trusted you, right? He called you to a secret meeting and had this file for you."

"Well, I'm not sure the meeting was secret, but…"

"Of course it was." Karen looked down for a long moment. When she looked back up, her eyes were round and scared. "I'm afraid of this place—of what's happened in the past and of what is going to happen."

"What does that mean, Karen?"

"That damn vault is what." Karen's voice lowered. "With William dead, I heard there might be an audit. And I could get into trouble if I don't tell someone. And I don't know if I should tell Mr. Thorne or Marshal yet, or the police. So I'll tell you."

"Tell me what?" Angel asked. "What's got you so upset?"

Karen slumped back in her chair. "About eight months ago, William had me open a new account. And since then, I've been moving money in and out of it. A lot of money."

I said, "Moving money in a bank isn't unusual, Angel. There's more to it." Angel said as much.

"The account was someone else's business account—not his. He was very secretive about it. Money moved all the time, but not the way a normal business does. You know what I mean? And on the withdrawals, there was never enough for me to have to file a CTR."

"A CTR?" Angel asked.

I knew that one. "It's a currency transaction report. Banks have to file them for any transactions over ten grand."

Karen said that, too, adding, "It's to monitor for possible money laundering, fraud, and other suspicious activities—and of course for taxes. I guess William didn't want anyone looking into the withdrawals on the account. And that's all I'll say. You have to do the rest yourselves."

Angel asked, "What did he tell you about this account?"

"Nothing. He told me when I opened it for him that it was a confidential, personal matter with a special client." She lowered her voice again. "I was never to discuss it with anyone—under any circumstances. He promised I'd be 'taken care of' when the board took up the vacant vice president position next month. If I helped him, the job was mine."

Oh, sure. There was nothing suspicious about that.

"Karen," Angel said, "I'll need the name on the account."

"There's something else, too." Karen shot a glance toward the doorway and then turned back to Angel. "I checked this morning and someone locked me out of the account last night after I left work. I can't even see the account register—it's been totally secured. Now only whoever has the password can get in. Then—"

Someone knocked on the conference room door and we all looked up.

Thorne stood in the doorway with a big wolf-like grin on his face. "Ah, Professor Tucker, I see you are busy."

"Yes," Angel said. "What can I do for you?"

"I hoped to have a private word with you." His smile was disarming. "Perhaps in my office later on? I'll go see Detective Braddock first."

I said, "Gee, Angel, first William wants you early in the morning. Then Karen, now the Masked Manly-Man…"

"Yes, of course. I'll find you soon as we're done here." She shot me a quick glance that wasn't hard to interpret—thumb screws, electricity, hot coals.

She waited for Thorne to leave before turning back to Karen. "I need more information, Karen."

Karen's face was pale, and she was still staring at the doorway when she slipped a folded piece of paper across the table. "Here's the account number—I don't dare give you anymore." She stood up.

"Please, don't tell Mr. Thorne or Marshal. You have to make something up about me speaking with you just now."

An icy finger traced my spine. "Angel, there's something big she's not telling you."

"Karen, you should tell the police about this."

Karen hesitated and bit her lip. Her voice was but a whisper. "Marshal will tell you that William kept lots of secrets. Like his private vault—even though everyone in the bank knew about it. He'll even say that William went senile or crazy or something. He wasn't. William is a good man—*was* a good man. But he was scared of something...or someone. He was terrified."

"Who? What was he scared of?" Angel motioned for her to sit back down, but Karen didn't budge.

"William was a strange man but kind to the staff. A few months ago, he became very bitter and short-tempered—terrified of something. Then he opened this account and began working all night long. Sometimes he never went home. But that's not what I'm worried about, Professor."

I said, "Then what?"

Karen didn't wait for Angel's question. "I need that promotion—I'm in nursing school at the hospital but have to drop out. My whole life I've had to scrape by. My stepfather couldn't work and was a drunk. We never had anything. It killed my mom a few years ago. I've earned the promotion—I need it. You understand, right?"

"I do. But, you have to understand, too, Karen."

"William trusted you, Professor. There are a lot of things going on here. And I know most of them."

"Let me get Detective—"

"No." Karen held up a hand. "Not until I have assurances." Then, without another word, she left the conference room.

I watched her walk out. *"Assurances?* Somebody needs to cut down on the caffeine."

"I need to get her confidence a little more."

Something struck me odd. "Does it strike you odd that Karen calls Mr. Mendelson by his first name when everyone else—even Thorne—calls him 'the Chairman' most of the time? But no one calls Marshal anything but 'Marshal.'"

"I did notice." Angel picked up the file from the table. "This bank always impressed me as an old-world institution. Like a men's society club that's all about status and position."

"Old money can be like that—secret rings and handshake stuff." I pondered that. "I think Karen wants her own club ring. And I think she has a few secrets to swap for it. I'm not so sure Marshal knows about them, either."

"Do you think William knew?"

Oh yeah, William knew. "I'm pretty sure Karen got her secrets *from* William."

Chapter Ten

Bear needed to know about Karen Simms's revelations. I went to find him. He was back in the sub-basement, standing near William's vault, talking with Thorne as the crime scene technicians gathered their equipment. The look on Bear's face was foul and I thought it best to stay quiet and let him work.

"We'll have to drill the safe unless we can find that combination," Bear said when the tech signaled they were done with the scene. "We'll get to that this afternoon."

"I'm afraid I still haven't found Marshal, Detective." Thorne watched a tech tapping notes into a tablet computer. "He isn't answering his cell phone, either."

"Keep trying."

"Of course. I hope nothing has happened to him."

"Yeah, me too." Bear went into the vault and stood looking at William Mendelson's body. He spoke to Thorne without turning to face him. "Any talk from your staff? Any rumors? My men are interviewing, but we're not getting much."

"Nothing." Thorne hesitated a moment, then added, "Detective, I just learned that the entire staff knew about this vault. I had no idea. But, as I told Angela, they don't take to me very well."

"No?" Bear said. "Why's that?"

"No one likes authority, Detective. And they like security and the police even less."

"Yeah, I get that. I need William's home address and any close friends,

47

contacts...the works. Can you get that for me?"

"I'll do what I can." Thorne turned and went back upstairs.

I waited for him to leave and walked up behind Bear standing over William's body. "Weird, huh?"

He jumped. "Jesus, don't do that."

"Do what?"

He lowered his voice so the crime tech couldn't hear. "Sneak up on me."

"Sorry. I thought you saw me."

He glanced out of the vault to ensure the crime scene team was out of earshot. "I was concentrating on the dead guy in the room."

"Then you *did* see me."

"No." Bear rolled his eyes. "*Him*—the one who isn't arguing with me."

"Gotcha." I took a long look at William's body and did what I used to do when I was a living, breathing detective—I tried to find what the body hid. "Want to hear what I think?"

"Do I have a choice?"

"A choice of what, Detective?" one of the crime techs asked at the vault door. "The medical examiner's done and said to call when you're ready. He'll transport the body."

Bear looked back at him. "What did the ME say about time of death?"

Billy Villary, a seasoned crime tech, looked at his notes. "TOD is estimated at two a.m. The body's core temp was 86.6 degrees when he took it—down 10 degrees from normal. The body loses about 1.5 degrees per hour, and we figure the vault had a constant temperature, too. That sets TOD at just eight hours ago. Full rigor has set in and that's normally between six and twelve hours, so that fits, too—he died about two a.m."

"Okay. Any evidence or prints so far?"

"No prints at all. Not even the vic's. The killer was real careful and wiped everything down. A few tiny fragments of glass and what you see on the table—blood, wound splatter, and a missing something from the table. Maybe we'll find more when we get into the safe."

"Glass?" One of Bear's eyes narrowed like he had something in it. "No prints at all?"

"A few very small shards of plain glass—at least that's what it looks like. No prints, no fibers. We vacuumed up the shards and were about to bag the hands."

I said, "I think I have something."

Bear walked over beside me and waved Billy away. "Okay, Billy, I'll bag the hands. Tell the ME to take him out of here. Why don't you take a break until we get into the safe?"

"Thanks." Billy clicked off his tablet computer and went upstairs.

Bear turned to me. "What did you find?"

I pointed to William's right hand, which was clenched in a fist. "He's got a small piece of cardboard or heavy paper in his fingers. Looks like something was ripped out of his hand postmortem."

Bear retrieved a latex crime scene glove and a penlight from a kit on the anteroom table. He snapped the glove on and gently lifted William's hand—his body was almost in full rigor mortis and the arm was stiff and difficult to manipulate. Bear shined the penlight over the body's fingers at a tiny piece of dull, dark paper—perhaps an inch square—caught between the fingertips and palm.

"It's something, whatever it is. We'll let the ME remove it." He retrieved two paper evidence bags from a kit in the anteroom and slipped one over each hand. Then he retrieved some tape from outside the vault and taped the paper evidence bags tight around William's wrists, sealing any possible evidence that might fall off his hands inside the bags. "You got anything else?"

I told him about Angel's conversation with Karen Simms. He was particularly interested in William's odd behavior. "Everyone around here seems to have secrets, starting with William. But I think he told some of them to Karen."

"Then we better find out what those secrets are before someone else does."

Chapter Eleven

Larry Conti filled his travel mug with coffee, tightened the lid, and left the break room. He headed deeper into the rear office area and checked twice to see if anyone was watching him. Across from the rear emergency exit, he used a key to open a door marked "Secure Storage" and went inside. The room was lined with a dozen rows of ceiling-high storage racks filled with file boxes. He maneuvered around them to the rear of the room, where a staircase led down to the bank's basement and the historical file storage.

In the basement, he found Karen already waiting for him in the middle of the room surrounded by more racks of files. She looked upset and anxious and jumped up from a metal folding chair when he appeared. Her face was pale and her eyes red and irritated, as though she hadn't slept in days. Nerves were getting the best of her.

"I was just about to give up," she said in a low, crackly voice. She crushed into him. "What took you so long?"

"I had to write my statement, Karen. The cops are intense, you know?"

She grimaced. "Yeah, right. I'm sorry. What have you found out?"

"Same question to you." He looked her over, trying to catch a lie. "What have you heard from Thorne and Marshal?"

"No one knows where Marshal is, but that's not unusual. Franklin told me what you already did: they found William dead in his vault but don't think the robber did it. We retrieved William's emergency instructions and get this—there was a file in his safety deposit box for Professor Tucker."

"Is that why she had the meeting with the Chairman?"

Karen shrugged. "I don't know. And I don't think anyone else does, either. Do you know how William died?"

"He didn't just die, Karen, he was murdered. And they think the murderer was someone he knew, too."

"Oh my God." Her eyes darted around. "He was right, wasn't he? It's all happening. Someone was after him."

"You gotta relax, Karen. It could all be a coincidence."

"Coincidence? I don't believe that and neither do you." She looked around again as though someone was listening. "Was it coincidence someone tried to rob his vault this morning and now William's dead?"

"I don't know. Maybe."

"What's wrong with you, Larry? You told me William asked you to protect him. Now he's dead. Don't you think he was right? Don't you think someone was after him?"

She was right, of course. More right than she realized. He said, "Yeah, yeah, I know. But who was after him? Who killed him? And why? Was it the vault or something else?"

"Do you think Marshal had anything to do with all this?"

"I don't know. Marshal asked me to spy for him. I thought that was to keep the Chairman from screwing up here at the bank. You know, like Alzheimer's or something—that's what he told me. But now I'm not so sure."

Karen bit her lip and blinked a few times. "That doesn't mean that's not the real reason he wanted you to spy on him."

"No, you're right. But I wonder, don't you?" He glanced back toward the stairwell and listened. Karen was holding back—he felt it and heard it in her voice. He had to find out what she knew and what Thorne knew. Karen was Thorne's favorite and he knew why. Still, jealousy had a way of getting in the way of common sense. He couldn't afford to get it all wrong.

"Somebody shot the Chairman in cold blood, Karen—sound like anyone you know? A cold-hearted bastard?" She looked away and he pressed her. "Did you meet Thorne last night? We were supposed to meet—you and me—remember?"

"No, I didn't see Franklin last night. Why would you think that? He was out of town." She reached out and touched Larry's arm. "I'm sorry about last night. I tried to call, but you didn't answer. Really, I did."

"What about Thorne? I heard you talking to him yesterday on the phone."

She pulled her hand away from his arm. "That was business—he asked me to check William's schedule about some meetings he wanted to set up. He and Marshal were gone until this morning and you know that." She looked away and tried to hide the redness on her cheeks. "I know what you think, Larry, but you're the teacher's pet, not me. Everyone in the bank knows William protected you."

Yes, that was true. "Then I guess we were both pets, right?"

"You listen to me, Larry." Her eyes grew fiery. "I live right down the street. You know what I see late at night—who I see coming and going. But you don't know everything I do. Maybe that's why Thorne is nice to me. Maybe that's why he doesn't trust you—you're kissing William's ass and sneaking around for Marshal at the same time."

"No, I'm not." He stepped into her and took her shoulders. "Careful, Karen—be very, very careful. Rumors and gossip can get you fired...or worse. And what about us? What would happen to us if they started poking around? I don't want that and neither do you, right?"

"No, of course not."

"Listen, you know I'll look out for you." He took her hand and touched the gold bracelet he'd given her. He ran his fingers over the raised letters of her name on one side and the Egyptian hieroglyphs on the other. It had cost him more than he'd ever spent on a girl and she'd accepted it on their second date. "I can't believe we're together. Do you think I want to lose that?"

She looked away. "No, I guess not."

"I'm worried about you. If whoever killed the Chairman thinks you saw or know something, you could be in danger. You could be next." He leaned in close, put his arm around her, and gave her a reassuring hug. "You should tell me. I'll protect you. Trust me."

"I do, Larry. It's just this place—this damn bank—it's cursed, I swear."

Karen kissed his cheek. "Look what it's done to William."

Larry watched her walk to the stairs and disappear. Yes, this damn bank was cursed—something the Chairman had said for years. And now he knew what the Chairman would want him to do. He had to protect his boss, even with him gone.

Larry took a heavy breath and breathed a sigh before taking out his cell phone. He dialed his voicemail. When it connected, he typed in his security code—52779, the numbers spelling his name—and waited. *"You have no new messages. You have twenty-five saved messages."* With a couple taps on his cell phone keypad he was done. *"All messages deleted."* Then he repeated the exercise by dialing a local number, reaching the phone's voicemail, and hitting the number key to access the phone's mailbox. *"You have two new messages. You have five saved messages."* He listened to all the messages and tapped the keypad again. *"All messages deleted."* He closed his phone.

William would have been pleased.

Chapter Twelve

Bear and I found Cal Clemens in the break room with a fresh pot of coffee. When Bear walked in, Cal poured him a cup. While he was scrounging for cream in a small refrigerator, Larry Conti walked in carrying a file folder.

"Detective Braddock?"

"Yeah, Larry, what do you need?"

"I thought you'd want to see this right away." Larry handed him the folder. When he looked at Cal, he cocked his head and gave him the once-over. After a long moment, he grinned. "Hey, aren't you Calloway Clemens, the Blues Man?"

Calloway the Blues Man?

"Yeah, that's me." Cal cracked a smile. "Do I know you?"

"No, no, but I know you." Larry thrust a hand out and almost wrenched Cal's arm off. "I listen to *Remember When* every weekend. I don't think I've missed more than three weekends since the Kit Kat opened. You sure can play."

"Play?" I watched Cal's face light up. "Bear, are you hearing this? Cal's famous."

Cal had always been a loner. He was an honest cop but not one of the first-call guys on Bear's team. He was more of a constant, steady hand—not the firebrand, go-getter type. If you gave him the task, you could trust it to get done—as long as his partner, the aforementioned Mikey Spence, didn't derail him. Except for the occasional choir practice after work—that's beer and bitching, not churches and singing—Cal didn't run with anyone from the department. He did his work, paid the minimal attention to cop functions, and went about his own way.

Now I find out he's the notorious Calloway Clemens—whoever that was.

Bear asked, "Cal, are you keeping something from us?"

"Not like you think, Bear," he said. "I told you about my pal Keys and his band. Well, I'm in the band. We play blues and swing out at the Kit Kat West."

"No shit?" Bear's face brightened. "The cat what?"

"The Kit Kat West." Larry waved in the air. "You're kidding, right Detective? That's the new nightclub out on Route 11 North. Been open for months and everyone is talking about it. Man, what a place—folks come all the way from DC, Baltimore, even Philly and New York. It reminds me of—"

"Yeah, right. The new club." Since Bear didn't have a clue what Larry was talking about, he changed the subject. "What about this file, Larry?"

"Man, Calloway blows a mean sax, too. Last weekend—"

"The file, Larry."

Larry slapped Clemens's shoulder again. "Okay, sure. But I gotta ask you about the band later, Calloway."

"Ah, Larry, it's Detective Clemens around here, okay?" Cal said. "But hey, I'll get you the CD we just laid down. Just tell us about this file."

"Great." Larry nodded at the file in Bear's hand. "Okay, listen, after your guys were done with me, I did some checking on our systems."

"Your systems?" Bear said, throwing some unhappy eyes at him. "You weren't supposed to touch anything, Larry."

"Yeah, I know. But Mr. Thorne told me to get you the daily reports from the building access control systems. That includes alarm system, the CCTV system, and the access control system." Larry waited for Bear to nod his approval. "So, I did some extra checks. Take a look."

Bear opened the file and scanned over the pages that had "Sancus Security Systems, LLC" in a marquee at the top of each. I peeked, too, and zeroed in on several yellow-highlighted entries on two computer printouts on top of the stack. Bear read them twice and looked up at Larry.

"Do I read this right? There were alarms at one thirty, two fifteen, three fifteen, and another at three fifty-one?"

Larry shook his head. "Not alarms, Detective—just activations of the rear employee door—the door opened, that's all it tells us. It was opened four times between one thirty and three fifty-one. If you look, the building alarm was set at seven thirty last night. The main vault was locked down and alarmed earlier at six, as always."

"Okay, I'm following. Go on," Bear said.

"The Chairman entered the annex again at eleven forty-five p.m.—the rear door was opened and the alarms deactivated. I know that because his access card was used on the doors and it was his pin code used to deactivate them. We track employees that way."

I looked over the pages as Bear re-read them. "Looks like someone came in and out a couple times. And what about that other annotation there?" I pointed to an entry on the printout that showed a five-digit code in red.

Bear asked Larry and Larry held up a finger. "That's a power flux. The main power went off for almost a minute and then back on. The alarm system sent a signal to the security company, but it reset right away. So, while Mr. Mendelson was in here, the power went out and came back on about a minute later—at one twenty."

"Hold it." Cal made notes on his notepad now. "The old man arrives at eleven forty-five and unlocks the offices. His access card and pin were used, right?"

"Exactly," Larry said. "But not in the bank—just here at the annex."

Cal jotted more notes. "Then more than an hour and a half later, the power goes off and on. Ten minutes later, the employee door opens—but no one's access card was used, right? So that means Mendelson opened the door from the inside and let someone in?"

Larry nodded. "Right, I figure he didn't leave because his card wasn't used again to re-enter."

"Then at two fifteen, the door opens again without an access card," Bear said, reading the printout, "so Mendelson went out, because an hour after that, the same door opens using his access card—he came back in. And then again forty-one minutes later the door was opened without an access card, so whoever was in here left. Is that it?"

Larry nodded. "That's right. Of course, all I can tell you is that the Chairman's card was used to enter, not that *he* used it."

Bear's face tightened a little as he read over the printout. His left eye always twitched and almost closed when he was deep in thought—or when his beer was too warm. "What was William doing at that hour of the morning?"

"And how did that get him killed?" Cal asked, looking at Larry. "You got any idea, man?"

Larry shrugged. "If someone propped the door open, say, to let someone come in without an access card, we wouldn't see that here. And there's more. The CCTV system went down last night and never came back up."

"Terrific." Bear flipped through a couple pages in the file and found the printout marked "Security Surveillance Report." He looked at the entries and found the last one time-stamped 0119. He looked up at Larry. "The cameras were turned off *after* the power flux?"

"Yes." Larry's voice was excited now. "Someone tripped the power at the main control box and stopped the system from recording. The cameras were still on when the power came back on, but they didn't record anything after one twenty this morning."

Cal looked at his notes. "Just in time for whoever to join William in the annex. So, let's see what was recorded before then. Like if anyone came into the building with William the first time."

"Can't," Larry said. "Someone took the hard drive that records everything."

Bear cursed. "Any backups?"

"Nope—too expensive. We run the cameras and record over them every other week." Larry headed for the coffee pot. "The cameras are recorded around the building on hard drives. That time of night, only the entrances and vaults are recorded. Office areas turn off when the alarms are activated and turn back on if the alarms go off. They were recording when the Chairman came back into the building just before midnight. Whoever turned off the recordings took the hard drives."

Cal said, "That would be William Mendelson—it would have to be. He was the only one in the building during the power flux, right?"

"Maybe not," I said. "William might not have come into the annex alone at eleven forty-five, or maybe he let someone else into the building. That person must have taken the CCTV recordings because they showed his or her identity."

Bear said as much, adding, "And that someone murdered William Mendelson."

Chapter Thirteen

Bear's words hung in the room like fog.

Cal asked, "Larry, where were the hard drives kept?"

"In the security room." Larry tipped his head toward the break room door. "It's locked all the time and only the Mendelsons and Mr. Thorne have complete access. We keep the alarm system, CCTV, and other security equipment in there. I can't even get in without Mr. Thorne's approval."

Cal noted that. "Any way to tell who opened the security room?"

"Should have been." Larry shook his head. "The room's recorded, too, but the recordings were on the hard drive."

"How convenient," I said. "The killer knew exactly how this place works."

Bear said, "Cal, get crime scene in there to check it over."

Cal made a note, gave Larry an exaggerated nod, and left.

Larry watched him go. "Man, Calloway Clemens is just too cool. You guys never knew he played? You don't know what you're missing."

"Let's focus on this, Larry. Who knows about the security system?"

He thought a moment. "Everyone, Detective. It's pretty standard stuff for banks. But if you're asking who has access cards, well, the Mendelsons and Mr. Thorne, of course. Karen Simms and myself are allowed access to certain things but it takes one of them to let us in."

"Certain things?" Bear asked.

"We have part of the alarm codes and vault combinations for opening in the morning and closing at night. It takes two people—we call them A and B people—each has half the alarm codes and half the combinations to lock and unlock the bank building and the vaults. The Chairman and Mr. Thorne are A people. Marshal, Karen, and I are B people. It takes one of each to unlock anything at the bank."

"What about this building, the annex?" Bear asked.

"No, the annex is different. The Mendelsons, Mr. Thorne, Karen, and I can all access this building alone."

I asked, "Why is that so different?"

Bear asked that, too, and Larry said, "No money stored in here. Well, none that we knew of. Now you gotta wonder about the Chairman's private vault, right?"

Yes, we did.

Larry went on. "In this building, only the security room is A and B access, Detective. So it takes dual control to get into it."

"Maybe the keys have been copied," Bear said, watching for any reaction from Larry. "Or maybe the door was left unlocked."

"No way. Mr. Thorne is a fanatic about that room. When he came to the bank a while back, he changed the locks, restricted the keys, and even put in a steel door so it couldn't be forced. He redid the security system, too. He trusts nobody."

Bear re-read the alarm reports several times and drained his coffee cup for a second time. "Larry, do you know where Marshal and Thorne were these past few days?"

"They were doing some audits or something at other branches. Yesterday, they were an hour south of here in Harrisonburg." His face flushed a little and he looked toward the open break room door. "Look, don't tell them— please don't—but I checked their access cards against the alarm lists. Neither of them came or went in the building for the past two days. They weren't around."

Bear looked at him. "Why'd you do that? Do you suspect one of them?"

"One of them?" Larry's eyes went round and his mouth cracked into a wide smile. "Detective Braddock, I wouldn't put it past either one of them. With their A-B access, they can get into anything in the bank together. Anything. But if I had to pick just one, I'd say Marshal."

Marshal? "Hey, I don't like these guys, Bear, but they're bankers. They're too boring to be killers."

"Why Marshal, Larry?" Bear watched Larry glance at the door again. "And don't cut any corners."

Larry lowered his voice. "The Chairman and Marshal have been fighting for over a year—real bad, too—about money, staffing, family stuff, even the Chairman's old pals from the war. Marshal threatened to have him tossed off the board."

"Can he?"

"No—I don't think so, anyway." Larry shrugged. "He also threatened to have him ruined. His reputation, I mean. Marshal kept saying the Chairman saw things and was mentally unstable. He threatened to bring that to the Board of Directors."

Bankers love scandals like rats love leaky ships. And nothing rocked your investments like a nut-job running the till. Marshal might not have had the power to remove him from the board himself, but he could stir up a scandal and just watch all the board members join hands to pack William's office.

"And Thorne? What's his deal?"

Larry looked down and sipped his coffee, making a face like it was cold. "Not really sure. I just don't like him. He's, well, flashy and pretentious. He thinks he's better than all of us—and that included the Chairman. He acts all respectful and such in front of others, but I've seen his emails and heard him on the phone. He thinks William and Marshal Mendelson are idiots."

"Being arrogant doesn't make him a killer," Bear said.

"It doesn't make him innocent, either." Larry watched Bear for a moment before adding, "And he dug around the Mendelsons' offices every chance he got. I've seen him several times coming out of them when they weren't in the building."

It struck me that Larry Conti, the mild-mannered suddenly-a-hero security guard had been keeping his ear tuned in to the bank's goings-on very well. Maybe too well. "Bear, Larry's playing at something. A promotion, maybe?"

"Yeah, yeah, I know." Bear chanced a glance at me but when Larry followed his eyes, he said, "What's your beef, Larry? You just threw your bosses under the bus. And now you're driving the bus."

"No, I'm doing my job." He went to the sink and dumped his coffee. "I resent being treated like a dumb-ass security guard—if you know what I mean. The Chairman understood me and treated me real good. Not friendly so much. Just good."

Bear considered that. "Okay, sure. Anything else strike you between Marshal and William that we should know?" Then he waited and watched for signs of a lie.

So did I, but neither of us found any.

"One thing." Larry took a breath. "Marshal asked me to keep tabs on the Chairman after banking hours. Marshal leaves around four and the Chairman works late. He even asked me to check the alarm and access card reports every morning and let him know if there was anything suspicious going on with his father."

Bear's eyebrows raised. "Did you?"

"Well, yeah, I had to. And if I didn't or if I lied, Marshal could find out anyway. I figured maybe it was a test or something."

"Did you see anything unusual?"

Larry nodded. "Yeah, but there was one thing, you know, I thought I should keep to myself for a while."

"Like what?" Bear leaned forward. "Come on, Larry. Quit playing games with me."

Larry took out his cell phone, clicked through a couple applications, and brought up a series of photographs he showed Bear. I looked over his shoulder.

The photos were of a woman dressed in a long green trench coat with a scarf wrapped around her shoulders obscuring her face. Only in one shot was her flowing black hair showing over the scarf. Never did any of the photographs unveil her face. In one of the photos, the woman was coming out of a house that Larry said was William's. In another, she was leaving the private entrance to the executive suite here at the bank annex. In others, she was around town—alone here and there.

"Who is she?" Bear flipped through the digital photographs again. "Did you ID her?"

"No, I have no idea who she is." Larry reached for his phone, but Bear held firm. "There was no record in our visitor logs. When I hinted around with the Chairman about the times I saw her at his place, he lied and said he was somewhere else. So I figured it was personal—you know, some kind of *thing*. I never told Marshal about her."

I said, "A thing? He's a billion years old and you think he has a thing?"

"He's loaded," Bear said. "What else happened?"

Larry walked to the break room door and looked out into the hall. He turned back around. "For weeks I've been telling Marshal about the Chairman's movements. He seemed fine with that. Then he asked me if I'd like to make some extra money outside of work. I told him sure, but only as long as it was nothing more to do with the Chairman. I didn't feel right checking up on him like I was—especially outside the office."

"And?"

"Marshal got weird and dropped the whole thing. He wanted someone to regularly follow the Chairman after hours. He said he was worried his father was losing his mind and memory—you know, like Alzheimer's or something. I refused and he let it go. Then when I asked him about it last week again—I thought maybe I should help after all—he said no, that he'd changed his mind."

Bear asked, "Larry, do you think he got someone else?"

"Yeah, I do. And so did the Chairman."

"William?"

Larry nodded. "Yeah. Look, I told you, he treated me with respect and I appreciated that."

"And?"

"And I told him everything Marshal was up to."

Chapter Fourteen

Bear finished with Larry and decided to check on the crime scene techs working the outside of the bank annex. "I wish we could find Marshal Mendelson. He's starting to worry me."

I agreed. "There're too many secrets around here, Bear. And the damn thing of it is, everyone knows everyone else's secrets—so far. And the one with the most secrets is dead."

"The uniforms haven't found anything on that bank robber yet. No one has checked in at the hospital with any gunshot wounds, and we're canvassing all the doctors in three states. He vanished."

He cursed again and headed outside.

Outside, Cal was overseeing two crime techs extracting bullet fragments from beside the employee entrance door where the robber fired at Larry Conti. Cal held up a small plastic evidence bag as we walked up. "It's a .22-caliber. And the round in Conti's book that saved his life is, too."

Bear nodded. "A .22-cal is an odd gun to rob a bank with."

"Maybe," I said, "but it's a nice quiet gun for a murder."

"Same caliber as William's murderer," Bear said. "Still, I'm having a hard time thinking the robber killed Mendelson. He would have had to be in the bank half the night."

Cal agreed. "Yeah, man, I was thinkin' that, too. Whoever killed him sure picked the wrong day. What are the chances someone offed him the same day someone else robs the place?"

Bear cursed.

Cal added, "So far, though, these .22s are our best evidence. Not sure about that cardboard from William's hand, but the ME gave it to me."

"Let me see it," Bear said.

Cal dug into his pocket and pulled out another small plastic evidence bag and handed it to Bear. In it was a one-inch piece of thin, dark paper or cardboard material. There was writing across one side of it and Cal noted that to Bear. "The ME took this out of Willy's—I mean William's—fingers before he transported the body. He said you asked him to."

"I did," Bear said, holding it up toward the ceiling light. "Cardboard? And what's that lettering on it?"

I looked but I'd never seen anything like it before. The cardboard was grainy and cracked. The lettering was faded and without any form I could distinguish. As we looked it over, Angel walked out of the bank and over to us.

She looked at the evidence bag in Bear's hand. "What do you have there, Bear?"

"Not sure." He showed her the evidence bag. "Some kind of cardboard I think."

"I don't think so." She examined the bag for a few moments, then started smiling. "It's not cardboard, Bear. Got a penlight?"

Bear handed her his from his pocket.

"Let's see." She used the light to inspect the contents of the evidence bag closer. "It's Egyptian papyrus. I'm sure of it."

"Papyrus?" It looked like scribbles on cardboard to me. "Like Noah's Ark papyrus?"

"Not Noah's Ark," she said, but when Cal's eyes got a funny squint to them, she added, "it has Egyptian hieroglyphs on it. We'll need an Egyptologist to examine it, but I'm sure I'm right."

Cal folded his arms. "Makes some sense, right? Willy's office is loaded with all that Egyptian stuff. He must have had more—maybe pricey stuff—in his vault. Maybe this is a piece of what his killer wanted."

"*Maybes* don't count for much." Bear handed the evidence bag back to Cal. "We need to find out. Find someone to get that safe open. Until we know what was worth killing over, we won't find the killer."

"You got it, Bear," Cal said. "Willy's cell phone is missing, too."

"He was an old guy, Cal," Bear said. "Maybe he didn't have one."

Angel shook her head. "No, he did. He gave me his number." She took out her cell phone, tapped a couple keys, and showed it to Bear and Cal. "Here it is. I had it in my contacts."

Cal jotted the number down. "Maybe he left it home. It's not in his office or car, or on his body."

Bear stood. "We'll check his house. I'm heading over there now."

"Bear, there's more." Angel dug out the folded piece of paper Karen Simms had given her earlier and handed it to Bear. "Karen Simms gave me this account number a little while ago. William had her open it a couple months ago. Since then, he's been moving money around. She's nervous about it all." She told them Karen's story.

Bear knew the details from me but listened anyway, then handed the paper to Cal. "Let's see whose account it is. And let's not let Thorne or anyone else we know we have it."

Cal cocked his head. "What if they ask about it? What if…"

"Lie." Bear threw a thumb toward the parking lot. "First, let's go to William's place and search it. You can follow that up after."

"You got it." Cal handed the two evidence bags with the papyrus and .22-caliber bullet fragments to the crime scene technician. "Get these logged, man."

As we turned around to leave, Franklin Thorne was standing three feet behind us.

"Ah, sorry," Thorne said and pointed at Bear. "I wanted to let you know I'm heading to the gym. Any objections?"

Bear eyed him. "I guess not. But check with me when you return. And don't be all day."

"Of course not." He pivoted and left.

"I wonder how long he was listening?" I asked, and Angel asked the same thing.

Cal said, "I don't like him much, Bear. Not sure why, but I just don't."

"Yeah, me neither." Bear watched Thorne walk around the side of the annex building toward the employee parking lot. "Something about him rubs me wrong. We've got a secret vault that isn't so secret, a dead Chairman of the Board, and a missing bank president. With all this going on, the VP of Security wants to go for a jog."

"Don't worry so much," I said. "None of us bank here."

Chapter Fifteen

"I don't like him either, kid," a voice said from behind me. "And I think he's got the hots for your girl, too."

The bomber jacket man was back. He stood beside the employee entrance door watching us. No one noticed him but me.

I walked over to him. "Okay, who are you?"

"Come on, kid," he said, tipping the ball cap off his forehead. "Doc said you were a little slow sometimes. I'm disappointed."

"Doc sent you?"

"I didn't say that. I said he said…"

"How do you know Doc?"

"How do you think? You're a detective—detect already."

This guy definitely knew my great-grandfather, Doc Gilley. He even played the same word games…no, wait…no…could it be?

The jacketed man's eyes had a familiar friendliness that reminded me of someone I'd seen before—as in more than seven decades ago. During my last big case—one involving the Russian mob, 1939 gangsters, and a few dead relatives of mine—one of my bizarre, unexplainable trips had taken me back to the forties. I was an unseen guest while two lovers said their wartime good-byes on the front porch of an old gangster's house. The beautiful young girl was pregnant and the dashing, off-to-war soldier was…

"You're my grandfather—Ollie Tucker."

He feigned a bow. "Captain Oliver Tucker—I guess the First, right? At your service. I wondered how long it would take."

"You were in the Office of Strategic Services—the OSS. You were a spy."

Ollie shook his head. "Not really a spy, kid. We were more, well, saboteurs. Maybe a little spying stuff, sure. I liked to blow stuff up and go after Kraut officers. And hey, I was good at it, too."

"OSS?" I said, looking at his penny loafers, bomber jacket, and baseball cap. "I thought all you spies wore fedoras, double-breasted suits, and trench coats."

He laughed. "Yeah, we did—in the forties. I checked out a little later and was more a fifties man. I was undercover a lot. This old jacket was a gift from Donovan himself after I landed a broken plane outside DC."

"You were a pilot?"

"Nope." He grinned. "I was with some other OSS fellas bringing in some important scientists at the end of the war. Pilot got sick and somebody had to land us. I got lucky and brought her down. That's why Wild Bill gave me the jacket."

"Wild Bill?"

He nodded. "General William Donovan—he ran the OSS."

Of course he did. "Why didn't you just tell me who you were before?"

"Tell you?" He laughed and patted my shoulder. "Doc said you always look for shortcuts."

Doc again—that would be his father and my great-grandfather. And boy, were they alike. "Give me a break. I've been a little busy with this murder."

"Too busy for family? Yeah, okay, I'll cut you some slack, kid. I know what it's like to get crap from Doc all the time, too."

I looked him over for the first time. He was about five-eleven and no more than one-seventy. He was thin and wiry, like many of the soldiers who returned home from the war several months ago, I'd seen him as a young soldier heading off to war. He'd aged since that scene. His hair was short and his face clean-shaven. But it was his eyes that gave him away; he had friendly eyes—Doc's eyes—dark blue, mischievous, and inquisitive.

"Does he give you a hard time all the time?" he asked.

"Of course he does."

Ollie nodded with a smile. "There were times I wasn't sure who was tougher—him or the Krauts. But old Doc is a smart guy—maybe smarter than me, even if he is my pops."

Doc was my mentor. He was a crusty, feisty old surgeon who'd lived in my den since forever. He was my great-grandfather by birth and my spirit-mentor by necessity. Of course, his idea of mentoring was torturing me with insults and chidings while I floundered my way through life as a dead guy. I always got the impression Doc knew far more than he let on and enjoyed toying with me. Now, talking with Doc's dead OSS agent son—my namesake—sort of proved my point. How long had Ollie been around and Doc never said? Doc had been close by for years, yet it took my murder to bring him out of the closet. Had Ollie been hiding in there, too?

"So, Granddad—"

"Oh no...nope, no way." Ollie raised a hand. "Cut that crap right now, kid. It's Ollie to you. Much as I don't like that name, it's better than Oliver or Granddad. I ain't old enough to be your granddad."

He wasn't wrong, of course. He didn't look more than mid-thirties. "So, how old are you, Gran—ah, Ollie?"

"Thirty-six, kid. Old enough to have had your dad and a few good years with him." He made a muscle with his right arm. "Not bad for a hundred and two, eh?"

I did the math in my head. Yup, a hundred and two. "What happened to you?"

"I dunno, kid." His face darkened. "Somebody hit me. Didn't see it coming, either."

"A car accident?"

He snorted. "No. Jeez, Doc was right about you. They killed me. Whacked, rubbed out, six feet under. You know—they *hit* me."

Earlier this year, a dead mobster, Vincent Calaprese came to me. His old book hid the secrets of the Russian mob in Washington DC and corruption that spread like peanut butter—sticky and gooey. Back in nineteen thirty-nine, the Russians killed Vincent and his girlfriend trying to get that book. Through the years, that book cost a lot of lives—lives that mattered.

Maybe it cost Ollie his, too. Maybe not.

I glanced around and saw that Bear, Cal, and Angel had left. "Was it the

Russians, Ollie? Could they have killed you? Doc told me…"

"Maybe." He thought about that. "But that would have been the Soviets, kid. Yeah, maybe them. Maybe old Nazis, too. Maybe somebody else. I rang a lot of bells in the OSS. And after, too—a *lot* of bells."

"What did you do after the OSS?"

Ollie straightened his ball cap. "That's for another time. For now, you got a big problem on your hands."

I do? Oh, yeah, William Mendelson. "Do you know who killed him?"

"No, do you?" Ollie faded—just a sliver of mist in the cold December air. "You think all you have is a dead banker?"

"And what do you think I have?"

"Well, the Egyptians would call it a *museeba*."

A museeba? "What would you call it?"

He was gone now, just a voice—a monotone, troubled voice. "A bloody disaster."

Chapter Sixteen

Yep, he was Doc's son all right. Drop a few hints, get me interested, and disappear. I wonder what they call *that* in Egypt?

I should have gone with Bear to search William's house but went instead to find someone who could give me some answers about my grandfather, Ollie Tucker. That meant finding Doc. I walked the few blocks from Old Town to our three-story Victorian. It was chilly and snowing off and on, but cold doesn't bother the dead. As I went around the back to the sun porch and passed through our wrought-iron gate, voices reached me from inside. One was Angel, of course, but the other surprised me.

Franklin Thorne.

I thought he went to the gym?

In the kitchen, I was met by my hundred-plus-pound black Lab, Hercule—named after the second-best detective in the world. Second after me, of course. Hercule bounded down the hall from the living room to the rear kitchen door with a few woofs and moans. When he reached me, he tried to plop his paws on my chest but found only the wall instead. You'd think after almost two years he'd know it was pointless. But he didn't care and it was the thought that counted. Hercule was nothing if not loyal and persistent. That's why he cocked his head toward the hall and gave me a low, unhappy moan.

"What's he doing here, Herc?"

Moan. Grumble. Moan.

"That's what I thought. Let's go say hello."

Woof.

Hercule stopped at the living room. He moaned, looked back over his shoulder at me—that caught Angel's attention—and then glared straight at Thorne, who sat in my good leather recliner sipping a cup of tea. Hercule took one step toward him and growled a steady, even warning.

"Stop it, Herc," Angel said, pointing toward the door. "Go."

Oh *hell* no.

"Hi honey, I'm home." I walked into the room. "What's he doing here? And in my chair, too? Well, at least he's not got my slippers on yet. That's good."

Hercule moaned again.

"Stop it. Go into the den," Angel said to Hercule, but it was meant for me. "Franklin was nice enough to drive me home because of the bad weather— don't start with me." The latter was also for my benefit. Hercule didn't care about the weather.

"I thought he said he went to the gym." I walked over and stood beside his chair. "Or was he thinking of working out some other way?"

Angel refused to look at me and said to Thorne, "Forgive Hercule, I'm the only one in this house with any manners—or common sense, for that matter."

Ouch.

Thorne set his teacup—one of Angel's "the Dean is visiting" fine porcelain teacups—on the coffee table in front of him. "Angela, I wanted some time to speak with you in, well, privacy. You understand—so the others wouldn't see us."

"Privacy?" Angel shot a glance at me, then at Hercule as he took another step and glared squirrel-death at Thorne. "That's enough, Herc."

Hercule is my hero.

"Well," Thorne said, trying to avoid eye contact with Hercule, "I know you're very close with Detective Braddock. And I hoped you might help me with a problem I have at the bank—a very delicate problem."

"It's a homicide case; he needs to go to Bear, Angel."

She said as much.

"Well, if I did, it would have to be official. And I'm not ready to do that yet. It concerns Marshal, who is now my boss. If he learned that what I have to say came from me, well, that would be unfortunate and I could lose my position."

I said, "Angel, this guy is playing you. He's going to do the tit-for-tat thing. You know, give you a little info and hope you keep him informed on Bear's case…"

"You want me to be a go-between with Bear?" Angel sipped her tea. "I'm not sure I'm comfortable with that. Tell me what's wrong and I'll help if I can. But if it's important to this case, you'll have to speak with Bear."

He nodded. "All right, but please consider the delicacy of what I'm telling you. Last night, Marshal and I were in Harrisonburg on business. We had dinner with the local branch manager and staff.

Later, we met for drinks with some other business people at our hotel."

"Dinner, drinks, swanky hotels. Life's hard for you, isn't it, pal?" I didn't like Franklin Thorne—not from the beginning and even less with him sitting in my good leather recliner sipping tea with my beautiful wife. "What do you think, Herc?"

Moan. Growl. Moan.

Thorne looked at Hercule. "I thought Labs were supposed to be lovable dogs."

"Oh, he is. But you're in Tuck's favorite chair." Angel shook her finger at Hercule. "He should learn to let some things go. And even though he's gone, he should have some manners."

"The dog?" Thorne asked. "Ah, I'm so sorry. I suppose my being here is making you both uncomfortable."

"Oh no. Not me." Angel gave him a big, warm smile. "Herc maybe, but he'll get over it."

I said, "That was for me, buddy. Not you." I patted Hercule on the head and took a seat on the couch opposite Thorne. "Okay, honey. I'll behave."

"Please go on, Franklin."

Thorne did. "So, this morning we were supposed to meet a client for breakfast, but the client never showed. I called Marshal's room and he wasn't in. The front desk said he'd left very late last night and had not yet returned."

"Perhaps he met someone else for a meeting." Angel knew what Thorne was suggesting and so did I. "Or the front desk was wrong."

He shook his head. "No, I think not. I called the breakfast client. He told me Marshal had canceled the meeting last night—I was never told."

Interesting. "Harrisonburg is just over an hour from here, Angel. Marshal had—"

"Marshal had enough time to drive back last night," Angel said, setting her teacup down. "Are you saying he could be involved in William's murder?"

Thorne nodded. "Yes, I'm afraid so. I checked out of my room and called his room but there was no answer. He was nowhere around. So I drove back here."

"Are you're suggesting he returned here last night?" Angel chanced a glance at me when Thorne reached for his tea. "And killed William?"

I wasn't *suggesting* anything. "Hell yeah, he could have."

Thorne shrugged. "I think Detective Braddock should know about this. But, as you can see, Marshal will know it came from me once he returns. And remember, he could really be on business in Harrisonburg. It could be very awkward for me."

"What would you have Bear do?" Angel asked. "He'll have to confront him."

Thorne already had a plan. "Detective Braddock could speak with the hotel clerk—you know, checking our alibis—and get the clerk to tell him that Marshal was out all night. Then it wouldn't have come from me. And if he presses me for confirmation about the meetings, I won't have any choice but to answer his questions. Surely Marshal would understand."

Wow. Franklin Thorne was not just a chair-stealing, tea-slurping little bastard; he was a *sneaky* chair-stealing, tea-slurping bastard. But he might be a smart one after all.

I said, "Angel, if Marshal's involved in William's murder, why is Thorne so worried about what the guy will think if he tells Bear all this?"

She asked him.

"What if he isn't involved? I find it difficult to think he is." Thorne's mouth tightened. "What if it's all very innocent? I'd be fired before the end of the day. Security men are supposed to protect their companies, not cause them damage."

Good point—weasely, but still a good point.

"I'll speak with Bear," Angel said. "Is there anything else?"

Thorne stood and straightened his silk tie, closed his suit coat, and buttoned one button—very *GQ*. It struck me once again that he looked like the centerfold for a men's fashion magazine and it irritated me no end.

He said, "Yes, but I need to do some checking myself, first. I need to ensure I've got all the facts straight before I discuss them with you. I would hate to look the fool with you, Angela. Not after just having met you. And it'll give me a wonderful excuse to call on you again."

"Oh, I see." Angel stood too. "I..."

"Angela, may I be forward with you?"

"No," I said, "you may not."

She said, "That depends, Franklin."

Thorne walked the long way around Hercule—who stood and followed him—and retrieved his overcoat from our antique coat rack near the door. "I'm new to Winchester and don't have many social opportunities. I work a lot, and, well, I'm not very good at social connections."

"Oh right, Joe-rich-and-perfect has a problem with women." Saying it made it sound so much sillier.

"I find that hard to believe," she said.

"It's true." He went into the foyer and stood at the front door.

Angel, Hercule, and I followed.

Thorne said, "What I mean is, well, would you have dinner with me tonight? That will give me time to sort out the concerns I have at the bank, and perhaps we can discuss them over dinner."

"Dinner?" Angel shouldn't have been surprised but was. "I'm not sure that's appropriate."

"Oh, yes, of course." His tone was low, perhaps a little...defeated. "Your husband—I just thought that it's been so long and..."

"I mean the case." Angel smiled. "I am a witness, after all. And you're..."

She gestured vaguely.

"Standing on the very spot where her loving, gun-carrying husband was murdered," I said and moved closer to him. "Back off, pal."

Hercule barked.

"Ah, I'm a suspect?" I swear Thorne had a twinkle in his eye. "But I saved you this morning."

"Yes, you did. Still, I'm not sure it would be wise to date."

Thorne's eyes brightened and he smiled a big, perfect-teeth smile. "All right, not a date. A business meeting. You were going to consult with the Chairman, and up until this morning, he was my boss. I think it wise that we discuss what you could have helped the Chairman with so that you can help me."

Was he kidding? "Oh, bullshit. Angel, this guy's—"

"All right, yes. Perhaps we could discuss the case." Angel opened the front door. "Seven?"

"Seven." Thorne's voice couldn't hide his surprise—and glee. "Wonderful."

Oh, puke. "Where are you taking *us*?"

Angel tried to hide a wicked smile but failed.

"I'll pick you up." He went outside onto the porch and turned around. "I have a table always reserved at a new place just outside town. You'll love it. And wear your dancing shoes."

"Dancing shoes?" I looked at Angel. "Since when do evidence consultants require dancing shoes?"

Angel bade Franklin Thorne good-bye and shut the door.

"I don't like him," I said. Hercule moaned in agreement.

"Well, I do. And you're just jealous you can't go dancing."

"Thorne's not my type." Then I added, "And he's not your type either. You know, the dashing French movie star type?"

"He's close." Angel went to clean up the teacups in the living room. Halfway across the room she stopped and turned to me. Her eyes were serious. "Tuck, you need to understand. We—you and me—we can't go out to dinner or dancing or even a movie. I need to do those things sometimes. Nothing romantic, just dinner and fun—in public with a live, breathing person. And I need this town to understand I'm not a nutty, *Ghost and Mrs. Muir* crazy person."

"The movie or the television series?"

She rolled her eyes.

I did my best imitation of her. *"A live, breathing person."* Okay, I got it. I did. So I added, "Okay, I know it's been tough on you. But no romantic stuff, right?"

She scooped up the teacups and headed for the kitchen. "No. I'm not ready yet."

"Yet?"

Chapter Seventeen

"You cannot be so selfish, Oliver." A gray-haired man in his sixties stood in my den doorway wagging his finger at me. "She's a beautiful woman. She's still young. She has life to *live*."

Doc. Just who I was looking for, but now the last person I wanted to see. "Doc, she's still my wife."

"Till death do you part." Doc was still in his 1950s surgical scrubs and had his stethoscope draped around his neck. His dark blue eyes singed me. "And you've reached 'do you part,' remember?"

Yes, I remembered. Every damn day I remembered. "She's still my wife."

"Yes, she is. And she has been loyal and at your side ever since your murder. But she has to have some time for herself, Oliver. Surely you understand that. And if you don't, stop being a whiner and get over it. Be thankful with what you have and forget the rest."

Shit. Shit. Shit.

Hercule trotted in and sat beside Doc for a head scratch. He moaned and threw a paw at him when he didn't begin immediately.

"Hey, Doc. Why didn't you tell me about Ollie?"

"I'm sure I did. You weren't listening, as usual."

"No, you didn't."

"You must have forgotten." He knelt down as Hercule rolled on his back for a belly rub. "What about Ollie?"

"*What about him?*" I dropped into my desk chair and spun around like I was thirteen again. "I meet my grandfather—my long-dead grandfather who was a World War II OSS operative—and you say 'what about him?' "

He ignored me—another shocker. He was busy fussing over Hercule and whispering soothing, pleasant things to him.

"Why is Ollie back, Doc?" I stopped spinning. "You showed up after I was murdered, to help me. Then there was Vincent and Sassy earlier this year. So, I guess Ollie is back for a reason, right?"

"Back? No, not back. He's been in and out for years. You just..."

"*Just noticed* him. Right. Like I *just noticed* you after I was killed. Okay, why have I *just noticed* him?"

"Didn't he tell you?"

"No."

"Then it's not my place." Doc sat in a high-backed chair facing me. His face was a mixture of omnipotent great-grandfather and steadfast Army drill sergeant. "In time, you'll figure it out. Well, at least you should. There's no telling with you."

Sweet peanut butter sandwiches—always word games. "Figure what out? Is there some kind of spook code of conduct I don't know about? Come on. I'll lighten up on Angel if you give me a clue."

"You'll allow her to enjoy life now and then without you tagging along? You'll regret it one day if you don't, Oliver."

Well...alone? "Sure. I'll give it a try. I'll do the best I can."

He eyed me with suspicion. "I'll hold you to that, Oliver. You have to learn to be less selfish. In the end, that could mean life and death."

"Why is everything with you a matter of life and death?"

He looked to the ceiling. "Have you looked in the mirror recently?"

"No." What a stupid question. "I don't have a reflection. I'm dead."

"Exactly." He took a long, deep breath—more exasperation than anything. "Ollie is here to help you, Oliver. He was a successful OSS man in his day. And better, afterward." Doc's blue eyes sparkled a bit as a proud father's do. "He went on to do brave and amazing things until his end."

Yeah, his end. An untimely end, apparently. That seems to be in our Tucker DNA. "Tell me about that part."

"No. That is for him to do." His eyes teared. "I'm not sure he even knows. Strange as it is, I don't know either."

Doc doesn't know? This was the first time in since my death he ever admitted not knowing everything, and I wanted to ring that bell. But the sadness in his face held me back. Instead, I asked, "Could it have been about that book—Vincent's book about the Russians?"

"I always believed that. But Ollie ruffled a lot of feathers during his OSS days. Even more after the war. Men like him often did."

"What do you mean, *men like him?*"

Pride trounced secrecy. "Your grandfather was a war hero. And after that, he was one of the first CIA men. He has a star at Langley. I've seen it myself."

Holy John Le Carré. Ollie had a star?

The CIA has its own Memorial Wall in their Langley Headquarters lobby here in Virginia. They memorialize every fallen CIA operative with a star—every operative killed in the line of duty. The names are a closely guarded secret, so the stars are their only way of memorializing them. A star was all the organization could share. A star was an honor—the *final* honor.

"He was a spook?" No pun intended. "A CIA agent?"

Doc wiped away a tear. "Yes, the CIA was built from the OSS after the war. Your grandfather was one of the first and one of the best. He laid the groundwork for many to follow—some of them very close to our family."

"Oh, yeah? Like who?"

"It doesn't matter. Another time. What does matter is that Ollie is here to help you and you can learn a lot from him. Perhaps you can help each other."

I leaned back and contemplated the old surgeon sitting across my desk. He knew more than he said—he always did—and the trick was to figure out what he knew and ask the right questions. But I was seeing a side of Doc I'd never seen before. His voice was soft and broken when he spoke about Ollie. I guess losing a son is like that. Normally, Doc was starchy and condescending, sharp-tongued and demanding—in a fun, loving kind of way. I'd never seen him emotional like this. Never. Not even when I died, his own great-grandson. But then, he had been dead for decades. Maybe that was it. Maybe not.

"How can I help him?" I asked. "How can—"

"Wrong question."

Of course it was. "Okay, how can he help me?"

"Ah, better." Doc stood and wandered to my bookshelf. Many of the books were his, handed down through the family over time. I learned that just recently. I never knew my parents and was raised in foster care. When I turned eighteen and inherited the deed to this house—something I never knew I had—cases of books and antiques dating all the way back to Doc's time were here, waiting. It would be twenty-five years later before I knew who Doc was, that my house was his house, and that he never left. It took dying for me to meet any of my family for the first time.

"And a good answer would be...?" I asked.

He gestured to two leather-bound books on the top shelf. "You're missing my good photo album, Oliver. In it are some photographs of Ollie and Frannie. You should find that album. There are answers inside."

Frannie was Ollie's wife and my grandmother. She was a beautiful woman and a strong, tough opponent. She died—was murdered—by the Russian mob.

What does it say about me that I'm related to gangsters and spies?

Doc went on. "Find that missing photo album and you'll learn a lot about Ollie *and* your father. Perhaps more than you want to know."

"Great, another book hunt. The last book got a lot of people killed—like Vincent and Frannie. It got you killed, too, Doc. Are you sure I should find it?"

"This one might save lives, Oliver."

I stood and went to the bookshelf beside him. "These were in the attic for years after my parents died. I got them when I turned eighteen and inherited this place. Maybe the album you're talking about is somewhere in the attic still."

"Your parents didn't just die, Oliver." Doc turned and leveled those deep blues on me. "They were assassinated."

"Assassinated?"

"It's time you understood our family's secrets. Starting with me—it's my fault our family has always taken on the hard challenges and paid the price. Me, Ollie, and your father—others along the way. And now, you."

What was he saying? "Are you trying to say we've been part of some grand conspiracy? Like the Lincoln assassination or Kennedy's? We don't have alien DNA, do we? Holy crap, Doc, you're not saying…"

"Be serious, Oliver. Focus." He returned to the chair in front of my desk. "I'm saying we've all met our end through violence. Violence we embraced all our lives. We were all volunteers. We've all been fated the same."

Christ, no more word games, please. "And my parents were assassinated? And there's some deep, dark family—"

"Yes, Oliver. I'm sorry. In time, you'll have to deal with that, too." He stared out the bay window behind my desk. "But for now, find my album and learn about Ollie. Then let him help you. It could be your only hope."

"My only hope?" I walked around the chair and faced him. "Come on, Doc. For once, just say it, will you? Just tell me what the hell you're talking about. Straight out."

"Yes, all right. This is too important to chance you understanding." He closed his eyes and leaned his head back. "Tuck, selfishness will be the difference between life and death."

Oh, yeah, that was much more straightforward.

Chapter Eighteen

Sometimes, talking to Doc was enlightening. Although his bedside manner was like brain surgery without anesthetic; every time he tried to enlighten me, my head ached. So I decided to return to the bank and find Ollie.

It was cold and still sleeting a bit by the time I reached Old Town, and I noticed a familiar black Mercedes sedan parked along Piccadilly Street near the entrance to the walking mall. The driver's window was halfway down and a few puffs of smoke rose from inside. The driver was intently looking down Loudoun Street and every time someone walked toward a small café two shops from the intersection, he perked up.

I glanced toward that café. "Thanks, pal. I'll be sure to tell Poor Nic you're enjoying one of his good cigars. No worries, what's he gonna do, kill you?"

Nicholas Bartalotta, alias Poor Nic, was a well-known—notorious, really—resident of these here parts. His former address was somewhere along the New York City skyline, where he wielded the instruments of thuggery as one of New York's most successful organized crime bosses. I say *successful* not because he amassed wealth and power—though he did. No, it's because in his sixty-something years he's never seen the inside of a cell for more than an hour, if that. A few years ago, Poor Nic—the media's idea of a clever mob name—returned to Winchester, where he'd spent his youthful summers on a local farm outside the city. Interestingly enough, that farm was a killing field for the same bastard who killed me years later. Poor Nic had a rival growing up—a rival for the affections of a young girl. He just didn't know it. Poor Nic won the contest and that started a secret killing spree that lasted fifty years. That secret cost me my life and the lives of several others along the way.

Poor Nic and me, we go way back. We're pals. Though he doesn't know that either.

The café smelled of fresh bread and rumbled with the bustle of a big lunch crowd. There were a dozen tables all filled with local businessmen and shoppers hiding from the cold. In the rear of the café, Bobby—Poor Nic's trained gorilla bodyguard—guarded the entrance to a small dining room off to the side of the café. Bobby ate lunch and monitored anything that moved in the café.

"You're looking fit, Bobby," I said and glanced down at the two sandwiches, soup, chips, double dessert, and heaping basket of fresh bread. "Go easy on the veggies though, pal, they're bad for your figure."

Bobby looked up and around the room. A scowl stopped a fistful of pastrami on rye from reaching his mouth as he sat scanning the room. He grunted and the pastrami proceeded unhindered.

Inside the private dining room were four more tables. Only one of them— the large round table in the far corner—was occupied by two beautiful women and one old, thin, pasty-faced, retired gangster.

I went over and slipped into an empty chair at the table facing Poor Nic. He was a battle-scarred, tough old man in his sixties with shallow cheeks and dark, brooding eyes. He was short and thin—by birth, not from the years of anxious existence he'd lived. What thinning hair he had was silver and immaculately combed back from his wrinkled forehead. He looked like anyone's aging grandfather with a light-hearted voice and eyes that could sparkle with kindness—or cut steel on demand. Poor Nic was a leathery chameleon of a man who charmed many, out-foxed most, and disappeared a few.

He was a swell guy, really.

"Hiya, Nic," I said. "Mind if I join you? Please, introduce me."

The dark-complected woman sitting opposite Poor Nic was beautiful and eloquent. She looked five-seven or eight and slender. Her face was pretty with large eyes that showed intelligence and savvy. Her skin was flawless—tanned, but not too—with flowing black hair. Her jaw and cheeks were pronounced, giving her an educated, sophisticated appearance. She was, perhaps, of Arab or Persian descent but as she spoke to Nic, her voice resonated with Western education. She wore black jeans and a loose-fitting black turtleneck. A heavy silver necklace adorned her neck and around her wrists hung gold and silver bangles.

The woman to Nic's right was stunning, too. She was forty-ish and hid her age beneath sandy blond hair feathered around a pretty, strong face. She had an athletic frame with noticeable body parts seeking male attention under an expensive cashmere sweater. She wore what looked like designer jeans, expensive leather boots, and a silk blouse that was a delight to admire. Her eyes sparkled like my own Angel's—I was, of course, analyzing the landscape for investigative purposes only. One must know his surroundings well.

"Boy, Nic," I said, "mobsters get all the babes, don't they?"

For a moment, Poor Nic looked up toward the entrance. Then he said, "Ah, Miss Raina, please go on. You were about to explain your interest in Ms. Hawkins's collection."

Raina, the dark-skinned woman, said, "Of course. Several artifacts have reached me from, shall we say, questionable sources these past months. I have been sent to find the source of these pieces and retrieve those belonging to our Egyptian people."

"I think you will find that Lee…" Poor Nic couldn't finish his sentence.

Lee Hawkins held up a hand and thrust a finger toward Raina. "The pieces my grandfather and I purchased are replicas, I assure you. All were bought and paid for as trappings for our club from an Egyptian dealer."

"Your club?" Raina smiled. "Ah, yes, the Kit Kat West? Interesting that you should name it that, no?"

"My grandfather was there, all those years ago during the war," Lee snapped. "Why?"

"I know of this." Raina's eyes rested on Lee. "Was he not involved in Operation Salaam?"

Operation Salaam? Interesting.

A blank look shadowed Lee's face. "Operation what? I don't…"

"No matter." Raina waved in the air. "Your grandfather met William Mendelson in Cairo, no?"

The name William Mendelson split the air like lightning.

"Raina," Poor Nic said, "tell me of your business with William."

"Business? No, I am afraid you misunderstand." Raina leaned back from the table and folded her arms. "I have no *business* with him."

I said, "She's lying, Nic."

Raina went on. "It is true I've been in touch with him—to examine his artifacts, and of course, to recover them if necessary."

"Recover them?" Lee tapped a steel finger on the table. "Just who the hell are you, lady? Where did you come from and why are you here? I'm not showing you—"

"My dear," Poor Nic said, placing a leathery hand on Lee's hand as he focused on Raina. "There is more here than you realize, Raina. I suggest you explain yourself or I will be forced to contact the police."

"The police?" Raina threw her head back and laughed. It seemed unnatural for her and she quickly recovered. "Mr. Bartalotta, don't think that I am a fool. I know who you are and I know of your involvement with Albert Hawkins and William Mendelson. I also know that they were in my country during the war. I know a great deal about them all."

Lee leaned forward. "If you know so much—"

"I am here to find that which was stolen from us over the years. You Westerners. You come to my land in the name of science and history and leave as thieves. You take and take and leave us with dust. No more. Egypt is not everyone's, what is the word... shopping mall. It has taken me two generations to find what is rightfully ours. Now you threaten me with the police? I think not."

Poor Nic leaned back in his chair and contemplated Raina. His face lightened and he smiled a smile I'd only ever seen on a dentist before he shoved a needle into my gums.

"Indeed." He patted Lee's hand and let his charm take over. "Raina, I agree with you. It has been a crime what has happened in Egypt—more so during the war, I am sure. I assure you, I will help you in any way I can. But, you must help us, too."

Raina didn't flinch. She sat watching Poor Nic with a thin, forced smile.

"Very good." Nic's voice was friendly and soft. "Please tell us about your dealings with William."

Raina scoffed. "That is between William and me. He—"

"William is dead." Poor Nic let no pleasantness mask his words.

I noticed he said "dead" and not "murdered." After years of playing chess with the police, a few detective skills rubbed off on him.

"Dead?" Raina raised her chin. "How?"

"He was murdered," Lee blurted out, slapping the tabletop. "What do you know about it?"

I was about to comment when Raina, the beautiful Egyptian goddess, did something totally unexpected—she stood and walked away from the table. At the entrance, she turned around.

"Of course he was murdered," she said in calm, dry tone. "The thieves of my ancestors deserve no less."

Lee jumped up. "Don't give us that ancient curse bullshit."

"No, not at all Lee Hawkins," Raina said. "The enemies of thieves are often their friends. And those friends are frequently other thieves themselves."

Chapter Nineteen

Bear wheeled his unmarked cruiser off the street onto a short cobblestone driveway. He never would have found it except for Cal's cell phone map directions—they argued about them like a married couple. He pulled to a stop in front of the three-story, white-brick Colonial home and waited for the Winchester police to pull in behind him.

William Mendelson's home loomed in front of them. It was guarded from the street by tall, aged oaks that had been growing for over one hundred years. The home's Civil War structure was two stories with twin gabled dormers facing the street. To the east was a framed glass sun porch, and to the west, a detached three-car, brick garage. The house and garage were in poor repair—paint was chipping, shingles missing, and the stone walk was in need of a mason for surgery. The two acres of landscaping were bleak in their winter undress. Barren trees and perennials, overgrown shrubs, and matted leaves in the gardens said the gardener had taken last season off. What had once been a garden tour stop for Winchester's elite was now a saddened, ill-kept shell whose owner's passing might be its salvation.

"All right, Cal," Bear said, taking long, slow eyefuls of Mendelson's estate. "Put one man in front and one in back. Have them search the grounds for whatever doesn't belong here. You and I will go inside. I've got the crime boys coming when they can, but let's get a head start. Maybe we'll find the good stuff."

"The good stuff?" Cal waved to the uniformed officers climbing out of their cars.

"Yeah, like the reason this old rich guy was killed in a private vault at oh-dark-thirty this morning." Bear started for the front door. "I guess the killer's confession would be too much to ask for."

Cal snorted. "Stranger things, Bear. You got the keys?"

"I've got William's key ring from his desk. I'm hoping it's on that."

At the front door—a wide, tall, double-wood door with large, beveled glass windows—Bear tried several keys before finding the right one. When he turned the lock and pushed, nothing happened. The door didn't budge; it was dead bolted from the inside and there was no keyhole to unlock the extra lock.

Cal watched him. "What gives?"

"Door's locked from the inside. Go around back and see if you can get in." He tossed him the ring of keys. "Pronto."

"Right." Cal disappeared but was gone little more than five minutes. "Same thing, Bear. I unlocked the lock but the door's not budging. I was able to see inside, and it looks like there's a high-security dead bolt on the inside there, too."

"Locked from the inside?" Bear cocked his head. "Since he's dead at the bank, how'd he manage that?"

At the front of the house, Bear worked his way across the four windows looking for a way inside. He found none. He did the same around the side of the house as Cal worked along the sun porch. They met in the rear of the home on a stone patio, where summer furniture, uncovered and badly weathered, was still sitting in the December chill. Neither of them found a way in.

When Bear walked the rear grounds beyond the patio, two floodlights turned on. Then, as he walked deeper into the yard toward a garden solarium at the rear of the property, a floodlight turned on above it, too.

At the rear patio door, Cal pressed his face against the glass. "Can't see much, Bear. But it looks like all the windows and doors are alarmed. Old Willy was one paranoid dude."

"He was. He's got motion sensors on all the outside floodlights. You can't move without setting them off."

Cal shook his head. "Man, that's paranoid."

"Paranoid or scared?"

"What's the difference?"

Bear frowned. "Paranoid is worry. Scared is dead."

"Looks like we break in." Cal went to another rear window at the corner of the house. "I'm smaller, so you do the breakin' and I'll do the snakin'."

"Deal." Bear pulled a short, six-inch black metal peg from behind his back and snapped his wrist, whipping it toward the ground. The telescopic baton extended out to its full sixteen-inch length. With a quick flip of his wrist, he shattered the small rear window and cleared the glass shards from its frame. He found the inside lock and released the window, boosted Cal up, and stuffed him through the opening.

Cal slithered through the window and dropped on the carpeted floor inside. He drew his handgun and listened. "Hey, Bear. You know what's weird?"

"Yeah, lots of things in this town. What in particular are you talking about?"

"Listen."

Bear did and shook his head. "I don't hear anything."

"Exactly." Cal frowned. "For a scared old dude with high-security dead bolts, motion lights, and an expensive security system, he didn't arm it last night."

No, he didn't—no beep-beep-beep, no shrill siren—and still the doors were locked from the inside.

"Be careful and get the back door open."

Cal disappeared from the room and a moment later unlocked the rear patio door leading into a large country kitchen. His face was tight and anxious. He held his 9mm at his side. He tipped his head toward a wide, grand hallway leading deeper into the house.

"Bear, somebody beat us here. The place is a mess."

Inside, Bear exchanged his baton for his Glock. Every kitchen drawer was open, every cabinet door ajar. "Okay, let's…"

"And they're still here." Cal pointed at the floor. "Somebody's moving around downstairs."

Chapter Twenty

"How do you want to play this?" Cal asked in a low voice—almost a whisper—as he inched to an open door in the grand hallway off the kitchen. "Do we wait for them to come up or do we go down?"

"There are no signs of a break-in from the outside, and somebody locked all the doors on the inside." Bear eased down the hall keeping his gun trained on the open basement door. "Let's find out if William has a maid."

"Yeah man, the maid."

"Did you see any outside basement access?"

"No."

Bear frowned. "Me neither."

In the hall, Cal eased the door shut and waited for Bear to nod. Then, he called out, "Sheriff's Department—identify yourself and come upstairs!"

Nothing. No one responded. No footsteps. No noise.

"In the basement—we know you're down there. Come up slowly. This is the Sheriff's Department!" Bear yelled again. When no one replied, he poked the air with his handgun. "On me."

"Good plan."

Bear eased onto the landing and found the light switch and flipped it on, but no light illuminated the room. "Shit." He kept his handgun trained into the darkness at the bottom of the stairs. There was a second landing below him, and the stairs turned out of sight. For a second, a faint light flashed on the landing from around the corner. Then it flickered and went dark.

"Sheriff's Department!" Bear called again as he reached the landing. He flipped on a small penlight and moved on. "Identify yourself and come out."

At the bottom of the stairs, the room was inky black. He stepped off the last step as Cal reached the landing behind him. Bear's penlight searched around the room as Cal's light turned on behind him.

No intruder. Just packing boxes, cabinets, old furniture, and wood shipping crates stacked around the cavernous room like a maze.

Careful to look for movement, Bear inched forward and examined one of three shipping crates. The sides of it had stenciled markings that read "Amphora Trading," and the ink looked much newer than the box. Deeper into the basement, he played the light throughout the room—where his light searched, his pistol aimed. He stepped around an old treadmill and some fitness equipment, then two bicycles that looked like they were ancient. A few more feet and his light beam landed on a steel door in the far corner of the basement.

"Over there, Cal," Bear said, "a door."

Cal moved faster now. "Got it." He stopped in front of the door and listened. Then he shook his head and turned to Bear. No sound.

"Okay," Bear whispered. "Let's take this one real slow—real careful."

"I like careful, man."

Bear checked the knob; it was unlocked and the knob turned in his meaty grasp. The door opened easily—noiselessly—and Bear shined his light inside. "Sheriff's Department! If you're inside, come out now."

Still nothing.

Bear waited for Cal to move in beside him. Weapon up and ready, Bear nodded and stepped inside. They both pivoted in opposite directions and swept the room with their flashlights in wide arcs, trying to capture as much of the room as fast as they could.

"Bear!" Cal's warning was a split-second late as something struck Cal with an audible oomph. He crashed through the doorway face-first onto the floor.

Bear spun around. A dark figure catapulted through the doorway onto him. A kick snapped away his flashlight and a knife-hand slashed down and sent his Glock clattering somewhere into the darkness. A second kick caught him in the abdomen and a flurry of three or four vicious punches followed to his midsection and face—the first and second stunned him, the third and fourth brought the damage. Bear was down before he felt the last kick knock his legs from beneath him and the boney elbow drive into his temple.

"Bear, the door!" Cal scrambled to his feet.

It was too late.

The metal door slammed closed. Wood crates banged against it and echoed in the darkness. Someone had barricaded the door on the other side.

"Shit." Bear hammered his fist on the door. "Call outside."

Cal was on his radio. "We're locked in the basement. There's someone…"

A gunshot cracked over the radio. Then another. A voice yelled, "Shots fired! Shots fired!"

Chapter Twenty-One

I reached William's house as the third police cruiser skidded to a stop. An officer bounded out, gun in hand, and ran for the back yard. Damn, I was late to the party. I can usually tell when Angel is in trouble—call it a spirit-vibe or sixth sense—and I could find her in seconds.

With Bear, not so much.

Bear and I had been best friends and partners for years. And there's a kind of brotherhood with cops. With partners, it's even deeper—a symbiotic connection, a family bond. Bear and I had that in the living years. But that connection was broken by my death. Oh, we were still pals—as close as any living cop partners are—but he and I don't share that same unspoken bond that we did before I took a bullet in the heart. Instead, something else connected us. Something strange and unexplainable. Like, he could see and hear me. That's a lot more special than sharing late-night beer and a gun-toting bromance.

I followed the cop around the house and through the open patio door.

"Son-of-a-bitch," Bear yelled as he burst from the top of the basement stairs. He jutted a finger at a Winchester police officer. "Tell me you got that bastard, Stark."

Stark stood in the kitchen listening to his radio. "Sorry, Detective. He got away."

I said, "Ah, hey partner. What happened? You looked a little frazzled."

"Unbelievable." Bear flashed a look at me when I sat at the breakfast nook table. He turned to Cal. "I want every car in the city and county hunting that bastard down. I want him found. Get on it."

Cal picked up his radio and issued the orders.

I noticed a dark swelling beside Bear's right eye. "Wow, pal. Somebody whipped your ass good." Cal limped toward me at the table, and I added, "Him too? How they get the drop on you?"

Cal seemed to say on cue to Stark, "Never even saw it coming, man. Damn, he was fast. One of those martial arts ninja dudes. Kick, whap, chop-chop-chop. We were down before we knew he was behind us."

Stark laughed but stopped when Bear shot him the death ray. "Sorry, Detective. But hearing you got locked downstairs in the dark was sort of funny."

"Funny?" Bear closed the distance to Stark and leaned in tight. He had to look down to connect with the officer's eyes. "As funny as you and Crosby missing the perp on the way out of the house? That funny?"

Stark backed up a step. "We got off two shots, Detective. That's more than you did. And Crosby hit him, 'cause we found a few drops of blood in the snow. The trail led nowhere, though. Followed it out back through another yard and to the street. Then it was gone."

"You hit him? Good. Get blood samples if you can, though it'll take days to get any kind of match from them." Bear calmed a little. "What's the perp's description?"

"Ah, well, that's something different." Stark shook his head. "We didn't get much. Just average height and wearing dark clothing. Perp had on one of those balaclavas, too. I couldn't get any facials—he moved fast. Nothing but a blur as he ran me over."

"What were you shooting at?"

Stark's eyes fell. "Well, I was on the back patio and coming into the house as Cal called for help. I drew my weapon just as the perp crashed out the door and knocked me on my ass. My gun went off. As he ran, Crosby came around and fired off a round thinking the perp had shot me."

"And you couldn't catch up?" Bear growled. "Two of you out there and nobody caught him?"

"We tried, Detective, trust me. Whoever that guy was, he was in good shape because he ran like a rabbit out of here, even in the snow. Tracks disappeared on the back street. He must have had a car waiting."

Bear cursed and poked holes in the air with an angry finger. "Dammit, you guys were supposed to be—"

"Whoa, man. Calm down now." Cal cut him off. "It was kind of funny seeing that ninja man kicking your ass, Bear. So give these guys a break. He whooped up on us real good. Did you see him coming? I sure didn't—he kicked my ass and tossed me around the room like a sack of potatoes. So be cool, Bear, we all got beat."

Bear's eyes singed the air between them.

Cops have a strange sense of humor. Even in the dark times. I said, "Bear, a ninja beat you up? Hey, could you show me how it happened? Maybe reenact it? You don't have to go back down to the basement, just have Cal…"

"Shut up," Bear snapped as he jerked a finger toward me. When Cal and Stark followed his eyes to my chair, he added, "Both of you shut up. If you're done having a good laugh, get your sorry asses out there and find that perp. And considering he caught us all by surprise, warn all units to use backup when they find him. No more ninja/kung fu bullshit escapes."

"Bear, ninjas are Japanese," I said. "Kung fu comes from China. You're thinking of shaolin—"

"Get on it!"

"Okay, Bear," Cal said. He had to stifle a snicker. "I'll have the units on the lookout for a big badass wearing ninja pajamas." He stood and shifted his weight a few times on his leg. "Good as new. I'll get the boys set up and be back to help search this place."

"You do that."

When Cal and Stark left, I said in the most endearing voice I could, "Bear, are you okay? You look like crap."

"I'm fine. It was dark. He took me by surprise and got a few good shots in." He rubbed his jaw and threw a chin toward the hallway. "He must have been hiding down among all the junk and we missed him. Damn, he was fast."

"Show me."

In the basement, Bear tried the light switch again, but the overhead light wouldn't come on. Then he shined his flashlight around until he found the light near the stairs. He turned the bulb and it lit. He found a second set of light switches he hadn't seen earlier beside the stair landing and illuminated the entire basement.

I looked around. "Looks worse than my basement."

"That's why I don't have one."

Near the steel door on the far wall were several wood crates knocked over. Two were broken into pieces.

Bear said, "The perp locked us in and pushed that stack of crates in front of the door. We couldn't get out."

"I wish I'd come along. I could have helped."

"Of all the times you were goofing off, you picked this one." He opened the crates. They were all empty but for their straw and foam packing materials. "And it's not like I can telephone you."

"Goofing off?" I told him about Angel's tea party and my suspicions of the handsome and suave Franklin Thorne. "He's cozying up to Angel just to get information. That's the only reason for it."

Bear grunted something—it sounded like, "Bullshit."

I told him Thorne's story of Marshal Mendelson disappearing from the hotel in Harrisonburg and ended with their plans to go dancing—Thorne and Angel, not Thorne and Marshal. Why would Thorne and Marshal go dancing?

His eyebrows raised. "Dancing? Thorne moves from 'my boss might have killed his dad' to 'get your dancing shoes on'?"

"Exactly what I thought."

"Smooth. I'll give him that." He thought a moment. "Maybe that's good for us. Angel might be able to get more out of him than I have. He's holding back I agree and there's something not right about him."

Huh, what? "You want Angel to go dancing with him so she can get information?"

"Sure, why not?"

"The only reason Thorne is taking her dancing is to get information from *you*."

Bear shrugged. "Come on, Tuck. Did you ever think that just maybe it's because Angela is smart and funny and drop-dead gorgeous?"

Some pal. "He wants information."

"I'm sure he does. But come on. She has to live…"

I was tired of hearing that. "Yeah, yeah. I get it." I pointed to the shipping crate he was looking at. "What did you find?"

Bear held out an empty hand. "Nothing."

I went to the steel door in the rear of the basement and looked inside. There was more basement junk inside along with the home's furnace and water heater. There were also two more shipping crates, each about four feet high, at least ten feet long, and three feet wide. These containers were empty, too, and there were no packing documents or manifests anywhere. Other than the missing paperwork, the one difference was the markings on the containers. The black stenciled printing read, "Nomad Air Freight–Cairo."

"Egypt again," I said, checking the other boxes in the room. "I don't believe in coincidences."

"What coincidence?"

I told him about my trip to Cairo and the Shepheard Hotel. It didn't seem to bother him that when I visited the hotel it was in 1942 or that the men in my trip seemed to be acting suspicious. It was when I told him about my long-dead grandfather visiting me that he drew the line.

"Whoa, whoa." Bear patted the air with both hands. "Why is it that every time we get a crazy homicide, your dead relatives are hip-deep in the case?"

"Luck?"

"And you're trying to tell me you went back to Cairo to some shitty hotel in 1942?"

"Hey, wait a minute." I threw a thumb toward the stairs. "If Cal Clemens can be a famous, hip jazz musician, I can be a time traveler."

Chapter Twenty-Two

Karen Simms flipped on her turn signal to make the right onto William's street. She saw the line of police cruisers two blocks down and changed her mind. She made a left instead, went farther down, and U-turned back toward the bank. One block away, she pulled into a parking lot behind a local attorney's office and maneuvered into her private parking space. There, she picked up her cell phone and dialed a number from memory.

"It's me. I didn't get there in time. It'll take me more time for..."

Curses. A pause. The voice on the line was monotone and low—one question.

"No, the cops were already there. I thought they'd still be digging around the bank but they're at his place."

Another short, angry question.

"I'm not lying. I know what would happen. They're there. I can't get close at all. You'll have to..."

More questions—jumbled, irritated, fast.

"It'll be pointless, but fine. I'll try back later tonight. I don't see what good it'll do."

Silence. Then, harsh words. A threat.

"I'm doing the best I can and so should you. Look, you don't get it, do you? You have to give me more time. I promise—"

The call went dead.

Chapter Twenty-Three

William's Colonial home was built sometime in the mid-nineteenth century—or so the framed photograph and local newspaper article smashed on the fireplace hearth reported. His tastes had been true to the era, too, with hardwood antiques and replicas throughout the home that, before it had been searched and trashed, would have been charming and rich. The walls were expensively papered above pristine hardwood floors. The ceilings were tastefully inlaid and framed in handcrafted crown moldings. Even the stonework around the fireplace was original and its wear spoke to the years it had provided warmth and light over the decades. All of it, like the outside of his home, showed signs of neglect.

Now the home also showed the consequence of a frantic search with no regard for discovery.

I stood in the middle of William's den and looked around. At my feet were piles of mail, books, and bric-a-brac from bookshelves now half empty. William's cherry desk was piled with the contents from drawers and more files—mostly household bills, banking communiques, and miscellaneous papers. All around the room, anything that had been hung on a wall—several paintings, framed photographs, even two wall lamps—was strewn and broken across the furniture and Persian carpet. William's CD player was pulled from the shelf and lay toppled over the credenza. Even the burnt remains of logs were pulled from the fireplace and scattered across the hearth.

"William needs a new cleaning lady," I said, kneeling to inspect a pile of papers. "Marshal is going to have to tell us what's missing—whenever he shows up."

Cal said, "William's computer is missing." He held up a long power cord in one hand. "Keyboard and mouse are here, but the computer is gone. And I didn't see it at his office earlier."

"Call our folks at the annex. Have them search for it again to be sure," Bear said. "And ask if Marshal has shown up."

Cal pulled out his cell and made the call.

"Any ideas what they were looking for?" I asked.

Bear shook his head.

"My guess is a safe or something." I walked over to the long, plush sofa on the far wall and looked at a painting smashed over the corner. "They pulled everything off the walls. They must have been looking for a safe. Or something hidden behind the paintings."

Bear turned in a slow, deliberate circle and mentally noted everything around the room. "But what? He's dead in his own private vault. If they were inside that, then they know whatever secrets he has, right?"

No, not exactly. "Maybe they didn't have any more luck with that railroad safe than we had. Could they have been looking for a combination?"

Bear snapped his fingers. "Yeah, right. Or a diary or journal or something with information on what was in the vault. If they emptied the vault, they'd want to cover their tracks. If we don't know what was in there, we might never figure out who wanted it bad enough to kill him."

I said, "Do you think they found what they came for?"

Bear saw Cal watching him and repeated my question.

Cal closed his phone. "No way, man. If they did find what they wanted, why were they still digging around the basement when we got here? I mean, if you just killed a dude, and you came here to get some evidence, why hang around after you find it?"

Bear took a long breath and squinted at Cal. He said what I thought. "You know, Cal, you get smarter when Mike Spence isn't around."

"Ah, hey, now." He waved in the air. "You leave my man Mikey out of this. He's not as bad as you think." He took a step over a stack of broken picture frames and turned back to Bear with a smile. "At least he doesn't discuss crime scenes and cases with his dead partner."

Touché.

"You know," Bear said as he looked over the desk contents littered around the desk, "William was really scared, right? He had alarms and locks and all kinds of security sensors. Whoever jumped us got in and relocked the doors to slow down anyone coming in behind them, right?"

Cal nodded. "Probably the second floor. Nobody ever alarms the second floor."

"And your point?" I asked.

Bear went on. "So, if you were a scared old man hiding your whatevers, you wouldn't put it in the obvious place like a wall safe, right? You'd put it somewhere no one would expect."

"And where's that?" Cal asked, looking around. "I've already checked the bathrooms—and there are five of them, by the way—and the kitchen, including the fridge and the freezer. Nothing."

I didn't see anything the perp had missed. If there was something hidden in this room, it was either gone or hidden very, very well. In the living room, I found the same slaughter of good taste and expensive trappings. Even William's collection of 33-speed vinyl records was dashed across the floor. Glenn Miller lay face down on the hardwood near the side window, accompanied by the Dorsey Brothers and the Andrews Sisters. Across the room were three torn album covers from big bands I'd never heard of, the black vinyl shattered by a collision with the wall. Even the record player—a 1950s Victrola—was pulled away from the wall and its mesh speaker covers slashed for access to any possible hiding space.

"Bear, do you think..." Vinyl records. Holy shit.

Bear glanced over his shoulder to see where Cal was. He was out of earshot, so he said, "What's wrong with you?"

"33 records, Bear. William was an old guy who still played 33s."

"So?"

I went into William's den where Cal sat on the floor going through the pile of books and papers. "Do you see any CDs anywhere around here?"

He looked. "No, I don't. Cal, do you see any CDs?"

Cal cocked his head and looked around. "No, man. But, this talking to Tuck thing is getting creepy."

I went to the CD player on the credenza. It was a metal and wood-framed player about a foot long and eight inches tall and wide. The player appeared normal—its knobs were intact and the digital readout was blank—its cord had been pulled from the wall. But I doubted it had ever been turned on.

I said to Bear, "He doesn't own any CDs, Bear. Check inside. See if there's a compartment or something."

"You're nuts." Bear ignored Cal's headshake, picked up the CD player, and shook it. Something weighty was inside. His big fingers struggled with the side panels, and he dropped it twice trying to find a latch or opening to pry free. All he succeeded in doing was to break a fingernail and curse like a drunken pirate. Finally, having cut another finger trying to lever open the back panel, he reared back and smashed the player on the floor, then stomped it with his size 14.

The player's frame surrendered and a side panel popped open on hinges.

"Voilà," I said.

Wires and computer circuit boards didn't tumble out. Neither did any CDs long left behind in the player. Instead, a black leather book the size of a paperback novel lay amidst the broken metal frame and plastic tuning knobs.

Bear picked it up and opened it to the first few pages.

I said, "Phew, I'm glad you found something. When you stomped on it, it dawned on me that he could have used the CD player just for its radio. Boy, that would have been embarrassing."

Bear mumbled something and read through the book.

"Good call, Bear." Cal stood up from his pile of books and mail. "How'd you think to look in there?"

"Just a hunch."

"A hunch? Sure, sure." Cal moved closer to look at the book. "What you find?"

"William's business journal." Bear held up the leather book. "And on page two is a list of passwords and combinations. One's gotta be for the railroad safe in his vault."

Chapter Twenty-Four

"What on earth is going on here?" An older, unassuming man—perhaps in his late-sixties—stood in the doorway beside a sheriff's deputy. It was Marshal Mendelson. I knew him on sight.

"Detective, he came to the door and gave me attitude," the deputy said. "This is Marshal Mendelson."

"Marshal? Where the hell have you been?" Bear asked and dismissed the deputy with a nod. "We've been looking for you all day."

"I am aware of that... now." Marshal was about five-eight and at least two hundred and fifty pounds. But what Marshal lacked in physique, he compensated for with swagger. His wrist was adorned with a Rolex and gold, diamond-studded cuff links. If I were a betting man, his suit looked like Savile Row and his shirt French silk. I'm not one on shoes—I wear old, tattered running shoes 24/7 now—but his were definitely Stefano Bemer. I know this not because I read *GQ* or the Washington gossip pages but because I heard gossip about him at the local diner last week while I watched Angel eat pancakes. Marshal Mendelson believed himself a prince with the ladies. The ladies think he's a toad in an expensive suit.

"I sincerely hope you policemen haven't done this damage."

"Where have you been, Marshal?" Bear repeated. "I'm sorry to tell you, but..."

"Dear old dad is dead." He waved dismissively in the air. "The Chairman is dead, long live the Chairman."

"The question was..."

Marshal snapped a cold glare at Bear. "In Harrisonburg on business. I arrived back just now."

"Just now?" Bear asked, eyeing him. "Or last night?"

"I said, 'just now.'" Marshal's face tightened. "I had a breakfast meeting that was canceled so I took on other appointments. But then, I'm sure Franklin Thorne informed you. Have you no leads? Do you have any idea what is going on, who is responsible?"

I said, "You know, your name has been brought up, Marshal."

Bear looked over at him. "I have leads and I have theories. Let's start with you, though, Marshal."

"Me? Whatever do you mean?"

"Do you have any idea who would kill your father?" Bear cocked his head. "Do you know what he did in his vault all night? And above all, what was in his vault? And why—"

Marshal did something neither of us expected. He threw back his head and laughed. "Oh, come now, Detective, surely you know by now."

"What now?"

"The Chairman was not well." He kicked at a broken knickknack on the floor. "Surely someone has mentioned that? No?"

Bear walked up to Marshal and stopped just a foot from him. He leaned in close and consumed his private space with one mouthful. "No, they didn't. In fact, the only weird vibes anyone gave me were about you."

Marshal's fleshy face scrunched up a little. He had dark, pudgy eyes with a perpetual eyebrow reigning over them—all of which were partially obscured by heavy, black-framed glasses too small for his round face. Now his eyes were darting around the room.

"Really? No matter." He backed away from Bear and breathed a heavy sigh. "The Chairman has been acting very odd of late. He's been babbling that someone was stalking him. He kept saying, 'They've come back for me. It's my turn.' I thought he was senile—or paranoid and delusional, at least."

"Senile, huh? An old man afraid of something doesn't always mean he's senile." Bear waved a hand around the room. "Especially when he ends up dead. Who did he think came for him?"

Marshal shook his head. "I have no idea."

"Do you know why he was in his vault last night? Or if he had anyone visiting him for any reason?"

"He took to some very bizarre behavior these past months."

"Bizarre like staying at work all night?" Bear chanced a glance at me and then added, "Or bizarre like talking to space aliens?"

"You have no idea how close you are." Marshal walked to one of the overturned chairs, righted it, and sat down. "Detective, the Chairman lost his faculties. He'd been that way for some time. He even thought he was being haunted."

"Hunted?" I asked and Bear repeated me.

"No, Detective, *haunted*."

"Haunted" sounded silly when Marshal said it. But it really wasn't silly at all. Not to me.

"Like, 'boo' haunted?" Bear asked.

"Yes." Marshal cringed, embarrassed. "The Chairman was nuts, insane. All right, I've said it. He saw and heard things and was completely paranoid."

"Well, maybe he wasn't after all, right?" Bear eyed him with a nasty *I don't like you* look. "Why did he think he was being haunted?"

"Good question—age, stupidity, maybe his obsession with Egyptian relics." Marshal shook his head. "He claims someone has been rooting though his office and the vault at night—moving things around and misplacing things on him, you know. But we have the entire building under closed-circuit television cameras and no one has been doing anything of the sort. He heard things, too. He even thinks something was following him. He was afraid to stay at home some nights. And..."

"Some*thing* following him?" I asked, and again, Bear repeated me.

Marshal's eyebrows raised. "Yes, some*thing*. He thought his life was in danger, but he couldn't—or wouldn't—explain why or how. I tried putting a security officer with him, but he wouldn't have it, either. He said there was nothing anyone could do."

"And now he's dead." Bear walked around the room and turned back to Marshal, grabbing Marshal's eyes in the Braddock death-stare. "Any idea who killed him?"

"No." Marshal looked away. "And frankly, as crazy as he's been, anything is possible. Are you certain it was murder?"

I laughed. "Well, William could have shot himself through the heart from the back, then ditched the gun and returned to the vault to bleed out. But I'm skeptical."

Chapter Twenty-Five

L arry Conti slid back from the steering wheel of his old blue pickup and waited to start the engine. Karen was a block down the street, parked along the curb around the corner from William's house. She said she was going out for lunch. But the closest restaurant or her apartment was five blocks away.

What was she doing? And why hadn't she included him in on whatever it was?

He started the truck just as Karen's coupe pulled from the curb and made an immediate right down a side street. He pulled out so fast he nearly sideswiped a school bus dropping off kindergartners after morning classes. The bus driver swerved, gave him a long, angry horn and a few silent expletives through the bus door window, and continued to the corner.

"Dammit, move."

The bus's emergency lights were on, and four small children stumbled down the bus stairs to waiting parents on the corner. The entire departure took three minutes—the driver waited while one little girl returned to the bus for some forgotten refrigerator art. Finally, after more hugs and more waves, the bus lights turned off and it moved down the street.

It was too late.

Larry stomped on the gas and slid around the corner trying to find Karen. Had there been dry streets instead of slush, he could have squealed his tires. Instead, he slid halfway across the road, recovered poorly, and fishtailed another half a block to a stop sign.

She was nowhere to be seen.

"Dammit. Stupid kids." He stomped on the gas again and kept straight, hoping to catch her ahead. Three blocks later, he cursed louder and banged his fist on the steering wheel. "Jesus, Karen, you better not be doing something with Thorne."

He dialed her cell number, but she didn't pick up. Stranger yet, it didn't go to voicemail.

What was she up to?

Larry slammed his cell phone down into the console between the front seats and cursed to himself. His temper blinded him from anything around him. Had he simply looked in the rearview mirror, he might have caught the gaze of the tall, dark-haired woman behind him. She hadn't done anything unusual—not for the five blocks she'd been following him since leaving William Mendelson's neighborhood. But he might have noticed that she'd also been watching Karen Simms. He might have also noticed her pull out to the intersection and wait until he'd made the right and fishtailed down the street trying to catch up to Karen—she stayed back three car lengths and easily kept him in her sights.

But he hadn't noticed her. And during his entire trip to Karen Simms's apartment, he failed to notice that the woman remained faithfully behind him, following his every move. Had Larry simply realized that while he followed Karen, someone was following him, the fear William had shared with him might not have seemed like just the paranoia of an old man.

It would have made him afraid, too.

Chapter Twenty-Six

"What about the gold and stones in the vault, Marshal?" Bear watched Marshal over his notepad. Marshal seemed disinterested in his father's murder, but the mention of gold and stones got his attention.

"Gold and stones? All he had in that vault—as far as I know—was that silly collection of worthless Egyptian junk he brought back from the war."

Bear narrowed his eyes on him. "And what in particular was in there?"

"I don't know."

"Why is that, Marshal?"

Marshal snapped to his feet and walked to the door. "Detective, my father and I did not get along. He'd always been a little difficult to live with, but lately, he's been impossible. He was always distant, always focused on anything but what he should have been. You've obviously been to the bank, to his office. He has tens of thousands' worth of Egyptian junk and old photos and memorabilia from his past. But, did you see one photograph of his family? His wife? Me?"

Damn. No, I hadn't. "This guy has daddy issues, Bear. He's on my list—him and Seth."

"Seth?" Bear asked before he could stop himself. Then to Marshal, he added, "I was thinking out loud. What about staff at the bank? Any issues with them?"

Marshal shook his head. "The bank has its problems, sure, but none that I would think anyone would want to kill him over. No, you'll have to look elsewhere. What about the robbery?"

112

Bear watched him for a long time and didn't answer. He wanted to rattle him a little and see if he showed any signs of stress or anxiety in the silence. Guilty people often did. Marshal did not. So either he was innocent, or he was a pathological psycho. There were other possibilities, of course, but those were my two favorites.

"The robber didn't kill William," Bear said. "At least I don't think so. I'm looking at other possibilities."

"Like what?"

"Other possibilities." Bear walked to a window and looked out. "Let's talk about the vault."

"It's been there for years. My family has owned that building and the bank property for generations. Apparently, unbeknownst to me, the vault was in the annex since before World War II, perhaps longer."

"*Unbeknownst to you?*" Bear asked. "What's that mean?"

Marshal cleared his throat. "My mother told me he was fine for a few years after he returned home. Then one day he became, well, different. Odd. He was often paranoid and secretive. Other times he was reclusive. It grew worse over the years until they eventually divorced. She died a few years ago."

"Okay, but what does that have to do with the vault?"

"I'm explaining."

"Explain faster."

"You're an impatient man." Marshal meandered through the room, stepping on broken items without care. "When he returned from the war, my father entered the family business—banking. This bank, to be precise. He apparently used the vault for his private collection since the war but kept its existence a secret from everyone, including me after I was born. It was some big family secret."

I said, "Why was that vault such a secret? What was he hiding?"

Bear asked those questions.

"I truly don't know, Detective." Marshal returned to his chair and sat. "I learned of the existence of the vault—as did some of our bank staff—in 1988 when a fire in the annex led to its discovery."

"A fire?" Bear said.

Marshal nodded. "The Chairman's cigar started some books and papers on fire and damn near killed him. He was in that vault at the time and the fire department had to rescue him. The fool. A fireman was seriously injured and it embarrassed my family to no end. What a disaster."

My vision. "Bear, remember what I told you about the fire in the vault?"

Bear nodded. "And everyone learned of the vault back then?"

"No, not everyone. It happened late at night. While everyone knew about the fire of course, only a couple staff learned of the vault. I never understood what was so significant about that vault, but he was obsessed with its secrecy. It wasn't until a few months after the fire that I was allowed inside at all."

"And you don't think that's a little nuts?" Bear asked.

"That is my point." Marshal allowed a short laugh. "I have only been in that vault three or four times since the fire, and I cannot recall the last time."

I said, "What was in it?"

Bear repeated me, adding, "And who knew about it besides you?"

"The only people who knew about the vault and safe were Thorne and myself—although I suspect Larry Conti and Karen Simms might also. The couple who learned of it after the fire retired years ago. As for the contents, he had a collection of old books and paintings—those I recall. He had a variety of junk from Egypt but nothing valuable, I'm sure. I think those items were in the safe, but I can't swear to it."

Bear changed tack. "Tell me about Franklin Thorne."

"He works for me."

Bear nodded. "Any problems between you two?"

"Has he said something? Is that it, Detective?"

Bear smiled. "Maybe."

"That bastard. What has he said?"

Bear cracked a thin smile. "I'm just asking, Marshal—hypothetically."

"Yes, *hypothetically*, there are issues." Marshal's face reddened. "I've had to warn him about taking too much authority. He made many changes and spent a lot of money that I did not approve of. He overstepped his authority. We've not seen eye-to-eye for a while now."

Bear said, "And then there's that other thing."

My guess was that Bear had no "other thing," but he baited Marshal anyway.

Some bottom-feeders will bite at anything.

"Oh, yes, you've heard," Marshal said in a low voice. "Yes. Several weeks back, I had to reprimand him for becoming too familiar with office staff—namely, Karen Simms. Rumors were going around they were seeing each other—and by seeing, I mean sleeping together. That is inappropriate given their positions. Especially Thorne's. I put an end to it."

"And what did Thorne and William say about that?" Bear asked.

Marshal shrugged. "The Chairman stayed out of it for the most part. Oh, he thought I was petty—poor Franklin was new to town and didn't have friends, that sort of thing. But the Chairman allowed me to exercise my own judgment."

"And Thorne?" Bear eyed him. "I bet he was pissed, huh?"

"He denied any involvement." Marshal raised his chin a little too high. "Yet, I saw them having lunch several times in Old Town. I think now he will have a better appreciation for my authority."

What a jerk. I said, "Imagine that, Bear, having lunch in Old Town—the swine."

Bear ignored me. "Any reason he'd question your Harrisonburg trip?"

"He questioned me?" Marshal jumped to his feet. "What did he say? Tell me what he said."

"Relax, we're being hypothetical, remember?" Bear couldn't conceal a wry smile. "And I advise you *not* to discuss it with him, either."

"I cannot confront him with his false allegations?"

"No," Bear said. "If you do, you and I will have a problem, Marshal. You understand that, right?"

"Fine—yes. But I suggest you look into his past, too, Detectives." Marshal looked from Cal to Bear. "The Chairman hired him without my knowledge. And when I objected, I looked into his background. I have to say, I was dismayed."

"Why?" Bear asked.

"I suggest you find out for yourself."

Bear eyed him. "All right, Marshal. We'll play your way for now. We'll be through here soon as we can. For now, I'd like you to go through the house and make a list of anything you find is missing—and anything you recall being in the vault."

"How would I know what is missing?" Marshal looked around with a wary, vacant stare. "I am rarely in this house."

"Try." Bear watched him. "And Marshal, what can you tell me about William's secret account at the bank?"

Someone call an ambulance.

Marshal's face tightened like a sphincter, and I could only imagine what that muscle was doing about now. "Secret account? What are you talking about?"

As if he didn't know.

"The secret account, Marshal. You know the one," Bear said, letting Marshal see the journal in his hand. "Or is there more than one? I can't remember."

"I don't know what you're talking about."

"He's lying, Bear," I said.

"You're lying, Marshal."

Marshal's eyes went wide and he turned and feigned interest in the broken bric-a-brac on the floor. "I am not lying, Detective. I'm not in the habit of that. If the Chairman had some accounts he was handling *personally*, I'm not aware. Nor would I imagine they were secret. But in any event, if this account does exist, it is bank business. I demand you—"

"So, you didn't know about them?" Bear pressed him. "Or you did? Pick one."

"I've said I did not."

"Then I guess they were secret—and that means we better take a good, hard look at them. Right?"

Marshal turned around and lifted his chin. "I don't know every account at the bank. I also am not privy to everything—every account—the Chairman dabbled in."

CHAPTER TWENTY-SIX

I said, "Oh, and here I thought you were the bank president."

Bear repeated me word for word.

Marshal's eyes went cold. "I'm sure I don't know in this case."

"*In this case?*" Bear lifted the business journal. "Then maybe I'll find the answer in your father's business journal."

Marshal reached for the book, but Bear held it firm. "If there is bank information in that book, I insist you release it to me. I will see you get a copy. It is bank property."

Marshal was a stiff, unfeeling guy in the wake of his father's murder. He was completely disinterested. Yet, mention the bank accounts and he turned into Mr. Hyde—and he didn't conceal it very well, either.

"It's evidence, Marshal," Bear said in a flat voice. "Evidence in a homicide."

Marshal didn't budge. "May I at least examine the book? With you present?"

"No. You understand—police procedure and all."

Marshal's face reddened even more. "All right. Have it your way." He turned to leave but only made it to the den doors. He turned back around and his eyes were sad and damp. His voice was distant, distraught. "I know what you must think of me, Detective. I know what everyone thinks of me—I'm cold and distant from my father and that somehow makes me a bad person. But being in his shadow has been difficult, especially since I hate this bank. I hate everything about it. And just when I think I have my way out—he ups and dies and traps me all over again."

"Murdered," Bear said.

Marshal blinked several times.

"William didn't 'up and die,' Marshal. He was murdered." Bear locked his eyes on Marshal's and the air rumbled between them. "You get that, right?"

"How could I not?" Marshal turned around to leave. "I simply don't care. You get that, right, Detective?"

Chapter Twenty-Seven

I followed Bear and Cal past the uniformed Winchester policeman and into the bank annex shortly after three p.m. There, Bear received an update from the crime scene team and noticed that the locksmith was ready to drill the railroad safe in William's vault. No one wanted to touch the safe until Bear was in front of it. Now, all the hand wringing was a moot point since we had the combination.

One of the detectives on Bear's team—Cheryl something—called Bear over to a desk in the back of the administrator's office area. "Hey, Bear, you know that Thorne guy?"

"What of him?"

She gestured toward the executive corridor. "He and that head teller, Simms, got into an argument and she went flying out of here an hour and a half ago. He followed her. Just a couple minutes ago, Thorne came back wearing running clothes, all sweaty and in a shitty mood. I tried to speak with him and he blew me off. I figured I'd wait to confront him until you got here."

Cal said, "Dark running clothes?"

"Yeah, I think black or dark blue," she said. "Mean something?"

Hell, yeah it could mean something. Deputy Stark's description of the tall, fast figure overrunning them outside William Mendelson's house popped to mind.

Bear headed for the executive offices.

I said, "Bear, let's not jump to conclusions. This could be anything." What was I saying? "Forget that, Bear, he probably kicked your ass in William's basement. Go kick his."

Bear didn't stop to knock as he stormed into Thorne's office.

Thorne stood in doorway of a small bathroom at the rear of his office. He toweled off wet hair and he was still wearing the bottoms of a black running suit.

"Detective, don't you knock?" Thorne asked, surprised when Bear and Cal walked in. "You could give me a little respect in my own office."

"Knock, knock," Bear snorted. "Where were you just now, Thorne?"

"Excuse me?"

Cal said, "Easy question, Mr. Thorne. Where have you been? You're all sweaty and jumpy like you just ran ten miles. Where you been?"

"Five miles." Thorne looked from Cal to Bear before leaning back into the bathroom to retrieve a clean, dry tee shirt off a towel rack. "I burned off some stress. I told you earlier I was going to the gym."

I said, "But he was at my house wooing Angel."

"Can anyone vouch for you?" Bear asked.

"I don't know." Thorne walked over to his office sofa and sat down. "Do I need someone to vouch for me?"

"It might help, yeah." Cal went to bathroom where Thorne had hung a fresh change of clothes. On the floor was a pair of dark blue running shoes. He picked them up and examined the tread. "Some dirt and mud in here, Bear."

"Dirt and mud, huh?" Bear eyed him.

Thorne nodded. "You got me. I ran outside. That's why I'm not sure who may or may not have seen me. I saw plenty of people, but I don't know if they noticed me. Why? What's happened now?"

Cal lifted a roll of bandages off Thorne's bathroom sink. "Bear—bandages."

Bear caught the bandages Cal tossed him. "You hurt, Thorne?"

"Detective, what's this about?"

"Are you hurt?"

Thorne pointed to his left knee. "Yes, I am. I slipped on some ice after a car nearly ran me over in an intersection. I cut my knee." He lifted his leg and showed a narrow tear in the outside of his running pants beside his knee. "I bandaged it when I returned a few moments ago."

Cal said, "We might have to have a doctor look at that for us, Mr. Thorne."

"A doctor? What the hell is going on?"

Bear sat on the corner of Thorne's desk and stared at him. "We were at William's place. Someone broke in and ransacked it. Then that somebody jumped us and ran through my men like they weren't there. Somebody strong, too, and well trained. You know any martial arts, Thorne?"

Thorne blinked several times and leaned back on the sofa. He returned Bear's stare with a crooked smile. "Yes, of course I do. I work in security. I'm a second-degree black belt in tae kwon do. I'm also very proficient with knives and firearms. I'm mean with a crossbow and can run twenty-five miles if I have to. I've done three decathlons and finished in the top ten each time."

Of course he had. In between, he graduated with honors from the Cordon Bleu and accepted the Nobel. Shithead.

"William was killed very neatly, and somebody almost took our heads off a couple hours ago, Mr. Thorne," Cal said. "And one of our guys got a shot off at the perp. Hit him, too. Maybe just a graze, but he hit him."

Thorne glanced at his knee. "And you think this cut is a bullet wound?"

Cal didn't answer.

"It's from a very sharp curb and a very bad driver. I assure you."

Cal smiled. "Then you won't mind giving me those running pants for examination, right? I mean, all this reads like an expert to me. Are you an expert, Mr. Thorne?"

"In some things, I am."

"Then that sort of makes you a good suspect, don't you think?" Cal's smile broadened.

"No, I don't." Thorne laughed—something strange for a man just accused of murder. "That *does* make me an Army Ranger, though. Nice try, Detectives."

I said, "Maybe they're one and the same."

Bear thought the same thing and said as much. "You know, Thorne, every time I turn around you're surprising me. What were you and Karen Simms arguing about earlier?"

"None of your business."

"It is my business. This is a homicide investigation."

Thorne stood and snatched his change of clothes from the bathroom door. "Perhaps it is, but not everything in this bank is part of your investigation. Now, if you'll excuse me, I need to change. I'll bring my running clothes to you afterward. So if you don't mind…"

"I do mind." Bear walked across the office and stopped nose to nose with Thorne.

The two men were roughly the same height, but Bear had fifty pounds on him. Given Thorne's Army Ranger training, that might balance the scale in a good fight. Not that I hoped that would happen…but I'd pay good money to watch.

Bear's voice was low and cool. "You're going to pen out the route you took on your little run this afternoon, Thorne. Then, you're going to rethink your stance on Simms and everything you've told us to date. When you're done with all that, come see me in the vault. And I suggest you have more than 'none of your business' on your mind."

And with that, Bear turned and left the office with Cal in tow.

But not me. I wanted to see just what Mr. Franklin Thorne would do next.

He didn't disappoint me.

After changing into his suit, he returned to his desk and picked up his phone and dialed. "This is Franklin Thorne—please confirm for seven thirty tonight. And have everything prepared as I requested."

But it wasn't the odd telephone call that got my spirit-blood pumping. It was when he took out a small, nickel-plated semi-automatic in a pancake holster from his desk and tucked it into the small of his back. Bear had confiscated the weapon he used to shoot the robber earlier this morning. Now he had another.

That had my attention.

Chapter Twenty-Eight

Downstairs in William's not-so-secret-anymore vault, Bear and Cal stood facing the old railroad safe with two other crime scene technicians standing nearby. Bear held the combination he'd transcribed onto a piece of paper from William's business journal.

Cal stood in front of the safe. "Read 'em off, Butch, and let ol' Sundance crack this bad boy open."

I watched as Bear read off the three numbers and Cal dialed them in. It only took two tries before the lock clicked and Cal turned the large brass lever to open the safe door.

"Here we go," Cal said. "I bet it's diamonds and gold. What are you bettin', Bear?"

Bear grabbed the door and pulled. "I bet it's..."

"Empty," I said as the door pivoted open. "Not so much as a crumb."

The safe had two distinct sections—a large, top cavity with three shelves, and a bottom cavity with three drawers.

Cal pulled out each drawer.

The safe was completely empty.

Cal stood up and stuck his hands on his hips. Bear pulled out his penlight and ran it over the entire empty cavity of the safe—first once, then twice, and even a third time. The crime technicians stood watching. As Bear shined his light on the bottom of the safe, I noticed something dark splattered on the lower part of the doorframe near the hinges.

"Bear, look there. I think it's blood."

"I think that's blood, Cal," Bear said, holding his penlight on two small blotches each no bigger than a dime. "Get a test kit."

One of the techs stepped forward and took several photographs of the spots on the safe door. The other retrieved a kit from their equipment outside the vault. He swabbed one of the splatters with a swab stick and then placed the swab in a thin glass vial, then left the vault. A moment later, he came back in.

"It's blood, Detective. We should collect the remainder as evidence. I'm assuming it's from the deceased."

Bear knelt down and scanned the entire lower half of the safe with his flashlight a fourth time. "Okay, there are a few small shards of glass inside, too. Maybe a match for what we found on the floor by the table. You guys process the entire safe. Take the damn thing with you if you have to."

One tech gathered their equipment while the other continued snapping photographs.

Cal said, "So, all this for nothing?"

"No," I said. "The blood is on the inside of the doorframe, right? The safe door was open when William was killed. The blood splatter proves that. Whoever killed him most likely got whatever was in this safe."

"Right," Bear said, but when Cal gave him that *Who you talking to?* look again, he added, "Stains inside the door, Cal. It was open when William was killed and the killer must have taken whatever was in here."

Cal agreed. "So, we're still at square one. We have no idea what was in here. No idea why it caused William's murder. No idea who the murderer is. Nada."

I wasn't so sure. "Bear, I told you about my trip to Cairo, remember? And it happened when I touched that scarab carving in William's office. This has something to do with William and Cairo."

"Cal, I think we're further along than you think." Bear went out into the anteroom with Cal behind him. "This has something to do with those crates at William's place and all his Egyptian junk upstairs. It has to. Some of the crates were from some Greek or Egyptian shipping firm named Amphora, and two were from a company called Nomad something. The ME found that piece of papyrus in his fingers, right?"

Cal nodded. "Right, man. Good thinkin'. Maybe it's about a mummy's curse or grave robbin'. Hey, maybe old Willy was an Egyptian tomb robber during the war, right? Maybe—"

"No, Cal, that's not what I meant." Bear cracked a smile. "Remember when I said you got smarter without Mike Spence? Forget I said that."

Cal folded his arms. "Oh, yeah? You think mummies and curses are weird, huh? Well, do I need to ask who came up with that idea about the Cairo connection or William's office full of antiques?"

Was he just pulling Bear's leg or was Calvin Clemens, alias Calloway Clemens, listening to our conversations?

Chapter Twenty-Nine

Y ou are responsible for this!" Marshal Mendelson's voice boomed down the executive corridor to Bear and me even before we reached the top of the stairs from the vault anteroom. "Explain yourself!"

Thorne's response was muffled—not quiet, mind you, just muffled. But I could tell by the few syllables that escaped through his office door that he was angry and fighting back.

When Bear opened Thorne's office door without knocking, we caught both men standing toe-to-toe ready to jab each other's eyes out with finger-daggers.

"Whoa there, boys," Bear said, walking in. "Everybody take two steps back and relax."

Thorne's face was tight with angry eyes narrowed on Marshal. But when he saw Bear, he stepped back and lowered his hand. "Of course, Detective. I'm embarrassed at having lost my temper. But Marshal is losing his mind."

Marshal wasn't as compliant. He lunged at Thorne again and threw something into his face that hit his cheek and dropped to the floor. "Explain it. Go ahead, explain it."

Bear leaned down and picked the small button-sized object off the floor. He looked it over and held it up away from Thorne for me to see. It was a tiny electronic device the size of a quarter with a short, thin wire protruding from it. "A bug? What's this about, Marshal?"

Thorne answered. "Marshal insists I tapped his phone. I believe all the anxiety is too much for him. Now…"

"Then explain it," Marshal yelled. "The Chairman put you up to this, didn't he? He hired you and still pulls your strings. Admit it. Come on, Thorne, admit it."

"I admit nothing."

Bear held up a hand. "Relax, Marshal. Seems you're the one around here who likes to do surveillance. Isn't that right?"

Marshal stood, blinking several times. Then he retreated from Thorne and straightened himself by the office window. "What are you talking about? I don't understand."

I did. "Liar."

"You were having your father followed," Bear said, setting the electronic listening device onto Thorne's desk. "Isn't that true?"

"No." Marshal's voice was edgy. "Whoever told you that is lying. Someone trying to stir up trouble. As though we don't have enough now."

"Detective," Thorne said, glancing at Marshal, "perhaps you could tell us what you know."

"That's not how it works," Bear said in a flat voice. "Now, where'd you find this bug, Marshal?"

"In my office. It was stuck under my desk lamp beside my telephone."

Bear looked at Thorne. "And you're sure you don't know anything about it?"

"Really? Bug my own superiors? To what end?"

He had a point. Doing it might be interesting; getting caught could be professionally fatal.

"Okay, gentlemen, I'll have my tech boys sweep the entire executive suite." Bear pointed a finger at Marshal. "And you don't know anything about surveillance on your father?"

Marshal snapped his arms folded. "I assure you, no."

Thorne took out a small ring of keys from his pants pocket and opened one of his desk drawers. He retrieved a small, hand-held electronic device the size of a large television remote control and turned it on. On its face was a digital readout and several buttons. When he waved the device over the electronic bug Bear had placed on his desk, the lights on the device lit up and it made a high-pitched whine. The readout began flashing numbers higher and higher.

"It's active, Detective," Thorne said, holding the device up. "This is an RF detector for doing TSCM sweeps. I'll need to bring in the rest of my equipment so I can check the offices myself."

Marshal looked at the device. "T… T… CM what?"

I said, "Technical Security Counter-Measures—TSCM. Jeez, everyone knows that."

Bear repeated me, and added, "It's for sweeping for electronic eavesdropping devices. Thorne's RF detector is a small portable device for radio frequencies—transmitters." Bear walked to his desk and watched Thorne move the device over the bug. "You have all the equipment?"

"Yes, of course."

"Why?" Bear asked. "It's pretty expensive and takes a lot of training. You don't look like a gadget guy to me."

Thorne lifted his chin. "I don't? Well, perhaps that's more a compliment than you intended, Detective. But the truth is, I'm well versed in TSCM and espionage—industrial espionage. I've spent the past fifteen years using this tradecraft. Quite successfully, too."

"*Tradecraft?*" I sat on the corner of Thorne's desk. "Now there's a word you don't hear very often."

"No, you don't—ah, you don't hear that term every day." Bear turned back to Thorne, who looked at him with a strange, awkward raise of the eyebrows. "Tradecraft, I mean. About that…"

The RF detector chirped again, and Thorne moved it over the listening device until the chirp became a steady tone. He handed Bear the listening device and began waving the RF device like a wand around his desk. The chirping started again, increasing in rapidity each time he neared a rectangular wooden box sitting on his desk. When he held the detector directly above the box, the chirping turned into a steady tone and the digital readout began flashing numbers again.

"Detective," Thorne said, opening the box. "Care for a fine cigar? They were a gift from the Venezuelan Ambassador. I save them for the most important occasions." When the box cover was lifted, three cigars were missing from the top row. "And I see someone has helped themselves, too."

Bear stepped closer. "Cuban?"

"Of course," Thorne said. "It's now perfectly legal." He smiled. "Unlike this." He gently closed the box and turned it over, careful not to allow the cigars to spill out. The bottom of the box was covered in dark felt and he ran the RF detector over it several times. Its steady tone and flashing readout continued. When he was done, he set the detector down, took a small folding knife from his desk drawer, and peeled the felt back from one corner of the box.

"Son of a bitch," Bear said.

I moved closer. "What do you have, Bear?"

Concealed beneath the felt, affixed to the underside of the cigar box, was a second listening device even smaller than the one from Marshal's office.

"Don't touch it," Bear said, "there could be prints."

"No, I think not." Thorne handed the wooden cigar box to Bear. "Anyone sophisticated enough to use this series of transmitter would have used gloves. But, by all means, have it processed."

"You're probably right but humor me." Bear lifted the box up and showed the underside and listening device to Marshal. "So, Marshal, you still want to blame Thorne for all this?"

"No, of course not." Marshal's face reddened. "I apologize, Franklin. Of course you understand..."

"Accepted." Thorne began moving his RF detector around his desk again. When he ran it over his credenza behind him, the chirping started again. "Detective, perhaps we should sweep the entire bank and annex. I think we have an infestation."

Chapter Thirty

The Kit Kat West Club belonged on the Las Vegas strip, not the outskirts of Winchester. The club could be seen miles away in the winter darkness outside of town on Route 11. It was like an oasis, both from the winter chill and the Virginia landscape—bright, dancing lights, music, and laughter.

The sand-colored stone building rose three floors above the ground and was fronted by two large marble pillars and rows of cauldron torches lighting the entranceway. Its windows were wide and tall, framed in dark red shutters, and light danced out onto grounds surrounded by sycamores and mulberry trees. There were four large chimneys protruding off the flat roof into the darkness—all belched smoke that seasoned the winter air with a rich, festive scent. Around the property, floodlights illuminated the club from every angle like a Broadway premier was underway. At the front entrance, two beefy bouncers fitted with tuxedos and bulging muscles checked guests between two pedestaled fire pits like the gateway of a great pyramid.

When Bear and I pulled up to the front of the club, we were greeted by a tuxedoed valet who waved at Bear to stop. The valet opened Bear's door—ignoring mine, of course—took one look inside the police cruiser, and opted for Bear to leave the vehicle beside the entrance.

At the top of the outside stairs, behind the two bouncers, we reached the fifteen-foot-high wood-plank doors that I expected Beau Geste to emerge from any moment. Inside, there was a grand reception area flanked by two large palm trees. As far as the eye could see there were more tuxedos, white dinner jackets, and buxom, classy ladies in evening gowns with long legs—not really, but it sets the mood, right? The floors were a high-sheened marble and the walls adorned with paintings and photographs of the pyramids, the Sphinx, and various Egyptian panoramas. Standing guard on the sides of the main ballroom entrance were a twelve-foot-high Anubis and his pal, the mummy from the black lagoon.

William must have helped with the Kit Kat's decor.

Bear walked to the ballroom entrance and was greeted by a short maître'd with a bushy beard and ill-fitting white dinner jacket. The man had a puffy face and squinty eyes, but when he saw Bear approach, his eyes bulged and a well-acted smile blossomed on his face.

Bear ignored him and looked around.

The ballroom was the size of a basketball court. It was two stories tall with dozens of linen-covered tables. There were flickering wicker and brass candleholders on tables clustered with guests. Liquor filled glasses and glasses filled tables for cocktail hour and dinner. The room was accented with more Egyptian relics and statues. Ferns and miniature date palms divided the room into four sections surrounding a dance floor. The band played beyond the hardwood—all dressed in black tuxedoes and bathed in a soft, backlit aura. To the left of us was a wide archway leading to a bar crowded with people and humming with conversation, laughter, and intoxication.

Music filled the air.

"Damn, Bear," I said. "This place is great. I wish it was here when I was alive. It's like Shangri La."

"Yeah, right, Shangri La."

"No, Detective Braddock—Cairo," the bearded maître'd said with an odd accent. "Our club is in honor of the original Kit Kat Club from my country of Egypt."

"You're Egyptian?" Bear looked the short man over. "You aren't selling it, pal—maybe Jersey?"

The maître'd smiled coyly. "I am Samuel—from Queens—and I'll be taking care of you this evening. I have your table all ready."

"My table? I didn't make a reservation."

Samuel's New York accent replaced his faux Egyptian one. "Calloway said you'd be coming this evening. And you're right on time, too. He's about to play. This way, please." New York Sammy didn't wait for Bear's response, just headed across the room, finger held up like a beacon for us to follow.

We did.

In the front row near the corner of the room Sammy pulled out Bear's chair and sat him at the table with a good view of the band and dance floor. The band finished a rendition of something from the 1940s, and the bandleader announced a break. Then he waved toward the bar and six new musicians—all dressed in 1940s Army uniforms—wandered out and took up their positions on the bandstand. A white-jacketed host picked up a microphone as a spotlight bathed him in a brilliant aura.

"And now, for our coppers in the audience, Keys Hawkins and Remember When."

A pale, puffy-faced, heavy man dressed in a World War II Eisenhower Army jacket and wool garrison cap stood up on rickety legs behind the piano—the trombone player helped to steady him—and waved to the audience. A raucous response of cheers and applause erupted. The old-timer looked a hundred if he was a day, and I was sure the Army jacket was his original issue from boot camp. The applause continued until he sat down at the keyboard and pointed to a black man in a sergeant's uniform standing with his back to the audience at center stage. The spotlight narrowed on the black sergeant as he lifted a trumpet skyward and began to play.

"Holy Omaha Beach, Bear," I said as the man turned around and leaned back into his opening riff. "That's Cal."

Cal laid into the bouncing opening bars of "Boogie Woogie Bugle Boy." Around the side of the bandstand, three ladies dressed in dark tan uniforms swayed out and lined the stage beside him. As Cal hit the end of the opening run, the three Andrews Sisters look-a-likes turned on the harmony and had the entire room on the dance floor.

Bear just stared.

I said, "Pinch me to make sure I'm still dead, Bear."

A waiter brought a bottle of champagne and two glasses. "Everything is on the house tonight, sir. Please enjoy your evening."

I was sure the second glass wasn't for me. Who, I wondered?

The music flooded the ballroom as waiters scurried around delivering drinks and meals. One of the bouncers at the ballroom entranceway looked our way. He turned to someone behind him and tipped his head toward us. I was about to comment on that when Jean Harlow appeared behind the bouncer and parted the waves our way.

This Jean—not the real Ms. Harlow, since she died in the 1930s—was a blond-haired vixen in a white satin dress that hugged her like a bed sheet in a rainstorm. Her hair was feathered back above her bare shoulders—not the only set of curves that I noticed, either. Her bosom made the entrance into the ballroom first but was tied for first place with long, toned legs that peeked out of her dress with each stride.

Bear noticed, too. While Cal blew his sax along to "In the Mood," Bear's foot tapped along but his attention fell to the swish of satin that stopped at our table.

"Good evening, Detective Braddock," the woman said in a low, soft voice. "I'm Lee Hawkins and this is my place. Calloway said you'd be coming in." A waiter appeared and poured the champagne, first in a glass he handed to Lee, and then one for Bear. "He's quite a player, don't you think?"

Was there music playing?

I gazed at her like a schoolboy. It's a good thing I was invisible to most or I'd have embarrassed myself. "Jeez, Braddock, offer the lady a seat."

Bear stood and pulled the linen tablecloth half off the table. "Please, have a seat. I guess the champagne's yours?"

Lee smiled with her eyes and poured herself into a chair across the table from him. When she leaned forward to set her champagne glass down, heaven opened up her dress and no doubt reminded Bear how long it had been since he'd been with a woman.

Lee said, "No, Calloway asked we give you the full treatment. He said you didn't get out much and that you'd been working too hard. You and your partner, that is."

"My partner?" Bear waved a hand over the champagne glass and looked at the waiter hovering nearby. "Bourbon, pal. Fast. A double—no, two doubles."

Lee leaned back with one arm over the back of her chair. She'd seen all the old Bogie and Bacall movies and had the sassy, confident girl act down perfect. "I'm teasing you, Detective. Calloway says you act like your dead partner is still around. I think that's charming. I talk to my dad all the time—he died in the eighties, working for this town, too. It's comforting, isn't it? Here at the Kit Kat, we all like to live in the past. It's somehow... safer."

"Bear."

"Excuse me?"

"Bear," he repeated and looked across the room for the wayward waiter with his glasses of hand-steadying elixir. "Call me Bear. Everyone does."

"Not Theodore or Ted?" Lee's eyes danced and her smile would have stopped my heart if I weren't already dead. It did stop Bear's when she added, "Maybe Teddy? Soft and cuddly?"

I laughed and that rankled him. "Teddy? Why do you think—"

"Just Bear." His face got serious and he held Lee's eyes. "I'm afraid I have bad news."

Her face darkened a little and her eyes drifted to the table. "Oh, I already know about Willy. I'm heartbroken. He was a strange old guy but sweet in his own way. He and my grandfather go all the way back to the war. They met at the Kit Kat in Cairo, did you know that? Do you have any leads on his killer?"

Bear shook his head. "Sorry, can't comment on the case. Keys is your granddad?"

"Yes," she turned and waved at the old man at the piano—he soloed now, shoulder-dancing to Tommy Dorsey. "He's very upset. He wanted to cancel tonight but Calloway talked him into playing. He said it was good for him. At his age, it's amazing enough he gets up and plays twice a week. With Willy gone, well, I wonder how long he'll stay at it."

Bear's two bourbons arrived, and the first one was gone before the glass ever touched the table. The second was poised for the same demise when

133

Bear's eyes locked onto someone being escorted up to a small mezzanine overlooking the dance floor.

The aged man—silver-haired and sallow-cheeked—was guided by a bodyguard who sat at the table nearest the short flight of stairs that led to the mezzanine. The older man was in a tuxedo and straightened his bow tie as he spoke to his bodyguard. For a frail-looking man approaching seventy, he was anything but doddering. His eyes were sharp and hard and his mind tough as nails.

Nicholas Bartalotta picked up the glass of wine the waiter served him, looked down at Bear and Lee, and toasted the air.

"Poor Nic." Bear nodded back and lifted his bourbon. "Does he come here often?"

That would have been a cheesy line from a bad B-movie except for what Lee said next.

"Of course." Lee waved at Poor Nic. "After all, he bankrolls my place."

Chapter Thirty-One

"Poor Nic owns this place?" Bear set his drink on the table. "Do you know who he is?"

"Yes, I know all about him. And he doesn't own it. Granddad does."

Bear let his eyes catch hers. "Your grandfather?"

"This club is his dream." Lee smiled and sipped her champagne. "Keys is the only family I have. My mother ran off when I was little, and as I said, my dad died in the eighties. This place is really his, but I run it. Poor Nic is a silent partner—he's the money behind us."

I laughed. "Never fails, Bear. If there's a scheme simmering in town, Poor Nic's holding the ladle."

Poor Nic claims to be retired from gangster life and enjoying the fruits of his hard-earned retirement benefits. And thank my stars, too, because Nic was pretty helpful a year ago when we had to stop a killer trying to keep Russian mob secrets still secret since 1939. Very helpful, in fact. I think at least one FBI agent and a couple other folks owe their lives to him. Angel did.

Poor Nic ain't such a bad guy—not really—once you get beyond that whole mobster-killer thing.

Bear gave Poor Nic another nod and returned his attention to Lee. "Nice place—a real charm. You build it yourselves?"

"Yes, we did. It took a year."

I said, "They didn't find any bodies buried here, did they?"

Bear almost spit his drink down Lee's cleavage.

"Or maybe they buried a few." That wouldn't be the first time for Bear and me.

"Bear?" Lee asked, laughing a little. "Are you all right?"

Bourbon threatened to come out of his nose. He grabbed a napkin and wiped his face. "Sorry." He changed the subject. "Tell me about William."

"Do you dance, Bear?"

Now I wished I had a drink. "Well, Bear? Do you?"

His face flushed. He took a healthy swallow of bourbon and looked at Lee over the glass. "No."

"No dance, no interview." She stood and extended her hand. "Come on, Bear, live a little. Calloway said you needed to loosen up. I think I got the right parts to help you do just that." She looked over at Cal who was just lowering his saxophone. She patted the air.

Cal swapped out his sax for a clarinet and soon had Lee's curvaceous body swaying to Glenn Miller's signature "Moonlight Serenade."

"Bear, if you don't dance with her, I will." And I would. I'm just not sure she would have let me lead.

"All right, Lee." He stood and finished his second bourbon. "A deal's a deal, right?"

"It is, I swear." She took his hand—hers lost in his massive paw—and walked him to the dance floor. In a few more bars of Cal's sweet melody, Bear looked like he forgot he was a cop and became the teddy bear I always knew he was.

His body moved awkwardly but Lee gave no notice. I sat at the table and watched my best friend melting in the arms of a beautiful woman for the first time in my life. With every step, his eyes closed a little more and her cheek sought the comfort of his chest.

Deep down, I was jealous as hell.

"Boy, she's a real peach, ain't she?"

"Huh?" I spun around. Ollie stood behind me, leaning against the wall. He smoked a cigarette and watched Bear and Lee among the half a dozen couples on the dance floor. "How long have you been here, Ollie?"

"Oh, almost seventy years. Give or take."

"No, I mean..."

"I know what you mean, kid." He tipped his ball cap back. "Keys's girl is a dish, ain't she?"

"A dish? Oh, yeah, she's hot. Do you know her?"

"I think so. She looks real familiar. She reminds me of this gal I chased around the USO back in '43. Man, could she dance. One night we were dancin' it up when this local tried to cut in. I busted his—"

"Yeah, okay. What are you doing here?"

He laughed and blew a smoke ring—he was a Bogie fan, too. "I do like swing. It takes me back. Way back, you know?"

Huh? "What's that mean?"

Ollie walked out on the dance floor and stood close to Bear and Lee. I followed.

He said, "Doesn't matter. She must be doing all right in this place, huh? Must have cost her a wad of dough."

He was playing games with me. "Poor Nic bankrolls them. He's..."

"A gangster. Just like old Vincent Calaprese. Of course, Vincent was one of the originals. Watch your gangster, though, kid. He's slippery—just like his new partners."

He was trying to tell me something, but like Doc, he wasn't going to tell me. "I get that. So, are you going to tell me why you're hanging around? There's always a reason. Doc says I can learn from you and maybe I can help you, too."

Bear made a turn on the dance floor. Lee, crushed to him, laughed and said something that made Bear laugh, too.

Bear, laugh?

Ollie wandered over to the bandstand and stood watching Keys playing the piano. "This old guy can play. He reminds me of..."

"Come on, Ollie, what brings you here?"

"Same as you, kid."

"And that would be?"

"A killer."

Obviously. "Don't start on Poor Nic, Ollie. Every time a body drops in this state, everyone points the finger at him. So far, he's been innocent."

He stuffed his hands into his pockets and turned to me. "Innocent and involved are two different things. You're a cop, you know that."

"I do. But, he's an all right guy. Even Angel likes him. And Poor Nic likes her, too, so…"

"Yeah, and your lady's a dish. You, Poor Nic, and that guy have good taste. Yes sir, you all got good taste."

That guy?

I followed his gaze across the dance floor to a couple just sitting down at a table. The tall, dark, handsome man in an expensive suit pulled the chair out for a beautiful auburn-haired babe in a long black evening dress. She laughed as he moved a chair around the table beside her.

Son of a—

Franklin Thorne.

And my Angel.

"Terrific. And I suppose he dances like Fred Astaire, too."

Chapter Thirty-Two

No, not Astaire. Thorne was more a Patrick Swayze kinda guy—suave, rugged, dashing, and a ballroom dancer. And as he glided Angel around the dance floor, some guests stopped and looked on. Some even applauded at the end of the dance. Just great. What was next, master chef and poet?

Thorne guided Angel off the dance floor for the second time as Cal put his sax away for a fifteen-minute break and headed for Bear and Lee at our table. As Cal sauntered up, he undid his Eisenhower jacket and tossed it on the back of the chair. Then he slumped down into the chair with a sigh and a grin.

"Man, oh man, what a crowd, eh, Bear?"

A waiter brought Cal a tall glass of something cold.

Lee said, "Calloway, you were wonderful tonight. How about some Dorsey Brothers next?"

"Yes, ma'am," he said. "You surprised me, Bear—you and Lee were really cuttin' a rug. Never thought I'd see the day."

Bear grumbled something, then said, "I guess you broke the news to Keys. I want to talk to him first chance, Cal."

"Yeah, he took it hard, too." Cal poured back half his drink and wiped his mouth. "Blowin' that sax makes me bone-dry. Keys knows you're here tonight. He'll be over. But he doesn't know much. They were pals and had drinks and laughs, not much more to it."

"I still want to talk to him."

Ollie was gone now and I was about to slip into the last chair at the table when Keys walked up and took it. He was pale and sweaty—his ninety-plus years and extra hundred pounds were taking a toll beneath bandstand lights. The waiter followed him with a tall glass of ice water and an even taller glass of scotch.

"You must be Bear Braddock." Keys extended a hand and a smile. He tipped back the scotch and easily swallowed half of it. The glass was barely away from his lips when he said, "Calloway and I talked—too many questions for me. But you're welcome to grill me again."

Lee stood. "I'll leave you to it, boys. Bear, save another dance for me. There's someone I have to meet." And she walked off toward the bar.

"You picked a feisty one, copper," Keys said. He slapped Bear's arm. "My girl will dance you into the floor and outdrink you, too. She's a tough one, my Lee. But you watch it, she's family."

"I'll keep an eye out," Bear said with a smile. He got serious. "Keys, I'll cut to the quick. Any idea who killed William Mendelson?"

"If I did, I'd kill the bastard myself. Slow, though. Real slow." Keys finished his scotch and lifted his ice water. "Doctor tells me no booze with my pills. Why? Will it kill me?" He laughed and sipped his water. "I played the clubs in Cairo during the war. Met and lost a lot of friends. Then, I lost a son not too many years ago. I've been fighting to put this club on the map—bankers, state liquor people, investors, even the damn zoning people. Screw 'em, all. I'm old and don't give a shit. So, I guess that makes me dangerous, right, Calloway?"

"Right, man, dangerous." Cal leaned toward him. "But hey, now. You and Willy were tight. If anyone can help us, it's you. So think, Keys. Think hard. Bear and me want his killer. We want him fast. So think."

He did. He sat back in his chair and looked out on the dance floor as waiters scurried about. His eyes didn't seem to see anything, and he looked lost in memories none of us could guess about. He took another swallow of water and fixed his eyes on Bear as his words bristled with a dry, heavy anger.

"I don't know who killed him, Detective. Oh sure, he's a weird old codger—just like me. But being a stingy old coot doesn't make you a bad man, does it? He's got all the money he needs and all kinds of baggage, too. Maybe somebody wanted that old Egyptian junk at his place for themselves. I just don't know."

Cal said, "Maybe, Keys. But what about the other stuff? Tell Bear what you told me earlier."

"Everyone has faults, Cal. Everyone has demons." Keys waved to the waiter for another drink. "I can't count or name all mine. Can you?"

Bear tapped the table. "No, I can't. But I'm not dead. So you need to tell me his so I can find out if they led to his killing."

Keys sat back and looked hard at Bear. He cocked his head a couple times back and forth like he couldn't decide what to say. Then he sighed and held up a finger. "Sure, sure. It's not like that shit son of his will help you. Look, me and Willy liked to go to Charles Town—you know, the track and casino—to do some gamblin' now and then. But one day, Willy refused to go back. He said he had issues with the races and slots."

I said, "Gambling debts? That could explain cleaning out his private vault, Bear. And it might explain someone killing him if he was in too deep."

Bear said the same thing and it sent a painful darkness over Keys's face.

"Willy didn't have markers. That bastard son of his, Marshal, did. And Willy tried to unbury Marshal from the hole he'd dug. I went to him last year and wanted him to invest in this club. We go back decades, right? He was loaded—or so I thought. So I went to Willy. Not as a banker, no, but as a private investor. A *friend*."

"And?" Bear asked, seeing Cal's mouth form the same word. "Did he invest?"

"Nope. Not one dime. Couldn't." Keys's drink arrived and he took a long sip. "He said he wanted to but didn't have the capital. And then he told me not to apply at the bank because he could never get the loan through without substantial collateral, which I ain't got. He gave me the bum's rush."

I looked over at Poor Nic sitting on the mezzanine. He watched us, too. "So, now you know how Poor Nic fits in, Bear. Nic loves the underdog. Or perhaps he loves the vig."

The vig is the ridiculous interest a loan shark charges for money lent. The vig also can include kneecaps, ankles, arms, and legs if payments are late. I don't recall where the nickname comes from, but I can tell you it isn't from a dictionary. My guess is that if it were in any book, it would be Poor Nic's operating manual.

Bear watched Keys. "And that's how Poor Nic became your partner? Alternative financing?"

"Not a partner," Keys said in a tight voice. "An investor. He doesn't own anything but my marker. And yeah, Nicholas has been good to me. And I'm good to him. And before you start all your cop bullshit, the interest ain't bad and he plays nice. It's all legal."

"Whoa, now." Bear patted the air. "Nic and I are good. Ask him. As long as he stays inside the rules, I'm a happy guy and he can invest where he wants."

A waiter left Keys another scotch, which he tossed back and stood up. "Gotta hit the latrine, boys. Look, I ain't sayin' Marshal's gamblin' is why somebody popped Willy. I'm just sayin' that hole was deep and Willy tried to fill it. Maybe somebody killed Willy to send a message. Willy couldn't invest in my place and that bothered him—all his money went to Marshal's debts. Willy was my friend back from the days friends didn't live so long, know what I mean? The war."

I did know what he meant. "He's holding back Bear. Nostalgia's got his tongue. And I think Nic's in this up to his vig, too. Just like always."

Bear watched Keys walk off. Then he turned to Cal. "Tell Bartalotta I want an audience—ten minutes."

"Sure, Bear." Cal stood, then threw a chin toward Angel and Thorne across the room. "Good to see Angela out, too, Bear. No offense to Tuck and all, but she's too young and too much of a catch to stay off the market. No matter where he is."

"I'm sitting right here, Cal," I said. "And she's off the market either way."

Bear grunted, then said, "Yeah, but Thorne?"

"Yeah, man, I hear you." Cal watched them. "Thorne's a little stiff. She's way out of his league, but I don't think he gets that. He's pretty enough and kinda slick, but… something about that guy just doesn't sit with me, you know?"

I did. And the way he leaned close to my Angel and refilled her wineglass didn't sit at all. And there *was* something odd about him. Not just that he had his own eavesdropping equipment or that he used words like tradecraft, either. He seemed a little too confident and righteous—like he knew something we didn't. And while bankers were often like that, he wasn't a banker. He was a security guy and ex-Army Ranger. If you put the two together, you get a professional soldier who knows about alarms, CCTV, and eavesdropping—someone who knows how to kill and cover his tracks.

The question was, was Franklin Thorne my best suspect or just my worst nightmare?

Chapter Thirty-Three

Ollie had disappeared to who-knows-where and Bear sat watching Cal and Keys on the bandstand. The way he glanced around the room looked like he hoped the steamy Lee Hawkins would return for another drink. Bored, I went to eavesdrop on Angel and Franklin Thorne—I'm sure I was the topic of conversation—I caught her looking around the room and keeping an eye on Bear. That meant she was keeping an eye *out* for me. Was she nervous about her evening without me? Should I be?

No, Angel would have to wait.

A dark-haired woman stood in the bar entrance and looked around the ballroom. After a third pan of the room, she turned and disappeared down the hall beside the bar.

It was the mysterious Raina—Poor Nic and Lee's lunch companion. If she were here to rekindle their conversation, I wanted to get a good seat.

I followed her.

It took me a moment to check two storage rooms and an employee break room before I found a door at the end of a long, L-shaped hall marked "Management Only." Since it was the last place Raina could be, I went inside.

Bingo. Or should I say, Gotcha.

The office was small, dark, and crammed to the ceiling with furniture, papers, boxes, and sundry office equipment. There was an old wooden desk with a broken coin-counting machine sitting on one side and a notebook computer on the other. Against a side wall was a table littered with papers and files and cases of printer paper. In the corner of the office, beside a door, were two filing cabinets. Beyond the clutter was a rear door that led to the outside employee parking area.

And there stood my Gotcha.

Raina was elbows-deep inside the filing cabinets and neither Lee nor Keys Hawkins were here. So unless she was recently hired as a bookkeeper or chambermaid, one might draw the conclusion that Raina-whoever was up to no good.

"So, Raina, we meet again." I love cheesy quotes from old movies. She didn't blink so I moved closer and watched her fingering the files one drawer after the other. "Tell me what you're looking for and maybe I can help."

Nothing.

"Oh, come on, what good is me snooping around if you're not going to give me a clue? Give a guy a break, will you? *BOO* already. *WOOO WOOO* and all that crap."

Nothing.

Raina finished with the filing cabinets and went to the computer on the desk. The system was password protected, but that didn't stop her. From a pocket somewhere beneath her black evening dress—my imagination reeled—she withdrew a small USB drive and inserted it into the computer and tapped a couple keys. A tiny red light on the USB flashed on. A few seconds later, a bar appeared on the screen and began counting down from one hundred percent. When it reached zero percent, the bar disappeared and the words "System Accessed" flashed on the screen. When Raina tapped the keyboard again, the words disappeared and the computer's desktop came alive.

"Ah, Raina—and I'm saying this to be helpful—that's illegal."

She went to work.

First, she searched through the computer directories like a pro. Here and there she clicked on folders —the email folder, accounting files, document folders—and typed in a command. The USB drive lit up again and she began copying files to it. Ten minutes later, she extracted the drive and tucked it into her dress from where it came.

"Raina, you need to tell me…"

Voices in the outside hall startled me but they didn't seem to unnerve her. She looked around the room and focused on a dusty, broken-framed photograph partially hidden behind a stack of files on the credenza. She picked it up and looked at it.

The photograph was very old—1945 from the hand-scrawled date in the lower right corner. In the photo was Keys Hawkins dressed in a light-colored linen suit standing on a street curb somewhere in what I could tell was Cairo. He was very, very young—barely an adult. Beside him was a beautiful, young Egyptian woman and a tall, handsome Egyptian man—both wore khaki trousers and loose-fitting shirts. The three looked chummy, with big smiles for the camera.

Raina turned toward the door as the sound of voices grew louder. Then, without a second thought, she took the photograph and slipped out the rear office door.

As the door closed, the main office door opened and Lee Hawkins walked in speaking with Sammy from Queens.

Raina's mission was apparently complete. Whatever that was.

Was it me or was everyone I'd met since finding William Mendelson's body acting suspicious? So far, the only one who hadn't was the bank robber. At least he carried a gun and hid behind a mask—his intention was straightforward.

Everyone else seemed to be hiding secrets and lies.

Chapter Thirty-Four

I returned to the ballroom just in time to see Bear stop Poor Nic and his bodyguard, Bobby, in the doorway. "Hey, Bear, I gotta tell you what I just saw in the back office…"

"Later." He offered his hand to Poor Nic. "I need a moment, Nic."

"Ah, Detective Braddock," Poor Nic said and held Bear's paw in both of his. "I'm afraid I don't have time for you this evening. Something's come up."

Bear frowned. "It's about…"

"William Mendelson's murder. Of course it is." Poor Nic nodded toward the club entrance. "I'm tired, Detective. And I ask your understanding to let an old man go home for the evening. I'll see you first thing in the morning, I assure you."

"Give me just a moment, Nic…"

Poor Nic raised a hand. "I wish to say good evening to Angela. Please, come see me in the morning."

I followed Poor Nic to Angel's table just as Thorne readied for another dance. Angel gave me those narrowed eyeballs that said *Don't say a word* when I emerged behind Nic. To Nic, though, she was all smiles and crushed into him for a kiss on the cheek.

Poor Nicholas Bartalotta was a lot of things—most of which had never been proven in court. One thing most people did not quite understand was that he was Angel's guardian—her self-appointed godfather. When I was murdered, Poor Nic was on the top of the suspect list. And perhaps for good reason, too, because Bear and I had been investigating him for another

147

murder just days before. In the end, though, Poor Nic saved Angel's life. Perhaps others' lives, too.

"Ah, my dear, you look beautiful as always." He gave her a long, familiar hug. "You should be out more. The light and music suit you well. Another time, I would welcome a dance or two."

She blushed. "Of course, Nicholas. Let me introduce Franklin…"

"Thorne." Poor Nic cast a brief glance at him but ignored Thorne's outstretched hand. "I am familiar with Mr. Thorne."

"You are?" Thorne motioned to a passing waiter for his bill. "I don't know you."

"No? Interesting," Poor Nic said, still holding Angel's arm. "Detective Braddock looked rather awkward on the dance floor, Angela. Perhaps he had the wrong partner, no?"

She blushed again and looked across the room at Bear waiting near the ballroom entrance. "I think he and Lee looked wonderful together."

"Perhaps." Poor Nic leaned closer. "My dear, it's been weeks since you visited. This week—promise me."

"I promise." Angel looked past him to me. "I'm trying to get out more, but it's difficult."

"I understand." Poor Nic kissed her cheek with a curt nod to Thorne. "Walk with me, my dear." He guided Angel toward Bear, leaving Thorne to pay their check.

Poor Nic is swell.

At the ballroom entrance, Lee Hawkins came up behind Bear and grabbed his arm. She leaned in close and gave him a hug, cheek-to-cheek. "Why don't you come back, Bear." She hooked his arm and walked toward the door behind Poor Nic with him. "There are a few things you might like to hear."

"Give me ten minutes with Nic and…"

"No, I mean later." She slipped a business card out of her cleavage—what was with these women tonight?—and handed it to him. "Say, three a.m.?"

"Too late for me." Bear was on uncharted ground.

Lee whispered, "The card's from some crazy lady—Raina something. She's trouble. Maybe you should check her out. Maybe send her back home, you know, or something."

Bear read the card. "'Egyptology and Archeological Research Group—American University, Cairo.'" On the back of the card were a scribbled, unreadable name and a telephone number.

"There's more, but like that dance, it'll cost you," Lee said and squeezed his arm. "Let's say lunch?"

"Deal." He pocketed the card. "I'll call you tomorrow."

She kissed him on the cheek and slinked away.

Bear watched her go—watched her close, too—and then caught up to Poor Nic and Angel at the club entrance as Thorne helped Angel with her coat. Bobby held the door.

"Angela," Poor Nic said, shooting a wry glance at Thorne. "I'll expect you for lunch—tomorrow? I'll be much better company."

Angel's finger scolded him. "It's not a date, Nicholas, it's business."

"Of course. How silly of me." Poor Nic kissed her cheek but said to Bear, "Detective, phone tomorrow for an appointment."

Bear and I watched Poor Nic—with Angel on his arm—pass through the double doors into the chilly night air. They stopped on the landing as Bobby continued to the car.

Angel said, "Nicholas, I want to ask you about William."

"My dear, I—"

The first shot cracked the cold, dense air like a firecracker. The bullet struck Poor Nic, and for a second, he didn't react. Then, as he turned toward Angel, he slumped backward against the doors, paled, and collapsed on the cold stone steps.

Chapter Thirty-Five

"Nicholas!" Angel dropped down beside him.

His bodyguard Bobby charged up the stairs.

Bear drew his weapon and dropped to one knee. He shielded Angel and Poor Nic with his hulking body and searched for the shooter.

Another shot flashed from somewhere across the parking lot. Seconds later, a pickup truck skidded across the rear of the parking lot, bounced over the curb, and lurched onto Route 11, gathering speed as it disappeared.

I ran into the lot, but in the dark and at that distance, it was impossible to see any details of the truck. When I returned to the valet area, Bear was on his cell phone yelling at Dispatch for backup and an ambulance. Angel knelt beside Poor Nic.

She said to Bear, "It's a shoulder wound and not bad. We need to get him inside and warm or…" But before she finished her sentence, Bobby bent, scooped up the gangster like a doll, and carried him through the club doors. She followed.

A crowd formed inside the open club door as Cal emerged, sax in hand. "You all right?" Cal called.

"Cal, keep everyone inside," Bear said. "Backup's five minutes out."

Cal nodded and disappeared back into the club. "Did you see anything?"

Bear was talking to me. "Nothing. And before you ask, no, I'm not *getting anything* either."

A voice called from the parking lot and a tall man emerged from the darkness. "Is everyone all right? Was anyone hit?"

Franklin Thorne—and in his hand was his short-barreled, nickel-plated handgun.

Chapter Thirty-Six

"Drop the weapon, Thorne," Bear ordered as he lifted his Glock. "Slow—real slow."

"What?" Thorne stopped ten feet from Bear. "Hold on, Detective. I was at my car when the shooting started. I pulled my weapon and tried to find the shooter. I'm sure he was in that pickup that tore out of here."

Bear prodded the air in Thorne's direction with his gun. "Drop the weapon—now."

"Fine. Here." Thorne turned the semi-automatic around and held it out, butt first. "It's not been fired. Well, last week on the range, yes, but…"

Bear snatched the gun away. "What did you see?"

"I heard a couple shots then the truck started up and flew out of here. I looked around and when I didn't see anyone, I came back. I didn't see the shooter. But my best guess is he's in the truck."

I watched Thorne. He seemed at ease, unshaken. "Cool as a corpse, Bear. He seems okay with gunfire around him."

Bear smelled the barrel of Thorne's handgun. "Not fired today." Then he bore into Thorne with skeptical eyes. "I thought I took your weapon this morning after the bank shooting?"

"I have several, Detective. I'm not going unarmed after the bank was robbed." Thorne reached for his weapon and after a long moment, Bear reluctantly released it to him. "Would you?"

"Maybe he's the shooter and that truck was just getting out of the way," I said. "He could have used a throwaway gun."

"Have a seat, Thorne." Bear pointed to the club stairs. "You're staying put for a while."

Two sheriff's cars—lights flashing—pulled into the lot and Bear went to meet them. He issued orders, pointed in all directions, and twice took one of the deputy's radios to issue more orders. A few minutes later, Bear returned.

I said, "What did you think of the shots, Bear?"

"Quiet," Bear said, "low-caliber I'm thinking…"

".22-caliber." I ran into the parking lot where the deputies were beginning a slow, careful search. "I'm sure of it. Not quite a loud bang—not like a .38 or a 9mm, right? More like a 'thwack.' Same as the bank annex."

"Just like." He thought about that. "No CCTV cameras within miles. As busy as things are around here, I doubt anyone noticed anything. That truck is gone—not enough patrols to check all these roads, but I have them looking anyway."

"Interesting string of events, right?" I said, "A botched bank robbery, a dead bank executive in a secret, private vault, and an attempted murder of our one and only gangster."

Bear was halfway through forming a word when Angel came back down the stairs. "Nicholas will be fine. It's a shoulder wound and not too bad. There was an ER nurse dining inside and she's tending him."

She looked over at Thorne sitting on the steps. "Franklin?"

"He's in a time-out," I said. "He doesn't play well with others."

She frowned. "Bear? What's this about?"

"Just questions, Angela." Bear turned to one of the bouncers standing by the door. "Club's closed. Turn off the booze sales and keep everyone in their seats."

"The club is closed?" a female voice said from behind us. "Come now, Bear, surely those inside can finish their evening?" Lee Hawkins walked through the small crowd beside the door and down the steps. "Bear, please."

Bear said, "Sorry, Lee. We have to speak with anyone who saw or heard anything."

"No one did."

"And how do you know that?" Bear asked.

She frowned and looked up the stairs. "Because until that gorilla, Bobby, carried Nicholas in, no one knew anything had happened."

I said, "She's right, Bear. But we'll have to interview anyway."

Bear waved to Cal who was organizing the deputies near the parking lot. "I'll have Cal talk to folks as fast as we can. I've got more detectives coming, too. I promise, Lee, it won't take long and maybe we can get things back to normal in a couple hours."

"A couple hours?" Lee checked her watch. "The night is over then. Okay, Bear, I'll serve up some coffee and pass the bad news. You owe me more than lunch, now." She turned and headed back up the stairs to the club.

Angel said, "Bear, what about Franklin?"

Thorne stood up beside her. "I was in the parking lot when the shooting started. I pulled my gun and looked around. Now the detective wants to make sure I didn't do the shooting."

"Really, Bear?" Angel said with a snarky bite. "Why would you think that?"

"Because it's my job to think nasty thoughts about people walking around parking lots with guns. It's procedure."

"It's all right, Angela." Thorne patted the air. "I only regret it ruined our date."

"Oh, puke." My eyes rolled in tune with my stomach. "I knew it was a date."

Angel asked Bear, "Is this necessary? Can you get his statement tomorrow? After all that's happened today?"

"No, I can't." Bear's mouth tightened a little. "But I'll have Cal get right on it. Then you go right home, okay?"

"Thank you," Angel said to Bear. "If it's not too late, come on by for coffee when you're done here."

I eyed Thorne. "Good idea, Bear. She'll be alone all night. She could use better company."

Angel closed her eyes and muttered something I'm sure I didn't want to hear.

"Detective, I'll wait inside." Thorne nodded to Angel and headed back into the club.

When he was out of earshot, Angel leaned in close to Bear. "Nicholas is involved again?"

"Why else would someone try to kill him?"

I coughed. "Oh, a million reasons."

"Seriously," Angel said. "He's lucky it's not bad."

"No," I said, "they're unlucky. If his people find them before we do, they'll be worm food."

Bear said, "Angela, I can have one of my men drive you home."

"Not yet. Franklin was just opening up to me."

"What did he tell you?" Bear asked. "Maybe this was a good plan."

I laughed. "A plan? This was a date. Plans don't involve dancing."

"Someone is just jealous they can't dance and drink champagne." She handed Bear a business card. "Franklin has his own ideas about William. He found this at the bank—and there's much more you need to know."

Bear glanced down at the embossed print on the card. "Amphora Trading—again. Like the shipping crates in William's basement."

"Franklin thinks William's death is connected to a couple others some years ago. Two old friends of William and Keys's—friends from the war. He also thinks something is going on at the bank. He thinks..."

"Of course something is going on at the bank," I said. "It doesn't take a genius to see that."

She grinned. "Good, so you see it too?"

Ouch.

Bear said, "Anything else, Angela?"

"No, not yet. But I'm working on it." Angel turned toward the stairs but stopped. She looked back at Bear but said to me, "I'll wait up for you, Bear. And I *will* be alone."

As she climbed the stairs, I said, "Partner, you know what's worse than a snotty, too-perfect Vice President of Bank Security?"

"No, what?"

My mouth went dry. "A wife who's too damn classy and alive for me but won't come out and say it."

Chapter Thirty-Seven

I got home a little after two a.m. and went upstairs to our bedroom to try and talk with Angel. When I went in, I found her fast asleep with my replacement lying beneath her arm on my pillow. My heart stopped for a beat—not really, of course—and I went in for a closer look at the betrayal.

It was worse than what I'd suspected. Much worse.

Hercule was cuddled with her, his big furry face snoring and drooling on my pillow. He should have been in my den, waiting in my good leather chair for me to return from a long and difficult night. He was supposed to be there to greet me and show his love and affection. But no. He betrayed me. He was my last rock of devotion and camaraderie. And here he was on my pillow.

"Traitor."

He opened his eyes, wagged a couple times, and returned to the land of steak tartare and adoring women.

"Angel?"

Nothing.

"Angel?"

She stirred and pushed Hercule's nose from her cheek. "I'm sleeping, Tuck. So, unless you're that dashing French movie star, it'll have to wait until morning."

What is it about this French movie star? "But I'm—"

"*Au revoir*." She rolled over and pulled the covers tighter.

Hercule moaned.

"Sure, okay. In the morning."

Our old Victorian was large, dark, and empty at that hour, and above all, it was lonely. I wasn't ready yet to go to the "time out" place I went to shut off my former life—it's just a dark, empty, nothing place. When I'm there though, it recharges me like I was plugged into a battery charger all night.

But not tonight. There was too much to do.

I remembered Doc griping about his missing photo album, so I popped into the attic to look for it. I hadn't been in the attic for years. And with good reason. When I'd first inherited the house, I found it fully furnished with antiques, shelves of books, and a basement and attic crammed with junk. Back then, I was a young man right out of high school struggling to pay for community college. I had no money and no family to fall back on. All I had was the few dollars I'd earned on weekends while I'd lived with an elderly foster family. So I sold as much of the antiques and old junk as I could and moved the rest into the attic.

Living in the house among those possessions was at first a trauma—an inheritance from a family I never knew—and I had sold part of it to make a living. And now, knowing what I did about Doc, Ollie, and the rest of my bizarre family, I felt worse. At first, walking around the house, I'd sworn I was not alone. The week after signing the inheritance papers, I'd gone into the attic to explore. Voices called my name. Shadows moved around me. I swore I saw an old coot in a mirror watching me. So, I did what any young cop wannabe would do in that situation: I ran back down the attic stairs, slammed the door, and locked it. Other than to move the extra furnishings and clutter up there with some college pals, I hadn't been back since.

Tonight, after all these years, the eaves and creaky wood floor seemed at peace with me. The voices and shadows were gone—one, at least, lived in my den. Others visited me from time to time as Vincent, Sassy, and Ollie Tucker. Now, it all made sense—in a macabre, unbelievable kind of way.

I rooted around the attic boxes and old shelves looking for Doc's missing photo album. I found only dust and spiders. On my way downstairs to wake Angel, I remembered an old wooden filing cabinet—the mate to the one in my den—whose drawers were locked and unable to be opened. The filing cabinet was buried in the rear of the attic behind several crates loaded with dishes, figurines, and other miscellaneous junk. I should have gotten rid of it years ago and Angel had implored me to. But I couldn't part with any more of my family's past, junk or not.

I popped back to the cabinet and considered my options. I could wake Angel and antagonize her into helping me open the drawers, or I could seek out some electricity somewhere and do it myself. The answer was easy—I took the route of least retribution. I went to the overhead light dangling on an old, worn wire, and took hold.

The euphoria was instant.

The current surged through me as screaming stabs of energy invaded my fingers, flashed up my arms, and exploded through my body in waves of power and light. I held on, quenching a thirst I didn't feel, until I could consume no more.

When I let go of the wire, my body tingled and pulsated and I felt almost alive.

At the filing cabinet, I grabbed the drawer and pulled. Nothing. I pulled again. Nothing. Frustrated, I found a dulled butter knife in a box of junk, pried the lock, and popped open the drawers. It wasn't exactly the spirited trickery one would expect of me, but it worked.

Inside, I found rows of files and papers in tattered brown folders marked with all sorts of numbers and letters. Many of the folders contained photographs, maps, and pages and pages of handwritten notes. In the rear of the top drawer, I found Doc's photo album. Behind it, I found another dark brown folder stuffed with notes, faded photographs, and typewritten reports. The pockmarked pages and irregular, fuzzy typeface told me they were prepared on an ancient manual typewriter.

"What in the world?"

I took my booty to a dusty wooden table near the stairs and spread it out. When I opened the photo album, a hand gripped me and held me firm. A flood of childhood memories—lost decades ago as a five-year-old thrust into foster care—flowed over me.

Faces. Ollie's face, no... my father's face, was everywhere. This house.

The backyard. Picnics and a birthday—my birthday party. Sounds rose all around. Voices. My father talking to someone... Doc? Ollie? The voices were mere whispers and the words not quite clear. But something told me what they meant—stories of my life as a child and before. The cloud of the past swirled, the images and voices dissipated and were gone. The photographs painted this house a different color and filled it with the old furniture I'd sold years ago. There was an old car in the garage—a fifty-something Chevy with big fins and white-wall tires. A woman, beautiful and happy, sat atop the hood flashing a leg and feigning surprise.

My mother?

Tears washed away the clarity and I moved on to other photos. There was Ollie in his Army uniform just back from the war. Doc stood beside his son, one arm wrapped around his shoulders and a finger pointing to his chest of medals. And among those was the bronze star. The bronze star?

"Holy shit, Ollie, you were a war hero."

The album was a treasure trove of forgotten memories and some I'd never had. I spent an hour looking at my family and embroidering their faces onto my brain. And in every photo of my father and mother—most with Ollie, too—was a large, bulky chocolate Lab.

Hercule was not the first. Boy, was I *not* gonna let him live that down.

I put the album down and opened a brown folder. Black marker labeled the file "Oliver Tucker, Captain, US Army—1945." I opened it and spilled its contents onto the table. Either fate or luck left three ragged black-and-white prints faceup before me. The photos were grainy and faded but I could still see the images clearly. Four men sat around a table littered with glasses and bottles. The walls were stark, dull stone. A beautiful veiled belly dancer sat on one of the men's laps. The other men were toasting her and laughing. On the back of the photo, the men's names were scrawled in shaky handwriting.

For Cy Gray, Claude Holister, Keys Hawkins, and Willy Mendelson, times seemed good in Egypt in 1945.

Finding this photograph wasn't any real surprise to me. What was a surprise was that it was in Ollie's folder in my parents' attic—and across the faces of two of the men sitting in the center of the photograph were black X's.

Chapter Thirty-Eight

I t was three in the morning when Bear pulled his cruiser into the parking lot at Three-A West at the Hunter's Ridge Garden Apartments just outside Winchester. He climbed out of his cruiser, stretched, and breathed in the crisp, cold December air. For a second, it invigorated him, but that lasted only as long as it took him to feel the ache in his back and exhaustion everywhere else.

When he reached the sidewalk, footsteps behind him sent alarm bells off. Other than old man winter, there was no one awake at this hour. As he moved toward his apartment, the footsteps synced with his. They stopped as he did at his stoop. They stopped again when he reached his front door.

He spun around, pulled his handgun, and peered into the night. "Who's out there? Come forward—easy."

A dark, long-coated figure stepped from the shadow of a tall spruce tree and into the stoop's light. "A little jumpy, aren't you, Bear? Afraid of little ol' me?"

Lee Hawkins?

The thermometer hit 100 and climbed.

"What are you doing here, Lee? Trying to get shot?"

She giggled and closed the distance. She carried two heavy, handled paper shopping bags and handed one to him. As she did, she pressed herself into him, kissed his cheek, and lifted the other bag.

"You left the Kit Kat at one thirty. Where have you been?" She smiled a smile that made him fifteen years old again. "I've been waiting an hour."

"Waiting?" Bear holstered his gun and fumbled for words to overcome the uneasiness rising inside. He found none. What was it about her? She was pushy and forward—a strong woman who put him on his heels and made him feel awkward. But she was beautiful and alluring, and above all, *interested*. That combination hadn't slapped him in the face—or kissed his cheek—in a very long time. The last woman to cross his stoop was almost killed by a madman. That attack sent her hundreds of miles away never to return.

Now, Lee's smile cut through the night like a beacon.

"Waiting for what?" he asked. "It's three a.m. You said lunch."

"I changed my mind. Now it's breakfast." Glass clinked against glass inside her paper bag. "Or dinner, whichever. You never finished yours and Calloway paid for it. So I brought it—for two, of course."

"Calloway?" He rolled his eyes and dug his house key out of his pocket. "Look, you should go home, Lee. I can't do this. I'm tired, and you're involved in my case. So you better go home."

Her face fell and her lips formed a pout. "Go home? Detective Theodore Braddock, since I was sixteen, no man has told me to go home at three in the morning."

"I'll bet that's true." Bear unlocked his door and opened it. "Sorry, Lee. Maybe after this case. Please, it isn't a good idea. Good night."

"But…"

"Good night, Lee—I'm sorry, really." He shut the door and realized he still clutched her shopping bag.

What was she thinking? More importantly, why was she thinking it? In all his years, he'd never been good with the ladies, least of all a lady like *her*—beautiful, successful, and, well, *beautiful*.

His doorbell rang. He groaned and opened the door. "Come on, Lee, I said…"

She pushed past him and strode into the living room. She set her bag on the small oval coffee table strewn with gun magazines and days-old takeout containers. Then she turned around, peeled off her Moncler coat, and tossed it on a chair. Gone was her sexy, satin dress that had earlier made his eyeballs bleed. It was replaced with tight jeans and a button-down silk shirt that was open to oh-my-God. She leaned down and took a bottle of Dom Perignon and two crystal champagne glasses from her bag. When she did, she had little beneath the silk but his imagination—and that was not a requirement.

"Three things, Detective Braddock." Her eyes melted his reticence and sizzled the air between them. "First, I've said I haven't been sent home in quite a while. Second, I have two wonderful filets and two lobster tails in this bag, buster, and this bottle of Dom is chilled just right—I should know, we've been chilling outside your apartment for an hour."

Bear peeked into the paper bag he held and found a rolled white cloth, some plates, and silverware. "What's all this?"

"You look like a guy without a maid—or plates."

He laughed. "You'd be right." He found her eyes again, unable to hold them, unable to break free. "You said three things."

With champagne and glasses in hand, Lee floated across the room. "Did I?" She crushed into him and kissed him—long and soft like he hadn't been kissed in a very, long time.

Without removing her lips from his, she whispered, "Third, I'm fragile, so be gentle with me."

Chapter Thirty-Nine

"Looks like they're having a ball, doesn't it?"

Ollie walked up the attic stairs and stopped in front of the table. He looked down at the photograph of Keys Hawkins, Willy Mendelson, and their friends.

"Yes, it does, Ollie. Why didn't you tell me you knew Keys and William?"

"Slipped my mind." He tipped his ball cap back. "And Doc said—"

"I was a little slow, yeah, he's mentioned it." I tapped the photo. "I can't ask questions about something I don't know about."

He smiled. "Noted. I'll try to remember to fill you in as we go."

"So, you knew Keys and William. You obviously know what this is all about, right?"

"Well, one thing doesn't always mean the other."

Holy shit, word games were a family curse. "And what does that mean?"

"It means, grandson, that those four in the photo are important. Yessiree. The question for you, though, is important to who? You or me? Or both of us?"

Huh? I picked up the other photographs that had spilled out of the folder. One was of a two-story house sitting on the water—a houseboat of sorts. On the street were Middle Eastern men in fezzes and turbans and long thobes. The other two photos were different street scenes at cafés and clubs with dozens of Middle Easterners and Westerners sitting around tables. I recognized one of the photos, too. It was of the Shepheard Hotel in Cairo. In fact, all the photographs were of Cairo.

"You were in Cairo, Ollie? I didn't know the US was in Cairo during the war."

"Oh, some of us. Not many, though."

"Why were you there?"

He walked around the table and sifted through several other photographs and papers. He pulled out a folded piece of newspaper and two photographs. He laid them on the table.

"I was OSS, kid. Remember? The Army had a few people there—mostly command staff and support groups for the Brits. And the Army Air Force flew combat missions and cargo in and out of there, too. I was there to keep the Krauts from mucking things up for them. And boy oh boy, the Krauts were trying."

The newspaper clippings looked up at me and I bent down to read. They were decades old. One was the story of a mysterious murder in Washington DC. A body found off River Road just across from the Congressional Golf club.

"Cy Gray? One of William's war pals was murdered in 1954? That's a long time ago, Ollie."

He nodded. "They never found the murderer, either. Keep reading, kid. It gets better."

The article went on to say Gray's body was found along the roadside in a ditch. His throat was slit and he'd endured a vicious beating. His wallet and belongings were untouched and the police were baffled as to the motive.

When I looked up, Ollie gestured to another clipping on the table. I opened it and read it out loud. "'The body of Claude Holister was found yesterday in the Shenandoah National Park on the Appalachian Trail, along the Clarke County line. Holister, a World War II veteran of the Army Air Force, died at the age of forty-seven of an apparent self-inflicted gunshot wound.'"

Things were tingling my brain. "Okay, so, Holister committed suicide. That was in 1969. What are you doing with this article? Doc and you were— well, I hate to remind you, Ollie—but Doc and you were already dead. How come…"

"Your dad, kid." Ollie lifted his chin and a thin smile cracked his lips. "He carried this on, too."

"Carried what on? What's this all about, Ollie?"

"All right, I'll give you this one. You know, a consolation prize." He went to the filing cabinet where I'd found the album and returned with something in his hand: a short, purple ribbon with a gold and purple heart at the end. In the center of the heart was a relief of George Washington. It was a military medal—the Purple Heart, given to those wounded in combat. "I got three of these in the war, kid. One of them in Cairo. It ain't like watching the flicks. I remember the first one. I got it in Algiers chasing this Kraut spy through the streets…"

He held the medal out to me, and when my fingers closed on it, the lights went out along with another war story…

The desert air was arid and smelled of charcoal fires and charred meat. The night was alive with rhythmic music and the clacks and creaks of carriages and trucks. But those sounds grew dimmer as the darkness ebbed—only a little—and I stood on a dirt street outside tall, pale stone-walled buildings. The music drifted with the dry breeze that brought little relief in the sweltering darkness and the sounds of Cairo's nightlife just blocks away.

Only darkness greeted me on my street.

There was no one but for a single horse-drawn flatbed cart being pulled down an alley. There were no lights. No sounds. Nothing that I could see. The cart stopped and a single man climbed down and went inside the house.

Ollie was nowhere around, and absent any clue for my visit to Cairo, I crossed the street and ventured toward the cart. The emaciated mare was startled and pressed backward, nudging the cart against the curb. She tossed her head and stomped the stone street, uncertain of me.

"Whoa, there, girl. Easy."

The mare settled down just as a light flickered through a window behind the cart. Inside the building, a man's voice called out in Arabic. Something crashed and shattered. The man's voice grew angrier and louder. More crashes.

The man yelled in Arabic again, then in broken English, "Swine! Get out!

167

Out of my house!"

I tried to enter the house through a side door beside the cart but could not. My body refused to move from the curb and I was frozen in place. The mare became more agitated with each violent outburst inside and twice nudged me with her muzzle and reared back.

A shot. The rumble of struggle. Another shot. Silence.

Inside, the light snapped dark and a moment later, the side door banged open. A figure emerged dragging a large chest and struggled to load it on the cart. He checked the street and returned inside. Moments later, he emerged again and loaded another chest. When he looked back at the house, the light inside flickered on and he stopped.

I couldn't see the figure on the street well—just a silhouette in the darkness—but I could make out his long, traditional Arab thobe and a scarf around his head. The darkness and his attire concealed his face. As a wail rose inside the house, the man bounded onto the cart and snapped the reins. The mare started forward, slowly at first then increasing her gait to the cracks of the reins. Moments later, the cart disappeared down the street and faded into nothing.

Another voice called out inside the building—a woman, I think—and her voice beckoned from room to room inside the shutters.

I drifted away now. The darkness swallowed the street around me and the sounds of nightlife had already disappeared. The building darkened and the inside light was no more than a wisp in the distance as I returned to my attic.

As I lost sight of the dusty street, the woman's wail flowed out from the darkness like a gathering storm. *"Laa, laa, laa! Youssif, laa, laa!"*

I did not speak Arabic. I didn't have to. The grief was enough—I knew what she had found. Her pain bridged the darkness between the 1940s and my time now. It explained my trip to Cairo at that late hour in the desert heat.

I was a witness.

A witness to a seventy-seven-year-old murder. Youssif's murder.

"Who is Youssif, Ollie?" I asked when attic eaves returned over me. "And where the hell were you just now?"

Ollie stood exactly where he was before I left—his Purple Heart outstretched to me. "So, kid, that's how I got my first medal. Lucky, huh?"

My trip to World War II Cairo had taken but an eye-blink. I repeated, "Where were you just now?"

"I wasn't needed." He shrugged. "And I wasn't there when it happened, now was I?"

My head spun. "Tell me what it means. And don't give me any of that Tucker-family doubletalk, either."

"I don't know what it means. Not yet." He stuffed his hands into his bomber jacket pockets. "Why do you think I came to you? If I had all the answers, why would I need you?"

"Because that's how this works, right? You guys on the dead-side cannot do things on the live-side. I can, through Bear and Angel. You all come to me to solve your problems, right?"

He laughed and folded his arms. "You got it all figured out, eh, kid? No, that's not always it. I don't have anything figured out. And neither do you. I just figured two heads are better than one."

Well, that was different—one of my relatives just gave me a straight answer. Even if he didn't offer any answers. Like who Youssif was and what it had to do with William Mendelson.

"Okay, Ollie. What now?"

He glanced at the photographs and newspaper clippings on the table. "You're looking into that Mendelson fella's murder and his pals, right? Back in the war, them fellas were in Cairo at the Kit Kat Club. Now they're here—a couple of them, at least—at the Kit Kat Club... *again*. There was a murder back then and a lot of other stuff, too. Now there's a murder here and a lot of other stuff."

"It's all connected."

"You have a way with the obvious, you know that, kid?" He picked up the photograph of the four men with the belly dancer. "She was sure a dish, wasn't she?"

She was and I told him so. "Did you know her?"

"She was the big name at the Kit Kat back then. The war raged just outside Cairo, but those Brits didn't let it stop them from having a party every night in the clubs. And a few of our boys led the fun, too." His eyes went smoky—he was back there, in Cairo. He looked up and saw me watching. "Yes sir, they knew how to have a good time."

"Who was she, Ollie—the belly dancer? A girlfriend?"

He laughed and slapped my shoulder. "Yeah, sorta. She was one of the most famous belly dancers in Egypt—hell, maybe even the world back then."

"Really?" I could only imagine a young Ollie Tucker loose in Cairo, far from home, befriending a sexy, slinky belly dancer. I wonder if Frannie found out. "How well did you know her?"

"Oh, she was a good dancer, don't get me wrong." He lifted the photo and his face brightened, admiring the young woman dressed in veils and gemstones. "But, that's not what made her famous. In fact, fame found her much later."

He grinned. I missed something. "Okay, tell me the rest."

"Her name was Hekmet Fahmy and she was pals with a guy named Hussein Gafaar." He held the photo up. "Mean anything to you?"

Yes, it did. "I saw a Hussein at the Shepheard Hotel yesterday after I touched that bug scarab thing in William's office."

"One and the same." He cocked his head. "Hussein's real name was Johann Eppler and he was with the German Abwehr. Hekmet worked with him."

He lost me. "The German Abwehr?"

"Kraut military intelligence, kid—Johann was a German spy. He and one of his spy-buddies got arrested just weeks after getting to Cairo."

I looked at the belly dancer frolicking at the Kit Kat with Cy Gray, Claude Holister, Keys Hawkins, and Willy Mendelson. "So, if Hekmet Fahmy the belly dancer was pals with Johann before he got arrested for being a spy, and she hung around with these guys later..."

He winked. "Then she was a German spy, too."

Chapter Forty

German spies. Dead bankers. Secret vaults. And a connection to Poor Nic Bartalotta.

Of all those things, one didn't surprise me—Poor Nic at the center of it. If there was a catastrophe around, there was always a connection to Poor Nic. He was a magnet for all things holy shit. I wouldn't be a bit surprised if his family held the mooring lines for the Hindenburg while they sold helium balloons nearby. And I think a relative was a lifeboat officer for the Titanic and another sold ice cubes on deck.

Why not now?

Angel stirred in our room, and I went down in time to catch her readying for a shower. She was elated, of course, to see me.

"Tuck, will you wear a bell or something? You're always popping in on me when I don't expect it."

What's with the bell, anyway?

"Angel, I need your help." I told her about my attic discovery and how I thought it all tied into my visit to Cairo's Shepheard Hotel.

She couldn't wait to help me and dropped her towel to climb in the shower. "It's six in the morning, Tuck. Your World War II belly dancer and German spies waited this long; another few hours won't hurt."

How silly of her. "Look, can you look up Hekmet Fahmy, Hussein Gafaar, and Johann Eppler for me? I'll see you later today to hear what you found."

"Why me?" her voice gurgled under the water.

"You're the history professor, honey."

"And you're the detective, *honey.*"

She had a point. "But it's sort of difficult for me to use a computer. And if I have to use electricity to build my strength to type all night, your electric bill will be outrageous."

Silence. "If I don't do the search for you, will you haunt me forever?"

"Too late for that. I'm going to see Poor Nic. I'll send him kisses and hugs."

"You do that."

As much as I loved our shower talks, there was work to do.

With a huff and a puff, I blew across town to the hospital and peeked over the shoulder of an ER nurse to find Poor Nic's room on the second floor. There, in a chair outside his door, was Bobby. He stuffed a breakfast sandwich into his mouth—in one bite—and gulped a mucho-extra-grande coffee at the same time. He probably had room for a side pound of hash browns and a half pig of bacon, too, if only his gargantuan hands could find the time.

I liked Bobby. He was both dependable and predictable.

Inside the room, I expected to find Poor Nic lounging in bed reading the Charles Town race forms and enjoying breakfast caviar or whatever mob bosses eat. I didn't find anything of the sort. He was sitting up in bed, one arm in a sling, the other holding the hand of the woman sobbing in his bedside chair.

Karen Simms.

"Now, Ms. Simms." He patted her hand. "I am afraid I simply do not understand your dilemma. Perhaps you should start at the beginning, no? Bobby said you were desperate to speak with me last night. I am sorry I was unavailable. Please, tell me now."

Karen sniffled, eased her hand away from Poor Nic's, and dabbed at her eyes with a handkerchief. "I'm embarrassed to be here, Nicholas. I was told to come to you if I was ever in trouble. I never thought it would be like this—and I'm sorry to bother you after what happened to you last night. But, that's precisely why I know I'm in danger. If they'll go after you, then I'm not safe."

"Ms. Simms, slow down. I do not understand. Who are you speaking of?"

"It's the bank." Karen straightened. "I'm in terrible trouble at the bank."

I said, "Oh, you are? Do tell, Karen. Do tell. And spare no details, please."

Poor Nic's eyebrows rose and he peered past her toward the door. Then he returned his gaze to her. "Tell me."

"With William gone, there's no one to turn to. I'm frightened—scared to death. I saw things, Nicholas. Things going on at the bank and in some of the accounts. Things I wasn't supposed to see and know about. Now William's dead. They're going to find out about me, too. I have to get out of town. I have to hide until this is all over and they catch the killers."

"Killers?" I said. "Come on, Karen, get to the punch line. What killers?" Nic asked her that, too.

"No, I can't say. I only suspect. You understand—I don't know for sure. But if you add it all up—the secret account, William's meetings, and the club—well, if you do, then I'm in big trouble."

She wasn't making any sense.

"You feel yourself in danger because of something you saw?" Poor Nic watched her and put on his best grandfatherly smile, and when she nodded, he added, "And the account? Which one?"

Karen's face paled and she slid back on her chair. She looked down at her hands on her lap. "Well, I think you know, Nicholas."

Poor Nic's eyes narrowed a little and a strange, thin smile etched the corners of his mouth. "Are you saying the Kit Kat West, my dear?"

She nodded.

Oh, really? The Kit Kat accounts are involved with William's murder? Funny how Marshal never brought that up.

"I assure you, there is nothing untoward with the Kit Kat accounts, my dear. I review those myself. Surely, you know I would not tolerate such possibilities."

"No, no, I'm saying—Well, I'm saying what happened to William and those accounts are all connected. And I know you're involved in the Kit Kat, Nicholas. Everyone knows. I have to get out of town. If I tell you what I know—it'll help you. If I do, will you help me?"

Poor Nic pressed a button on his bed control and the bed sat him straighter. He slid his aged legs over the side and eased himself into a sitting position facing her. "My dear, if there is something amiss at the club, I assure you I will get to the bottom of it. You have my word. And if it has anything to do with William's murder, I will deal with that most *directly*. Now, tell me."

"All I'll say is this: I was told to move money around, Nicholas. Lots of money. Every month I was told to take cash out and turn it over. Not enough to get anyone's attention, but plenty. And there's more. But, not until I'm somewhere safe, okay?"

Poor Nic reached a hand out, and when he did, he winced and touched his bandaged arm in the sling. "I assure you, Ms. Simms, you are quite safe with me."

"That's what William told me, too, Nicholas." She stood and went to the window. "Never mind, I'll find my own way. I'm sorry I came to you. I didn't know where else to go. I don't trust the police—after all, they're working with Marshal and Thorne. I don't trust them. I just thought..."

"No, no, you came to the right person, my dear." Poor Nic beckoned back to the chair and called out for Bobby. When Bobby entered, Poor Nic gestured to Karen. "Bobby, make arrangements for Ms. Simms to have, oh, let us start with five thousand. Is that sufficient for now?"

Karen blinked several times. "No, no, I wasn't asking for..."

"It is fine, my dear." He returned to Bobby. "Provide her with five thousand from the house money and give her one of our guest vehicles. Something small and low-key, you understand."

"Yes sir, boss. Want me to take her somewhere myself?"

Poor Nic glanced at Karen. "My dear? You are welcome to stay with me. It's the safest..."

"No." Karen stood and backed away from the bed. "I can't. No. You... Hawkins... Marshal. No. I can't. I..."

Poor Nic held up a hand and calmed her with that schmoozy smile of his. "I understand. Trust is important. Bobby, the cash and the car—for now. And perhaps get her one of our untraceable cell phones, too. She must be free to call and know the police are not listening."

Bobby nodded and looked at Karen. "I'll be outside." He left the room.

I said, "Geez, Nic, pretty generous. You know she's probably the key to this case, right? And if she is, hiding a witness is obstruction of justice. Except for you. I think you call it 'business as usual.' But you got class, Nic. Always helping out the lovely ladies."

Karen wiped away tears. "Thank you, Nicholas. William wasn't wrong about you."

"Who wasn't wrong about whom?" A voice said from the doorway. "The only person who's wrong is whoever thinks you're so sweet and innocent, Karen."

Lee Hawkins walked into the room like Patton returning to the Philippines—no, wait, that was MacArthur, but you get it. Bobby was behind her holding the door open for her entrance.

"I'm sorry, Nicholas, I have to leave." Karen retreated to Bobby and gave Poor Nic a faint smile. "I meant what I said. William wasn't wrong."

"Oh, please." Lee stood at the foot of Poor Nic's bed. She gave the old gangster a warm smile that metamorphosed into ice when she turned to Karen. "What are you doing here, Karen? Blackmail or another con job?"

"I don't have to put up with this, Lee." Karen snapped her arms folded. "I know all about you and your grandfather. I know..."

"You know what? Some deep dark secret?" Lee took a quick step toward Karen and split the air between them with a stiletto finger. "More lies and innuendo? Come on, Karen, when are you gonna be happy with what you have and go?"

Poor Nic patted the air. "Ladies, please. This is not the time or place."

A short, stout nurse brushed passed Bobby into the room. She took one look at Lee and Karen and stepped between them. "All right, ladies, everyone out. We need to discharge Mr. Bartalotta. You can take whatever this is elsewhere."

Karen stepped back near Bobby. "Hawkins, you twist everything, don't you? I know what you two were doing to William—and I know all about that woman, too. I won't let you get away with it." She looked to Poor Nic as tears welled in her eyes. "I'm so sorry. Good-bye." She spun on her heels and rushed from the room.

The nurse looked at Lee. "All right, Miss, you're next—*out*."

Poor Nic started to object, but the nurse held up a hand. "Not a word, Mr. Bartalotta. Not a word."

Poor Nic surrendered and lay back on his bed, arms folded, looking submissive.

Now, there's something you don't see every day.

Chapter Forty-One

"Somebody deleted all the evidence, Bear," Cal said and pointed to his computer screen. He leaned back, sipped his coffee, looking at Bear across the office. "They got into William's email and deleted everything."

I'd arrived at the Task Force office on the southwest side of town just before nine and found Bear and Cal at work. It was obvious they never went home last night—tired, bloodshot eyes, the same rumpled clothes, and an empty bag of breakfast takeout lying in the trash.

"Where are we then?" Bear propped his feet on his desk and closed his eyes. "Can you undelete the emails?"

"I'll have to check with the techies." Cal tapped away at his keyboard. "Whoever deleted William's email did it remotely—they used a computer outside the bank. So either they don't work at the bank or they're trying to cover their tracks."

Bear cursed. "The bank has everything backed up, right? How often?"

"Every morning at three a.m. They got to his account before the backup, though. He was killed around two a.m. and someone deleted his files just before the backup ran. We lost the day before his murder. Techs are sending what they found right now."

Bear stood and went to the coffeepot across the room to refill his mug. "And the crime scene report?"

"Right here."

I read over Cal's shoulder. "Nothing exciting, Bear. The glass fragments were from some kind of picture frame. And Angel was right, the paper in

William's hand was papyrus. Not enough to make any sense of but the lab thinks its old—like ancient-old."

"Skip the glass and papyrus," Bear said, "what about the .22-cal bullets, fingerprints, and everything else?"

Cal smiled. "If you already read the report, man, why are you asking?"

"Just tell me."

Cal muttered under his breath, then said, "They're gonna try to match the slug from Nic's arm to the .22-cal from the Agatha Christie book that took the bullet for Conti. We found fragments of the bullet that killed William, but not enough to ID. We'll have to send the two whole bullets to the lab in Richmond, but I think they'll match. And no prints in the vault or safe at all—wiped clean. The blood was all William's blood type. No surprise there. The ME won't be done with the body until tomorrow, so that's it for now."

"Shit." Bear sat back down and leaned back in his chair to contemplate the darkness inside his closed eyes. "And the bank perp? What's his status?"

"Nothing. No trace," Cal said. "No reported gunshot wounds around a three-state area. Nothing. We canvassed Old Town but no one saw anything. As for the pickup leaving the club last night—well, do you know how many old, dark pickups there are in this area?"

I said, "That would-be bank robber wasn't working on his own or thinking for himself, Bear. He knew about William's vault and then went after Poor Nic. That takes inside information and balls."

"I was thinking that same thing," Bear said.

Cal cocked his head. "What same thing?"

"Inside job." Bear shrugged and repeated me almost word for word. "He screwed up robbing the bank, and shooting Bartalotta was another big mistake. Two big mistakes in one day. That's not a pro."

"Sure, right. I get that." Cal sipped his coffee. "Thinking out loud—again."

I said, "This is about whatever was in that safe."

"And it's about what was in that safe," Bear repeated, closing his eyes again.

I added, "And it's about Keys, and Holister, and Cy Gray…"

Bear repeated me.

Cal watched him and shook his head.

"Oh, and it's about Cairo and Hekmet Fahmy, the belly dancer."

"And Cairo and the belly dancer…" Bear sat up. "Who the hell is Hekmet Fahmy?"

Cal loosed a loud belly laugh and spit coffee over his desk. "Belly dancer? Oh, man, you need some sleep, man. I'm going down to the tech boys. A belly dancer? Damn, man, get a grip."

As Cal walked off laughing, Bear turned to me. "Dammit, Tuck. I look like an idiot. What the hell are you talking about?"

I told him about Ollie and the files I found in my attic. He didn't have a big problem with any of it considering I was explaining about my long-dead grandfather showing me his photo album. But he almost spilled his coffee when I replayed my trip to 1940-something Cairo and the Youssif murder. He did spill it down his shirt over my theory that William's murder was linked to Cairo and the death of Claude Holister and Cy Gray—William and Keys's World War II buddies.

I finished with, "Oh, and Karen Simms paid Poor Nic a visit this morning at the hospital. He's helping her hide. And you missed this great catfight between her and Lee Hawkins—"

"Lee was there?"

"Sure, she came to see Nic. They're pals."

"Pals, huh? What did Lee have to say to Nic?"

I gave him the details. "Karen knows something, or thinks she knows something. She promised to tell Nic as soon as she found someplace to hide. He gave her a car and—"

"I'll send Cal to talk to Lee."

"Why don't we go?"

"I'm busy."

"So's Cal. Let's—"

"No. You stay clear of Lee, Tuck. Cal knows her pretty well from the Kit Kat. He'll have better luck."

What was wrong with him? "Are you afraid of Lee? What's up with you?"

"Nothing."

"Bullshit. Give. What's going on?"

He retrieved another cup of coffee. He took his time stirring it—odd, since it was black—and stalled long enough for Cal to return to the office.

"Tell me you have something, Cal—please."

"Okay." Cal laid a thick file on Bear's desk and spread several of the pages out. "I think Lee Hawkins has some explaining to do, Bear.

And I gotta tell you, I'm blown away. I always thought she was a sweet, hot lady—a tough one, but still sweet, ya know? But according to the little I read, she and Willy were really having a battle."

Bear picked up several emails and read them. I stood beside him and read over his shoulder. The first few were an exchange between William and Lee four months ago. Lee was upset that he wouldn't invest in her grandfather's business. In another, things got heated and she used words like *traitor, coward,* and *backstabber*. A few emails later, as early as last month, Lee threatened to go to the board of directors and tell them about his "secrets and betrayals." Nowhere did she say what those were, but she made it perfectly clear she'd ruin him with them.

When I looked up, Bear's face was sullen. His eyes were sad, and I could tell by the way he put the papers down that the contents upset him. If I didn't know any better, I'd say the big lug was truly smitten with Lee Hawkins and now her being a suspect killed him.

So goes life as a detective.

"This might track with what Karen Simms said," I said. "But, then again, people say vicious things in emails and they don't mean most of them. I used to get email offers from big shots in Nigeria who wanted to give me ten million dollars."

"Dammit," Bear said, closing his eyes.

Cal handed Bear another email. "You better read this one, Bear."

Bear hesitated, then took the paper.

This one was pretty clear. It was an email from Lee to William just a week ago. It warned him that if William didn't control "that bitch Simms," Lee would take matters into her own hands. In plain words, it read, "I'll deal with that bitch myself if you don't put her back on her leash."

"I think it's time we look a little deeper into Lee Hawkins and Karen

Simms," Bear said in a low voice. "Let's start with Lee. Go see her, Cal, and get to the bottom of this. Ask her about her visit with Poor Nic this morning and these emails."

"Her what with Nic?" Cal's face twisted. "You get something while I was gone?"

Bear nodded. "She was at the hospital this morning. Karen Simms was there, too. They got into it."

"Oh?" Cal looked around the room. "And I suppose an informant told you this?"

"I got a call."

Cal laughed. "Yeah, okay, man—you got a call."

There was a knock on Bear's office door. A uniformed deputy stood in the doorway behind Angel.

She walked in. "Good morning. I just spoke with Nicholas. He's doing fine and on his way home from the hospital. He said for you to call him later today to compare notes. He has something, but he wouldn't tell me what."

"Oh, he wants *me* to call *him*?" Bear growled. "To *compare notes*?"

"You know what he means, Bear." She looked over at me leaning against the wall behind Cal and gave me a "humph." That meant I was still in trouble after last night. She said to Bear, "I got a voicemail from Karen Simms, too. She asked me to come by her apartment later. She was very upset and said that she had some important things to tell me about the Kit Kat Club."

I said, "Did Nic mention seeing her and Lee this morning?"

Bear asked her that, too—for Cal's sake.

"No, nothing about them. Maybe Karen will tell me about it. I think she feels safe talking to me—woman to woman. I'm going over there later this morning. I just thought you should know."

I said to her, "What about your pal Thorne? Maybe you can interrogate him over a movie or a show next."

"Now, that's the best idea I've heard in a long time," she quipped, then smiled when Cal looked at her and snorted a laugh. "The idea that I get going to see Karen, that is."

Cal grinned and picked up his coffee. "Oh, yeah, Angela, go see Simms."
He laughed all the way out of the office. "You guys crack me up."

Chapter Forty-Two

I tagged along with Cal to the Kit Kat West—for professional reasons, of course. It was not, as Angel had suggested, to have another peek at the voluptuous Lee Hawkins. Now, if the ghost of Norma Jean or Jayne Mansfield were hanging around the club, different matter.

We arrived at the club just after ten a.m. and parked in the rear employee lot. Cal walked to a rear door marked "Delivery" and went inside. I followed him to the back office where the mysterious Raina had snooped around last night. He knocked on the door.

"I'm busy," Keys Hawkins bellowed from inside. "Shove off."

Cal pushed the door open. "It's me, Keys—Calloway."

"What are you doin' here so early? You boys got a rehearsal I don't know about?"

Calloway—er, Cal—dropped into an old wooden chair beside the door. "No, man, sorry. It's official. Is Lee around? I need to speak with the two of you."

I stood near the window beside Keys's desk and listened.

"Lee?" Keys picked up a cup of coffee and took too long to sip it. "What's she got to do with anything you'd be asking about?"

"Oh, come on now, Keys." Cal stretched his long, thin legs out in front of him, trying to appear as casual as he could. "You know I gotta do this, right?"

"Do what?"

"Investigate, man. You know, about Willy." Cal smiled a big, genuine smile. "It's me or Bear. You got the long straw, be happy."

Keys grunted a laugh. "Sure, okay, Calloway. Shoot. Just remember who signs your weekend check, though. And we both know it's more than your deputy pay."

"Yeah, it is."

They both laughed.

Cal leaned forward and put his hands on his knees. "I hear Lee got into a little pissin' contest with Karen Simms this morning. What was that about?"

"Oh? Don't know about that. Who told you that? Nicholas didn't."

"I never mentioned Poor Nic." Cal let a crooked smile out. "Bad play, Keys. Come on, now. What's the deal between Simms and Lee? And give me the straight story. Don't make me regret playin' here."

I went over and looked around Keys's desk. He had a thick notebook open with a three-inch stack of papers inside. On the edge of the binder, printed in wide, black marker, was, "Sancus Security Invoices."

That name tickled my memory, but nothing floated to the surface.

Keys said, "Listen, Calloway, you know about me and Willy. We were close. Real close. Brothers, even—from the war. He and me were trying to work some things out."

"What kind of stuff, Keys?"

"Personal stuff. I ain't sayin'. It has nothing to do with anything you need to know."

Cal shook his head. "No, it might have something to do with his murder."

"It doesn't."

"How do you know?"

"'Cause I do." Keys rested himself on his elbows. "Look. He wanted to invest in the business and couldn't come up with the capital. He was heartbroken and so was I. We always talked about being partners and all. He was worried the Kit Kat wouldn't turn a profit and he'd be stuck. The bank and that kid of his drained him, so I told him not to worry about it. But I knew he would. That's all."

"What about Lee?" Cal asked. "How'd she fit into that? And what's it got to do with Karen Simms?"

"I really don't know, Calloway. Honest. I think Karen was sort of kissing up to old Willy. You know, like trying to work her way up the chain at the bank. A couple times, Lee met with Willy on our accounts. Every time Lee showed up, that Simms dame wiggled into the meeting. Lee had the idea Simms was up to something—something no good."

Funny, that's exactly what Karen suggested of Lee.

Cal watched Keys for a while and squinted at him like he was dissecting his every word. Finally, after crossing his legs for the second time, he said, "Okay, Keys. But I know you're not tellin' me everything. So let's agree on somethin'."

"I'm listening."

"I'll cut you some slack. You find Lee so I can talk to her. And you think hard about Willy and Karen Simms. Don't be holding out on me, man. Music or not, it's my job and I'm gonna do it right."

Keys laughed, "You're a better musician than a cop."

"Serious now, Keys. I gotta do my job." Cal stood up to go. "And I'm a better cop. Trust me. Remember, we're talkin' about Willy, your best friend. Do him right."

Keys stood up, too. "I hear you, Calloway. Lee hasn't been in all morning. I swear. She must have had a late night. I'll let her know you're looking for her. Now, nothin' personal, but I gotta get back to my books. Nicholas might be an investor, but he don't like me payin' his own company's bills late." He tapped the notebook on his desk and thrust out a hand across to Cal.

I looked at the binder again. Sancus Security Systems, LLC—of course. Sancus was also the bank's alarm company. The name appeared on the records Larry Conti showed us yesterday morning.

Poor Nic owned Sancus?

"I'll be waitin' on a call, man." Cal shook Keys's hand.

"You do that."

When Cal shut the door behind him, Keys stared after him for the longest time. Then he picked up his office phone and dialed.

I wasn't fast enough around the desk and missed the number.

"Mornin', it's me. We gotta meet. Soon. The cops just left. No, it can't wait.

And if my granddaughter is there, send her to me. She kicked a hornets' nest this morning and now I'm getting stung." Silence. Then, "I don't know anything about no deal with William. That's got nothing to do with me." He hung up.

Poor Nic?

Keys sat down and took his cell phone out of his desk, hit a speed dial number, and opened the Sancus notebook. "It's Keys. We got more than one problem and it's time you did your part, fast. That account is what I'm sayin'—you find out what the devil was going on there? Oh yeah… really? Then fix it. And fix it fast before Calloway Clemens forgets he plays in my club."

I waited but I couldn't hear any more. Being dead has a lot of advantages. Like now: I can hang around and listen in on conversations without anyone knowing. I didn't need a warrant or probable cause, either. The downside was, well, I don't have any magical hearing or crystal ball. In other words, I can't hear both sides of the call. And unless I knew who Keys was talking to, I couldn't poof over to the other caller and hear their side of the conversation.

Good and bad. Yin and yang. Ice cream and liver and onions.

When Keys tapped off his call and returned to his records, I snooped around a little more. Just as I got ready to go and find Angel to make nice-nice, something sent a bolt of "holy shit" through me.

Sitting on top of a stack of computer printouts on Keys's credenza was a small hand-carved stone figurine inlaid with gemstones and trimmed in gold. A scarab beetle—identical to the one in William's office. I hadn't noticed it last night.

"Oh Keys, you have some 'splainin' to do."

Chapter Forty-Three

I caught up to Cal a few blocks from the Kit Kat on his way back to the office. "Hey, Cal, I think you better turn around and go see Keys again. Poor Nic owns his alarm company—Sancus something—and it's also the alarm company for the bank. Get it? Somebody had to know about the alarms to deactivate them and play around with the CCTV cameras and backup systems, right? So, someone who knows the Kit Kat's alarm system might know the bank's alarm system. Get it? There could be…"

Cal's cell phone rang. "Calloway—er, Clemens."

He was lost in his call for a few moments and when he tapped off his cell, his face tightened and he banged a bony finger down on the "3" speed dial key. He placed the cell phone on a holder on his dashboard and put the call on speaker.

"Braddock."

"Bear, I got something." Cal's voice was rapid, almost frantic. "Thorne called. Karen Simms never showed up for work this morning—neither did Larry Conti. Neither has missed a day all year. Thorne called Simms's cell and no answer. Same with Conti. Thorne also checked their computers, and somebody deleted all their emails and records last night—just like William."

"Right around the time he was murdered," Bear said. "Dammit, Cal, get to Simms's place pronto."

Cal flipped on his siren. "And, Bear, Angela said she was going to Simms's place this morning."

"I'll get units to meet us there and someone looking for Conti."

"Right. Do I wait on a warrant when I get there?"

"Hell, no. Kick in the damn doors if you have to."

Chapter Forty-Four

Karen Simms's apartment was located south of the bank on the second floor of a nineteenth-century brick-and-clapboard house. An attorney's shingle hung on the first floor and there was only one other apartment in the building. I beat both Bear and Cal there, and just in time, too. Angel's Explorer sat in the building's small parking lot, and she had already climbed the outside stairs to Apartment 2 on the second floor.

"Angel, wait," I called as she reached the apartment's streetside balcony. "Bear and Cal are on their way. There could be trouble inside."

She was startled when I appeared on the balcony landing beside her. "Tuck, what's wrong?"

I told her what I'd witnessed in Poor Nic's hospital room and the Kit Kat West, and about Karen's absence from work. She listened but still knocked on Karen's apartment door. "If Nicholas gave her money, maybe she left town. Let's find out."

"Angel, someone deleted her emails and work files. Just like William the night he was murdered. They deleted Larry Conti's, too. That's got *You're next* written all over it. Just wait for Bear, okay?"

She knocked again and peeked in the windows beside the door. "I don't think she's home. I want to look around."

If she wouldn't listen, I had to stall her until Bear arrived. "Did you have time to do the research on the belly dancer, Fahmy, and those other two—Gafaar and Eppler—for me?"

"No. I'll do it later. Let's see if there's an unlocked window or door."

She was a dog on the scent. I knew what would get her mind off Karen Simms. "So, you like Thorne. I get that, but..."

"Now? Here? Fine." She turned and faced me with fiery eyes and a bullet finger. "You're acting like you don't trust me. You're acting like..."

Gulp—it worked too well. "I'm acting like I'm afraid you might actually want a warm, breathing man beside you." The words stung, for both of us. "I'm being childish, I know. I'm sorry."

For a moment I thought she might rescind my invitation and send me away—no, that's only for vampires. Instead, she looked down and turned away. When she looked back at me, tears filled her eyes. Those tears stabbed me like a knife. And when they rained down her cheeks, the knife turned and thrust me again.

"No, Tuck. You're right. I do think about that. I won't lie." Her eyes lowered and couldn't settle on any one point. Her voice quivered a bit as a shadow enveloped her face. "But you're still my husband—as childish as you are, *and* as dead as you are. It's difficult for me. I don't know how to handle this. Do you?"

Hell no. "No, I don't, but... *childish? As dead as I am?* That's harsh, Angel."

She allowed herself a little giggle. "Try to understand. It's not like you're dead and I'm alone trying to move on. And it's not like you're still here—not totally. So I'm as stuck as you. I don't want to do anything to hurt you and I don't want you to leave—God, I don't want that. But..."

I knew what *but* meant. "Okay, okay. Just don't be mad at me for being jealous and worried."

"That's hard, Tuck."

I touched her arm. "And if you have to, you know, have a friend for dinner or a show or something from time to time, two rules."

"What?"

I hugged her and she cried harder. "First, I have to know about it so I can haunt you."

She giggled again.

"And, he has to be ugly and stupid. Grossly fat would help, too. And have only one eye—no, an eye patch."

190

She tried to laugh but couldn't as something else took over. "We'll talk about this later." She wiped her face dry and with that, gone was my emotional wife and standing on the porch now was Professor Angela Tucker, Special Police Consultant. "Come on, Tuck, we need to get inside."

Damn, she was stubborn. "I quit. Okay, let's go."

"I'll check the other side of the porch for another door." She walked to the corner of the balcony and peered around to the other side of the apartment balcony. "Oh my God, look."

The balcony floorboards were in poor repair. They were painted a dull gray and the paint and wood were chipped and peeled from age. Several of the boards needed to be replaced where rot had set in. That wasn't the problem—there was a trail of reddish-black ooze that ran from a side door and along the balcony to a rear stairwell that led down to a side parking lot. The trail of ooze looked like something had slithered across the porch, down the stairs, and disappeared in the gravel below.

"Angel, I think that's blood."

She maneuvered around the blood trail to the balcony railing just as two unmarked police cruisers screeched into the parking lot below us. "It looks like something was dragged out of the apartment and down the stairs."

"Or someone."

Chapter Forty-Five

"Let's go." Bear stepped in front of Karen's apartment door and pulled his handgun. Then, without warning, he drove his right foot into the door beside the doorknob. The door splintered and he went through it all in one movement. "Sheriff's Department! Show yourself!"

I was already inside. "It's clear, Bear. No one's here."

Angel waited for Cal and a uniformed Winchester officer to follow Bear in before she appeared in the doorway behind them. When they each yelled "clear" and reappeared from the different rooms they'd searched, I waved Angel inside.

As I turned to look around again, something tickled my nose. "Bear, I smell smoke again. Do you?"

"No. Look around."

I walked around the room and the scent was nowhere. Maybe it was in my head. "No sign of Karen, Bear," I said. "There's a blood trail that starts in the kitchen then goes out onto the porch and down the stairs."

Bear hooked a thumb at Cal. "Check the kitchen—get men searching the area."

"Got it." Cal disappeared.

Karen's apartment had a cozy two-bedroom layout with lots of windows and the aforementioned wraparound outside balcony. Her furnishings were few but in good taste. The living room had a big-screen television, matching sofa and loveseat, a wingback chair, and numerous clocks and art prints on the walls. One bedroom was used for storage and held a couple pieces of furniture, some boxes of dishes and glasses, an ironing board and iron set up in the back corner, a rack of videos and music CDs, and two mismatched lamps. The rooms were disarranged and had been searched. Karen's bedroom was the same—the mattress was askew from the box spring. What had been atop her dresser—assorted combs, brushes, and pieces of jewelry—was scattered about the floor. Her bathroom was the same, everything strewn about. There was a small walk-in closet with its door open. Most of the hangers were empty and there was only one pair of shoes on the floor. Spring clothes remained hung up but were pushed to the side and several items lay on the closet floor in a pile among fallen hangers.

The kitchen told the rest of the story.

Cal called out, "Bear, in the kitchen."

I knew what was there and still, it chilled me to look. In the center of the kitchen floor, right beside an inexpensive round breakfast table, was a large smear of blood. The smear looked like someone tried to clean up but hadn't finished, leaving a residue of gooey, dark-red ooze. The blood trail crossed the kitchen and went out the side door onto the balcony. From there, it led to the stairs and halfway down to the parking lot, where it disappeared.

The uniformed policeman on the balcony came into the kitchen. "Detectives, the car in the parking lot is registered to Simms."

"Oh shit," Bear said as he contemplated the blood trail. "She never left. She's dead."

I said, "Hold on, Bear. Remember, Poor Nic gave her a car. Maybe…"

"Maybe." He looked around the kitchen. "But car or not, it looks like somebody got to her here. First, they erased her emails, and second, they erased her. Just like William. They were cleaning up behind themselves. Whatever she knew, it cost her."

Angel said, "She could be still be alive. You have to have hope, Bear. Call Nicholas. He'll help, I'm sure."

Yeah, Nic… he could help. "There's no forced entry. Not even a scratch on the door frame—what's left of it after Bear's big foot." Bear shrugged and I went on. "Somebody got in with a key or she let them in. Whoever it was overpowered her before she knew what happened. There's no sign of a struggle—just the ransacking and blood trail. They dragged her out of the apartment like a sack of potatoes. And they didn't clean up all of it afterward, so they were in a hurry. Maybe they were such in a hurry they left something outside. Her car's here. So maybe they took Nic's loaner."

"Maybe again—all maybes. Like, maybe she was injured and made it out on her own—*maybe*." Bear gave orders to the Winchester policeman to begin a search of the surrounding areas. "Go three blocks in all directions. Get more officers if you need. Move."

One officer made notes. "Detective, there's some construction going on next door. And there's a construction dumpster across the parking lot. I'll have a unit see if any of the workers were around earlier and might have seen something."

"Good and search the entire site." Bear turned to Cal. "Get ahold of Nicholas Bartalotta. I want cell phone number and car information on what he gave Simms. Then get it on the air in Virginia, West Virginia, and Maryland. Put a BOLO on Simms as a possible kidnapping. Get someone checking all the hospitals, clinics, and doctor's offices. And find out if Larry Conti has surfaced—if not, find him."

"On it." Cal pulled out his cell phone and walked into the living room.

I said, "Simms stirred up trouble with Lee Hawkins this morning. You don't suppose…"

"No. Yes. Hell, I don't know." Bear's voice was hollow. "Karen Simms was tight with William and had information about his secret bank account and money moving around, right? And she had issues with Marshal and Lee and Keys Hawkins, too—maybe even Thorne. We gotta figure out what she knew. Whatever it was might give us the who and the why."

Angel said, "There are too many *who's*."

Bear grunted something and began a more detailed search of the apartment.

Out on the porch, I looked down at the two uniformed Winchester officers dumpster-diving across the parking lot. It took them several minutes of moving wood, old wiring, empty bags of sand and concrete, piles of plaster board, and old wall slats. After ten minutes, one of them called out.

"Detective. We have something."

Cal stood at the foot of the apartment stairs talking on his cell phone. He pocketed his phone, jogged over to the dumpster, and climbed up for a better look. He reached down and moved something around, then jumped back onto the ground. While he wiped his hands and dusted himself off, he gave the policemen instructions to empty the entire dumpster.

Bear emerged behind me. "What you have, Cal?"

One of the officers inside the dumpster lifted something above the edge for Bear to see. It was a dusty, trash-covered suitcase.

"It's full of women's clothes," Cal yelled. "Simms's name is on the luggage tag."

Angel closed her eyes. "Oh no. Not her, too."

"There's more." Cal's voice was edgy. "There's a bunch of towels and old clothes in here with blood on them."

"Dammit." Bear turned to go inside. "So, she ran from someone and might not have made it out of the apartment alive. If she did, she's on the run."

I looked north up the street a little more than a block. "Bear, Karen's apartment has something very interesting. Don't you think?"

"What?" He joined me at the railing.

"A nice view of the bank's employee entrance and parking lot."

Chapter Forty-Six

"Hold him there, Thorne," Bear said into his cell phone a few minutes later. "I'm sending Cal over. Put him in the conference room and lock the door. No one talks to him. No one goes near him. And Thorne, that includes you."

Cal walked into the living room. "Bartalotta gave me Simms's car details—a blue Fiat two-door. One of those classy new ones. And I have the burner cell phone number, too. We'll start trying to trace both."

"Larry Conti just showed up at the bank," Bear said. "Two hours late and he's been drinking."

I said, "Cut him some slack, Bear. He got beat up and shot at yesterday morning."

"That's not all." Bear shook his head. "He's got blood on his shoes."

"I'll take him in." Cal headed for the door. "We can question him when you get through here. I'll have him sobered up by then." He didn't wait for an answer and left.

Bear looked around and, seeing no other officers inside, turned to me. "Do your thing, Tuck. Whatever it is you do, do it now."

Really? "Yesterday I was a crystal ball. Now I'm what, a scent dog? A medium?"

"Christ, quit bitching and do it. You know what I mean."

Of course I did. So as he followed me room to room, I went in search of clues he'd never find—the kind with a link to the dead or a connection to the crime that were, ah, *not of this world.* But after thirty minutes wandering the apartment, touching every personal thing I could, all I found was Karen's

196

key ring under the edge of a kitchen cabinet beside the trash can.

"Sorry, Bear. I struck out."

He called one of the officers standing guard on the balcony. "You guys wait for crime scene to get here. I'm going back to the office. Keep hold of anyone who shows up and call me. They don't leave unless I okay it."

"Yes, sir."

Bear examined Karen's key ring. It was a collection of five average-looking keys, including her car key, with an embossed medallion that read "BC 053" hanging off the ring. One of the keys had her apartment number, 2, on it. He mumbled something I didn't catch and tossed it into an evidence bag before going to his cruiser.

On the way back to the office, his phone rang twice—both times he looked at the number and ignored it. Both times I asked him why and he cursed and ignored me. When it rang the third time, he answered.

"Braddock—oh, hey, good morning."

When whoever it was spoke, his eyes lit up and he smiled—not something you often see from him. But seconds later, his voice turned all business. "Sorry, I'm onto a few things right now. And we can't do lunch because I need to speak with you. No, *officially*. No, sorry. It'll have to be in my office. Yes, I'm afraid so."

When he dropped the phone on the seat beside him, I said, "Lee Hawkins?"

His foot hit the floorboards and we made it to the office in less than ten minutes.

"How do you explain the blood?" Cal asked as he tapped the interview room table with his finger. "How do you explain it, Larry?"

"I can't." Larry's face was pale and his eyes red and tired—a combination of alcohol and something else—what, I didn't know. He emptied his coffee cup and leaned forward into his hands. "I told you, Detective, I don't remember. I got home last night and sort of freaked, you know? I almost got killed yesterday. I drank too much."

"When's the last time you saw Karen Simms?" Bear asked.

"Karen?" Larry sat up. "Did something happen to her?"

"What makes you think that?" Bear asked. "You feeling guilty, Larry? *Did* something happen to her? When's the last time you saw her?"

"When's the last time I saw Karen?" Larry repeated the words like he was trying to translate a foreign language. "At work when I left last night. About five, I think."

I stood near the door and couldn't decide if Larry's angst was the booze unsettling his stomach or something else. I was about to say as much when another detective knocked on the interview room door and called Cal into the hallway. When Cal returned, he pulled out his cell phone and showed something to Bear.

Bear nodded. "Larry, a couple more questions. Let's start with your black pickup truck, shall we?"

"What about it?" He watched Cal's eyes narrow on him. "Hey, come on guys. I stopped a robbery yesterday, remember? And I saved Professor Tucker, too."

"Maybe," Cal said. "Unless you were in on it from the beginning. Maybe you weren't jumped like you said, Larry. Maybe you were helping them along until Angela Tucker stumbled into the robbery and things got out of control. How am I doin', man?"

"What are you trying to say? I didn't do—"

Bear snapped forward and drummed his palm onto the table. "Then why do you have Amphora Trading crates in the back of your truck? And what's all the surveillance gear in your house? You've got microphones, cameras, video... everything to bug someone's office or do surveillance on them."

"You guys can't search my house." Larry's voice was angry and his eyes flashed from Cal to Bear. "You need a warrant. You can't just..."

"Right you are, man," Cal said. "All that security training is paying off for you, huh?"

Bear waved the cell phone Cal showed him in Larry's face. On the screen was a photograph of Larry's truck bed with two large wooden shipping crates identical to the ones in William's basement. "I got a warrant, dipshit, as soon as you showed up to work with blood on your shoes."

"Blood? I got beat up yesterday, remember? It's probably blood from that guy Mr. Thorne shot—or from me, remember? Maybe I didn't clean up enough." Larry gripped his empty coffee cup with both hands. His knuckles were white and strained. "Maybe it's mine."

"No," Bear said in a low, matter-of-fact voice.

"I must have not cleaned them or something."

"No."

Larry lowered his head. "Come on, this isn't what you think."

I'd heard that before. Recently, too.

"What should we think, Larry?" Bear asked. "Look, we're gonna run that blood from your shoes against what we found at William's house and some other blood evidence. If there's something you want to say, say it."

That was a bluff, of course. With the crime techs running between crime scenes, it would take days before the evidence got processed and came back from the lab. Maybe weeks.

Cal tossed Larry's car keys on the table in front of him. "What else are we gonna find at your place, Larry? We found your surveillance gadgets. Come on, tell us. What did you do to Karen Simms?"

"Nothing! I didn't do anything to Karen. Nothing."

I looked at Larry's car keys and noticed several large keys on the ring. One key stood out—the number 2 was branded on the side.

I said, "Bear, he's got Karen's apartment key on his ring."

Bear glanced back at me across the room and dug into his pocket for the folded evidence bag with Karen's ring of keys. He laid the bag on the table and took Larry's keys and compared them. The moment he did, Larry pushed back from the table and folded his arms. The key on Larry's set was a perfect match for Karen Simms's apartment key.

"Uh oh, Larry." Bear leaned forward and forced him to meet his eyes. "What are you doing with Karen's apartment key?"

Larry's face fell. His eyes snapped shut and his mouth quivered. For a moment, I thought he was going to be sick. Then, in a near-whisper, he said, "We're very... close. Look, we're dating and I have her key. That's all. Can't I have—"

"No, you can't." Bear leaned in even closer—inches from Larry's face. "Were you at Karen's house early this morning?"

"No."

"You're lying, Larry." Bear put his index finger against Larry's forehead and held it there. "Listen to me, if you're mixed up in something—anything in these murders—then now is the time…"

"Murders?" Larry jumped up from the table. "What the hell are you talking about? I didn't kill anyone! Karen's dead? Oh my God…no…I should have called. No…no…no!"

Cal grabbed his arms from behind. "Easy, man. Easy."

"He knows, Bear," I said as Larry began his meltdown. "He knows what happened to Karen."

"Larry, what did you do?" Cal sat him back at the table. "What do you mean, you should have called? Called who? About what?"

Bloodshot eyes glistened as tears flowed down Larry's cheeks. "I want a lawyer. Now. You don't get it—you don't." His hands shook as he buried his face in them. He quaked and mumbled, "Please, just get me a lawyer. You won't understand—you just won't."

Chapter Forty-Seven

While Bear and Cal waited for Larry Conti's public defender, I went looking for Angel. I found her at my favorite coffee house, where she'd just arrived after a walk with Hercule. Hercule didn't much care for leashes, mind you, but he loved the café's blueberry muffins and the owners loved him.

A few months ago, Angel had been sitting outside at the café when a young couple got into a heated argument beside her. The boyfriend—a large, wiry guy who needed a bath far more than he needed the beer he carried into the café—happened upon his girlfriend and was enraged that she'd walked out on him. Angel didn't blame her. She was a pretty little thing about half the guy's size and clearly outclassed him. When he knocked her coffee into her lap and readied for a punch at her face, Sylvia, the owner, stepped in. Sylvia took the brunt of the guy's right cross intended for his girlfriend. That was the last punch he threw. Hercule had been lying beside Angel and launched himself atop the drunk boyfriend in a second. He grasped the guy's wrist in his mouth, put him on the ground, and growled a warning. The boyfriend was reduced to a whining, crying little…You get the idea.

Hercule was the girl's hero. Hercule was Sylvia's hero, too. And Hercule was welcome in the café any time—free muffins included. It was a welcome he revisited a couple times a month just for the fame.

A hero has responsibilities to his followers, after all.

Now Hercule sat inside the doorway as Angel picked up her mocha-Frappuccino-latte-caramel-double-espresso-something-orother, and, of course, two blueberry muffins.

"Larry's copped for a lawyer, Angel," I said, as she scooped up Hercule's leash and coaxed him away from Sylvia's affections. "Looks like he's neck-deep in all this. And Karen hasn't been found, either."

She waited until we had walked half a block from the café and turned to me. What she said surprised me. "Tuck, I'm sorry about what's going on with us. I'm having a hard time with it all."

"Me too. I get it."

"Do you?" She stopped Hercule and turned to me. In a soft, almost pleading voice, she told me what I already knew. "I'm sorry you're dead. I'm sorry things are the way they are. And, I'm sorry we can't have sex. Believe me, I'm sorry about everything in our lives right now. But I'm not dead. I'm not able to pop around and do the strange things you can. But you have to understand I'm not able to have any normalcy in my life. I'm thirty-six and I'm too young to stop living. I don't know what to do."

Wow, maybe the silence was better.

"You're right. And I'm sorry."

"All right, then." She smiled and blew me a kiss. "Just give me time, please."

Herc moaned.

We walked along for another half block and I changed the subject. "How about telling me what you found out about Hekmet Fahmy and Eppler?"

"I don't know what it all means, but Eppler was connected to a World War II German mission called Operation Salaam." She sighed, relieved to be talking about something else. "Operation Salaam was in those papers William left for me. It started in 1942."

Another connection. "William was researching Operation Salaam and he turned up dead. Except he, Keys, and their old pals Holister and Gray, weren't in Egypt until 1944 or '45. How could they be connected?"

"I don't know." Angel shrugged. "The story goes that in '42, the Germans sent two spies across the desert to infiltrate Cairo and spy on the Allies. The spies were Johann Eppler and Hans-Gerd Sandstede. They used the names Hussein Gafaar and Peter Monkaster."

"Hussein and Peter were the spies?" Those names rang a bell. "They were the two guys I saw at the Shepheard Hotel on my first visit to Cairo. It was in 1942. Now it makes sense—they were passing messages that day."

She gave Hercule more leash as he tugged on it and pulled her along. "The spies snuck into Cairo but were caught a few weeks later in '42. And the belly dancer, Hekmet Fahmy, was famous at the Kit Kat Club. She spied on the Allies, too. That's all I've had time to find out."

Yep, German spies, dead bankers, and secret vaults. William and his pals weren't there for another couple years, but it's all connected.

"Thanks, Angel. I'll have to talk to Ollie and Doc again. Maybe they know what the connection is."

Hercule strained on his leash as we turned the corner down our block. Angel was having trouble keeping up with him and was trying to pull him up when she looked down the hill at our house.

Our front door was open.

Hercule knew something was wrong and pulled the leash from Angel's hand, bounded through the open wrought-iron gate, and charged up the porch stairs. He stopped there on the front porch and stared inside the open door. He growled and lowered himself on his haunches as his tail snapped straight out.

"Call Bear, Angel." I ran to Hercule.

Angel reached the top of the porch. "I got voicemail but I left a message." She didn't wait for a reply and slipped inside.

"Angel, no."

Hercule bounded forward and positioned himself in front of her. He braced himself against her legs and stopped her in the foyer. As he did, he pointed his nose into our living room, growled, and barked a warning. Angel eased into my den and returned with a 9mm semi-automatic I kept hidden on the bookshelf beside the door.

"Who's in here?" she called.

"Angel, get back." I moved in front of her and Hercule. "Go back outside."

Hercule let go a ferocious bark and lunged into the living room. Someone was around the corner and hadn't moved in time. Hercule had them by the arm and whipped them sideways and off balance and drove them to the floor. He followed his captive down and stood on top of them. He held an arm and growled.

"Hold him, Herc!" I yelled.

It wasn't a *him* at all. It was a woman dressed in dark jeans and a dark blouse beneath a black peacoat. She cried out and struggled beneath Hercule but was pinned down and at a disadvantage. Her free arm covered her face, protecting it from any attack Hercule might launch.

Angel was behind me now and aimed her gun at the woman. "Who are you? What are you doing in my house?"

"Please. I ask you—remove your animal. I mean you no harm."

I recognized her the moment she lowered her arm. "Raina?" I reminded Angel of the woman who met Lee and Poor Nic at the café and of her foray at the Kit Kat Club last night.

"Okay, Hercule." Angel waved her pistol at Raina. "Let her up, boy."

Hercule growled a second opinion.

"Herc, back."

Hercule stepped off Raina and released her arm. He backed up two steps and kept his eyes fixed on her—*Don't try it lady, I'll kick your ass.*

"Thank you, Professor Tucker. I—"

Angel waved the air with her gun. "What are you doing in my home?"

"Professor, I assure you. I did not break in. I arrived just moments ago and your door was open. I knocked and called out. Then I heard someone in your home—it did not sound right to me. I called out again and heard them inside. So I came inside and checked. They ran out the back and are gone. I am afraid I interrupted a crime, but perhaps I stopped it in time."

I said, "Hold her here, Angel. I'll look around."

Much of the house appeared untouched. My den was the exception. Someone had been searching for something. My desk drawers were open ever so slightly. My filing cabinet had two open drawers and files lifted but not removed. A few books were pulled forward on the shelves and others looked like they had been pulled out and hastily shoved back into place. But the biggest problem was Angel's notebook computer. It was gone from my desk.

Luckily there didn't appear to be any damage—a neater break-in than

William's home or Karen Simms's apartment. Either Raina had interrupted someone before they could finish, or we had interrupted her before she could.

Back with Angel and Raina in the living room, I said, "Nobody's around. The den's been searched and it looks like your notebook computer is gone. The rest of the house is okay."

"What are you doing here?" Angel asked Raina. "I've called the police."

Raina looked down at Hercule and rubbed her arm where his teeth had torn the heavy wool. She favored the arm, too, and I wasn't sure it was from Hercule's bite or something else.

"I am a friend of William Mendelson." Raina held Angel's eyes. "He told me to seek your counsel if anything befell him."

Chapter Forty-Eight

"*If anything befell him?*" Angel lowered her gun. "You know he was murdered?"

"I do," Raina said. "He told me he was consulting with you about a matter most urgent to us both."

I said, "And what would that be?"

Hercule growled when Raina stepped forward. She stopped.

Angel said, "Back, Hercule." He sat down. "Now, explain."

"The retrieval of Egyptian antiquities and the arrest of those responsible, of course." Raina didn't blink. "Did he not explain this to you?"

Angel glanced out the window. "Why don't you sit down and we'll wait for Detective Braddock. What was your relationship to William? When did you last speak with him?"

"Good cop questions, babe. I taught you well."

Raina said, "I spoke last with him two days ago. He said he was bringing you to his office for a consult. Did he not do that?"

"He tried."

"And he told you that he was involved in many matters regarding my country—Egypt—and worked with others to make right a great wrong?"

Huh? "Maybe she means Lee and Keys Hawkins and the others—Holister and Gray?"

Angel asked her.

"You are acquainted with these people?" Raina cocked her head and narrowed her dark, penetrating eyes on Angel. "They were friends, perhaps?"

"The Hawkinses are acquaintances. We didn't know Holister and Gray."

"We?" Raina looked around.

Something poked my brain and I gave Angel a few questions for Raina.

"Raina, what do you know about Operation Salaam?"

Raina's eyes went wide but she recovered quickly and forced a thin, phony smile. "Salaam? William told you?"

Her response was just what I expected. "Angel, ask her..."

"No matter." Raina held up a hand and pointed out the window toward the street. "I have brought papers for you to see. Papers that will explain what William and I have been negotiating."

"Negotiating?" Angel looked at her phone. Bear had not called back. "All right, let's see what you've brought."

Hercule growled when Raina moved toward the front door.

"Hush, Hercule. Stay here" Angel patted his head.

I said, "I'll go with her. You two stay on the front porch."

"Please, I will show you everything." Raina walked down the porch stairs, out the gate, and down the sidewalk to a dark blue Nissan. At the driver's side of the car, she turned and looked back at Angel watching from the porch. "You will see, Professor Angela Tucker. I will show you."

And I stood there, dumbfounded, as Raina unlocked her door, slipped behind the wheel, and promptly drove off.

"Nice plan, Tuck," Angel called. "I waited here while you helped her with a getaway. Great plan."

"Did you get her license plate?"

"Who's the detective in the family?" She didn't wait for a reply, just walked back into the house and slammed the front door.

I guess she didn't get the license plate number.

And neither did I.

Chapter Forty-Nine

"Williiam's death changed everything," Lee snapped and slashed the air with a sharp finger. "Why don't you see that?"

"You mean his murder?" Keys stood behind the Kit Kat's bar and poured her more coffee. They'd been arguing all morning and neither had won. Of course, Lee wasn't sure what her grandfather knew, and he felt the same about her. Such was their complicated relationship since her father had died.

"You have to understand, Lee. That woman isn't going away until this thing is put right. I don't expect you to understand. But I expect you to do as I wish."

"Why, Granddad? Because of William?"

"No." He reached across the bar and took her hand. "Because there are things in the past that must remain there. This—all this—has stirred up the war again. I can't… I won't take any chances on it stirring things any deeper."

"Then tell me what you're so afraid of and I'll help you fix it."

"You can fix it by letting me make this right with that woman. When she has what she wants, she'll go away."

"That's Willy talking. You're stronger than he ever was." Lee watched him as he leaned back against the counter and sipped a cup of coffee made stronger with a shot of Irish whiskey. "Until now."

"Lee, please." Keys came around the bar and took a barstool next to her. He patted her hand and tried to soften her anger. "Willy was right and you have to know that. If we give it all back—if we make good on what's

208

left—what more could anyone ask of us? Even she has to know there isn't anything else for us to do, right?"

"But, Granddad, what makes you so sure? What about Cy and Claude? You told me that's what got them killed. If she already knows about you, then let's make a deal for some money at the same time. We could pay Nicholas off if the deal is big enough. How good would that be? Kill two birds with one stone."

"I'm afraid who those two birds might be." He looked down. "And I'm sure Marshal will agree with you, too."

"Yes, he would, but…"

"No matter." Keys' voice lowered and the bitterness was thick. "I don't give a damn what he thinks."

Lee smiled an almost imperceptible smile. "Well, he doesn't matter anyway. And with Nicholas, once he's paid off, there's more profit for us."

Poor Nic was the least of his worries. Lee taking matters into her own hands was his biggest. Cy and Claude had not listened to him before and they died for their mistakes. William didn't listen and now he was dead, too. Now Lee—it could happen to her.

"Lee, tell me what you found out from Braddock."

She blushed and tried to hide it behind her coffee cup. "He likes his eggs sunny side up."

"You know what I mean."

"Nothing, Granddad." She glanced away—he knew her too well. "No, really. He wouldn't talk about the case. I tried to get him to loosen up and after all the bubbly, he still wouldn't talk. He's tough, Granddad, and sweet at the same time. I like him a lot."

"I guess you do." Keys glanced at his watch. "You just got in an hour ago. Come on now, girl, did you learn anything?"

"A little, I guess. He doesn't trust Thorne at all. And I'm not sure he likes the guard or that bitch, either."

"Conti and Simms?"

She shrugged. "I said I knew them and that I didn't like any of them. Anyway, he wouldn't even comment about them, but he talked about

William—how his friend, Angela, really liked William and how William had problems. But, when I brought up Thorne, he shut up fast. Just like the bitch and Conti."

"Interesting." Keys thought for a while. "You need to lighten up on Simms, Lee. You really pissed William off with those emails. Cal's already asking questions about you. I'm afraid that he'll think…"

"Let him think." She smiled wryly. "Bear likes me—a lot. It'll be okay, Granddad. And don't worry about Simms, either. Trust me."

Keys had kept things safe for nearly eighty years. But now, with Willy gone—and Cy and Claude—would things ever really be okay again?

Keys slid off the barstool. "Come with me, girl. I want to show you something."

He led her down into the basement where the extra liquor, kitchen supplies, and dining room paraphernalia was stored. In the back of the room, against the wall, was a covered stack of containers halfway to the ceiling. He pulled on the large tan tarpaulin that covered the boxes and revealed a dozen wood crates marked "Nomad Air Freight–Cairo." Beside the crates was an old steamer trunk secured by a heavy padlock.

Lee went over to the Nomad crates. "You hid your trunk in with this order of replacements for the replica pottery upstairs?"

Keys laughed. "Sure, who would look? Only you and me handle this stuff."

He took a key out of his pocket and unlocked the steamer trunk. Inside were small cardboard boxes with papers and photographs and keepsake memorabilia. He picked up one of the boxes and carried it to a round banquet table off to the side and opened it up.

"You're finally going to show me all the family photos you've been hiding all these years, Granddad?"

He crinkled his brow. "You know about the trunk? How? I just had it delivered from my place."

"Sure I know." She dug into her pocket for her key ring and produced an old, narrow-barreled key. "I found Dad's key years ago. It took me two years to find the lock it went to. But I finally did a few summers ago when I was over at your place taking care of you when you got sick. I didn't tell you because I know how secretive you are."

"I'm not secretive, Lee."

"Yes you are, Granddad, and so was Dad." She hugged him. "And I understand—I do. And it doesn't matter to me. It's a long time ago and those days are over. Everything is different. You're different. I love you no matter what."

Keys looked at her for the longest time. What an amazing woman she'd become. Her mother and father would be proud. Very proud. Her father never understood, never forgave him. But then, those were different times— too soon after the war. He kept the secret but never allowed himself forgiveness.

Thank God for Lee.

"One day, my dear," he said, embracing her again, "I'll explain all of it. I don't want to die and have you wondering. I was a hero of sorts. But a hero nonetheless. And yes, the past should stay in the past—I've done terrible things to keep it that way. Things I'm not proud of. They were necessary, though. And because of all that, and a little help from our new benefactor, you'll inherit this place."

"Okay, Granddad. But I don't need anything. You've been everything to me since Mom and Dad passed." She dug through the faded black-and-white pictures in the box until she found her favorite—a young, handsome man with sharp chiseled features, sitting behind a piano. Standing beside him, arms wrapped around his shoulders, was a beautiful, dark-haired woman dressed in veils and silk wraps. On the bottom, handwritten in the white border, it read, "Kit Kat 1945."

"This is my favorite, Granddad." She held up the photo. "You looked so happy. Who is the dancer? She was beautiful."

"A dear friend, Lee, a very dear friend."

Chapter Fifty

"Doc? Doc? Where the heck are you?" I stood in the middle of my den. "Come on, Doc."

"Oliver, stop shouting. I'm right here." And he was, *now*. He stood in the doorway, arms folded, with that perpetual scowl on his face. "What on earth have you been doing?"

"What have *I* been doing? You're supposed to be my watch-ghost. Did you see who broke in here? Was it a pretty Arab woman?"

Doc sighed. "If it had been, I would know that. No, I was not here. I was resting."

"Resting?"

"Yes. As you do, I need to get away and recharge. You've become something of a handful lately, Oliver. And now you've got Ollie all worked up about your bank murder. I thought I was prepared for this."

How in the world do ghosts prepare themselves? "You're saying you didn't see or hear anything?"

"Nothing."

"Then what good are you?" I sat behind my desk. "You never answer a direct question. You always nitpick. And now, you can't even hang around to see who burglarized the house."

Doc stood in front of my desk. His eyes bore through me. "First of all, I answered your question. I didn't see or hear anything. Second, I don't nitpick, I guide. I motivate. I curtail your ego. And..."

"You curtail my ego?"

"And third, I also provided you the clue about my old photo album." He cocked his head and let a thin, wry smile slip out. "And I see it helped you already. So, what more assistance should I be? After all, I'm a doctor, not a detective. You play that."

"Right, sure." Doc was obviously well-rested. "All right, then. Someone broke in and stole a computer. We caught an Arab woman."

"She was beautiful."

I eyed him. "So you did see her."

"No."

Oh, brother. "Okay, Doc, what about Operation Salaam? Do you..."

"Never heard of it. But, there is one important thing." He sat on the arm of the chair and scratched Hercule's ears. "Raina was not Arab, she was Egyptian. Of course, technically, those born of the pharaohs are Africans, but I understand they feel themselves Arabs and foremost Egyptians. But..."

I held up a hand. "You're kidding me, right? Arab, Egyptian, African? And you know a lot about someone you didn't see."

"Raina is not who, or what, she pretends." He smiled. "That is my point, Oliver. If you would pay attention."

Huh? I looked at him. He had a very self-satisfied smile on his face.

"Oliver, she was not a friend of William. Do you understand?"

"Of course I understand. The questions are, why did she lie and did she kill him?"

"No, Oliver." Doc faded. "The question should be—why were you so irresponsible as to allow her to escape?"

Chapter Fifty-One

When Bear arrived, Angel had already inventoried the valuables in the house and determined that only her computer was missing. Her jewelry, china, silver, a few pieces of art, and even my 9mm were untouched. Someone came to the house for information, not profit.

"I'll have a crime scene tech here to check for prints," Bear said. "But it'll be a while—too many scenes working right now. I didn't see any signs of a break-in, so someone must have picked the locks. Did you get the license plate number on Raina's car?"

Ouch—sore subject. "No, we didn't have a chance…"

"I was on the porch," Angel said. "Tuck walked her to her getaway car."

Touché.

Bear snorted. "All right, I have to get back. Cal's got information on Marshal from the hotel in Harrisonburg. He's found something hot. Are you okay here?"

"Yes, I'm fine, Bear. I'll wait on your crime scene people," Angel said.

"I'll go with Bear," I said. "What are you going to do alone here, Angel?"

"I'll call my office and get a new laptop ready." A car pulled up outside in front and she looked out the den's bay window. "Oh, Franklin's here."

Thorne walked up the front porch stairs and rang the doorbell.

I said, "What's he want?"

"Lunch, I hope."

Bear headed for the door. "I'll be leaving. Come on, Tuck, it's better if you're with me."

"Or you could come along, Tuck," Angel said, "and watch us eat a good steak-and-cheese sub with lots of French fries."

"Now you're just being cruel."

She grinned and taunted me by blowing a kiss. "Perhaps just a little."

At the front door, Bear said to Thorne as the door opened, "What are you doing here?"

Hercule slipped into the foyer and greeted Thorne, too—with a growl.

"Hercule, lay down." Angel apologized and told Thorne what had happened at the house, ending with, "And yes, let's get lunch after the crime scene people leave."

"Sure, yes, lunch. Terrific." He looked from Bear to Angel and back. "I'll wait with her until your technicians are through—for her safety, of course. Then we'll get some lunch."

"Of course," I said. "And take Hercule to lunch, too, Angel. For his safety."

She ignored me.

Bear said, "Thorne, I may need to speak with you later. Keep your cell phone handy."

"Of course, Detective. I am at your disposal." He glanced over at Angel. "I am at everyone's disposal."

Cal clicked the video player's pause button on his computer. "Did you catch it? Did you see the vehicle that comes into view when Marshal walks out of the hotel?"

"No, play it again." Bear leaned closer to the computer screen.

The video was from Marshal Mendelson's hotel in Harrisonburg. It was shot on their security system the evening before, and early morning of, the day William was murdered. The readout said "0012"—twelve minutes after midnight. The video camera was mounted somewhere outside the hotel and focused on the lobby entrance and hotel parking lot in front of the hotel. When the video played again, Marshal Mendelson walked out the hotel lobby doors at precisely 0012. He proceeded to the sidewalk and turned right. As the video continued, Cal stopped it as a vehicle entered the camera view from the right and drove in the direction Marshal had walked.

Bear stared at the video for a long time. Then it hit him. "That's Larry

Conti's pickup truck."

"Maybe," Cal said. "It's a pickup truck for sure, man. And it's the same description as Conti's—and it also matches the one fleeing the Kit Kat last night. I can't be sure they're one and the same, Bear, and can't say they're not."

"So, Marshal left the hotel at twelve after midnight." Bear leaned back and opened the case file on Cal's desk. "And William opens the bank door at oh-one-thirty. Presumably to let someone in, right? That's plenty of time for Marshal to leave the hotel and drive back to town. And the ME says William was murdered at oh-two-hundred. That would give Marshal plenty of time to drive home from Harrisonburg, kill his father, and get back to the hotel by breakfast."

I said, "Yes, it does. Whoever was in the pickup is connected to Marshal. Which means it could be William's killer and whoever tried to kill Poor Nic."

Cal turned the video off. "Marshal's back in the suspect pool, right?"

"He never left," Bear said. "What else you got?"

Cal pointed to a second file on his desk. "I ran backgrounds on Conti, Simms, Thorne, and Marshal Mendelson. Jeez, man, these people are something."

"What's that mean?" I asked and Bear repeated me.

"Conti was fired from his last two jobs as a security guard. Guess why?" Cal waited but Bear didn't want to play "I've got a secret." Cal went on. "He harassed some young sweetie-secretary every night. When her boyfriend stepped in, Conti beat the shit out of him and had him arrested for trespassing. The boyfriend *was* trespassing, but he sneaked into the building where the girl worked to catch Conti harassing her."

Bear nodded. "And Simms?"

"She's been at the bank for years, ever since high school. She's in college part time—a nursing student at the hospital—and ran up some big tuition bills. Never married. No criminal record. Had a disabled stepfather who became an alcoholic, and her mom died a year before she got out of high school. No father on record. But Thorne is the odd one."

Bear opened the file and found the yellow legal pad page with Thorne's name at the top. Below it was his date of birth—he was thirty-six. Then there was a second date of birth making him thirty-five. His address was listed as a condo on the northwest side of town and he had two driver's license numbers. One in Washington DC and one in Virginia—hence the two dates of birth. There was no car registered to him, no previous addresses, and no credit history.

"What the hell is this?" Bear asked. "This guy's…"

"A ghost," Cal said.

"He is not," I said.

Cal went on. "I cannot find any reference to him before he joined the bank seven months ago. Poof, nothing."

"*Poof?*" Bear said. "I don't like *poof*."

"Then you're gonna love this." Cal leaned forward and flipped the yellow legal pad page to the one with Marshal Mendelson at the top. "Read on."

The notes provided Marshal's normal information—age, address, three registered automobiles, education, etc., etc. But it was the financial notes that had Bear's eyes popping. Marshal had over $100,000 in credit card debt and there was a note circled at the bottom of the page. It read *Private debt—$250,000.*

"His gambling debts," Bear said. "Like Keys said?"

Cal nodded. "I contacted the track in West Virginia. Marshal was a big player there until about eight months ago. His credit crashed and then he came in with a private marker and ran up another quarter mil. They tossed him two weeks later and he's not allowed back until he squares his debts. Somebody paid down about fifty thousand a month ago—in cash, man. *Cash.* I'm guessing that was William."

"I have a pretty good guess who owns his marker, too." Well, maybe it wasn't a good guess; it was the only guess I had.

"Poor Nic is loan-sharking these days." Cal smiled, nodded, and leaned back on the corner of the desk. "Marshal's into him for some big money. Now you know why William couldn't invest in the Kit Kat."

Bear read the file. "So, we have one goodie-two-shoes who claims to have some dirt on everyone, one nut-job security guard, one mystery-man security executive, and one asshole in debt over his eyeballs. And of them, one is probably dead, one is in custody, one is now running the bank, and the other is courting Angela Tucker."

I cringed. "Thanks, Bear."

Cal nodded. "That's about right."

"Oh, and the suspect pool just got bigger." He told Cal about the break-in at my house and the mysterious Egyptian beauty, Raina. "Might as well add her to the list."

Cal picked up the two files from the desk and stuffed his notes back inside. "Well things could be worse, Bear."

"How?"

"We could have *no* suspects, man."

Chapter Fifty-Two

Angel waited for the waitress to refill her tea and walk off. "Franklin, where did you work before you came to the bank?"

"Oh, around." Thorne bit into his BLT and took his time as he chewed. "Nothing spectacular. If it had been, I'd be in a better place than this small-town, family-owned bank."

"Like where?"

He smiled. "I thought you were a college professor, not a detective."

"Oh, I'm just curious. You can't expect a lady to consider a date and not know anything about him, right?" Was she being too much the detective? Since sitting down, he'd asked every conceivable question about her past. Wasn't turnaround fair play? "So, tell me more about yourself. I know you were an Army Ranger and you've been with the Mendelsons for a few months. That's not much."

"No, I suppose not." He took another bite of his sandwich and followed it with a long, slow mouthful of coffee. "I'm from a military family and I've lived around the world. When I was old enough, I enlisted. I got out a few years ago and went into private security and landed a couple good jobs in corporate work. That's how William found me. We met at a banking conference in New York."

She watched him over her teacup. "Wow, did that hurt to tell me?"

He laughed. "I don't talk about myself. Sorry."

"Have you ever been married?"

"No."

"Close?"

"Never."

She thought a moment. "How about now? Seeing anyone?"

"I was, but it got too complicated and I had to break it off." He leaned back and folded his arms. "How about you? Is that big-lug Braddock on your radar? A past fling, maybe? Future one?"

Now she laughed. "Bear? None of the above. He's been, well, my rock since Tuck died. More, but never that. No, I've not seen anyone and have no plans to. Tuck is gone, yes, but he's still here with me. If you know what I mean."

"I do."

No, you don't. And good Lord I can't explain it. She glanced around the café hoping Tuck had not popped in. "Good. So, you'll understand if I say dinner and dancing is fine, but it ends on the sidewalk, right?"

"Well, okay for now." He sipped his coffee and looked at her over the rim. "Can I see you tonight?"

"You're seeing me now. Sorry. I have to drive into DC. I may not be back until late. Maybe another time."

Thorne finished his sandwich and played with the last of his French fries. "What's in DC? Your uncle, what was his name, Cartier?"

"Yes, as a matter of fact." She glanced around again looking for Tuck. Franklin was a charming, handsome man. He was the only man she'd had more than a few minutes of real conversation within months, Bear and work notwithstanding. The university was full of educated, eligible men but she dared not even consider any of their offers for an evening out—and there were many offers. None of which Tuck was aware of. But was that really the reason—Tuck's jealousy? Or was it her? Was *she* not ready to move on with her life? Her living-life?

The answer eluded her.

"And?" Thorne asked.

She looked around the café.

"Angela? Hello?" Thorne waved a hand in front of her. "Are you embarrassed to be seen with me?"

"What? No, no." She blinked and looked at him. "Sorry. DC...yes. My uncle, André Cartier—he's with the Washington museum circuit—used his contacts at the Smithsonian and found this woman, Raina. Her real name is Raina Iskandr."

"The woman at your house?" He stopped eating his last fry. "Tell me you're not going to look for her."

She nodded. "According to André, Raina was an adjunct professor with American University on loan from Cairo for the past two years. But, get this, there is no Egyptology and Archeological Research Group at American U, and she hasn't been active on campus for the past year. She left for some special research project. André found an old address for an office she used. I want to check it out for our investigation."

Thorne leaned back, folding his hands in front of him on the table. A smile turned into a brief laugh.

"What did I say?" Her face flushed.

"You said, 'our investigation.' " He laughed again. "You mean the police's investigation."

"Well, yes, of course." Heat rose in her cheeks. "You know what I mean."

"No, actually, I don't. Isn't that Detective Braddock's job?"

"Well, perhaps. But he's busy with other things and I can handle myself."

"I'm sure you can. Are you going alone?"

"André may tag along."

Thorne waved for the check from the waitress at the counter flirting with a regular. "Why don't I go with you? The bank is still closed to the public so I can play hooky for a few hours."

"No, no." She sipped her tea. "You should stay close here—Bear may need to talk with you, remember? And I don't know how long I'll be. Depending on André, I might stay over at his place tonight."

"Even better." Thorne handed the waitress some cash. "We can have a nice meal in DC. I'd love to meet your uncle."

She shook her head and forced a faint smile.

Thorne reached across the table to her hand, not quite closing his fingers around hers. "Angela, what's wrong? Am I such a beast? I know I'm not your husband, but he's gone and I'm here. Just dinner. I promise. And I'll leave you on the sidewalk if that's what you want."

Why didn't she pull her hand away? Why was she trembling? Was his warmth so bad?

"No, no. I need to find Raina and find out about her connection to William." She waited for him to let go of her hand; he took forever, but she couldn't bring herself to move first. "I promise, another time."

He stood and gazed at her for a long time. "All right, Angela. But be careful you don't wait too long. Who knows, I might just disappear one day."

Chapter Fifty-Three

Cal and Bear decided to split up to cover more ground. Bear went looking for Marshal while Cal stayed behind to research William's business journal and follow up on the hunt for the bank robber and Karen Simms. The search for Karen was looking more like a search for a body—the crime scene boys were able to verify with the hospital that the blood at her apartment was the same type as hers. And so far, a tristate search for the Fiat she was driving turned up nothing.

I stayed with Cal hoping for a break. Besides, Bear was in a foul mood and wouldn't be much fun.

Cal opened the investigation file on his desk and looked over his notes. I read over his shoulder. It wasn't polite, mind you, but it was necessary. Cal couldn't see or hear me, and thus he wouldn't tell me what he was doing, thinking, or reading. I'd have to do all that on my own.

Sometimes being dead is a pain in the ass.

The first thing we came across was the annotation on the secret bank account William had Karen Simms open at the bank. Cal only had the account number Karen provided and Bear had to find Marshal and get access to the full account. If Marshal balked, a warrant would follow.

"Hey Cal," I said, even though he couldn't hear me. "You've got the business journal and the account number. Maybe William's journal has the passwords to get into them online. You know, like he had the safe combination in there." I put my hand on his arm and repeated what I'd said very slowly, trying to will my words into his head.

Cal just read his notes.

"Okay, let's try something else."

Then Cal did a funny thing. He reached across his desk and turned on a small MP3 player, disconnected the headphones, and plugged the player into his computer. He turned on the player to some Duke Ellington hits from the 1940s. Then he went into Bear's desk and rummaged around the papers stacked there. When he returned, he had the photocopies of William's business journal in his hand. Next, he went on the Internet and typed in the URL to the First Bank and Trust of Frederick County.

"Hey, Cal," I said. "Do you hear me? Are you listening to me or what?"

Nothing. Not even a smile.

"Sure you are. You're just shy. Don't worry, pal. Just like Bear, you'll come around."

Cal navigated the bank's website to the accounts section and stopped at the entry for account number and password. Then he fanned out the copied journal pages on his desk and went to work. He found one page with columns of letters and numbers side by side. The column on the right had two numbers and one special keyboard character on the other—accounts and passwords was my guess. It was Cal's guess, too, and he scanned down the columns looking for a pattern or sign of the secret bank account number.

"William was an old dude, Cal. He'd use a real simple code of some kind, right? How about an alpha-substitution code?"

An alpha-substitution code, or whatever the real pros call it, is simply substituting the letter A for the number 1, B for 2, C for 3, and so forth. Sometimes, it's in a different order, but the concept remains the same. Some substitution codes could be tricky and more sophisticated, but others were not.

Oddly enough, Cal did what I suggested. He started by substituting numbers for the letters beginning with A and the number 1. Still, none of the column's numbers matched up to the account number we had. Then, he reversed it—Z was 1, and Y was 2, and so forth. When he applied the substitution, the fifth entry from the top of the first column was a hit; the substituted number matched the bank account number.

Next Cal turned to the second column of numbers and special characters.

He started with 55 and the percent symbol with it. He tried the reverse, substituting letters, but nothing seemed to make sense. No password would be only two or three characters, whether it was numbers or letters. After a long time, he sat with the pages spread out in front of him again. For another hour, he tried every conceivable combination of letters, numbers, and symbols he could find in the journal using the columns. Nothing worked.

He was at a dead end.

I wasn't. "Cal, what about simple stuff he wouldn't forget? Try *Cairo, Egypt, 1945,* and *Kit Kat Club.* Heck, even try the names of his pals."

Cal rubbed his eyes and gathered the papers up and laid them aside. Before I could say another word, he went to work.

Kit Kat. Cairo 1944. Kit Kat 1945. He even tried *Seth 1945.* But it was after running Holister and Gray's names that I thought he reached the end. Until he entered the last one.

He typed in *Hekmet Fahmy 1945.*

The administration page of an account belonging to Nostalgia, Inc. appeared. The account listed a local Winchester post office box for an address. According to the information on the screen, the account was opened the first week of February this year. When Cal clicked on Account Details he nearly fell out of his chair.

The account balance began with a deposit of $155,000 and was followed by smaller deposits of $25,000 to a little over $60,000—significantly over the $10,000 threshold Karen told us about. They were all wire transfers. And all the deposits were transfers from the Amphora Trading Company. Then the account changed. In May, withdrawals of cash and cashier's checks began to be made the same day or the day after each deposit. The withdrawals were all under $9,000, just as Karen had said. Even with money moving out of the account, the balance steadily grew until one week ago, when it reached $521,511.22. A nice, not-so-round number. Then, just two days ago, the account was closed and the money transferred to an offshore account.

Cal jumped up from the computer. "Holy shit, man, Bear's gonna love this one." He performed screen saves of each of the account's pages and copied

225

them onto his computer. Then he printed the account transaction reports.

It struck me that other than the withdrawals that accompanied each deposit, there were no other transactions. No checks drawn. No online bill payments. Nothing you would expect from a normal business account. Someone had been moving money around—transfers of large amounts in, small cash amounts out. That sounded like trouble to me—money laundering, drugs, and a list of other crimes ran through my head. And if I was right, whoever took their cut from each deposit might have made someone very, very mad.

Had William been skimming money from a money-laundering scheme involving Nostalgia Inc.? Is that why he was murdered? Or was the scheme his and someone cut themselves in and decided to kill him to take the whole thing?

I said as much to Cal, but he wasn't listening. He had accessed the online Frederick County business records and had looked up the Nostalgia company records. He examined Nostalgia Incorporated's records and made notes on the company officers, incorporation date, and business filings.

"Holy shit, I thought so," he said. "I wonder..." His fingers flew across the keyboard until he found the Washington DC business records for Amphora Trading. The records listed several corporate officers—all Egyptian names— none of which were familiar to either of us.

Then he called Bear.

"Just tell me what you found, Cal." Bear had lost his patience halfway through Cal's explanation of *how* he found the information. Then, when Cal got to the punchline—$521,511.22—Bear's patience got a second wind. "I'm at the bank now and Marshal's not here. I'm heading over to his place. Meet me there with those printouts. I want to see Marshal's reaction to all this—firsthand."

Cal hung up and scribbled some notes on his pad. Then he gathered up his papers, stuffed them into his investigative file, and slipped the file into his ballistic nylon briefcase.

"Nice work, Cal," I said. "I never knew you were a numbers guy."

"We did okay, didn't we?"

Chapter Fifty-Four

Marshal Mendelson was at home, sitting in his den at an antique cherry desk in northwest Winchester. One hand lay on the handwritten note in the center of his desk blotter and the other hung at his side. He was slumped in his leather desk chair with his head to one side. In his right temple was a jagged bloody hole and a piece of his skull was gone from his left. The gun lay on the floor beside him where it fell after dispensing the single round that ended his life.

Marshal couldn't take the guilt and shame over what he'd done—or so his note said.

Bear stood in front of the desk. His eyes worked the scene right to left, back, forward, right to left, like a typewriter clicking away on a report. I'd seen him work this way before and my own method wasn't so different. Stand still and just *see*.

No speaking. No guessing. Just observe and record.

After several minutes and his fifth time performing the technique—I'd already done the same thing when I arrived ten minutes ago—he took out a fresh pair of latex gloves, pocketed the ones on his hands, and slipped the fresh ones on.

I said, "Looks like suicide, Bear."

"Looks like. But I don't like it." He walked around the side of the body—the side without the blood and bone fragments—and read the suicide note for the third time. "He doesn't admit to killing William or Simms. All he says was he couldn't live with the guilt and shame. That could be anything."

"Or it could be two murders and embezzlement. Did you really expect

227

him to wrap this all up in a nice little letter for us?"

"It would have been nice."

"Marshal was a pain in the ass even at the end." I looked around his home office but didn't see so much as a paperclip out of place. "No signs of a break-in. No signs of a struggle. Just his body, a note, and a lot of goo to clean up."

"I've got uniforms canvassing the neighbors. Marshal told everyone he was working on William's arrangements..." Bear lifted his nose a little. "Do you smell?"

"Excuse me?" I stopped poking around Marshal's desk. "What kind of a question..."

"Do you smell? You know, can you smell things?"

Oh, sure. Okay. "I've been smelling smoke all day. You thought I was nuts."

"This time I smell it."

He was right. So did I.

"Burnt paper." Bear walked over to the fireplace and knelt down. "I wasn't sure when I came in—the body was already putrefying—but I smell it now. Look." He picked up the fireplace poker in his gloved hand and pulled back the chain-link fireplace screen. "He burned something."

Inside the fireplace was a small pile of fresh ash that had fallen below the center of the grate. The rest of the fireplace was clean and ash-free.

Bear stirred the ashes and pulled out a half dozen pieces of unburnt paper from the bottom of the ash pile. He carefully laid them on the hearth and examined them with a penlight from his pocket.

"They're some kind of serialized papers."

As Bear examined them, Cal walked in carrying a leather notebook. He stopped in the doorway, staring at Marshal's body across the room. He closed his eyes and shook his head. "Ah, shit. What the hell is going on in this town, man? Now Marshal?"

"You got me, Cal." Bear pointed to the charred pieces of paper on the hearth. "But I found something. Take a look."

Cal knelt down beside him, set the leather notebook down, and examined the papers. "Let me see a couple of these." He gloved up his hands and took out a piece of blank notepaper from his notebook. Using a pen from his pocket, he maneuvered the charred papers from the hearth onto his blank piece of notepaper, where he could examine them easier.

"I know what these are," Cal said. "They're cashier's check receipts. Marshal destroyed evidence, Bear."

I looked over his shoulder. "He's right."

The remains of the paper were a fine, translucent onionskin paper. The few numbers still left along the bottom of the papers appeared to be MICR numbers—Magnetic Ink Character Recognition numbers—that identify the bank.

I said, "Check the printouts from the secret account and see if anything matches."

Bear repeated me and Cal took out the papers we'd printed from William's account back at the office. He handed Bear the collection of charred papers still on the paper from his notebook.

"Bear, read off the last few numbers of each one you can." Cal held up the printed papers. "I'll check them against William's account."

Bear flashed his penlight on the papers and began reading the numbers out loud. As he did, Cal scanned through the printouts. "Oh yeah, man. We got him. Read a couple more."

A few minutes later, the remaining numbers printed on six of the charred papers matched up against the withdrawal entries on William's secret account.

Cal said, "Marshal didn't want us tracing these, did he?"

No, he didn't. That was bad news for someone. Back at the office, Cal had run Nostalgia Inc. through the Frederick County business records database. The result was the list of corporate officers—and now those names were on top of the suspect list.

Bear looked at the printouts in Cal's hand. "I'm running short on crime scene people. We'll have to wait a while to get this place processed. Seems like Marshal siphoned money from William's account. Maybe Karen knew, too. He killed her and it all got too much for him. What do you think?"

"You think Marshal embezzled from William's Nostalgia account?" Cal asked. "You think he'd screw over his own father?"

Bear shrugged. "Got any better ideas? If you're right and these are cashier check receipts, then it fits. Why else would he be burning them?"

"He had a lot of gambling debts, Bear," I said. "To the tune of a quarter million dollars. And his credit cards were over a hundred K.

That's a lot of motivation for taking chances with Nostalgia. And a hundred K is enough of a reason for somebody to send a message by killing William—pay or you're next."

"You're saying somebody kills William and that sets Marshal up to be in control of the bank. And in control means access to more money to pay his gambling debts or for other uses?"

Maybe. "Or…maybe Marshal helped himself to get in control of the bank. He whacks daddy and takes over the bank. A few months later after the dust settles, he's in control and can play with all the money he wants. Solves all his problems, right?" I said.

"Son kills dad over gambling debts. Head teller knows too much and son kills her. Remorse sets in and he kills himself, too. Pretty evil—I like the theory." Bear turned and looked back at Marshal's body. "Okay, we can check to see if he paid bills with these cashier checks and try to trace money wherever we can. But my guess would be he cashed them out and paid his bookies in cash. That's gonna be tough to trace."

"Why not just take the cash out of the account directly?" Cal asked. "Wouldn't that be easier? After all, it's his bank."

"Marshal or William taking cashier checks already got Karen Simms's attention. But one of them taking big sums of cash all the time would draw everyone's attention. Someone would have reported him."

Cal reminded him of the details from William's secret bank account, ending with, "Looks like someone was skimming money and was into something very illegal. Then they moved all the money to an offshore account I can't get to."

Bear started pacing. "William got deposits from Amphora Trading. But for what? Then the money disappears offshore. And someone skimmed off the top after each deposit. Maybe that was Marshal."

I thought about that. "Why didn't Karen just tell us?"

"Maybe Karen found out Marshal was skimming," Bear said. Then his eyes darkened. "Or maybe she was the one skimming and that's what got her killed. Either way, all three of them were involved."

I walked over to Marshal's body. "Nostalgia's involved, Bear. There's no way around that—and Poor Nic's on the corporate filings as a company officer. But I cannot believe he'd kill William and Simms. It would lead right to him. What about Hawkins from Nostalgia?"

"Damn." Bear's face dropped and he stood staring at nothing. "Okay, Cal, we gotta go talk to Nic Bartalotta—then Keys Hawkins."

"Ah, shit, man," Cal asked, "every damn time there's a body, Nic is on the list. It never fails."

No, it didn't. But, that's what happens when you're a retired mob boss and you *are* involved in every murder in town.

Bear pulled out his cell phone and called for more uniformed officers to secure the area and wait on the crime scene team. When he hung up, he pointed at Cal.

"You stay here until the uniforms arrive." Bear headed for the door. "Then meet me at Poor Nic's."

Chapter Fifty-Five

"I repeat, Detective, I did not kill William Mendelson." Poor Nic sat in his living room in a tall wingback chair.

Bear smiled at Nic across the room. "I didn't say you killed anyone, now, did I?"

"Ah, not yet, Detective, but you will. Every time there's mischief about, you come calling. I'm an old man. And I make an honest living—these days at least. And killing bankers isn't on my resume." He turned to Bobby, who stood off his right shoulder. "Please bring Detective Braddock and me some tea, won't you? And my medications. My arm is quite sore."

"Sure, boss." When Bobby ambled from the room, the crystal glasses on Poor Nic's corner bar rattled.

"You are the president of Nostalgia Incorporated, aren't you?"

"I am." Poor Nic smiled a warm, friendly smile that could sell bridges. He was a master of charm—right up to the point where he inserted the knife into your heart. Or at least, that's how his reputation had it. Since he'd retired to Frederick County, Poor Nic seemed to have, well, mellowed. "What of it? I own a security guard company, a construction company, a storage firm—all of which you've already investigated at one time or another, no?"

"What's Nostalgia about, Nic?" Bear asked. "Let me guess… nightclubs."

Poor Nic let a thin grin escape. "Nothing gets by you. But then, that was an easy one."

"Tell me about Nostalgia Inc., Nic, and about your investment in the Kit Kat."

"Delighted to." Poor Nic settled himself back in his chair and rested his

232

injured arm on the armrest. "I incorporated Nostalgia less than a year ago to facilitate my investment into the Kit Kat West. There is no physical company—no brick and mortar, if you will. It's a paper company to allow me to have legal protection as a corporation, properly pay my taxes, and have anonymity in my business dealings."

"What else?" Bear hadn't bothered to take out his notepad and that meant he already knew the answers to his questions. Or he figured Poor Nic's answers weren't worth writing down.

"Nothing else, Detective. I assure you. Did I not cooperate with you and provide you information on the car and cell phone I loaned to Miss Simms? Has that information been helpful?"

Bear shook his head. "No, we're still looking for her. What about noncash assets?"

"A few."

"Like what, exactly?"

Poor Nic cocked his head and thought a while. "I believe I've declared a computer or two. Maybe some office furniture. Oh, and I'm sure I've written off one of my Cadillacs as a company asset—you know, just for business trips, should there be any—and two Fiats. One of those you're looking for."

"You have many business trips with Nostalgia?" Bear asked.

Poor Nic just smiled. "As you know, I use the cars as loaners for special friends."

"And if you have no office, why do you need computers and furniture?" Bear watched as Bobby returned with the tea.

"Because I can legally offset some expenses. Although at present, I have very few." Poor Nic seemed bored with the questions. "But then, Detective Braddock, the Kit Kat just caught on, hasn't it? My investment will pay off in short order."

Bear nodded. "Any other assets?"

"Some investments. A loan, to be precise."

Bear recited the post office box address for Nostalgia that Cal gave him. "How much do you have in that account, Nic?"

Poor Nic squinted a little and sat in deep thought. "I do not have an account with that address. I think you're mistaken."

"No mistake, Nic. That's the address."

"Detective, I assure you. That address is not mine." Poor Nic leaned forward. "No matter, let's dispense with the innocuous questions, shall we? You wish to know about my business with the Mendelsons."

Bear didn't blink.

"It's very simple. William was in financial trouble. His bank was in jeopardy. He came to me for help."

I was confused. "Nic propped up Keys and William both? And he owns Marshal's gambling markers, too?"

Bear asked him those very questions. "They're all into you?"

"No, no, not *into* me, Detective." Poor Nic waved in the air. "You already surmised, I see, that Marshal got into some very heavy gambling debts and as a result, William could not invest in the Kit Kat. William asked me to assist with some financing for Keys because he could not. I was delighted to invest in such an enterprise. There's nothing like it in the area."

"We know all that. And I still don't get how you got past the state licensing board," Bear said. "Your history, is, well, rather well known. I'm surprised they didn't balk at your being on the Kit Kat books."

"Why, Detective, I'm simply a passive investor. I own nothing. My name is on nothing. And if it were, do not blame the victims, Detective. After all, when your police retirement account was devastated in '08, did the FBI and SEC arrive at your house to blame you? No, of course not. My record is clean. Except, of course, for those pesky false allegations of yesteryear. Allegations that were never proved in court, I might add."

Bear cracked a smile. "Yes, pesky allegations. How silly they were."

"Ah, you do understand." Poor Nic waited for Bobby to serve the tea and leave the room. "It is all legitimate, Detective. I can promise you."

"And Marshal?" Bear asked.

"Ah, yes, Marshal. After William confided in me about Marshal's gambling debts, I also interceded. I paid off the debts and acquired his marker."

"Out of the goodness of your heart," Bear said in a matter-of-fact tone.

CHAPTER FIFTY-FIVE

"That's loansharking, Nic."

"No, it is not." Poor Nic stood and went to the hall, calling for Bobby to retrieve a file from his den. A moment later, file in hand, Poor Nic returned and handed it to Bear and sat back down. "This is our loan contract—Marshal's and Nostalgia's. Nostalgia, on paper, held Marshal's gambling loans and had specific repayment terms for the amount of just over $255,000. It's all right there in the file. And you may keep that, Detective. I prepared it for you earlier."

Bear read through the first few pages. Then he skimmed over the remainder and closed the file on his lap. "You had this ready for me?"

"Of course."

"Why?"

Poor Nic laughed. "Come now, Detective. I invited you here, did I not?"

I said, "Summoned, more like."

"Speak with Marshal, Detective, he'll…"

"Marshal Mendelson committed suicide this morning." Bear watched the old gangster with deadpan eyes. "Or maybe you know."

"Suicide?" Poor Nic's jaw tightened and for a long time he sat staring at nothing across the room. Then he touched his forehead, his chest, and each shoulder, and said a silent prayer. "No, Detective, I was not aware. But, now that I am, I am not so sure it was suicide. And before you blame me, remember the old adage."

"What adage is that, Nic?" Bear asked.

"Dead men pay no debts." Nic lifted his narrow chin. "Tell me about Marshal, Detective. Tell me what you found."

Bear did, finishing with, "Looks like suicide. First William was killed, now Marshal commits suicide. Things sort of all wind up on Marshal's lap, don't you think?"

"Ah, very convenient, Detective." Poor Nic stood up and went to the doorway to summon Bobby again. When he returned, his jaw was set and determined—the grandfatherly eyes were gone and in their place was steel and fire. "Detective Braddock, I insist you place policemen at the Kit Kat Club immediately."

"Why?" I asked and Bear repeated me, adding, "What are you worried about?"

"Marshal Mendelson did not commit suicide." Poor Nic pointed a bony finger at Bear. "Murders—William and now Marshal. And there were two before them. That means, Detective, that there is only one left. Keys Hawkins is in danger."

Chapter Fifty-Six

At Poor Nic's insistence, Bear followed him and Bobby to the Kit Kat West. I tagged along with Bear, and we had a good chat about what Poor Nic had just told us. Neither of us was sure that the former gangster wasn't holding out on us.

"The old guy knows," a voice said behind me as we walked past the Kit Kat's bar toward the management offices in the rear. "He knows, kid."

Ollie sat on a barstool and looked at me.

"Poor Nic knows about what?"

"He's known a lot since this thing started, kid." He slipped off the barstool and walked over to me. "I just don't know how much he knows. You gotta find out—and fast—before this gets away from you. Now, just listen to old Keys."

"But…"

"Zip it and listen. Let's hear what Keys and the old guy have to say. And when they're through, you and me are going for a walk."

Poor Nic stopped at the entrance to the hallway leading to the back offices. He whispered something to Bobby that sent him back outside. To Bear, he said, "Please, follow me. Keys will be in his office this time of day."

"Nic," Bear said, holding him up. "Before we see Keys, I have to ask you something."

"Yes, Detective?"

"You said Marshal didn't commit suicide."

"I do not believe he did."

"Why did you say that?"

237

Poor Nic walked to the rear door marked "Management Only" and stopped. "Detective, it's very simple. Marshal was in financial difficulties and everything seemed lost—at least, that is why he came to me. William attempted to help him and could no longer manage. I inserted myself. Marshal and I came to terms and that is that."

"What the hell does that mean?"

"Don't you see?" Poor Nic's grandfatherly smile blossomed. "Marshal had my protection. His debts were gone, except those to me. No one would dare approach him. Nor would anyone allow him to gamble again. Except for dealing with his father's demise and sorting out issues at the bank, Marshal's problems were over."

He had a point. If Marshal's money issues were solved and all he had to do was pay off Poor Nic—and the terms of the loan documents he gave Bear seemed pretty easy to me—then life was looking up.

"Bear," I said, "when did these two make their deal?"

Bear asked him.

"Last week," Poor Nic said. "As of then, his burdens were lessened. Our terms were rather generous, since Keys asked me to help the son of his long-time best friend."

Poor Nic opened the office door and walked in. Ollie and I followed behind Bear. Inside, we found Keys behind a desk facing the doorway. On his desk were stacks of papers and files and an uneaten sandwich and a carafe of coffee.

Keys looked up. "Nicholas, what are you doing here? It's Wednesday, we're closed. I thought you…"

"I have brought Detective Braddock. He is here both as a policeman and as a friend." Poor Nic shut the door. "Marshal has been murdered and I fear you are in danger. I can protect you, but Detective Braddock must find the killer and put this to an end."

Keys's mouth dropped open. "I…I…are you sure? Marshal called me last night. He wanted to come by the club tonight and mend fences—other stupid shit, too, of course. You know Marshal, always wanting to be a player and worm his way in here somehow. Anyway…"

"He's dead, Keys," Bear said flatly. "Nic says you can shed some light on it. So start shedding."

Chapter Fifty-Seven

"This is about stealing ancient junk from Cairo?" Bear said after Keys waxed and waned through memories about the war for over an hour. "You guys smuggled out a bunch of old Egyptian junk during World War II and you think somebody's killing all of you over it?"

Keys sat in his chair. His eyes were distant—memories of life stories still difficult to put into words. He looked at Poor Nic, then at Bear, and his face strained trying to conceal his emotions. "Not junk, Braddock, antiquities— ancient Egyptian antiquities. Gold, jeweled relics, artifacts worth a fortune in the right hands. In today's market, that 'junk,' as you call it, would be priceless—tens of millions at least."

"Priceless?" Bear glanced at Poor Nic. "You buy that?"

"I do." Nic folded his arms. "And Detective, stolen art and antiquities are like blood to sharks—there are those who deal exclusively in such transactions. After all, who would report the theft of already stolen goods? If word of these treasures got to the wrong places, the art and antiquities thieves would be in a feeding frenzy to get to them."

Keys stood and went to a small safe in the corner of his office, buried under a pile of papers and an overcoat. He spun the dial a few times and opened the door, pulled out a round, heavy object, and handed it to Bear.

"See kid, I told you," Ollie said from the doorway. "Look familiar?"

It was the stone-carved scarab outlined in gold with tiny gemstones identical to the one in William's office. I reminded Bear of that fact.

"And you guys stole it?" Bear examined the scarab. "You're kind of vague about that part, Keys. How about filling in the details."

Keys sat back down and took a long breath. "I'm not proud of my involvement, Braddock, but what's done is done. I told you, I was playin' at the Kit Kat in Cairo—in '45. My father work in the oil fields before the war and died there. I was in Egypt—a teenage, smartass kid. I got a gig banging the keys for the Brits in some of the clubs. Pay wasn't good but it was a good life, you know?"

Bear nodded.

"Anyway, I got in with Willy and a couple of his pals..."

"Cy Gray and Claude Holister," Bear said.

"Yeah, yeah, that's right." Keys nodded. "How'd you know?"

"Investigating. Go on."

Keys took down an old black-and-white photograph hanging on his wall behind his desk. It was of Gray, Holister, and William Mendelson when they were young men during the war. They were sitting outside at a café—the Shepheard Hotel—drinking from tall glasses and smiling for the camera.

"I took this." He handed the photo to Poor Nic. "I started pallin' around with those three. Then one day Willy tells me he's in good with some Egyptian professor. This professor planned to come to the States for that university that was over there—American U—running from the war and all that. The professor wanted to arrange to *privately* move a few crates of his personal stash of artifacts and antiquities here ahead of time. The professor didn't want the university or the Egyptian government knowing he was, well, helping himself to a few crates of the loot he'd found over the years."

"Wait." Bear held up a hand. "You're telling me this professor asked you to smuggle his own archeology treasures out of the country?"

"Well, yes and no." Keys leaned forward and smiled. "The stuff wasn't really his, see. He found it all right—he was a big-shot archeologist. But the stuff belonged to American University and the Egyptians—mostly the Egyptians. But when the professor found out he was headin' to the States, he wanted to keep a bunch of the loot for himself."

Bear and Poor Nic sat in silence.

Keys continued. "Look, Braddock, the old guy stole from the university and museums—all them professors did. You know, early retirement and mementos and all that. He wanted us to help get it here without the university finding out. So we did."

"How?" Bear asked.

"Willy and them were cargo guys flyin' with them C-54 Skymasters, Braddock," Keys said. "You know how much cargo you can get on them things? And they had pals everywhere who would help. They were headed back Stateside, so they decided to bring some extra cargo back with them. The spoils of war. Everyone did it. They made the arrangements. It was easy."

Bear looked over at Poor Nic, who caught his gaze and nodded. Bear said, "So, what happened when this professor came to claim his already stolen treasures?"

"That's the thing." Keys played out a strange, awkward smile. "He never did. I jumped a ride out of Cairo and came back with some university types about a month after Willy and the others left. It took me forever to get passage out of that hole. Anyway, Willy had moved the stuff back here already, to Virginia, and hid it in his father's old vault..."

Bear leaned forward. "At the bank annex?"

"Yeah, that one." Keys waited for Bear to nod before going on. "Anyway, when I got back, Willy had it all stashed. It stayed there until the war ended. Then, me, him, Claude, and Cy all got back together. Claude lived outside DC, and Cy, I think he settled somewhere south of here."

Poor Nic raised a hand. "Keys, do get to the professor, if you please."

"Like I said, he never showed up. Willy and I looked for him in DC—Claude helped too. Turns out that he got himself killed in Cairo and never made it out."

Bear watched Keys with a skeptical look. "How fortunate for you guys, huh?"

"At first, yeah." Keys's smile turned into a vacant, distant stare. "We just let the stuff sit for a while—we figured we better not touch it and see if anyone comes looking for it. We waited years. Then, Cy decided to test the waters and took a couple small pieces—an old dagger with some jewels on it and a couple other gold pieces—I don't know much about it. Anyway, he sold them."

I watched Keys's face go ashen. "That's what got Cy killed, Bear."

Bear drew the same conclusion.

"You bet it did." Keys poked a hole in the air with his finger. "Cy was found murdered outside DC. We weren't sure it was all related. DC has always been a dangerous place. And old Cy had a habit of finding trouble. So we laid low again. Years later, Claude Holister did the same thing—he tried to sell some of the loot. And you know what happened to him, I guess."

"Suicide?" Bear asked.

"That was bullshit." Keys sat back and watched Bear for a long time.

Bear asked, "Ever heard of Amphora Trading or Nomad Air Freight?"

"Yeah, why?" Keys's face looked like he was constipated. "Nomad is the outfit that shipped all my replica Egyptian statues and artwork for this club. They make the fake stuff over in Cairo—Willy put me onto them—almost identical to the real deals. My basement storage is full of that junk. He got those big ugly statues in his office from them. Why?"

"And Amphora?" Bear watched him as Keys's constipation got worse.

"Yeah, them too."

"Would you please explain to Detective Braddock, Keys?" Poor Nic wasn't asking. "It is the key to all of this, after all."

Keys's eyes were red and teary. "Not quite a year ago, Willy got a call from American U asking about being stationed in Cairo during the war. It spooked him so he decided to give the stuff back. We wanted it gone for good, Braddock. He got back in touch with American University and told them he had the professor's stuff. He played coy and didn't let on any of us were involved—just that he knew where the stuff was and that he would help them recover it. I know they probably figured it all out. Then all this started."

Ollie said, "Ask him about Operation Salaam, kid."

I relayed the question to Bear.

"Operation Salaam?" Bear's face twisted a little and Poor Nic glanced over at him. He covered with, "It was on some papers William left for Angela Tucker. What do you know about it, Keys?"

His eyes settled on nothing in the distance. "Salaam? That old German spy job from the war? Hell, I don't know anything about it, 'cept lately it's been real popular."

"What do you mean?" Bear asked.

"You're the third one askin'. First, Willy became obsessed with researching it a while back. It had something to do with the Germans sneaking around Cairo, I think. But hell, it all happened before we were all there."

Bear asked, "When did William start researching Operation Salaam?"

"About eight months ago. Right after he was contacted by the University."

I asked, "And what happened next?" just as Bear asked the same question.

Keys's face flushed and his voice got dry and angry. "Then she showed up."

"Who?" Bear asked.

"The granddaughter of that old professor from Cairo—the one that Willy knew. It was his loot, right? And she showed up. And when she did, all kinds of bad things started happening. Bad things to all of us—illy, Marshal, even Lee and me. Jesus, we knew we were in trouble. That's why we asked Nicholas to help us out." Keys looked over at Poor Nic and his face fell, defeated. "But it was too late. That professor's granddaughter had already found us."

"Who?" Bear asked leaning forward and demanding Key's eyes. "Give me a damn name, Keys. Who's behind all this?"

"Raina Iskandr."

Chapter Fifty-Eight

"This is not about stealing junk from Cairo, kid," Ollie said as Bear and Poor Nic continued interviewing Keys in his office. "It's about revenge. I guess it's time to clear some of this up."

I looked at him. "Yeah, that would be nice."

"Come on, kid. Follow me." Ollie led me out of the office to the rear of the Kit Kat West and down into the basement. There, he made a beeline to an old, covered steamer trunk sitting beside a wall full of Nomad Air Freight boxes like the ones we'd found in William's basement. He opened the trunk without difficulty.

"Ollie, how come you can move things without any juice or anything?" I asked.

"Age, kid. And experience." He reached in and pulled out a shoebox full of old papers and photographs and dumped them onto a nearby table. "Take a look. Keys and me share a lot of history. And somewhere back there, there's a killer and a spy."

Ollie's face was sullen and sad and in his eyes I could see him reminiscing over the pile of old black-and-white photographs. "A spy—like Eppler and Fahmy? Like in my vision when somebody killed Youssif?"

"Yeah, exactly," Ollie said, handing a photograph to me. "Youssif was a good man—smart, a family man, and he didn't like the Jerries. He didn't like the Jerries one bit."

"Tell me about him." I looked at the photograph. It was of Cy, Claude, Keys, and William again. They were standing together on a stage surrounded by beautiful belly dancers. Between them was the mysterious belly dancer,

Hekmet, from the original Kit Kat Club in Cairo. "What do these four have to do with Youssif?"

"Youssif was an archeology professor at the American University in Cairo. He was also a big-shot with the Egyptian Antiquities people—that much, Keys got right." He reached out and touched the photo in my hand. "But that's not why he was so important."

His fingers closed on the photograph and mine at the same time. The room snapped shut.

The woman's wail sent chills down my spine like fingernails on a chalkboard. "*Laa, laa, laa!*"

We were back. We stood in front of the three-story, pale stone building I'd visited last time, when the old mare and her rickety cart had waited while a strange man loaded it with two heavy chests. The mare and cart were already gone, and this time Ollie was beside me.

But the Ollie I'd left the Kit Kat's basement with was not the man beside me now. His face was covered by a dark shroud—sad, removed, fearful.

"Damn, Ollie, I've already been here."

He went toward the house and hooked a thumb at the side door. "Coming?"

"Inside?"

"Yeah, you should know how this started."

"Sure. Okay. Start at the beginning." I followed him and found what I didn't want to.

Youssif lay face down on the floor. He had close-cropped graying hair, and dark leathery skin—life had already left his eyes. His thobe was matted in blood from his shoulders to his waist. The room was a shambles of broken pottery, toppled stone statues, and papers littering the floor. Above him, a woman of indeterminable age lay above his head, holding it delicately as though she could retain the life that had already poured from his wound. Her wailing continued, and each cry stabbed me deeper and brought back my own last moments on this earth two years ago.

In the corner of the room, at the foot of a staircase, stood a toddler and his older sister. They stood there, mouths agape, staring at their mother as she erupted over and over with the sorrow the murder had delivered. Their faces were blank—stone—uncertain of what lay ahead without their father.

"That's Tahira." Ollie pointed at the woman holding Youssif. "His wife. I don't know why she and the kids weren't killed." He turned and threw a chin toward the children on the stairs. "Tahira, Malek, and Aalia were hiding upstairs."

The door banged open behind us and a man ran in. I recognized him even through the dark Egyptian night. He was younger, thinner, and wearing baggy tan cotton pants and a sweat-stained tan shirt, but it was OSS Captain Oliver Tucker.

"Oh, dear God, no, Tahira," the younger Ollie yelled as he went to the Tahira's side. He bent down and rolled Youssif over. "I'm so sorry. What happened? Who did this?"

The woman spoke in rapid Arabic and thrust her finger out, pointing outside. Then she stood and went to her children, gathered them before her, and delivered slow, moving words. When she was through, she addressed each child until they nodded and said, *"Na, 'am, umm."*

"What's that all about?" I asked.

"Revenge," spirit Ollie said. "She swore them to a blood oath. They must hunt down their father's killer no matter how long it takes and no matter how many generations of their children it takes. He will be avenged."

"Damn, they did that?"

The younger Ollie spoke to Tahira in Arabic and then bolted from the house.

We followed. But when we stepped out of Youssif's house, we were not standing beside his dusty three-story home, but along a busy music-filled street where the aroma of grilled meat and fish hung in the air. Ahead of us, Ollie-the-younger stood in the shadows of a doorway and watched two men unload the horse-drawn cart the murderer had escaped in. The second man was neither Arab nor American and both men spoke unguarded in dulled accents. An occasional loud word hinted of Germanic heritage and for the first time, I understood.

Youssif's murderer was a German spy.

When the cart was empty and the two chests moved down into a dark alleyway, Ollie-the-younger moved in. He crept through the darkness—a .45 handgun now at his side—and disappeared down the alley after the two men.

"Remember," spirit Ollie said, "we're observers. We cannot interact. We cannot do anything. We watch and listen. Got that, kid?"

"I get it. I've got a little experience in this."

We maneuvered down the alley for a hundred yards deep behind a row of dilapidated stone buildings. Spirit Ollie led me in a back door and up to the top story of the building that was empty but for a few broken pieces of furniture and stacks of discarded trash. On the second floor, in the corner of the room, the two men from the cart sat at a table dialing in a whiny, fuzzy military radio. They spoke German. One of them wore headphones and gave instructions over the radio, then he sat waiting for a response.

Of all I heard, the only words I understood were *Salaam* and *Hekmet*. I looked at Ollie. "Did you find out who the spy was?"

"Back in '44—right now, that is—I was just about to when I ran into a little trouble." Spirit Ollie winced when an outcry reached us from the first floor.

"What about—"

"Shush."

Him, too?

We returned to the first floor in time to see two new men—both dressed in Arab attire—kicking and stomping Ollie-the-younger on the floor. His face was bloodied and his body contorted as he took the savage attacks over and over.

"No! Stop!" I tried to rush forward, but my feet wouldn't take me. "Stop this, Ollie, stop it!"

"We can't, kid. You know that. It happened over seventy-seven years ago." He turned away. "And it happened to me. Trust me, it's gonna happen—it *did* happen."

The attackers rained down kicks and brutal heel-stomps. One of them found an old board amongst the trash and used it for a thorough thrashing.

When Ollie-the-younger stopped moving, the men continued their attack for another few moments. They tired and stopped, then retreated to the front window and looked outside—checking that his torment hadn't attracted any unwanted passersby.

He made his move.

Ollie-the-younger staggered to his feet and made a hobbled run for the back door. He'd made it into the doorway when the pistol shot cracked from behind him. The shot slammed into his back. He staggered through the door and into the darkness.

"No!" I tried to run to him, but the room was already spinning. "We have to help him. We have to go back."

"No point, kid, no point. It's been over for decades."

The photograph wavered in my hand and its dull black-and-white images drifted in and out of focus until they coalesced into the men and the belly dancers. Ollie sat on the steamer trunk watching me.

"Understand now?"

Did I? "That German spy killed Youssif. The killer was part of a spy ring. So how do Keys, William, and the others fit into all this? Are you saying…"

He nodded. "You know about Operation Salaam: Eppler and Sandstede, the two German spies, sneaked across the desert into Cairo."

"I get that."

"What you don't know, and what no one knows but me…" His face formed a wry smile. "There was a *third* German spy with them. Eppler and Sandstede were captured early on, but not the third one. He was never caught—never. In fact, he stayed in Cairo a long time after Eppler and Sandstede were captured. He kept operating for the Germans. Sly bastard."

Holy Mata Hari. The images of Ollie-the-younger being beaten, the German shooting him in the back—it all sent a wave of anger raging through me. "Do you think Keys and William and their pals had something to do with that? Are they part of it all?"

He shrugged. "Somebody was. I got wind the third spy set up a new network out of a houseboat on the Nile. Me and Youssif were hunting him." He tipped his ball cap onto the back of his head. "Youssif knew Eppler years before when he went under the name Hussein. He also met several of Eppler's old pals and he worked those contacts trying to find this third spy. That's why I went to see Youssif that night. He thought he found the third spy and had arranged a meeting. He never should have involved his home and family. But he told me about it too late to change it."

"That's why Youssif was so important to you."

He stuffed his hands in his pockets and looked away. "After the war, OSS became the CIA. So did I. I kept looking for him. I used CIA's resources and networks. I owed Youssif that much; OSS owed him that much."

"So, they didn't kill you that night?"

"No, kid." He smiled a faint, hollow smile. "I told you, I don't know who killed me. But, I didn't die in Cairo. I did get that purple heart, though. No, somebody did me eleven years later."

"Your murder has to have something to do with Youssif, right? That's what's so important about him?"

"No, that's not why." Ollie turned and walked away into nothing, leaving only his tired, sad voice behind. "Youssif Iskandr is important because he was my friend."

Chapter Fifty-Nine

I caught up to Angel as she crossed DC on New York Avenue. She headed into northeast DC and paralleled the railroad tracks as I popped into the Explorer beside her.

"Enjoy lunch with the Amazing…"

She swerved, cursed, and straightened the SUV in time to avoid a head-on with a taxi. "Dammit, Tuck. You scared me to death."

"Then we could be together, babe. How cool would that be?"

"Or, you could possess—"

"Yeah, yeah, the body of a dashing French movie star." I thought about that. "Why French?"

"Why not?" She looked pleased with herself as she slowed on New York Avenue and turned right on Fairview and weaved down a semi-industrial area. "If I were to pick who you possess, I'd pick someone more handsome and dashing and, well, very *French*."

"Forget I asked." I looked around at the rundown, fenced-in buildings around us. "Hey, what are we doing down here?"

"I have Raina Iskandr's address. At least an old one for her Egyptology research office. She left earlier without explaining herself and I intend on finding out what she knows."

"Then let me tell you about Youssif Iskandr, her grandfather."

"Grandfather?" She pulled up to the curb outside a rundown industrial building.

"Yes, grandfather." I told her the whole story of what I'd just witnessed in Cairo and what I learned about Professor Youssif Iskandr and his family. I ended with, "Raina Iskandr is Youssif's granddaughter. She could still be on that blood oath to find Youssif's killer. Maybe she already did."

Angel looked out the window, thinking. Then she said, "You think William killed Professor Iskandr back in the war? And after seventy-seven years, his granddaughter came six thousand miles for an old blood feud?"

"Oath—blood oath."

"Whatever." She jumped out of the Explorer.

I followed. "I think as a history professor, the difference between blood feud and blood oath would be significant to you."

Her silence proved me the winner.

The cement block building had a one-story office area with narrow, security-screened windows in the front and a windowless two-story warehouse affixed behind it. The premises were surrounded by a chain-link fence in poor repair, with a pedestrian and vehicle gate just down from where we parked. There was a heavy chain and lock around the gate. Inside the fence, parked along the side of the building, was a dark-green late-model cargo van with its engine running. "This is a bad idea, Angel. Let the cops…"

"You're getting chicken being dead, Tuck."

"I'm not chicken. Don't you want to make it to your next date and…"

"Just shut up, Tuck. Or should I say, *ta gueule?*"

"No, really, but I was just thinking about being that French movie star on a date with you. You know, not for the sexy dialogue or snails or anything, but for the anatomy."

"Oh yes, the anatomy." She turned around and faced me—there was sadness in her eyes. "You're right, Tuck, it's been nearly two years." Tears welled in her eyes and she turned away.

Sometimes, my wit and lips collided in a very bad way. "Sorry. I'll shut up now."

Angel walked to the pedestrian gate down the sidewalk and grabbed the heavy security lock affixed to the end of the gate chain. She tugged. The lock hadn't been properly secured and popped open. Without a word, she pulled the chain free, opened the gate, went inside, and closed it behind her. In a few steps, she stood at the brown, paint-chipped steel front door.

I followed behind like a puppy seeking forgiveness for peeing on the rug.

There was a buzzer button beside the door and she pressed it several times. Neither of us heard anything and she pressed it several more times. Nothing. The windows were a heavy opaque glass with a steel mesh lining between the glass layers.

"I'll go in and look around," I said.

She tugged on the doorknob. It was locked. "I'm going around back." She headed around the side of the building as I slipped through the steel door inside.

I don't know what an Egyptology research office looks like, but I was pretty sure this wasn't one. The place looked like a bad advertisement for government surplus sales. The office was large and drab with stark, dull-tan walls that were void of any homey touches. There were two battleship-gray metal desks on opposite sides of the room and a large rectangular metal table in the center with four metal chairs around it. Against the far wall were four mismatched metal filing cabinets—one gray, two green, and one brown. The overhead fluorescent lights were off and the little bit of light coming through the security windows gave the room an eerie, shadowy feel—shadowy as in monsters about to spring out and attack me.

There was a dark hallway off the far wall that I assumed went back into the warehouse area. Another doorway on the opposite wall led into a smaller empty office. I snooped around the desktops and found stacks of business letters, faxes, and files that began to connect the dots. The papers were from various businesses, individuals, and several museums around the country. They were all addressed to the Amphora Trading Company, with a Washington DC post office box—the same address Cal found earlier.

"Of course," I said to no one. "Amphora, the Department of Egyptology and Archeological Studies, and Raina Iskandr are all one."

Something crashed in the darkness down the hallway. Something crashed again and metal rattled against concrete. Then someone yelled, "Stop!" and a second later came the sharp crack of a gunshot.

"Angel!"

I ran down the hall, around a corner, and reached the small warehouse behind the administrative offices. The room was filled with metal shipping containers and wooden crates similar to those in William's basement and the Kit Kat West. In the far corner, perhaps a hundred feet from me, Angel lay across several toppled wood containers—an open window twenty feet above her explained why. She had climbed through it and tried to navigate the containers to reach the floor. Somewhere along her route, she'd lost her footing.

Her fall was the least of her worries.

Raina Iskandr stood in black jeans and a colorful turquoise tunic just feet from where Angel struggled to sit up. In her hand was a small-framed semi-automatic pistol.

The gun was aimed at Angel's head.

Chapter Sixty

"Raina Iskandr, I presume?" Angel said as she pushed a small wooden crate out of her way. "Put the gun down. I came here to talk to you—*again*."

"I do not think so, Professor Tucker." Raina's eyes locked on Angel. "Have you not come here to do me harm?"

"No, I haven't."

"Then why did you break in as you did? Those who come to talk come through the front door, no?"

I said, "Don't do anything to piss her off. Let's talk our way out of this."

"Raina, listen." Angel eased up onto her feet. "I've come here to find out what you have to do with William Mendelson's murder. Is this because of your grandfather? Did you avenge him for your blood oath?"

Great plan—antagonize a murderer holding a gun to your head. "Nice, Angel. Maybe you should accuse her of being Lizzie Borden's reincarnation?"

Raina took a step back and lowered her gun a few inches. "William Mendelson's murder was a debt long overdue and it matters not how it was paid. For that reason, Professor, you have wasted your time."

"No, I haven't. You've been lying to everyone since you arrived, Raina." Angel walked around two of the fallen shipping containers and opened the distance from Raina another three feet. "You claimed to be with the Egyptology and Archeological Research Group at American University. American U hasn't heard from you in over a year. Care to explain that?"

"I need not explain anything to you, Professor Tucker." Raina's eyes

255

flashed a little, and when she tried to move a box out of the way, she held one arm down and favored it. "Now, please do not move again or I may have to shoot you. You are, after all, a burglar."

I walked to Raina and looked at her arm. It looked like it was bandaged beneath her tunic sleeve. "Angel, her right arm is injured. My guess is one of Bear's deputies grazed her at William's house yesterday. She broke in there."

"You got shot, Raina?" Angel pointed to her arm. "You were at William's house yesterday. You broke in. For what?"

No response.

"It must hurt."

Raina lifted her chin. "Yes, I returned to the Mendelson house to retrieve the rest of what was promised to me. The police interrupted. No matter. It was a wasted trip, and I've made other arrangements."

"And she's holding a .22 handgun," I said. "Same caliber used in the bank robbery and to shoot Poor Nic. You need to get out of here, Angel, fast. I can't help, either. There's no electricity for me to use in here. You're on your own for now."

Angel's eyes dropped to the handgun. "A .22? You shot Nicholas? And the bank robbery…"

"Nicholas—the old man? The… how do you say it, the gangster? No more of this." Raina backed up a step. "I suggest you do not play games with me. Now, tell me, why are you here?"

"I told you. Just to talk." Angel looked for an escape. "I want to know about William. If you killed him, I understand—and I can't say that I blame you."

"You do not know anything. You understand nothing."

"Did you kill him because of the vendetta?"

"Blood oath, Angel." Geez, she sounded more and more like me.

"Blood oath," she corrected. "Because William killed Youssif—your grandfather—back during the war?"

The name Youssif set Raina's eyes ablaze. She stepped back again, lowering the handgun. "What do you know about my grandfather?"

"Why don't you tell me about him," Angel said. "All I know is that a German spy murdered him in Cairo during the war and that your family swore revenge."

"Not revenge—justice." Raina's mouth tightened, her jaw lifted, and she prodded the air with her gun. "Surely you understand that. You sought justice for your husband, did you not?"

"She's well informed, Angel," I said. "Ask her if—"

"Yes, I wanted justice. And yes, I got it." Angel took another step back. "Did William kill your grandfather?"

Raina wet her lips. She seemed to be sizing Angel up—perhaps to answer the question or perhaps to see which Amphora Trading crate her body would fit into. "He sought forgiveness for my grandfather, yes." Her voice softened. "And he wished to make amends. Yes, guilt told me what I needed to know."

I said, "Amends?"

Angel asked her that, too, and added, "So you met with William?"

"It does not matter." Raina stiffened and waved the gun around the room like a magic wand. "This has been my life's work and it is nearly over. I swore to my mother that I would find grandfather's killer. She witnessed it—so many years ago now—and it consumed her entire life. A life wasted. My grandfather helped you Americans. He helped them with the Nazi spies. And for what? To be murdered and have his life's work stolen?"

"Keep her talking, Angel," I said. "I have to find you a way out of this."

"Raina, I know it was unfair. I know—"

"You know nothing. My family was ruined when grandfather was killed and his work stolen. *Ruined.* It has taken my family almost eighty years and me two decades of reclaiming my country's stolen antiquities to reach this point. And after all this time and so many false hopes, someone found me and led me to William. Revenge is a wondrous motivation, is it not, Professor Tucker?"

Angel stared. "You've been searching for Egyptian artifacts around the US?"

"Yes, and the world. I have searched for them wherever they were hidden."

"I don't understand."

I did. "Angel, Raina didn't know who killed her grandfather, but her mother knew the killer had a fortune in his antiquities. If she found the stolen artifacts, she might be able to trace them from seller to seller and maybe find out who first stole them from Cairo. She might find the killer."

"I know about Youssif, Raina." Angel retold my story of Youssif's murder and my own grandfather's role. When she was through, she said, "Raina, it's not a coincidence that my husband's grandfather and yours worked together in Cairo. Please, I understand. But murder isn't the answer..."

"Did you learn of my grandfather from your husband and his family?"

"Yes, sort of. It was, well, you won't understand..." Angel stuttered trying to find an answer—her face showed the strain and fear that grew each time Raina waved the gun at her. "It was..."

"William told you," I said.

"William," she said. The words calmed her.

"No matter. It is not murder if you are avenging murder. It is justice." Raina smiled a faint, painful smile and lowered her gun to her side. "But you are correct, Professor Tucker. Many Egyptian antiquities were looted during the war—and afterward, too. Stealing from my country has been a pastime of those who came for science and learning and left as simple thieves. It has been that way for generations—for millennia. I found many stolen antiquities, and often, they had been passed along, sold, and stolen again. It has been an endless journey."

"And you followed the trail here?" Angel asked. "To William?"

Raina shook her head. "No. Years ago, my family learned of a man selling one of my grandfather's pieces—a jeweled weapon he'd found during a dig south of the Valley of the Kings. My father found the man here in Washington and tried to learn where he had obtained the piece. He refused to provide the information. He died for his resistance."

Cy Gray.

She went on. "Many years later, a similar discovery brought us back to America. But my father was impatient and did not get the man to talk in time. Once again, silence kept the truth hidden."

Claude Holister.

"Angel, she just admitted that her family murdered Cy Gray and Claude Holister."

"I know." Angel stepped back beside a ten-foot-high stack of shipping crates. "Raina, you said someone led you to William. Who?"

Raina lifted the gun. "It does not matter. Soon I will have the last of my family's possessions and I'll be through. I'll go and you will never see me again. So for now, Professor Tucker, you will have to stay here." She waved the gun toward a steel door in the far corner of the warehouse. "It will be uncomfortable, I'm afraid. But it is necessary. I require a day to retrieve the remainder of my grandfather's possessions, complete my duty, and leave this country. You know too much, and I have but a simple choice—kill you too, or lock you here for the time it takes me to be done."

Kill her too?

Angel didn't move. "I want to know more about William. Who led him to you?"

"Revenge, Professor Tucker, and guilt." Raina made a show of pulling back the handgun's hammer. "Last April I found someone selling my grandfather's artifacts and they led me here, to Washington, where the others had been as well. I purchased many items—for very large sums of money, too. It took time, but I was able to find the source in Winchester."

"William sold some of the antiquities?" Angel asked.

"I purchased the items over the Internet—the seller refused to meet me but emailed photographs of some of the items and provided small pieces to establish their authenticity. I transferred payment and the items were shipped here." She raised her chin. "Amphora has been my, my...my front company for recovering stolen items. I communicated through here until I was sure I had located the person who had the rest of my grandfather's treasures. When I did, I arranged a meeting to make a considerable final payment for the rest."

I said, "That's the payments Cal and Bear found in the bank account, Angel. The money's been coming from her."

Angel repeated me.

Raina shrugged. "It was not my money. The Ministry of Antiquities provided me with resources to purchase items in order to find those responsible for our country's thefts. Then, in time, they take action against those people."

"You mean they kill them." Angel's words were icy.

"No—it is not that way." Raina shook her head. "It does not matter that you understand. Into the back room, Professor. It does not matter the how and why of my business. It only matters that it is ending."

Angel didn't budge. "When did you first meet with William?"

"You ask too many questions—but fine, I will explain." Raina watched her with an interested-killer sort of look on her face. "After I received several of my grandfather's artifacts from someone here in Winchester— *and* already paid nearly half a million of your dollars—William contacted my embassy. He told them he wished to return many artifacts. He sought no payment. He claimed he had come by them innocently during the war. He wanted assurances he would not be prosecuted and his name would remain anonymous. I have worked through the Consulate over the years and this information was passed to me."

"Raina, didn't it strike you odd that you'd been buying some of the pieces for months and then suddenly William comes forward and wants to give them back? For free?"

Raina looked down for a moment. When she looked back up, her eyes were back to their angry, determined stare. "Perhaps, yes. But it did not matter. And it does not matter now. Move back toward the room. Now."

Angel refused to move and Raina stepped forward and reached for her arm. Angel blocked Raina's arm and jabbed a punch into her bandaged right arm, knocking her back a step as she cried out in pain. Then Angel made a jump toward the stack of shipping crates.

But Raina was too agile and skilled. She recovered and sprang forward, delivering a leg sweep that buckled Angel's knees beneath her. As Angel fell sideways and down, Raina pivoted on the ball of her left foot, twisted her body in a crisp spiral and snapped out a right kick into Angel's jaw, sending her crashing to the floor.

"Angel, stop! You can't take her!" I rushed forward and tried to grab Raina's gun, but my fingers found only air. "Stop it, Angel!"

Raina jumped forward and landed beside Angel, grabbed her arm, and twisted it behind her. Then she pressed the pistol to the back of her head.

"Enough, Professor."

"Angel, are you okay?" I could do no more than watch Raina's performance. "Don't move. She'll shoot. Do as she tells you. I'll get you out of this somehow."

"Professor, do not anger me further." She tugged Angel to her feet, wincing as her right arm took the weight. "To the back room, quickly, before I change my mind."

Angel threw scared, defeated eyes at me. "Change your mind about what?"

"Letting you live."

Chapter Sixty-One

By the time Bear returned to the Task Force office it was early evening. He'd spent hours going over Keys's story and chasing down false leads on the bank robber. So far, nothing made sense and the questions were piling up. As he walked in and tossed his coat over a chair in the bullpen, Cal spun around in his chair and held up a handful of documents.

"Bear, you're not gonna believe what I found, man." He handed him the documents. "This whole case is messed up. Really messed up."

Bear frowned, dropped the pile of papers onto a desk, and headed for the coffeepot. "Your pal Keys thinks it's all about a fortune in stolen World War II Egyptian relics." He told Cal the story as Keys had told it to him and Poor Nic, ending with, "And that junk is worth a fortune."

"And ol' Keys has known about it all this time? He never let on." Cal leaned back against one of the bullpen desks. "I got that beat, man. The crime scene team said Marshal Mendelson had no gunshot residue on his hands or arms. I'm confirming that with the lab now."

"Then he didn't pull the trigger," Bear said. "And that means it was murder, not suicide. Anything else?"

Cal's cell phone rang and he took the call. His face grimaced and he nodded several times. "Can you email me a photo and any distinguishing marks? Thanks." When he tapped off his call, he stared at the screen, waiting for the email he'd asked for.

"What do you have, Cal?" Bear asked.

"That was the West Virginia State boys. They found Karen Simms. Poor

Nic's small blue Fiat went down a ravine outside Morgantown. Someone rammed it off the road a couple hours ago—the wreck is pretty bad, man. There was a witness and the body has Simms's ID, too—they'll send everything over soon as they can."

Bear's mouth tightened. "Dammit."

"They're sending a crime scene photo and a scan of her ID now."

"So, Simms isn't a missing person anymore—she's a homicide. That's three murders in two days." Bear returned and picked up the papers Cal had given him and took them to his office with Cal in tow. There he slumped into his chair, took a long sip of his coffee, and started reading. After two pages, his eyes widened; he'd gotten to the background report on Franklin Thorne. "Are you saying Thorne's a phony?"

Cal shrugged. "Don't know and that's the problem. I ran his background like I told you and got nothing—no credit, two IDs with different info. So, I got a copy of his resume from the bank HR department and had one of the guys check his references, college, the whole shootin' match."

"And it's all bogus?" A knot formed in Bear's stomach. "All of it?"

"All of it. The phone numbers for his former employers all went out of service within a month of his starting at the bank. The college numbers too. But when I cross-checked the college telephones on the Internet, none of the numbers were what he gave out. His resume is all bullshit, Bear. Pure bullshit."

"What the hell is going on here, Cal? Thorne's in on this?" Bear stood and went to his window to look out. The sun was already down, and the parking lot lights were on as it began to snow again. "Is Larry Conti downstairs in the holding cell?"

Cal nodded and picked up the desk phone. "Roberts, it's Cal. Bring Conti up to Detective Braddock's office, pronto."

Bear retrieved another cup of coffee for himself and Cal along with a third cup. They waited for the deputies to bring a handcuffed Larry Conti to the office and sat him down in the corner as Cal received a message on his cell phone and looked it over.

Bear took the handcuffs off Conti. "Okay, Conti. Time for you to man up."

"I didn't kill anyone, Detective Braddock. You have to believe me."

"I do, pal. But you can help yourself, too." Bear handed Conti a cup of coffee and waited for him to take a few sips. "Larry, we have a body. We want you to take a look."

Cal nodded and held his cell phone up for Conti to see. "It's bad, man. But tell us what you think."

The photograph on his cell phone was of a badly damaged car on its hood. All the windows were shattered and a body was crumpled half in, half out of the driver's window with an arm and long blond hair hanging out amidst glass and debris. The woman's face was obscured but she had been pretty and young—features masked by bluish-gray bruised flesh and broken bones.

"They're sending more photos, Larry," Cal said. "But do you think..."

Larry took the phone and fanned through to a close-up photo of the body hanging out the broken car window. He stared and manipulated the photo to enlarge it around the body's arm and hand—specifically the body's gold bracelet. As soon as he did, he burst into tears and looked away. "Oh, jeez, no. I gave her that bracelet when we started dating. Her name in hieroglyphs..." He couldn't finish the words and dropped his head into his hands. "I loved her. I do. Who did this to her? Who butchered her like this?"

Bear looked at the cell phone photograph and took it out of Conti's view. "We were hoping you'd help us find her, but not like this. And there's more. Thorne is a ghost—none of his references check out and no one can find a trace of him before he started at the bank. Marshal Mendelson was found murdered..."

Conti jumped up. "Marshal's dead? Holy shit, no, no, no. You gotta believe me. We didn't think this would happen."

"*We?*" Cal took Conti's shoulder and sat him back down. "Start talking, man. Maybe you'll walk out of here tonight."

Conti's face was ashen and he looked from Cal to Bear and back several times. Finally, he closed his eyes and dropped his head. "Karen and I have been dating off and on, I told you that. Well, she confided in me a few months back about stuff at the bank. Thorne made moves on her and she was worried about her promotion so she didn't stop him. She sorta played along, get it? But then one night, in the summer sometime, she noticed Thorne and Marshal coming and going all hours of the night at the bank. So she cut him off. Was it him? Did Thorne kill her? Did he?"

"Karen watched Thorne and Marshal from her apartment balcony?" Bear asked.

Conti's face turned into rage. "Was it Thorne? Was it him and Marshal? Shit, I told you that Marshal wanted me to keep following the Chairman and I refused. Well, I kept the Chairman aware of what Marshal was doing, too. Karen saw him and Thorne in the bank before midnight a few times—staying for hours. I kept the Chairman advised, and after he was killed, I deleted all the voicemails between him and me so you wouldn't find out. I should have told you. But for two guys who hated each other, Marshal and Thorne were doing a lot of overtime together."

Bear sat back. "I'm thinking Karen knew about William's secret account and caught someone skimming, right?"

"She said it was Marshal," Conti added. "I should have told you all this before, Detectives, but I was scared I'd be next. Now Karen's dead and it's all my fault. I screwed up, didn't I?"

"Yeah, man, you did," Cal said. "But you're helpin' yourself out now."

Bear went on. "You said you told William about Marshal wanting you to follow him around. Maybe William confronted Marshal and Thorne—maybe that's why he was in the bank so late all the time. He tried to catch them doing whatever they were doing. Maybe he did and they killed him."

"You think they found out what Karen knew about the account and what she'd seen?" Cal asked. "So they killed her? Then Thorne decided he was scot-free without Marshal, and..."

"Thorne tried to make Marshal look like he committed suicide." Bear looked at Conti. "Anything else, Larry? Don't make me ask twice."

A uniformed deputy knocked on Bear's office door. "Detective, someone here to see you. He says it's urgent."

Poor Nic walked past the deputy into the office with his left arm in a sling. His face was pale and his voice hard and tight. "Forgive the intrusion, Detective Braddock, but there is a matter most urgent."

"Glad you're here, Nic." Bear cast a glance at Cal, who slid a chair over for Poor Nic to take, but he refused it. Then Bear had Cal show him the cell phone photograph of the blue Fiat at the bottom of the ravine. "We found your Fiat. And…"

Poor Nic took one look at the photo and nodded. "I thought she had found refuge somewhere. I had hoped, anyway."

"She's dead, Nic," Cal said. "If you'd told us sooner…"

Poor Nic held up his hand. "It is not my responsibility or yours. It was not you, nor I, who killed her."

Cal shrugged.

"Detective, in light of Miss Simms's murder, I am concerned for Angela."

Bear's eyes flared. "What about her?"

"Mr. Thorne tells me she went to DC this afternoon—investigating leads regarding Raina Iskandr." Poor Nic waited for questions but when Bear had none, he continued. "That is troubling, no?"

"Yes, it is," Bear said.

Poor Nic raised his chin. "I fear Angela has located Raina Iskandr—and that woman is hungry."

Cal looked at Bear and both of them stared at Poor Nic.

Cal asked, "Hungry for what, Nic?"

"A dish that is best served cold, Detectives: revenge."

Chapter Sixty-Two

"And now you'll do what, Raina?" Angel fixed her eyes on Raina's gun. "Kill someone else? First William, then Karen Simms, then…"

"Quiet." Raina reached out her hand. "Now, Angela Tucker, give me your cell phone."

Cell phone? Good idea. "Yeah, Angel. Give her your cell phone. And turn it on when you do."

Angel hesitated but Raina jammed her gun against her chest. In a slow, careful movement, Angel slid her cell phone out of her pocket and tapped the side button to turn it on. Then she held it out to Raina.

The cell phone lit up.

And so did I.

As Raina took hold of the phone, I grabbed hold, too. The small surge of electricity was all I needed. The charge stung my fingers and started up my arm, surging through me like fire. In seconds, the current filled me and Raina's eyes locked onto mine as fear electrified the air between us.

She saw me.

"What?" Raina yanked the cell phone from Angel's fingers and backpedaled. "Who… no, no… *shabah, no!*"

"Hi, Raina." I stepped toward her. "Boo, bitch."

Raina stumbled back another step and tripped over one of the fallen shipping crates behind her. "No, *shabah*… it is not possible. *La, baaid 'annee!*"

I jumped forward and kicked at the gun in her hand. The little juice I got from the cell phone wasn't enough to kick it free, but it startled Raina and she dropped the gun amid the fallen boxes around her.

"Run, Angel! Run!"

Before she did, she took a step toward Raina, reared back, and drove a vicious kick into Raina's jaw. It jarred her head and sent her eyes rolling back. Without looking back, Angel dashed for the warehouse office and was gone.

I stayed long enough to make sure Angel was clear of the building and safely to her Explorer. As we drove away from the warehouse, the last of the energy in me faded and was gone.

"You did good, Angel. Real good. Get out of the city fast. Find a convenience store and call Bear. Let him know what happened and he can get some DC cops down there. Maybe we'll get lucky and catch her packing."

Angel floored the Explorer, veered out onto a wide boulevard and continued for three blocks, checking behind her the entire way.

"I don't think she followed us, Tuck," she said and slowed. "You need to get back to Winchester. You have to figure out who got into William's vault and sold those artifacts to Raina. I don't think she killed William, or she'd already have her grandfather's antiquities.

She'll head back there when she wakes up and God knows what she'll do. She'll stop at nothing to get those artifacts back—nothing." She was right. If I couldn't find who led Raina to Winchester, that person would be long gone once Raina got what she'd come for. Long gone or worse.

Chapter Sixty-Three

Angel left the Washington Metropolitan traffic thirty miles behind her and began the climb up Mount Weather along Route 7. She crossed the Blue Ridge Mountains out of Loudoun County through Snickers Gap and into Clarke County to the west. She'd stopped at a convenience store and called Bear to warn him about Raina Iskandr. During the trip back to Winchester, she fought the fear that each set of telltale headlights behind her might be Raina.

The road was slick as the winter night took hold and froze the inch of new fallen snow and ice. Twice she almost lost control as her Explorer drifted lanes as she headed down the mountain to the bridge spanning the Shenandoah.

"Tuck? Are you here?" She knew better—he'd gone ahead. She felt foolish calling for him, especially since she'd wished him away so many times in the past week. "Damn." She wiped tears away and wished him back.

She eased off the gas and glanced into the rearview mirror as bright lights glared from behind. "Come on, pal, go around…"

The crash into the Explorer bucked it forward in a violent surge. The rear end fishtailed, and Angel frantically struggled to regain control a hundred yards before the Shenandoah River Bridge. A large vehicle—its bright lights blinding her through her mirrors—slammed into her a second time. This time, it stayed against her rear bumper and plowed her forward.

She tried to regain control, but the wet roads and assault made it almost impossible. The vehicle behind her slowed and she gained a few feet of distance before it rammed her again. As she started to slide, she looked for escape—nothing but trees and darkness ahead. The river fast approached, its embankment dropping away as it led to the water's edge. Cold, icy water waited.

No cars to offer help. No homes to seek shelter in. No rescue.

The vehicle rammed again, pushed her, and tried to spin her off the road.

The bridge was almost beneath her. She began to slide.

She dared a glance into her side mirror just as the dark vehicle smashed into her again.

"Tuck!"

Chapter Sixty-Four

The Kit Kat West was dark. The outside floodlights that normally bathed the club were off and the parking lot—overflowing any other evening—was empty. The club was closed Wednesdays and it was Wednesday, or so said the sign posted near the entrance. The oasis of light that lit up the sky for miles around was a dark, empty shell now.

I'd spent the past two hours looking for any missed clue that might lead me to William Mendelson's killer. I'd been to the bank annex and William's vault. I'd searched William and Marshal's homes again for any scrap. I'd even returned to Bear's office, but he and Cal were nowhere to be found. So far, I'd come to one big conclusion: I hadn't a clue who killed him.

The Kit Kat was next on my list.

I wasn't as certain as Angel that Raina Iskandr hadn't killed William. Maybe she hadn't recovered her grandfather's antiquities, but that didn't mean she hadn't killed William trying to. Or maybe it did. Raina Iskandr was one crazy lady—albeit sexy—and anything was possible.

But I'm a pro and couldn't let good looks, brains, and a little case of whacko cloud my judgment. Four people came out of Egypt in World War II who knew about William's stash. Cy Gray, who was dead. Claude Holister, who was dead. William Mendelson, who was dead. And Keys Hawkins, who was, last I checked, *not* dead—yet.

As I stepped off the spook express and onto the front steps of the club, Ollie was waiting. His normal upbeat smile and easy mood were still gone. In their place were concern and angst.

" 'Bout time, kid. I thought I was gonna have to deal with this on my own."

"Deal with what?"

"That crazy Egyptian skirt." He hooked a thumb over his shoulder. "She's inside with some party guests."

"Okay, what's the plan?" I asked.

He shrugged. "I don't have a plan. How about you?"

"Me?"

"You're the detective, kid. I've been dead too long. And all I want to know is who killed Youssif. After I find that out, well, I'll make it up as I go along."

"Make it up? I thought you were a big hero? OSS, CIA. What kind of spy makes it up as they go along?"

"The best ones." He winked. "I remember back in the Sudan, I was…"

"Later, Granddad. Let's go see the crazy Egyptian skirt."

We walked into the Kit Kat's bar and into a gathering of very unhappy people.

We were definitely going to need a plan.

Keys was bound to a chair near the bar with heavy gray duct tape. His face was swollen and bloody. His head rolled from side to side, and he mumbled something I couldn't understand, but the man standing in front of him did—he was interrogating him and Keys's answers weren't stopping the onslaught.

Raina stood across the room. She seemed unconcerned about the pain inflicted on the elderly Keys, and her attention—along with her gun—was focused on Lee Hawkins sitting in a chair six feet away and crying.

Raina and the man—a short, muscular man dressed in jeans and a dirty sweatshirt—readied for another round of "questions." If I were a betting man, I'd make two wagers. First, the thug beating Keys had a balaclava in his wardrobe, and second, he also had a bandage around a gunshot wound on his arm.

This was the bank robber who'd tried to take Angel hostage.

Lee was unblemished—for now—and tried to run to her grandfather to comfort him. The thug grabbed her and pulled her away, pushing her back into the chair she'd been sitting in.

Raina walked slowly to Keys and leaned down, face to face. "I do not like this violence, Keys Hawkins. I regret B.C. must use it. But he and I have a new arrangement and how he fulfills his end is not my concern. B.C. is a dangerous man, is he not?"

"What do you want, Raina?" Keys's words slurred together. "I don't have your grandfather's loot. I told you, this thug stole it from William's vault before he killed him."

Raina tapped Keys on his leg with her gun. "I want the truth, Mr. Hawkins. Which of you killed my grandfather—William or you? Whoever did that to my family is a murderer *and* a traitor."

"William!" Lee shouted. "I already told you a dozen times. It was William!"

"I am not so convinced. A granddaughter will do many things for family. Lie, perhaps? Worse?"

Keys coughed a strange, nervous laugh. "Or kill, like you, Raina?"

B.C., the thug and bank robber, landed two powerful punches into Keys's midsection. The blows on an ordinary man would be painful, but at his age, they could be deadly.

Keys gasped for air—almost failing—and spit blood. He cried out and went limp.

"Stop it. You'll kill him," Lee cried, and ran to him again. "You *bitch*! B.C. has what you want. Leave us alone."

"For now, perhaps it is enough." Raina waved her gun at B.C. "When will I see the rest of my possessions? I was promised they would be here."

B.C. shrugged and rubbed his knuckles. "I told you, lady—I ain't got that junk. I never did. I left that bank empty-handed."

"I think you are all lying. Unless you provide me my grandfather's property, I will have to convince you. For now, get to the truth." Raina moved close to Keys and placed the barrel of her gun against his forehead. "Consider your next words carefully, Keys Hawkins."

Ollie walked over to Raina. "This dame's serious as a heart attack, kid. You better find a way to get your cop pals here, fast. If you don't, Keys is a goner. But not too fast, you know? I want to know the truth, too. I want Youssif's killer. I think maybe she can find out."

"Are you insane? They'll kill him."

"Naw." Ollie grinned an evil grin. "Not yet anyway."

Keys lifted his head and tried to steady his eyes on Raina. "Kill me then. What difference does it make now who killed your grandfather? I'm dead either way. You can go to hell wondering, bitch."

"We had a deal, Raina!" Lee yelled. "You said if we helped you get your grandfather's treasure, you'd leave us alone. I'll do anything for Keys, anything. Just tell me what you want."

Raina turned the gun on Lee. "That was before William's passing. Now there is only *your* grandfather to tell me the truth about *my* grandfather. How fitting, is it not? Be quiet and don't force one granddaughter to kill the other."

I said, "Ollie, you can do more than I can. I'll get Bear and you..."

Cold fingers jabbed into my head and stole my breath. My vision went fuzzy and if I weren't dead, I would have vomited. Then, from far away, a whisper grew into a long, hollow cry.

Tuck! Help me! Tuck!

Chapter Sixty-Five

O h, dear God... *no!*

The dark, overcast sky was assailed by a kaleidoscope of dancing red, blue, and white lights. The circus of emergency vehicles was parked along Route 7 at the Shenandoah River bridge. The air gurgled with radios, voices, and the mayhem of adrenaline. The wind blew snow and ice. Clouds of anxious breath billowed out from the firemen and sheriff's deputies circling the ambulance.

At the ambulance's doors—pale and drawn—stood Bear.

He was crying.

The ambulance left the roadside and headed toward Winchester. Either slick roads or a lack of urgency kept the vehicle from progressing quickly. A sheriff's cruiser pulled out ahead of it and began the escort westward.

"Angel?" I tried to reach her—tried to will myself to her—but I couldn't move. "No. No. No. Not you."

I never should have left her—dear God what did I do?

"Bear?" I turned as he collapsed onto the side of a cruiser and waved two deputies away. He turned his back to them and slammed fists into the cruiser's hood. He let loose a howl that silenced the dozen onlookers and froze them in their tracks.

Pain.

I ran down the bank from Route 7, through the cracked scrub trees and lifeless bushes, to where the Explorer lay dead on its roof. A tall oak tree had stopped the vehicle's tumble deeper down the slope. Two doors were open—one bent back and crushed—and the glass had scattered from two

275

or three rotations as the vehicle rolled over and over until it found rest on the oak. My heart exploded at the sight of the open driver's door and the seatbelt that hung where it had been cut to remove my Angel.

I walked around the vehicle and with each step, my fear turned colder and colder. The cause of the crash was obvious. The Explorer's flesh was crumpled and torn. The vehicle's sides were mangled from its death roll. But it was the rear of the vehicle that told me what I wanted to know. The rear bumper, broken free before leaving the road, was crushed in, showing signs of a violent impact—something strange given the vehicle had rolled sideways down the embankment. The Explorer's rear hatch was twisted and crushed in—again, unlikely the result of rolling. And even without a flashlight, I could see the scrapes of darker paint that had transferred from one vehicle to another.

Someone did this. Someone rammed Angel from the road.

"Bear!" I ran back through the group of deputies over to him. "Is she alive?"

Nothing. Tears and more assault on his cruiser. "Bear, tell me she's alive?"

"Tuck?"

The voice behind me was weak and disconcerted—familiar, though I willed it not to be. That one word—my name—cast disbelief and agony so thick that I feared it would consume me.

No, not Angel.

"Tuck, I'm here. I'm right here."

I turned away from Bear and prayed I was wrong.

Angel.

"No, babe. No... no... no."

She came to me and wrapped her arms around me. I felt her—not in any physical sense—but a bond of essence and love deeper than any embrace could provide. "It's all right, Tuck. Things will be better now. You'll see. You and me now."

"No." I pulled away. My beautiful Angel still wore her jeans and long wool overcoat. Her eyes danced and sparked—like they had after our first kiss. The contentment in her smile...happiness? She had no bruises or cuts. Her long auburn hair was combed perfectly—even the blowing wind couldn't dishevel it, and the falling snow couldn't find her.

Two firemen walked past her without a notice. A deputy taking photographs would have collided with her, but he passed through her on the move. Even Bear was oblivious to her.

Angel was in my world. And I'd never felt so alone before.

"Angel, what happened? Who did this to you?"

She embraced me again, and when she released me, she looked confused. "I don't remember. I don't know what happened. It's all so confusing. I was driving home. Then, I don't know—I was very cold. Freezing. It all went black until the lights and noise, and then I was here, waiting for you. I knew you'd come for me."

The dead don't cry, but I did. Tears streamed down my cheeks as I took her hands. "No, Angel. This isn't right. Not you, too. You can't be..."

"It's all right, Tuck." She was just a whisper in the snow now, fading and nearly gone. "I'm so confused... wait for me, Tuck. I'll be right back."

"No."

"Tuck? What the hell?" Bear spun around and stared at me. He turned to the deputies who watched him and said, "Get to work, dammit! Find me evidence. Move!"

The mice scurried about.

"What the hell, Tuck? Who were you talking to?"

The answer choked me. "Angel."

"Oh, shit. They said there was a chance. Dammit." He turned away. The living cry, too.

The tow truck strained pulling Angel's Explorer back to level ground. Over the groans, I said, "What happened, Bear? Who did this? Someone pushed her over the bank. Someone murdered her."

"A lawyer heading home saw the bridge apron railing broken in and vehicle tracks going over the side of the embankment. He called it in. A Clarke County patrol was close by and got here fast. He yanked her out, but she was... was... The paramedics thought she was gone but they worked on her the whole time anyway, Tuck."

"She was here, Bear. Right here." The tow truck righted her Explorer and it punched me in the gut. "She's gone—with me, now—at least, I hope with me." For the first time I wondered what my days would be like if Angel died and moved on without me. My brain skittered away from the thought. I needed to focus now, and thinking like that would only slow me down.

Bear erupted again. He covered his face with his meaty hands. He shook and fought the emotions that rushed from him in torrents of rage and grief.

"We gotta get those bastards, Bear—listen…" I told him about Lee and Keys Hawkins, and Raina and her new pals at the Kit Kat. It took time to fight through the words—a battle with grief—but I told him everything that had happened since Angel and I were in DC. "I'm going back, Bear. Send a patrol to the club but don't let them go in unless I tell you to. Maybe that crazy bitch Raina will confess or give us some clues."

His voice was a quiver of edgy, raspy anger. "Okay. But no matter what happens, I want whoever killed Angela."

"Only after I get through with them."

Chapter Sixty-Six

"Yes, I am Albrecht Klaus Falke," Keys Hawkins whispered with a faint German accent—his words mixed with spittle of blood and saliva. "And yes, you bitch, I killed Youssif Iskandr. I had no choice."

Keys lay on the hardwood floor, still taped to the wooden chair by his left arm, beaten and bloodied. His eyes were swollen nearly shut and Lee knelt beside him, holding his head on her lap. Her face was unbruised—unblemished by any assault—but it showed the pain and agony Keys had endured.

"Well, I'll be damned," I whispered to Ollie beside me at the bar entrance where I'd arrived. "Keys Hawkins was your German spy."

"And a murderer." Ollie slid his ball cap onto the back of his head. "I figured it out a little while ago. It only took me seventy-seven years. I thought it was William. Damn, I'm getting slow in my death."

Lee looked up at Raina across the room and defiantly ripped the final piece of tape off her grandfather's arm. "What now? He's an old man. That was a lifetime ago. What's the point? He's been here most of his life. He was a boy back then. A boy, dammit."

Raina sat on a barstool watching. She seemed removed from it all—distant and unfeeling. Her eyes held no regret, no emotion, for the pain she was causing.

Beside her, B.C. leaned against the bar and drained a tall glass of booze he'd helped himself to. Perhaps he was getting drunk. Perhaps he was waiting for his final orders and readying his resolve.

279

B.C. said to Raina, "Okay, I did what you wanted. Now give me the cash. I'm done with this shit, lady."

"I think not." Raina turned to face him. "I want my grandfather's possessions. Bring those to me and I shall deliver your money."

B.C. slid away from the bar. "And I told you, lady. I ain't got that junk. Never had it. How many times—"

"Lies." Raina gestured to Keys. "Just like him. A liar, a traitor, and a murderer."

"It was war," Keys grunted. He pulled himself to a sitting position beside Lee. "Damn you to hell. It was war." His German accent was gone and he was a Virginian again. "Your grandfather pulled a gun on me. I never intended to kill him."

Raina thrust her gun at him. "Lies! And for what did you kill him? Treasure? War profit? It was not for your country—you abandoned Germany, did you not?"

"Please." Lee's voice was gravel. "You're just like William. He wanted to dredge it all up just for the truth. Why? What difference does it all make now? The truth won't bring anyone back and it won't change anything."

"Raina, it was a hard time—for everyone," Keys said and coughed blood. "The Abwehr recruited me as a boy-soldier from the Hitler Youth Corp. They sneaked me into Cairo with Eppler and Sandstede. Those two were idiots and got picked up within weeks. Not me. I stayed and kept working in Cairo. Who would think a young, musician was a German spy? Especially a teenage boy playing the clubs. The Yanks and Brits couldn't hold their tongues when beautiful dancers and booze were around. I thought Youssif wanted to help us against the Allies, like so many Egyptians did. Lots of them helped, you know. But when I met Youssif that night, he pulled a gun. I had to kill him."

"You murdered him." Raina's eyes drilled through Keys.

"No." He shook his head. "Yes, I took his trunks of treasures to create the illusion it was a robbery. But in the end, that loot was my ticket out of Cairo and away from those Nazi fanatics. I am sorry. I am truly sorry."

Raina walked back over to Keys and pressed her pistol to his forehead.

"You murdered my grandfather. How... when... it does not matter."

"It was war," he grunted again. "I was a boy and realized too late that the Germany I went to war for was not what I'd thought." He coughed and took a heavy breath. "It wasn't what many of us thought. It was an accident with Youssif, I swear." Keys took several more breaths and steadied himself. "I couldn't return to Germany. Hell, I knew I'd never leave Cairo alive if I didn't find a way out. When Willy and the boys headed back here to the States, well... I used the loot as a way to hop a ride." Another long pause and several breaths. "The rest you know."

Raina's eyes hardened. "A spy and a murderer."

"You're a murderer, too," Lee yelled. "Claude Holister and Cy Gray were innocent men. Your family murdered them. William knew you were coming for him and wanted to make things right. I tried to convince him there was another way, I tried to keep him from going through with it. But he had to tell and he died trying to."

Raina flashed dead eyes at her. "Justice is better."

"Justice?" Lee stood up between Keys and Raina. "Gray and Holister had nothing to do with your grandfather's death. They didn't steal anything. They thought they were helping your grandfather come to the States. You still killed them—your family did. You're worse than my grandfather ever was. You killed for no reason at all. Where is their justice?"

Keys looked at B.C. "Did you kill Marshal and Karen Simms, too?"

"I didn't kill anyone, mister—yet," B.C. said with an evil, dark grin. "But I'm up for it."

"Not yet." Raina turned the pistol on B.C. "Now, give me my possessions."

"And I told you, I ain't got them." B.C. walked away from Raina as she cocked her handgun. "Screw you, lady. I never found that damn vault. I never got past the lobby."

"Liar." Quick as a flash, Raina shot B.C. in the leg. He went down in a surprised squeal of agony. "I've dealt with others who got in my way. I was promised you would cooperate. I was promised you would assist in finding my grandfather's killer and that afterward, you would deliver my possessions. You failed me."

Dealt with others? My blood—if I'd had any—ran cold. "Ollie, did Raina kill Angel? Did she run Angel off the road to stop her from getting back to warn Keys?"

"Slow down, kid." He put a hand on my shoulder. "Let this play out. You'll get your answers—and if we're lucky, so will I."

"Please," Lee yelled as tears flooded her face. "If you're using us as hostages…"

"Hostages?" Raina laughed a strange, crazy laugh. "You are prisoners. Now move away from your grandfather. My family has waited too long and I will not wait any longer."

"Shit, Ollie," I said, "what now? Time for one of those unplanned plans of yours. Like, right now."

He bit his lip. "Why? Keys—*Albrecht*—deserves it. He killed Youssif—he killed my friend. I'm not worried about your murder, kid, I'm worried about mine. And maybe this crazy bitch is right. Maybe it's justice."

No, it wasn't. "Murdering Keys isn't any better, is it? Are you that sure she's right?"

He looked at me and then at Keys and Lee. "Oh, crap. Come on." He walked over and knelt down beside Keys. When I joined him, he took hold of Keys's shoulder. He said, "A Jerry spy is a Jerry spy to me. But I'll give you one chance…"

The Egyptian heat washed over me like a wave and when my eyes adjusted to the darkness, I was inside Youssif Iskandr's home in 1945. Shelves of pottery and artifacts lined the walls. Two long tables were stacked with papers, books, and more stonework. Beside the tables were two heavy trunks. Their tops were open, displaying trays of bundles wrapped in cloth and paper. I recognized the chests—they held Youssif Iskandr's Egyptian treasures, and soon they would be loaded onto a rickety cart drawn by the old mare outside.

Ollie stood beside me. "We're back again, kid. This is—"

"I know."

Two voices rose from the other room—men's voices. They argued in broken English. One had a German accent and the other a thick Egyptian one.

"What have you done, Youssif?" the German demanded. "You play these games with me? Who? Who is behind this?"

"No one. I don't know what you say. Stop it now. Let me make some tea—"

Youssif crashed through the door across the room from us and landed against one of the chests. The German—a stout, hefty man dressed in khaki pants and a loosely tucked-in cotton shirt—followed. He was a very young Albrecht Klaus Falke—Albert "Keys" Hawkins. He was young and strong—yet barely more than a kid himself—and much stronger than the aged Youssif Iskandr.

Keys grabbed Youssif by the arm and dragged him back to his feet. "Answers. I want to know, Youssif, who is behind you? What have you done?"

Youssif broke free and lunged for a nearby bookshelf, but Keys was on him. The two struggled and knocked the table over. Several pieces of pottery and statues shattered on the floor. They crashed into the second table and continued the battle. Youssif knocked Keys backward into a shelf, and books and papers cascaded down. Then Youssif dashed to the first shelf, took something from behind a large, wide volume of work, and jutted it at Keys. A gun.

Ollie grabbed my arm. "Oh, shit. I forgot about the gun I gave..."

Keys dove onto Youssif and they grappled for control of the gun.

Youssif yelled, "Swine! Get out! Out of my house!"

A shot.

They fought for the revolver—twisting and pulling—grunting and sweating. Youssif kicked him hard in the groin and Keys faltered. But as he did, Keys wrenched the pistol sideways.

Another shot.

Youssif slipped to the floor and lay unmoving. He was facedown, his life flowing out onto the stone floor around him.

Keys fell to his knees, the pistol still in his grasp, his face twisted with fear and uncertainty.

"Oh, no. No, no, no." Spirit Ollie's chin dropped to his chest. "It was my fault. I gave Youssif the gun just in case. I was supposed to be upstairs, but Keys got here too early. He must have been testing Youssif. Damn, I gave Youssif the gun, kid. It was me."

The room spun and the darkness ebbed and flowed around us. The air cooled and the desert turned to barroom hardwood.

The ceiling fan settled into a soothing rhythm above me. I stood beside Ollie and looked over at Keys and Lee as though we'd never left. Ollie's face was defeated and dark—the pain of the history he now found himself responsible for welled inside him. "Dammit, kid. This was my fault. I gave Youssif the gun. If I'd only been earlier…"

"I'd put that down, Raina," a voice said from behind us. "I've got a gun on you. If you move, I'll shoot."

Raina whirled around, fired off two quick shots toward the bar entrance, then bolted down the hall beside the bar. A second later, a door banged—first open, then closed. Two more shots rang out.

She'd made her escape.

"Ah, one less to worry about." Franklin Thorne eased into the bar behind us. He brushed the snow off his head with one hand and leveled a semi-automatic at B.C. with the other. "If you kindly do not move, you might live the night."

"Thorne?" Lee said. "What are you doing here?"

He glanced at her and Keys. "I trust you are both all right?"

Lee shook her head and took Keys by the arm, helped him stand, and walked him to a barstool nearby. "He needs an ambulance. What are you doing here? I don't understand."

Neither did I.

"Thorne ain't Thorne, kid." Ollie laughed. "And he ain't no bank man, either."

My head spun. "So, Raina is a whacko revenge-seeker. Keys is a World War II German spy. And Thorne…"

"Thorne came here for William's loot."

Chapter Sixty-Seven

"Tuck?" Angel walked into the Kit Kat's bar behind Thorne. She was dazed, confused—her face was pale, and her eyes darted around the room trying to find familiarity, but she couldn't. Her voice trembled and the words stuck in her throat when she said, "Tuck? I don't understand. One minute I'm with you and then... nowhere. What's happening to me?"

I didn't know. "You're here now, with us—Ollie and me. It's all right."

She looked at Ollie with eyes more uneasy than friendly. "Ollie? You're his... grandfather, the OSS man? Oh, Tuck..." She ran to me and threw her arms around me. She kissed me long and hard. When she pulled back, she smiled as though it all suddenly made sense. "It's over. The hard part, right?"

"Yes, I think so." Hell, I didn't know. I glanced at Ollie. "Is it, Ollie?"

"No, kid. Be patient. This one's new to me, too."

There was a crash of wood splintering outside the bar and Bear and Cal burst in, weapons drawn.

Bear yelled, "Everyone freeze, Frederick County Sheriff's Department."

Thorne lowered his handgun. "Ah, Detective Braddock, good. I was worried I would have to entertain this one myself." He pointed to B.C., who lay bleeding on the floor. "And dear Mr. Hawkins needs an ambulance as well."

I pulled Angel close. "It's okay, babe. It's over."

"Ah, no, kid," Ollie said. "Keys was a German spy who killed my friend. Raina's family killed Claude and Cy. And if I'd not given Youssif that gun, maybe none of it would have happened. But it still isn't over. Not yet."

Angel whispered, "Tuck, we can be together now. It's all right, isn't it? No… Tuck!" Her voice trailed off and she was gone.

"What happened to her, Ollie?" I looked around but she was nowhere again—just gone. "Where'd she go? Is she coming back?"

"I don't know, kid. I'm a spook—I mean, a CIA man—not a spirit master. Remember what Doc told you."

I wanted answers and that wasn't one of them. "Bear, Raina Iskandr might have killed Angel. I'm not sure…"

"Angela's in a coma," Bear said to no one in particular. "The cold saved her life. She went into hypothermia and it kept her from bleeding out—maybe."

Relief flooded my not-quite-there body.

"Angela?" Thorne turned to Bear and his face paled. "Will she live?"

Bear shrugged. "Where's Iskandr?"

"She ran out the back," Lee said. "She's gone."

"Raina?" Thorne asked. "But why?"

It struck me that Thorne had called Raina by name. "Bear, Thorne shouldn't know Raina unless he was working with her somehow, right?"

Bear looked over at Cal tending to Keys. "Cal?"

"He's in rough shape, Bear. He needs a doc." He pointed to B.C. just as his radio squealed and he listened. "This one will live. One of our deputies was hit out back trying to stop Raina from escaping. She's gone. I've got ambulances on the way."

"Get them here faster." Bear looked back at Thorne. "What are you doing here, Thorne?"

"Saving the day—again." He didn't skip a beat. "You recall Marshal's ire at me over the eavesdropping devices in his office?"

"I do. You said it wasn't you."

"Actually, no, Detective." Thorne walked to the bar, reached over it, and retrieved a glass. He poured himself a drink from the bourbon bottle B.C. had been emptying. "I never actually denied it."

Bear watched him.

Thorne took a long, deep pull on his drink. "I have been working this case right along with you. You were not aware, I know. I've had listening devices in this club, just like the bank, for months. It seems someone—an accomplice of this man, B.C.—dispatched him here to assist Raina as part of a grand bargain for William Mendelson's treasure and the identity of her grandfather's murderer. An hour ago, B.C. and Raina arrived and begin interrogating the Hawkinses. They were in serious danger; thus, I decided to end my charade and intercede. I regret Raina escaped. I'd hoped your young deputy in the parking lot would have stopped her."

"The charade?" Bear didn't lower his weapon.

I said, "Bear, Thorne's not Thorne."

"Thorne's not Thorne?" Bear didn't seem surprised, nor was he worried about the odd looks he got from everyone. "Okay, pal, let's have the gun. Then you can explain your charade."

"Yes, of course." He handed the gun to Bear and returned to his drink. "I'll want it back later. You understand."

Bear turned to Lee. "Are you all right?"

"I'm fine—shaken, but all right." She put a hand on Keys's shoulder as Cal worked on his wounds. "He's got busted ribs, I'm sure. But I think he'll be okay."

I said, "Keys's real name is Albrecht Falke, not Albert Hawkins. He was a Nazi spy in Cairo in 1945. He killed a man named Youssif Iskandr—Raina's grandfather. He was just a boy-soldier—a teenager—that German Intelligence sent with Eppler and Sandstede. Afterward, he and William and others smuggled Iskandr's Egyptian antiquities back here. Keys started all this back in the war."

I gave him the condensed version of everything Ollie and I knew. The entire time, Bear stood there and absorbed the details—oblivious to the others in the room who looked at each other with raised eyebrows and smirks. Everyone but Cal, that is. He nodded right along with Bear.

"Albrecht Falke—Albert 'Keys' Hawkins? A Nazi spy?" Bear's face twisted when he looked from Lee to Keys.

"That was 1945, Bear." Lee went to him and took his arm in both hands. "He's been an American ever since. He never did anything in this country but be a good man. Surely you'll understand."

"Dammit, I wish we had normal murders around here." Bear bit his lip and grumbled for a long time. Then he said, "Last time it was Russian mobsters and now it's German spies. What's next?"

I knew. "Zombie apocalypse."

He didn't think that was funny. Ollie did.

Bear said, "Okay, so we know about Keys. But who robbed and killed William? And what about Karen and Marshal? Someone is behind all three murders."

Damn good questions. "I don't know yet, Bear. We haven't worked that out."

Cal handcuffed B.C., wrapping a bar towel around his leg wound all the while reading him his rights. After he searched him, Cal dumped the contents of B.C.'s pockets into a ceramic bowl on the bar that had hieroglyphs and Egyptian drawings on it. Then he sat him on the floor.

Bear walked over to Thorne. "Who are you, pal? You're no bank man, that's for sure."

"No, I am not." Thorne laughed and emptied his drink. "Interpol. I've been on William's trail for a year. I was sent under cooperation with the Egyptian government after some of the stolen antiquities surfaced. I was to identify the thieves and return the antiquities. I'm part of an international smuggling unit."

"Oh, yeah?" Ollie raised his eyebrows. "A smuggling unit?"

Bear said, "Prove it."

"Of course." Thorne reached into his coat pocket and withdrew a black leather credential case and tossed it to Bear. "I have a contact number for you to call, too. But perhaps we should try and catch up to Raina Iskandr first. I believe I know where she is headed."

Bear studied the credentials and handed them to Cal. "You could have identified yourself sooner, Thorne."

"Perhaps. I didn't want you locals screwing up my investigation. I've been on it too long." Thorne hooked a thumb toward the door. "Raina won't get far, gentlemen. But I insist you allow me to apprehend her. I have more jurisdiction over her than you."

"Go with him, Cal," Bear said, handing Thorne back his handgun. "I'll stay with this bunch."

"Right, I'll call you on the way—jurisdiction or not." Cal holstered his gun and looked at Thorne. "Let's go, Interpol Man."

Thorne marched out of the bar with Cal close behind.

Bear looked down at Keys for several minutes. "What am I supposed to do with you?"

"That depends, Detective Braddock." Keys tried to smile but winced in pain. "Is forgetting the past out of the question?"

"Please, Bear, for me." Lee put a hand on Bear's shoulder and kissed his cheek. "He's so old. How long can he last?"

"Bear!" Cal staggered back into the bar holding his head—blood streamed between his fingers. In his other hand was a small-framed revolver.

"Cal?" Bear helped him to a chair. "What happened?"

"Son of a bitch." Cal looked at his blood-covered hand and felt the gash in the side of his temple. "He was yakking about being an Interpol cop. He just stopped and came at me—about took my head off. He took my piece and drove off. I didn't find my legs or my backup gun until he was already gone."

Bear shook his head. "Interpol my ass."

"When I was on the ground, he gave me a message for you." Cal balanced himself on the barstool. "He said, 'Tell Angela I'm sorry.'"

"He's sorry?" Bear looked at me.

"International thief," Ollie said. "I tried to warn you."

He did? "No, Ollie, you said Thorne wasn't Thorne. You kept saying…"

"Details, details," Ollie said.

"I need some ice, man." Cal found the ceramic Egyptian bowl on the bar that held B.C.'s pocket contents. He fumbled with it using only one hand and it dropped on the floor and shattered.

"Easy, Calloway." Lee went over and scooped up the pieces. "It's all right. We got tons of this junk in the basement. Let me get you some ice."

Ollie looked down at B.C.'s key ring amidst the ceramic pieces on the floor. "Hey, kid, you thinkin' what I am?"

I was. "Yes, and it's been in front of our faces the whole time."

Chapter Sixty-Eight

In the basement of the Kit Kat West, Ollie and I showed Bear the back wall stacked with Nomad shipping crates. Well, I showed Bear; Ollie just tagged along. Sitting beside the crates was Keys's old steamer trunk partially covered with a tan tarpaulin.

Bear said, "Okay, Tuck, what's this all about?"

"Show him, kid," Ollie said.

I pointed to one of the crates already pulled from the stack. It was about two feet square and nailed shut. "Open it, Bear. Unless I'm slipping, there's a bunch of gold and jewels waiting in there."

Ollie added, "It's kinda like a rainbow—Leprechauns with a pot of gold."

He was trying to compete with my Zombie joke.

Bear pulled out a pocketknife and levered open the crate. It took him a few minutes and he broke his knife blade in two, but he continued until the wooded lid was on the floor beside him. When he pulled back a layer of plastic padding, the glint of gold and gemstones peeked out from inside.

The end of the rainbow.

Bear stood back. "Holy shit, Tuck. It's here."

"I know." I didn't, really; I'd guessed. So had Ollie. "Check a couple more."

Bear searched around the basement and found a handyman's toolbox in a cabinet by the stairs. Then he went to work on several of the Nomad crates until all but a couple were open and their contents laid out on three folding tables.

The tables were covered with Youssif Iskandr's Egyptian treasures. There were gold amulets laden with emeralds and what I think were rubies. I say amulet because that's what they call those things on the science channels I often watch late at night. There was also a small box that resembled a sarcophagus (History Channel Thursday nights) with a carved pharaoh's head on one end. The box was the size of a shoebox, and it too was decorated with gems and gold with hieroglyphs carved on its sides. There were dozens of small stone statues, some artifacts covered with gems and others with gold. The boxes weren't empty yet and in front of us were millions of dollars of antiquities hidden in William's secret vault for eight decades.

"Damn, Tuck," Bear said. "I can't believe it. It's like some old movie or something."

"Think Charlton Heston," I said. "I did."

Ollie stood in front of the table and looked down at the loot. "Yeah, a fortune. But it ain't worth all this killin'. And it wasn't worth Youssif's life to start."

Bear's cell phone rang and he took the call. A moment later, he stuffed it back into his pocket, frowning. "My men just hit B.C.'s place out in the sticks. Empty. But they found an old dark blue pickup truck parked in the back. And get this, they found a smashed-up cellphone in the trunk. It was William's. And it looks like B.C. doctored himself after getting shot. They found a couple plastic medical containers in his trash—for blood—and other medical supplies."

I nodded and watched Ollie as he looked over a stack of gold and ceramic statues. "What did you find, Ollie?"

"The jackpot, kid." He touched my shoulder with one hand and one of the statues—a sphinx-shaped ceramic piece—with the other. "William's missing bookends."

The room flashed black.

William Mendelson sat behind the small steel counting table inside his vault. He was bent over, examining a glass frame. He held it up to the light for a better view. It was a papyrus scroll. Beside the table, his safe was open, and it was empty.

In fact, the entire vault was empty—the treasure was already gone.

Ollie and I watched as William laid the glass frame on a file in the middle of the counting table.

"Do you know what this is?" William asked as he looked toward the vault door and tapped the file.

The killer stepped into the vault. "Your inventory."

"Precisely—and it tells me much." His voice was soft, calm, and without worry that his life was about to end. He tapped the framed scroll. "In this frame is a scroll that dates back to the time of Khufu in the Fourth Dynasty— I'm sure of it. To think that Keys and I have kept these treasures to ourselves. They belong with their people. And I am going to rectify that."

"You'll expose Keys. Do you want him dead, too?"

William lowered his eyes to the file. "No. And I don't want to die, either. His secret weighs heavy on us both. Those were dark times and he has more than atoned for his sins."

"Then why?" the killer asked.

William folded his hands and looked at the killer with sad eyes. "I know about the account. I know you stole some of these treasures and sold them. Did you think I wouldn't find out? I'm consulting with someone who has the credentials to assist me—Professor Tucker, from the university. She has contacts with the police and will help me sort this out. I will not press charges—how could I?"

"You've consulted with an outsider?" The killer moved closer. "You should not have done that. This treasure is worth tens of millions. You owe me, William. You don't get that, do you? You—this bank—destroyed my family. It's not about the millions—oh, I'll take that, too—but it's about family. And I'm getting revenge."

"Revenge? I don't understand, but then, neither do you. By selling those pieces, it is you who have brought the danger to us—to Keys and me. We were going to return those treasures and end this madness." William slammed his hand down on the framed papyrus scroll and cracked the glass, sending shards sliding off the table. "Don't you see? We have to make this right."

"All right, William. If it's that important to you. Show me the scroll. Khufu, you think?" The killer moved behind William and put one hand on his shoulder, then drew a .22-cal revolver with the other.

William raised the scroll. "Khufu was—"

The sharp *crack* inside the vault was not as surprising as the look in William's eyes as he saw the last seconds of his life spill onto the desk before him.

"I understand, William. And I'm sorry. But you can't tell. Not about Keys. Not about this treasure. Not about me."

Footsteps ran down the stairs into the anteroom behind us.

Marshal Mendelson ran into the vault, sweaty and out of breath. "Dear God, what have you done?"

"You knew I had to." The killer's voice was calm, relaxed. "You knew."

"No." Marshal stared at his father. "I just wanted out. I needed the money. Nicholas bailed me out—I told you it was over. I didn't want this."

The killer laughed. "You sound like Keys. We have to get out of here before that idiot B.C. shows up. He'll get the blame and I'll be gone. You can play the grieving son and the score will be almost even."

Marshal peered down at his father's body. A strange, eerie calm flooded his face. "It didn't have to be this way."

The killer grabbed the Khufu scroll. "Yes, it did."

Chapter Sixty-Nine

Angel lay silent and unmoving in her hospital bed. A labyrinth of wires and tubes invaded her body. The rhythmic *beep-beep-beep* of the life machines filled the stillness while their lights and dials illuminated the room like eerie eyes and demonic fingers. Three times over the past hours the doctors revived her, and three times she'd returned to my world. On her fourth resuscitation, her vitals fell and her breathing became almost imperceptible. Whatever thread of life she grasped escaped us both. Now she stood beside me near the window and watched herself slip in and out of worlds.

I stood waiting for her decision. Silence was my only vote.

Outside her room, a nurse wearing surgical scrubs came down the hall and stopped at a portable computer terminal outside her door. She glanced up and down the hallway, checked the terminal's monitor, and scrolled through the screens. She tapped here and there on the keyboard and got busy with work. Twice she looked through the ICU window and rechecked her watch before she returned to the computer screen.

Everyone was on deathwatch.

"Tuck, I'm staying with you." Angel looked from her dying body to me. "Bear will take Hercule. He'll be fine. We can both be with him like you've been. It'll be better than before."

I put a finger to her lips. "No, Angel. You belong here now—and for a long time. Fight back. Fight back and you can still make it. We'll work things out."

"No. It's my choice, not yours."

I touched her face and let my finger linger on her cheek, a feeling I hadn't truly felt for a very long time. I missed that. "I wasn't given a choice, but you have one. Fight back, Angel. Stay with Bear and Hercule. Please? Do this for me."

The nurse walked into the room and over to Angel's body lying on the bed. She checked more monitors and electronic devices standing guard. Satisfied, she turned to leave.

The heavy, acrid odor of smoke reached me as the nurse made her move. And just then, I understood.

The nurse closed the curtains on the observation window and returned to Angel's bedside. She withdrew a syringe from her smock, slipped it into the IV bag's port hanging above her bed, and depressed the plunger. The contents flowed into Angel's IV line.

Angel and I watched from across the room.

"Bear!" I yelled and grabbed the electrical line Bear had purposely left snaking from a wall junction panel. It took but a second for the electricity to take effect. The euphoria was instant and the power overflowed from me. My world opened and collided with the living.

And I was there—beside Angel's bed—staring into Karen Simms's eyes.

"What the hell?" Karen's eyes exploded. "Who are you? Where did you come from?"

I grabbed her hand, yanked the syringe from it, and tossed it onto the floor. "Hello, Karen. I thought you'd never show."

"No... no. It can't be."

"I'm Detective Oliver Tucker of the Frederick County Sheriff's Department—well, formerly at least. Angel, my wife, called me Tuck." I shoved her backward against the glass observation window just as the door swung open and Bear Braddock rushed in.

"Oh, hell no." Karen tried to find escape behind her. "You're dead. William told me you were dead. This can't..."

Bear wrenched Karen's arms behind her, pressed her face-first into the wall, and snapped handcuffs on her wrists. Then he spun her around and held tight to the handcuff chain to leverage her arms high and keep her off balance up on her tiptoes.

Karen settled and stared at me, her face wild and frightened. "You're dead. Aren't you?"

"Oh, I'm dead all right, Karen." I walked over and locked eyes with her. "I'm just not gone. And that's the trick, don't you think?"

Chapter Seventy

"Get me out of here, Detective." Karen pressed back into Bear. "Get me out of here, *please*."

"Karen Simms," Bear said as he stooped and picked up the syringe, "you're under arrest for the murders of William and Marshal Mendelson and, after this trick, the attempted murder of Angela Tucker." Bear finished the conventional Miranda rights and pushed her down into one of the chairs across the room.

"Attempted murder?" Karen pointed her chin at Angel. "She won't be testifying."

"Sure she will, Karen." Bear lifted the IV line she had poisoned. The end of the line should have been attached to a needle in Angel's vein but instead it was affixed to a small plastic bottle hidden in the bed linens. The bottle had already captured the syringe of poison Karen injected.

"Glad you like needles," Bear said in a dry voice. "The Commonwealth has one for you."

Angel—Angel in my world—said, "Tuck, I thought Karen was dead."

"Yes, Angel, me too." I told her what Bear's men found at B.C.'s house. I ended with, "Karen found out about William's treasure and was selling it piece by piece until he caught her. But by then, Raina had traced it and found her, then found William and Keys. William called you to that meeting to ask for help—he needed your contacts at the Smithsonian to sort it all out with the Egyptians before anything happened to him and Keys."

Karen stared at me as I began to fade. Her eyes darted to Bear, me, and back to Bear. "Detective, it was all Marshal. He was over his head with some

298

loan sharks. He…"

"Bullshit, Karen," Bear said as Cal walked into the room with another deputy. "You found his treasure and set up that secret account to sell it. You tried to frame Poor Nic and Keys by putting the account under their company name—Nostalgia—except the address went to a PO Box that wasn't Nic's. Marshal may have helped you, but you did the killing. You killed William to keep him from revealing his secret to Raina before you could sell all his treasure. And then you killed Marshal. Why, did he get cold feet?"

Karen's eyes were steel. "That stuff was worth millions—more, even. Marshal was a bastard and he killed his father to get the treasure. I just helped with the bank account to sell it. And then he was gonna turn me in for William's murder, like he was all innocent and shit. Do you believe it? He committed suicide…"

"No, Karen." Bear eyed her. "You killed William. And you're going down for Marshal's murder, too. But hey, that was a neat trick pouring your blood all around your apartment to make us think you were dead. If we hadn't found the containers at B.C.'s place, we might have never figured it out. I guess being a nursing student paid off."

Karen cursed and turned away.

Cal said, "And we have B.C. He's talking so much we can't keep up. Seems he didn't like you setting him up with Raina just to get him shot and arrested for murder. You used that .22 to kill William, then you gave it to B.C. for the phony bank heist. You set him up to look like he'd robbed William's vault and killed him. Then you sent the poor sap to help Raina get Keys to confess. What, did you figure she'd kill him and Keys to cover her tracks and yours at the same time? And why try to kill Poor Nic?"

Karen's face flushed. "That was meant for Professor Tucker. Bartalotta got in the way—dumb luck, right?" She looked up at Bear and her face dissolved into a cocky, nasty grin. "But I figured, what the hell, Bartalotta will find B.C. to pay him back. Then, there won't be any witness to rat me out."

"Angel?" I said, and Karen looked for me but couldn't find me. "Why kill

Angel? She wasn't involved with all this."

Karen lifted her chin. "William told her everything. She had to go. She even found Raina at that Washington warehouse—I followed Angela there. I figured that crazy Egyptian bitch would finish her off once and for all. But she didn't, so..."

"That's the funny thing, Karen," Bear said. "Raina may be a crazy bitch, but she never killed anyone. Oh, her family did, but not her. You're the murderer."

"She's no saint, Braddock. It was her fault I had to do it. Angela Tucker would have figured out it was me sooner or later. What was I supposed to do? Just wait around for her to figure me out?"

Bear leaned forward. "So, you followed Angela out of DC and drove her off the road."

"I had no choice. It was William's fault for talking to her." Karen let a sly grin escape the corners of her mouth. "Look, I have a deal..."

"William didn't tell her anything," Bear growled. "He never spoke to Angela. She was heading to see him for the first time the morning you killed him. Angela never knew what William wanted."

She stared for a moment. "But... he told her before, in emails. She had to know."

"No, he never told her." I leaned close to her and whispered, "I'm gonna haunt you for the rest of your life. Me and every ghoul I can find—maybe William and Marshal..."

"Come on, Braddock, let's make a deal." Karen's eyes darted around the room looking for me—or others. "I'll confess everything. I'll give the money back—"

"Give it back?" Cal took her arm and stood her up. "Willy knew you were stealin' and he moved the treasure to Keys's club for safekeepin' until they could return it. He knew you'd make a move on the rest."

"Money? You think this was just about money?" Karen's face chilled to ice again. "My stepdad was a fireman. He saved William when he started the annex on fire years ago. William was down in his secret vault—no one knew it was there back then. My stepfather and another fireman had to hunt

300

around to find him. But then my stepfather got trapped behind the vault gate. He was burnt so bad he never worked again. William was untouched—didn't have so much as singed hair. My stepfather drank himself to death and mom died trying to make ends meet. William Mendelson and that damn treasure destroyed my family. Sure, I wanted his money; I earned it. And I got them—I got their money and them, too."

Tommy. Fire. Smoke. *Revenge.*

Bear looked over at me and then at Karen. His face softened a little. "For your family, I'm sorry, Karen. But you're still going down for the murders. Now, if—"

"Look, I know things about Franklin Thorne." She wet her lips and looked from Cal to Bear. "I saw him in the bank at all hours of the night. He was up to something, I'm telling you. He—"

"Thorne's an international jewel thief, Karen," Bear said and laughed when her face paled. "He was there to rob William, too. And I suspect he was onto you. In fact, I wouldn't be a bit surprised if your stolen money is long gone from your offshore account. It's probably in *his* Swiss bank about now."

"Thorne…a thief?" Karen shook her head as her eyes raged. "He used me. I led him to it all. That miserable lying bastard!"

"She's loonier than a clown on steroids," I said.

Cal pulled her toward the door. "Let's go, Karen. Your old boyfriend, B.C., made a deal that'll keep him off death row. Maybe being nuts will save you."

Cal paraded Karen from the hospital room.

Angel sat beside me on the couch. When her eyes rose to me again, she was crying. "It's time—I have to choose. It's so hard, Tuck. It's so hard."

"Stay alive, Angel. Stay with Bear and Hercule and your life. I'll be fine. And I promise, no more snooping around on you. Well, maybe a little."

She laughed between the tears and took my hand. "I know Hercule would be fine with Bear. And we'll both be with him… always."

"No, Angel."

"Being with you is all I want, Tuck." She leaned forward and kissed me. "I know what I have to do." She kissed me a second time, long and hard, then smiled as she slipped away into nothing.

A moment later, her life machines beeped and cried out. Lights flashed everywhere. Footsteps ran up the hall and anxious voices grew louder and louder. When the doctor and nurse burst through the doorway, they went straight to the life machines. The doctor scanned the readouts, checked numbers, and slowly turned off the alarms.

The doctor looked down at Angel. "Dear God."

Chapter Seventy-One

"Tuck?" Angel's voice startled me. "Are you here?"

"I'm here, babe. Right here." I reached out and took her hand. Her warmth was something I'd have to get used to, now that'd we'd shared my side of life and death. In those short hours, we had bonded so much that the link between us was stronger—better—unbreakable. "You fell asleep again. I haven't left."

It had taken days for Angel to do more than sip water through a straw. In that time, neither Bear nor I had left her side. Even Cal stood a couple all-night vigils so Bear could sack out on the guest couch in her room. This morning—a week after Karen Simms tried to kill my Angel for the third time—she was getting back to normal. Not bad for a woman who'd died and almost didn't return.

Almost.

In the end, she'd chosen life. Life as she had it before. Life as she would have it for a very long time. Life as we both knew it since I lost mine.

Bear had just left for breakfast and it was just the two of us. My feet had been propped up on the couch waiting for her to awaken from a late-morning nap. I hadn't taken my eyes off her for days.

"Tuck," she said as she eased her legs over the bed, "who was the woman the West Virginia police found in Poor Nic's car in Morgantown?"

I shrugged. "They don't know yet. No ID. No prints on file. They're thinking she was just some homeless gal Karen found. They're working it."

She thought for a while. "So, Karen tried to shoot me at the club the night Nicholas was hit? And she ran me off the road?"

"Yes. She thought William told you everything that was going on at the bank and about Professor Iskandr. She figured you'd eventually put it all together." I was guessing of course. "You were a popular girl, babe. What is it about you that so many people want to kill you?"

"Maybe it's you, *dear*." She grinned and rolled her head to relax her shoulders. "What about Franklin Thorne? Raina? What came of them?"

Good questions. "Raina's gone—probably back to Egypt. Her government won't say. Funny how a little seventy-seven-year international murder spree has them all hush-hush."

"Franklin?"

"Gone, too." I went to her and put an arm around her. Strangely, I felt her arm around me, too. Feeling her touch was new—like our first time all over again. "He got the money from Karen's offshore account and poof, he vanished. Karen thought she played him for inside information on the bank security system, but he played her for over half a million. I doubt the bank will give him good references, though."

Angel laughed and tried the few steps from her bed to the window. "And what will happen to Keys and Lee Hawkins? He *was* a spy and he *did* kill Youssif Iskandr, right?"

Ah, another good question. "The FBI doesn't know what to do with him. Other than his confession—and he's recanted that—there's no proof of anything. Ollie can't testify and Raina sure won't. So, all we have is an immigration mess. After all, as Lee keeps saying, that was war. He killed Youssif all right—in self-defense." I told her about my last visit with Ollie to 1945. "And Youssif wasn't an innocent civilian, not really. He worked for the OSS, and that made him fair game during the war. Sort of. If Ollie hadn't given him that gun, maybe things would have been different. Maybe not."

"If the FBI doesn't want the case, does Keys stay?"

I shrugged. "The FBI punted to Immigration. Germany doesn't want him and claim they have no record of any spy or citizen named Albrecht Falke. And after Poor Nic got ahold of him when he got to the hospital the other day—I bet that was an unpleasant meeting—Keys won't talk to anyone. He's in legal limbo."

Angel steadied herself by the window and looked out. The sun shone for the first time in days and the few inches of snow had already melted to nothing.

She turned and took my hand. "I can feel you, Tuck. I feel your touch without you playing with the light cord or anything silly like that anymore."

"I hope it lasts."

"You could have convinced me to stay, you know. You could have kept me with you." She pressed against me and kissed my cheek. "I would have."

"I know."

"Will you two knock that off? Jeez, I'm right here." Ollie stood in the doorway holding his Washington Senators ball cap. "Doc's looking for you, kid. He wants the full scoop."

I laughed. "Why don't you fill him in?"

"Oh, no." He slipped his ball cap onto the back of his head. "I can't take his nitpicking. Damn, kid, I've been listening to it my whole life—and death. It's your turn. So hurry it up."

I gave Angel a squeeze. "You know, if you can feel my arms around you and my kiss, maybe then..."

She blushed. "It has been two years. Do you think?"

I did think. "What about the suave French movie star?"

"Let's hope we don't need him."

Later, we'd find out. Another secret to keep.

Thinking about the past days reminded me of the book that saved Larry Conti's life, *Murder on the Orient Express*, one of Agatha Christie's best. In that story, they all did it—every one of them. Just like here and now. Keys was a German spy who killed Youssif. William Mendelson unknowingly helped steal Youssif Iskandr's antiquities, and by that, was an unwitting accomplice in his killing. Karen stole from William. Marshal plotted to steal all William's treasure with Karen. Then Karen killed William for revenge and then killed Marshal; he was the only witness who knew the whole story. She tried to kill Angel, too. Franklin Thorne planned to steal the vault treasure and did steal over half a million bucks. And Raina Iskandr's family took revenge over and over.

The irony, though, was that Raina Iskandr came here to Winchester to avenge her grandfather's death. She came to kill. Yet, in the end, she never did. Oh, she was a crazy bitch—as Karen had deemed her—but she never took a life. She just followed all the old secrets and they consumed her.

They all had secrets, I guess. They all told lies to keep them—and some of them killed for them. Those secrets hurt a lot of innocent people. Cy Gray, Claude Holister. Even my Angel.

And it cost them all.

In the end, everyone got what they deserved—it's like that sometimes. Except Franklin Thorne, who tried to take my Angel. That suave, handsome, thieving son-of-a-bitch was somewhere laughing over his $521,511.22. But that will end. The formerly unidentified master thief now has a face and fingerprints. They'll find him one day.

I hope I can be there when they do. *Bastard*.

Angel and I have our secrets, too—her more than me. And we're going to keep them. Sure, there are a few little white lies—like who she talked to at the café and strolled with through Old Town. Who made her laugh when it was only her in her University office. Many around town know about me—or think they know—yet, no one will come out and say it.

Except Cal "Calloway" Clemens. He wrote a song about me. He called it the "Dead and Back Blues." It's a real hit at the Kit Kat Club where Angel, Bear, and I have a reserved table. Lee Hawkins loves to buy the drinks, too. And most times, Bear stays late and sees her home—for the job, of course.

But hey, like Cal's song, I'm dead and back. I'm just not so blue. I've got my job, my dog, my beautiful wife, and my... well, no, not my health. Three out of four ain't bad. Is it?

The end

Acknowledgements

Writing is not a team sport—not until you reach the "The End" and your agent, personal editors, personal publicist, publisher, and publisher's editors jump in. Then it's all hands on deck. This novel is no different. And to all of you who joined the fray to put this one on the shelf, so many thanks I cannot begin to list them all. This time around—the second issue of the Dead Detective Casefiles—is even more of a team effort.

The usual suspects—Jean, Nicci, Gina, Annie Rose, Sawyer, and Mosby, Toby, and Maggie. As for my companion pets, several of whom I lost during the work on this series, inspired me for their gentleness, kindness, and devotion.

Also, never-ending thanks to Kimberley Cameron for support, wisdom, and friendship. More than anything, she's my hero for her belief in me and my stories.

A huge thanks Gina Hott—publicist extraordinaire—for all her enthusiasm and drive to help get my name out is so much appreciated and I couldn't do it without her.

In memory of my best friend, mentor, hero, and best critic—Wally F. who would "one more edit" me to oblivion if he could have. "Good Enough is not Good Enough" was his mantra. It's that quest that drives me still; oh, and his puns.

It goes without saying that without Shawn Reilly Simmons at Level Best Books, I would not be here again telling Tuck's continued adventures. Thank you and I look forward to a long and wild ride. For many reasons, you're an inspiration.

To all I haven't mentioned in this post—and there are many, I'm sure— thank you. Writing may not be a team sport, but I have a great one nonetheless.

About the Author

Tj O'Connor is an award-winning author of mysteries and thrillers. He's an international security consultant specializing in anti-terrorism, investigations, and threat analysis—life experiences that drive his novels. With his former life as a government agent and years as a consultant, he has lived and worked around the world in places like Greece, Turkey, Italy, Germany, the United Kingdom, and throughout the Americas—among others. In his spare time, he's a Harley Davidson pilot, a man-about-dogs (and now cats), and a lover of adventure, cooking, and good spirits (both kinds). He was raised in New York's Hudson Valley and lives with his wife, Labs, and Maine Coon companions in Virginia where they raised five children who are supply a growing tribe of grands.

AUTHOR WEBSITE:
  www.tjoconnor.com

SOCIAL MEDIA HANDLES:
  Web Site: www.tjoconnor.com
  Facebook: https://www.facebook.com/tjoconnor.author2
  Blog: http://tjoconnor.com/blog/
  Twitter:@tjoconnorauthor
  Instagram: https://www.instagram.com/tjoconnorauthor/
  Amazon: https://www.amazon.com/author/tjoconnor

Goodreads: https://www.goodreads.com/author/show/7148441.T_J_O_Connor

Youtube Channel: @tjoconnorauthor3905

Bookbub:https://www.bookbub.com/profile/tj-o-connor

Also by Tj O'Connor

Dying to Know

Dying for the Past

New Sins for Old Scores

The Consultant

The Hemingway Deception